"I'VE NEVER SEEN YOU NAKED, ALISA."

"I've touched you through clothing, I've held you against me in the dark, but you've never shown me your body," Pace said, his voice barely a whisper. "Show me now."

With shaking fingers, Alisa undressed. Pace did not help her. When she stood before him, naked in the soft lamplight, he reached out for her hand and brought it to his mouth, placing a tender kiss in her palm before he laid it on his cheek.

Looking in her eyes, he leaned down to repeat the kiss, as soft and gentle as Delta rain, on her mouth.

"You're so very beautiful," Pace whispered, his voice full of reverence as he cupped her full breasts.

"Don't ever leave me," he moaned as they moved together. "Please, my love, don't ever leave me."

ABOUT THE AUTHOR

An idyllic but isolated childhood in the Mississippi River Delta of North Louisiana fostered Jean DeCoto's early love of literature, which eventually led her to try her hand at writing. This, her second Superromance, is redolent of the Delta she so loves. The region provides the perfect backdrop for her characters' tender romance.

Books by Jean DeCoto

Jean DeCoto

DELTA NIGHTS

Harlequin Books

TORONTO • NEW YORK • LONDON
AMSTERDAM • PARIS • SYDNEY • HAMBURG
STOCKHOLM • ATHENS • TOKYO • MILAN

Published December 1984

First printing October 1984

ISBN 0-373-70145-4

Printed in Canada

In honor of my grandfather, Joseph Carrol Cobb,
in his one hundreth year.

PROLOGUE

THE PILOT OF THE CROP DUSTER scanned the ever-brightening horizon. He knew that the full-blown day would be clear and hot, typical of early May in Northeastern Louisiana. It was good weather for maturing wheat and for breaking ground for soybeans. And it was perfect weather for aerial applications of the insecticides, herbicides and fertilizers that enhanced the productivity of the fertile land. The aviator dropped his sight to the earth below where the Mississippi River Delta stretched rich and flat. The patchwork of tender young cotton, ripening winter wheat and verdant pastures was beautiful. But Sonny Carter had not come out this early in the morning to enjoy the scenery. He had a job to do. Checking his landmarks, he turned his yellow Ag-cat in a lazy loop over the Bayou Macon and made his first assessing approach to a stretch of Little Fork Farm's eastern pasture land.

ON THE GROUND, the first rays of morning sun beamed through uncurtained windows into the airless three rooms of a tiny house nestled on the banks of the Bayou Macon. In the bedroom, that presummer sun heated rumpled sheets and reflected off a thin layer of perspiration coating the fine-grained skin of a woman who, in her sleep, noted the faint hum of the powerful skyborne engine counterpointing the early-morning sounds of birds and frogs and chirping insects.

As Sonny Carter's aircraft drew nearer to the farmhouse, the iridescent sheen on the woman's honey-gold skin gave way to full beads of sweat, and her eyelids, fringed with inordinately long dark lashes twitched, as concealed green eyes made the rapid movements indicative of deep slumber. Long sun-kissed limbs twisted without coordination, and the sweat began to run from her body, to pool between her full breasts, to puddle in the deep indentation of her navel. It dampened the thin nightgown of pale-blue batiste until the fabric stuck to her body. Suddenly, the dewy complexion paled. The sleeping woman muttered a broken cry of alarm. "Run! Oh dear God, run!"

Sonny, flying at rooftop level, saw a distinctive red-and-silver pickup truck on the gravel farm lane and knew that his brother-in-law was in the area. Before he made his last turn, he saw Pace Lofton at the edge of the boundary ditch just beyond the shade of an ancient oak. Pace stood easy, his booted feet spread wide, his arms crossed over his broad chest and his head tilted back as he peered skyward from beneath the brim of his pale straw hat. Sonny assumed that Pace had come to watch how well the new fertilizer spread, as well as to check the maturation of the vast acreage of Little Fork's winter wheat. Daringly, he tipped his wings in salute. Sonny caught a quick glimpse of Pace's arm lifting in return.

The bold pilot wasn't too sure of what he saw next. He had his hands full of controls and his mind on the power line that crossed near the end of the pasture. He did allow a tight grin to play beneath his bushy red mustache, and had a fleeting thought that if that near-naked female streaking across the gravel lane wasn't a mirage, ol' Pace Lofton would have his hands full in about ten seconds. Sonny pushed the lever that released a rain of fertilizer pellets and kept his eye steadily trained on the up-coming power line.

CHAPTER ONE

ALL THAT ALISA FAIRLIGHT COULD SEE as she tore out of the doomed building was the outline of a lean, dark-haired man and the ominous plane bearing down at him out of the brilliant sunrise. Intuitively, she knew a shouted warning was futile. Her command of the language was too halting. Besides, he would never hear her above the deafening sound of the diving plane. With one final burst of energy, she hurled herself at the unsuspecting man, catching him hard around the waist and tumbling them both, head over heels, into the ditch and beneath the protective screen of shielding oak limbs.

Alisa searched frantically for the words. *"Señor,"* guerrilla avion!" She corrected herself. *"Avion guerrilla!"* she screamed as she fought the resisting man, trying to keep him pinned beneath her wildly trembling body. She wanted to tell him that they would be relatively safe in the natural shelter of the ditch's embankment. In the open they were as good as dead. If only she could get the man to understand the danger, to keep his head down before it was shot off.

"What in the sweet hell!" Pace cursed, when for

the second time he hit the squishy earth with a thud and felt the dampness ooze through his shirt. In a natural reflex he tried to pry the clinging body from him. It was as if he were in the clutches of a lunatic. Finally Pace gave a mighty lurch, which broke the woman's hold long enough to let him roll on top and try to wrestle the flailing arms and legs beneath him into quiescence. Throughout their struggle, the crazed woman kept shouting unintelligible words at him and pulling him closer to her own body, breaking free from his firm hold to wrap her legs around his thighs, to pull his head hard against her bosom. Twice she had scratched him as he tried to crawl up out of the dank ditch, the second time drawing a fine line of blood across his cheek. Pace's agile mind knew that he had only two possible courses of action. He could knock the hysterical female loose with a sharp clip to her jaw, or he could give in to her dementia.

Pace Lofton had never hit a woman in his life, and insane or not, he wasn't about to hit this one, either. He gave in. He sank his full weight onto the taut body beneath his own, bearing them down into the muddy recesses of the drainage ditch.

"I don't know what your game is, sweetheart, but it's a little rougher than I like to play," he muttered into the golden hair that tangled itself around his throat and spread like a silkened web across his nose and mouth. Still the woman held him in a vise-like grip.

As the minutes passed and Pace stopped fighting

her, the woman gradually eased her hold to lie quietly beneath him. Sonny made his third pass over the ditch, and Pace could feel the hard pounding of her heart against his chest. He lifted his head enough to focus on her wild green eyes and saw the absolute terror there. Whatever was going on in the woman's mind, it was something happening at another place, at another time. She was not here.

Pace also knew that the feelings created by having a woman beneath him in such a compromising posture and wearing nothing but a thin nightgown, which was now riding high on her hips, were inappropriate to the present. Very gently, inch by slow inch, Pace slid his weight from her, but he wisely and cautiously kept within the limits of the ditch. Carefully, after he had turned his assailant with him until they lay on their sides facing each other and he no longer felt threatened by the suggestiveness of their positions, he eased the gown down her thighs. At last Pace took an easier breath.

The woman did not. Each time Sonny made a pass, a pulse thudded visibly in her throat and in her temple. Pace smoothed the sun-streaked hair back from her face with a muddy hand and crooned soothing words to her, much as he did his horse when it was spooked. And this woman was spooked. He had seen that look before. He had probably worn it before. . . when he was in Vietnam.

God, how big was that damn pasture anyway, he silently questioned. How many more passes did Sonny have to make? He tucked the woman's face into the relative dryness of his shoulder and mentally calculated how much longer Sonny would be.

"It's not real, is it?" The soft, husky words were breathed into the hollow of Pace's throat. The breath that bore the words was soft and disturbingly warm against him, but he made no answer as he continued to hold her until the sound of the Ag-cat faded. Sonny had laid his layer of fertilizing granules across the grassland. Just as quickly as his noisy plane had come, it was gone, and the sounds of rural morning returned. The birds sang, the squirrels chattered, the insects chirped and the Bayou Macon gurgled over a fallen log on its way to the Tensas River. In the new stillness the feminine body gave a hard shudder against Pace, and long shapely limbs untangled from those longer and more muscular. Her biting clasp eased, and slowly her slender arms around Pace's manly shoulders relaxed.

For a long time she lay quietly in Pace's embrace. Once more the muddy hand came to her face and brushed against her cheek. "It's okay." It was all Pace said, but it seemed enough. Then he pulled back to let her rise before he lifted his own lithe frame from the confines of the boggy ditch. She stood on the shoulder of the road and waited.

For the first time Pace had a complete view of his assailant, and his night-colored eyes narrowed beneath blue-black lashes. Even heavily splotched in rich delta mud, her beauty shone. The morning sun highlighted pale streaks in her golden hair, enriched the healthy glow of those expanses of honey-tinted skin that had escaped their roll in the earth, gave a strange luminescence to her eyes, eyes the crisp green of early summer. Light outlined her trim body, barely concealed by the wet gown that clung to the thrust of her full unbound breasts and accented the ripe curve of her hips, the dark valley of her femininity, the long length of tapering legs. Pace caught an appreciative breath.

Alisa Fairlight knew exactly what the man was thinking, and nervously she plucked the clinging folds of her nightgown from her body. Telltale color rose in her cheeks, and in embarrassment she turned, not knowing that she presented the man with the perfect sculpture of her rounded derriere.

"I'm sorry," she offered in weak apology, and then with an elegant shrug of her shoulders, she wrapped her arms about her torso and took the first step toward the house from which she had bolted in absolute fear.

"Wait," Pace ordered sternly as he popped open the snaps of his Western work shirt. The folds of his sopping garment enveloped her, and she felt the warmth of his hands on her upper arms as he held the shirt in place until she clasped the edges with her own stiff fingers, until he was assured that some of her modesty had been restored. It was a generous act, for he was as wet and probably as uncomfortable as she. It was his generosity that caused her to quell the uneasy feelings he created in her with his bold, assessing stare. So Alisa spoke without turning back to look at him.

"I do have hot water, if little else. You might like to take a shower or at least to wash up," she offered. Without waiting to see if the man followed, she gingerly picked her way across the sharp gravel of the lane. A wry smile played about her mouth as she thought of how her bare feet hadn't felt those stones earlier. She had felt nothing but the utter urgency of survival.

Pace wiped the fingers of one hand on the leg of his jeans and carefully retrieved his undamaged hat before following the woman across the road, through the overgrown yard that merged with his own wheat fields and onto the screened porch. He wondered who she was and why she was living in such isolation. He noted the recently repaired screens, the fresh coat of paint, the new board on the center step, the shiny electric meter near the kitchen window.

He caught the screened door and eased it closed behind him as he surveyed the orderliness of the shady porch, the comfortable-looking chairs pulled up to a small table, the cushions artistically tossed in a swing suspended from the ceiling, the pots of ferns and blooming house plants. Then he looked down at his muddy boots, retraced his steps to the door and tugged them off. His socks and his briefs probably contained the only dry threads in his clothing, he decided, as he crossed the neat porch toward the double French doors where the woman waited. Then he revised his opinion about his briefs and stepped over the threshold into the center room of the little house.

Although it was barely six-thirty, the house was hot, and it was in total chaos, in complete contrast to the cool order of the porch. Boxes and packing crates, furniture and accessories were everywhere. From the cartons that had been opened, excelsior, shredded newspaper and once carefully packed contents spilled onto freshly polished floors. His quick glance to the right showed him that in the bedroom there were still more boxes stacked helter-skelter as well as a single-sized mattress lying flat on the floor. That mattress was made up in crumpled sheets, which proclaimed the restless night its sole occupant had spent.

Pace pulled his sight from the telltale bed and watched as the woman picked her way through the crates, watched her carelessly stirring already-disturbed goods in the opened boxes and bending to read the labels on others. Finally, she grunted with satisfaction and stooped to pick up two large, thick emerald green towels and matching washcloths.

"The bathroom is through here." She indicated the bedroom door with a nod of her head as she shoved aside a huge box with her hip. Pace followed her direction through the narrow path she created through the living room and into the bedroom.

At the bathroom door she stood aside for him to enter the small room that, like the rest of the house, had recently received a fresh coat of white paint.

The green towel and washcloth she laid on the edge of the basin were the only color in the stark room. Even the bar of soap that she paused to peel was white.

"All the windows are painted shut." She explained the oppressive heat as she nervously wadded the soap wrapper in a tight ball. "I haven't the strength to break the seals. Maybe you can." With that she stepped back through the door and closed it behind her, leaving him to stand in the stuffy little room.

The first sound Alisa heard coming from her tiny bathroom was not the noise of a running shower, but the crackle of a protesting paint seal breaking. It was immediately followed by the groan of a swollen wooden window sash being forced upward. Calmly assessing those sounds, the enormity of her early-morning actions finally hit her.

She had thought she was over the worst of the nightmares, that they had attenuated to merely bad dreams. But she had been wrong again.

On weakened legs she turned to an open suitcase and found clean clothes. She crossed to the kitchen, shut the door behind her and with shaky fingers she stripped off the chambray shirt. Dropping it into the sink, she squeezed out a generous squirt of dish soap and turned on the water. While the muddy shirt soaked, she hurriedly peeled the gown over her head and sluiced the dirt from her body. Quickly she tugged on her clothes, rinsed the man's shirt, then thrust her hair beneath the flowing faucet. The

cold water not only washed the mud from her hair
but it jolted her nerves and restored the energy that
the vivid dream had stolen from her. The surging
blood stimulated her thoughts and she became
aware, suddenly, of what she had just done.

Whatever must the man in her shower be thinking
of her? She had come at him like a wild woman,
hurling her body at his, wrapping her legs and arms
around him in her desperation, clasping him in the
most intimate and suggestive of positions. Color,
not brought on by the cold water, rose in her cheeks
as she thought of the man who had fit his body so
well against hers.

He was a handsome man, tall, dark, leanly muscular. She could still see him poised over her, his strong
arms holding him just inches away before he finally
laid his body onto hers. Even in the shadowy ditch,
his healthy hair had gleamed as it spilled over his
forehead, straight and sleek, like the costliest of
sables. She could still smell him, the soap of his
early-morning shower, the spicy shaving cream, his
own body aroma. She remembered his cheek pressed
against her bosom, how smooth it had been. But she
knew that smoothness to be short-lived. By midafternoon, the blue-black stubble would be raspy,
and he would again need the razor.

Her mind shifted to his wary eyes, eyes that had
matched his hair—the secret black of night. And
she especially remembered the feel of his strong
body on hers. Gasping at the boldness of her
thoughts, she turned the water off and wrapped the

towel around her hair. She needed to decide how she would explain her bizarre behavior.

Alisa sat on the steps cleaning his muddy boots, resolved that she would simply tell him the truth. She heard him leave the bathroom then heard her bedroom windows being forced open. Leaving the boots to dry in the sun she went into the kitchen and unpacked two glasses, filled them with ice and poured the orange juice she had squeezed the night before. She looked up to find the man watching her from the living-room doorway. She tried not to notice the breadth of his bare chest, the strength suggested by his muscular arms, the way his dark body hair arrowed down his hard, flat abdomen to disappear beneath the wide leather belt hung low on his trim waist. She tried to ignore the long line of his legs. It took a lot of effort.

"You didn't have to clean my boots," Pace scolded gently before giving his name and asking hers.

"I think I owe you more than a shoeshine."

"The only thing you might possibly owe me is an explanation. What happened?" There was more gentle concern than curiosity in his voice, but still her green eyes shifted uncomfortably beneath Pace's assessing look. Alisa picked up the two glasses and turned away.

"Let's go onto the porch. It's my point of reference until I get this place whipped into shape."

Pace followed the path of her slim, bare feet. He selected a chair at the table, tossed out the colorful cushions in deference to his damp, dirty jeans and settled his narrow hips onto the bare wooden seat.

He tried to remember the last time that anyone had lived in the house, tried to remember if he had heard of its being sold. As far as he knew, it still belonged to the O'Neill family, the people from whom his father had bought the pasture land across the lane and the adjacent wheat fields that he had come to check. Besides, he knew from her slight accent that she wasn't a local. She had the crisp pronunciation of an Easterner.

"Then you're not a relative of the O'Neills?" Pace asked after he had sampled the chilled fruit juice. It was freshly squeezed, not frozen, and it was pulpy, the way he liked it.

"No, I'm renting the house. In a few weeks I'll join the Louisiana State University summer field school on their archaeological dig at Poverty Point. At the same time I'll be conducting some independent research for my doctoral dissertation."

"Is there something new there?" Pace's mind quickly catalogued what he knew of the square mile or so of ridges and mounds called Poverty Point. He knew it was one of North America's most significant archaeological sites, one which drew anthropologists and archaeologists to conduct studies into the lives of a community of people who had lived there more than three thousand years ago. He silently admitted his lack of any other pertinent information.

Alisa didn't know if Pace was genuinely interested in her work or if he was merely being polite, but she treated his question seriously. "A recently built weir on the Bayou Macon shifted the course of the waterway. It cut into the southeast bluff of the site, taking a tree and exposing a deep layer of midden. That's where we'll be digging." Her green eyes sparkled with anticipation. "I'm anxious to see what we'll find."

"And the topic for your dissertation?"

"'Common Ceramic Traits of North American Mound Builders.'"

Pace raised a dark eyebrow, but made no comment. He took another sip of the orange juice. "I thought all the university people who come to work at Poverty Point stay in the dormitory on the site."

He watched the sparkle fade and that uncomfortable look wash over her again. "Yes, generally." Her tone was edged in self-deprecation. "But first of all, I'm not an official member of the Louisiana State University team. When my own dig, which was necessary to fulfill the requirements of my postgraduate program was—" she searched for a term "—disbanded, I was fortunate to get myself into the summer program here, but the dorm was filled already. As to the second reason why I'm staying here instead of on the site.... I think you were a victim of my poor sleeping habits. How much rest do you think the other crew members would get if they thought that at any time I might come sailing out of my bed to rescue one of them from imaginary guerrilla soldiers?"

Alisa rose restlessly and moved to the far end of the porch to lean against a support column. She had changed into a pair of white shorts that left her long tanned legs bare. Over them she wore a camp-style shirt of an unusual pink. It reminded Pace of mimosa blossoms. Absently, she jammed her hands into the pockets of her shorts.

"In January I was on a site in Central America gathering data for my dissertation when, without warning, I found myself on the front lines of a very violent, very bloody revolution. There was fighting all around us and frequently amidst us. We were completely cut off, with no way out and no way to get help in. If we wanted to live, it was to be by our own wits. So we worked our way out, traveling at night, resting during the day, eating what we could find." She looked down at her slender form. "It wasn't much," she muttered. In the same small voice, she concluded, "Of a team of twenty-five—seven archaeologists and anthropologists, the rest support crew—only nine of us survived. I was one of the three archaeologists who made it to the border alive." The shudder ran through her body, but she denied the power of the black memories by throwing back her elegant shoulders and thrusting up her pert chin. It was a stance of total defiance.

As Alisa collected herself, Pace continued his silent study of her. Even with her hair drying in straight heavy strands and her face devoid of any makeup, he thought her to be unutterably beautiful. And he felt the urge to go to her, to hold her, not only to give her comfort, but to appease some alien appetite within himself. Pace shifted in his chair and suppressed that desire, just as he suppressed the urge to label the emotion that this woman called Alisa Fairlight had inspired.

Alisa stood in the same stiff stance for a while, and then she turned to front Pace. "Before we could sneak into the jungles, our camp was repeatedly strafed by small aircraft. It's been several weeks since I've had such a vivid nightmare. This morning's dream must have been triggered by the heat and the sound of that low-flying plane. When I awoke, I couldn't separate reality from the dream. I thought you were going to be cut in two." She added in a tight little afterthought, "I saw one of my best friends cut in half." She looked off again at the stretch of mature wheat, and he knew she was reliving the experience. "I'm sorry," she whispered. For the second time Pace received her heart-felt apology.

Pace rose from his chair and took three steps toward her, reaching out his hand to touch her shoulder in understanding and perhaps in something more. He didn't know.

Immediately, Alisa ducked beneath his arm and moved toward the kitchen. She was not oblivious to the embryonic emotions stirring within Pace. Subconsciously she had registered every nuance of his actions and reactions within the confines of the ditch. She might not remember everything, but the primitive level of her brain had computed and inter-

preted everything about him, and it now bled coded
messages into her conscious thoughts. She responded accordingly, and the excuse she needed to leave
him came. "I'll check your shirt."

Even with the blow-dryer humming on high, the
kitchen was cooler than it had ever been. Pace had
opened the short window over the sink and the two
others near where she had planned to set her small
drop-leaf dining table. Deftly, Alisa rearranged his
shirt, unaware that Pace had followed her inside.
She turned to find him directly behind her, reaching
around her to unplug the hair dryer and collect his
shirt.

"But it's still damp in places," she protested.

"It doesn't matter," Pace claimed as he pulled
the air-heated shirt over his shoulders. "It will
match my jeans."

They were standing very close, and for the first
time Alisa noticed the inflamed scratch down his
cheek. "Oh no," she breathed on a thin wail. "I
didn't do that, did I?"

Pace reached up a lean finger to trace the small
wound. "It doesn't seem fatal." He tried to smile
reassuringly, and he produced the beginnings of a
breathtakingly handsome grin, an expression further enhanced by the play of hard muscles in his
dark cheeks. But that movement stretched the tissue
beneath the scratch, and the wound that Alisa had
inflicted began bleeding again. Pace winced, and
Alisa immediately hurried to dig through the packing crates in search of a first-aid kit.

By the time Pace had his shirt buttoned, Alisa was dragging him back to the porch and shoving him down into the chair he had vacated earlier. "There's no telling what bacteria was in that ditch water," she muttered as she set down the metal kit and popped open the lid. Still mumbling about staphylococcus and other dire infections, she rummaged through its contents until she found a sterile cotton swab, a bottle of tincture of merthiolate and an adhesive bandage.

Positioning herself behind Pace, she drew his head back against her midsection while she painted the angry red scratch with the orange antiseptic. When the stinging medicine touched a line of especially raw tissue, he inhaled a hissing breath and instinctively thrust his head back.

"That hurts worse than the scratch, Alisa. What are you doing?" he complained as he reached up an assessing hand to his face just at the exact moment Alisa leaned over him for the bandage to place over the deepest gouge. Pace's hand touched the soft side of Alisa's breast, instead of his cheek. His eyes flew open, and both he and Alisa jerked back as if the merthiolate had touched something more than a small streak of raw tissue.

Black eyes locked with the dark-fringed green of hers. Both of them stopped breathing. Suddenly, parallel memories played across their minds, the memories of the intimacy of the morning in the close confines of the earthen walls: soft comforting words spoken against a damp temple, her thinly clad breasts protectively cradling his dark head, his pinioning leg thrust between her thighs. Slowly his hand dropped and fumbled for the bandage she held between slack fingers.

Pace's voice was husky as he peeled back the wrapper. "I'll put this on in the bathroom. You're too damn dangerous, Alisa Fairlight." He didn't know how he meant the words; he didn't know how she took them. He knew only that he had to move.

Pace rose again and picked his way through the jumbled rooms to the bathroom where in the mirror of the old-fashioned medicine chest, he examined the minor scratch. He doubted that it warranted the bandage, but with a dismissive shrug, he stuck the plaster to his cheek.

When Pace returned, Alisa was in the kitchen rinsing the juice glasses. He watched her for a moment before he asked from the doorway, "What do you intend doing with all of this...this stuff?" Without turning around, Alisa knew he gestured widely at the confusion of her belongings.

It took her a moment to find her voice. She had never met a man like Pace Lofton. He was too open, too...she searched for the word and settled on *earthy*. "I don't really know. There was a mixup in my instructions to the moving and storage company. When the van arrived late yesterday afternoon, the shippers unloaded everything from my old apartment, including the things I had separated for storage. I don't think that everything will fit in this tiny house.'' She dried the glasses and set them in a freshly lined cabinet.

"Do you have someone coming to help you get organized?"

Alisa shook her head as she neatly folded the dishtowel and searched for a non-existent rack on which to hang it.

"Well, come on and I'll help you put the bed together and up off the floor." His voice grew significantly quieter and heavy with suggestion. "It just might give you a new point of reference."

Alisa sucked in her breath in a soundless gasp and whirled to face Pace, but he was back in the living room searching for the bed frame. She stood listening to him whistle thinly through his teeth as he rummaged through the scramble. She couldn't repress a smile at his buoyant "Eureka" when he located the metal frames and supporting slats. The suggestive moment had passed, besides, she had spent half of yesterday wondering how she would manage without some muscles. She had literally landed a Good Samaritan; it would be foolish not to use him.

Acknowledging that if the bed were off the floor she could catch more of the cross ventilation from the newly opened windows and that assembling the bed was one of the tasks that would prove almost impossible without help, Alisa joined her newly acquired helper. Soon she was listening to Pace softly curse the inadequacies of the meager supply of hand tools she had unearthed at his request. Finally, in disgust, he threw the little screwdriver back into the plastic bag and stomped out to his truck. When he returned, he carried an impressive array of wrenches and screwdrivers, as well as a hammer and a metal measuring tape.

Pace assembled the bed frame, and together he and Alisa wrestled the box spring and mattress into position. Next, Pace attached the hardware to the bathroom and bedroom windows so that Alisa could hang blinds and draperies. He repaired the flimsy night bolt that she had ripped off in her panic, warning her to replace it with something stronger as soon as possible. "You may be out in the country where the crime rate is practically nil, but your nearest neighbor is four miles away. There is no reason to invite trouble," he explained as he tightened the latches.

While he wrestled her chest of drawers from the living room into the bedroom, Alisa found the coffeepot and proudly served her first guest. After one look at the contents of the cup she proffered, Pace volunteered to take a look at her electric percolator, innocently suggesting that maybe he could find out why it had only heated the water instead of brewing coffee. There was no time for Alisa to stop him before he poured the contents of the pot down the drain, popped out a screwdriver from his back pocket and removed the covering plate over the heating element. He poked around inside, replaced the panel and brewed the second pot himself. When Alisa grimaced at the bitter beverage, Pace realized his faux pas. He grinned sheepishly and muttered something about colored water as he opened the refrigerator to get cream for the strong coffee he had made. He stopped abruptly.

Inside, there was only the remains of the orange juice, looking even more forlorn because of the vastness of the refrigerator that she had purchased the previous morning. There had been nothing smaller in stock at the appliance store, and in the subtropical heat she couldn't wait a week or more for delivery of a special order.

Slowly Pace closed the refrigerator door. "Would you like to come home with me for lunch?" Pace offered as he thought of the meal his mother would have on the table.

"Oh, no. I couldn't. Besides, I don't think your wife would welcome a drop-in guest."

Pace smiled as he spoke softly. "I don't have a wife, Alisa, but I have a mother who always prepares enough for at least three extra mouths."

Alisa blushed and restated her denial. "I really can't. I have too much to do here." She grimaced at the clutter that had only worsened as she had opened more boxes in search of the things Pace requested as well as the coffeepot and cups. He turned to the sink and splashed tap water into her cup in place of the cream he had sought and returned it to her. Then they moved to the porch to drink the black brew.

Pace finished his coffee and moved to the steps to tug on his boots. "I hope you take a break this

morning and ride into town for something to eat,"
he spoke over his shoulder. "And if you won't take
that much time, at least run to that little store across
the bayou. It's right over the bridge, directly in
front of the turnoff to Poverty Point." He looked
out over the fields then down at his watch. The
wheat would have to wait. He should have been at
the farm-equipment dealer nearly two hours ago,
and he would be late for his appointment with his
banker. He wouldn't even have time to go home for
clean clothes. Oh well, he thought, they were used
to seeing farmers in worse condition.

With that thought Pace rose and stuffed the long
shirttail into his Levi's before turning to raise a
hand in a last farewell to Alisa. After settling the
straw hat low on his forehead, he cut a trail through
the overgrown yard and leaped the ditch beside his
truck. He wondered where the time had gone. He
hadn't realized that he was staying so long with
Alisa Fairlight. And more importantly, he had
never known himself to be so reluctant to leave any
woman's company. That bothered him. He jammed
the keys into the ignition and shook his head in
wonder. For the first time ever, something had
taken Pace Lofton's mind from his beloved good
earth.

CHAPTER TWO

IT WAS WHAT THE LOCAL PEOPLE CALLED dark-thirty when Pace pulled his silver-and-red pickup truck onto the edge of the wide cemented parking deck that jutted off the driveway at a right angle to the triple garage. The garage was full, as was the driveway and there was no way he could properly fit his truck onto the parking deck. Somebody had left a vehicle in the center of the lane, so that he had to edge onto his mother's lawn. Mary Alice wouldn't like that, Pace mused as he fondly identified the inconsiderate owner of the obstructing station wagon as his sister Lou Ann, who was married to Sonny Carter.

On the driveway, Pace skirted his brother-in-law's truck and wondered if Sonny and Lou Ann ever went anywhere in the same automobile. Winding between his mother's car and his father's pickup, he finally reached the door of the mud room where he left his boots and his hat. He barely made it into the main hall when he was tackled by his niece and three nephews. With a kid hanging from each leg and one under each arm, he noisily wrestled his way into the spacious living room.

There his father, J.D., and his brother-in-law sprawled in comfortable reclining chairs as they watched the tail end of the news blaring loudly from the television. Each man greeted Pace with an absent wave, sparing only a fleeting glance from the glowing screen.

"You kids let go of your Uncle Pace," his sister Lou Ann ordered as she blew Pace a kiss from the dining room where she was arranging place settings along the long table. "Pace hasn't had time to sit down, and already you're all over him," she grumbled sympathetically as she tossed a swath of sable-colored hair over her shoulder and reached for the napkins.

Reluctantly, her own two youngsters let go of Pace and flopped directly in front of the television to resume their wait for the anchorman to sign off so that they could switch on the Intellivision and play electronic games. But two little blond boys lingered. John David and Daniel were the children of Pace's older brother David, who had abandoned his sons to chase after the boys' mother.

Dropping down on one knee, Pace draped his arms about their thin shoulders to hug both boys close. "How did it go today, fellows? Did you help grandma?" he asked gently. As Pace attentively listened to the report of their adventure-filled day, he retied the sneaker of one child and examined the scraped elbow of the other with tender concern. When the tale wound down and each in turn had given him one more "sweet hug," he rose and ruffled their blond heads. The gentleness faded from his eyes. Every time he settled his bronzed hand on those golden crowns, so different from the darkness of the rest of the family, he was reminded of their mother, and that memory always brought a surge of bitterness up the back of his throat.

David should have known better, he told himself yet again. Like the rest of the people who had lived their lives in the isolated Delta country, David had seen time and time again the outcome of marriages between their friends and the women who had grown up in the cities. And it didn't matter if the brides came from nearby Monroe or Shreveport. The adjustment to rural life was simply too much for them. David had been warned repeatedly of what to expect from Linda, even before any of the family really knew about her. But David had listened to no one, and he still wasn't listening, even when the problem had proved larger than any of them had anticipated.

Now Pace and his family didn't even know where David was or if Linda was with him. All they knew was that there were two little boys left in the care of the family—J.D., Mary Alice and Pace. At the thought of the burden two active young boys placed on his mother, Pace's bitterness intensified, but with practiced control he managed to hide it as he gave each boy an affectionate pat on the rump and nudged them toward the television.

Five-year-old John David took the hint and crossed to join his two cousins, but little three-year-old Daniel lingered. He still clung with devotion to the leanly muscular leg of his beloved uncle. Big chocolate-colored eyes, incongruous with the child's fair hair and light complexion, studied Pace carefully. "What happened to your face, Unc Pace? And why are you so dirty?" he lisped as his tiny hand brushed ineffectively at the embedded streaks on Pace's Levi's.

Daniel's words caught Sonny's attention, and he laughed knowingly beneath the bushy red mustache. "I think Unc Pace tangled with a she-cat this morning, little Daniel. And I'm thinking that your ol' Unc Pace may have gotten the worse end of the deal." At Sonny's words, Pace immediately had more attention than he wanted as J.D. eyed him closely.

"Sonny!" Pace growled threateningly.

"A wildcat, Unc Pace? A real wildcat?" Daniel's eyes grew big at the awesome thought of his uncle wrestling a wildcat, and he clung even more tightly to his tall hero.

"Sonny's teasing you, Daniel. I fell into a ditch," Pace explained with gentle patience. At the same time he glared a warning at Sonny over Daniel's head, a warning that went unheeded.

"Fell!" Sonny whooped and nearly tumbled from his chair in laughter.

"What's this about a wildcat?" Mary Alice spoke from directly behind Pace as she wiped her hands on her apron and reached for her son's shoulder to turn him toward her for close inspection.

Lately, Mary Alice had spent a lot of time worrying about her second son. Ever since David had left, Pace had pulled more and more into the family and more and more into himself. He spent every free moment with John David and Daniel, all too frequently foregoing outings with his friends and evenings with the ladies in the towns. It wasn't fair, she protested to the other members of the family. It should be David caring for the boys. They were not Pace's responsibility. If he must tend a family, it should be his own, not his brother's. But Mary Alice did not say those things to Pace.

"I thought the game warden trapped that panther and took him deep into the Tensas preserve," Mary Alice muttered in worried tones as she examined her son from head to toe, assuring herself that none of his vital parts were marred or worse, missing.

Pace sent Sonny a look that should have singed his eyelashes. Sonny only laughed louder.

"There was no panther, mom. I fell into a ditch, that's all," Pace reassured his mother. "Worry about Sonny. He must have flown his plane too high one time too many. He seems to be brain-damaged from oxygen deficiency."

Homing in on the source of confusion, Lou Ann stuck her head inside the living-room doorway, bringing with her more of the rich aroma of Mary Alice's kitchen. She, too, looked askance at Pace. "What happened to you? How did you manage to get your pants so dirty while you kept your shirt clean?" Again Sonny howled with laughter.

Pace rolled his black eyes toward the ceiling. "Do

I have time for a shower before supper?'' He evaded the questions in all the eyes resting on him, especially the silent question on the face of J.D. Not waiting for an answer to his own query, Pace took the stairs two at a time, stripping off his shirt as he went.

Inside his room, he fleetingly wondered what it would be like to come home to a quiet house. Then he laughed at himself. He might complain about the way his extended family wandered in and out of the Lofton house all hours of the day and early night, but he would have it no other way. Well, maybe, just maybe, he might make one or two alterations. He grinned wryly, as he tugged off his clothes and dropped them into the laundry hamper. He might consider a reprieve from Sonny every now and then. Even before Sonny had begun to romance Lou Ann, he had been a constant visitor in the house. As best friend to both the Lofton sons, he had probably eaten more meals at Mary Alice's table than he had at his own mother's. Then Pace reversed the train of his thoughts. He couldn't even think of getting rid of his best friend, brother-in-law or not, especially a man as good as Sonny Carter, no matter how big a pain in the backside he could be with his teasing. With that admission Pace stepped into the shower and began to steam away a few sore spots he had acquired in his headlong sprawl into the ditch.

By the time Sonny entered the bathroom, Pace stood before the steamy mirror, a towel carelessly knotted around his lean flanks and a thick layer of shaving foam masking a day's growth of his heavy black beard. Sonny proffered a frosty bottle of beer.

"Peace offering," Sonny explained before he plopped down onto the toilet lid and stretched his stocky legs across the narrow bathroom floor. Pace wiped the shaving cream from around his mouth and took a deep swallow, watching Sonny warily from the corner of his eye. There was a tension about the other man that caught in the pit of his stomach. Pace carefully completed the shearing of his beard, flipped out the used blade from his razor and swished the handle beneath a hard flow of water. He wiped the remaining cream from his face, reexamined the thin scratch down his cheek, took another swallow of beer and waited.

"David called me around five o'clock this afternoon," Sonny began baldly.

Pace's hold on the bottle tightened, the muscles in his chest tightened, the knot in his stomach tightened. Even his voice tightened as he asked, "Where did he call from?"

"Las Vegas."

"Is Linda with him?"

"He didn't say."

Pace didn't hesitate before he clipped out the next question. "What did he want?"

Sonny noted his displeasure. "Capital. M-o-n-e-y!"

"How much?"

"As much as I can raise."

"Against what?" Pace snapped as he carefully realigned his shaving equipment on a high shelf in the medicine cabinet.

"Pace...." Now there was total reluctance in Sonny's voice.

Pace slowly turned to face him and repeated more demandingly, "Against what?"

Sonny's words were low. "His anticipated share in Little Fork Farms."

Suddenly the steamy room felt cold. Later Sonny would swear that he had heard the electronic pulsation of Pace's watch resting on the edge of the basin, had heard the blood pounding in his veins and been palpably aware of the absolute anger surging through his body. Later he would swear that he had not been afraid. At the moment, he certainly could not make the last of those claims, especially when he thought the beer bottle would burst in Pace's hand. He thought Pace would rip the towel bar from the wall when he snatched at a fresh towel to wipe the beaded sweat from his brow. He became especially alarmed when Pace shoved him aside and stood over the toilet, waiting to see if the two swallows of beer were going to stay inside his churning stomach.

"She's with him," Pace muttered through the cold water that he splashed onto his face. "There's not a doubt in my mind that he finally found her."

Sonny took a slightly easier breath. "What makes you so sure?"

"You know David almost as well as I do. Does bargaining away our forefathers' sweat, J.D.'s sweat, and my own sweat sound like something that David would think of on his own?" Disgust permeated his every word. His vision narrowed as he posed his next question. "Did he ask about John David and Daniel?"

He knew the answer to both questions and delivered it before Sonny had a chance. "Of course not," he snapped. "Could the David that we know mention his sons and talk about selling their inheritance in the same breath?" Again he answered his own question. "He could not. He was mouthing Linda's words."

Stripping the towel from his waist and hurling it in the general direction of the clothes hamper, he stalked naked into the bedroom and pulled on low-riding briefs, clean Levi's and a knit shirt. Sonny followed close behind, bringing Pace's nearly full beer bottle with him.

"Do you want any more of this?" He held up the brown bottle.

"No, you finish it. You haven't said anything about this to mom and dad, have you?" Pace asked as he stepped barefoot into a pair of soft loafers.

"I didn't think you would want me to."

"I don't. They're both hurting inside, especially dad, and you and I aren't going to make it worse." His anger flared anew. "Dammit, when you get to be nearly sixty years old and you've earned what almost anyone would consider the good life, you shouldn't have to eat your heart out over your thirty-six-year-old son because he is so hung up over a two-bit piece of human trash...." Pace's description of his sister-in-law became so vivid that Sonny's blushes matched his hair.

Pace slammed the closet door violently, breaking the stream of obscenities, breathing deeply in a valiant attempt to gain control. After a moment he spoke more calmly. "I assume that David is calling back."

Sonny nodded. "Same time, same station, Friday."

"The first thing you do is tell him that the corporation still stands. Our grandfather set it up to protect the family, and even if we could, we damn well wouldn't dissolve it to please that woman, not even after dad is gone. Just because Linda whistles doesn't mean that the rest of us jump like trained dogs through a flaming hoop. I'll see to that." Pace's anger resurged, but he forcefully kept it in control as he laid his plan to Sonny.

"Before dad's father died, he moved into the house with us. At that time poppa deeded the old house and homesite to David, but I'm sure that Linda doesn't know that. You remember the first time David took her there; you remember the raging fit she threw at the idea that he would dare to suggest she live in such isolation. She ranted and raved that it was bad enough living here with mom and dad. There was no way that David was settling her in that house. David's suggestion that they live in the old house triggered her first little side trip. Remember? She went to Houston for two weeks. Came back with a new wardrobe and a couple of friends in tow. You remember.''

Pace didn't wait for confirmation. "I'm almost positive that David never mentioned the property again and Linda still thinks it's part of Little Fork. That is probably the only reason she didn't make him sell the house and land along with the acreage he had bought before they married," he snarled bitterly.

Then his voice became demandingly cold. "I want that house, Sonny, and if I can't have it, I want to make sure that it doesn't leave the family. You know what it's worth. Make a deal with him without bringing my name into it. If Linda is with him and she learns that I want it, hell will freeze over before she will allow David to sell it to anyone without a rider that the property never reaches me."

They discussed the fair market value of the old house and the three acres of land on which it sat, finally settling on a price to offer the absent David that they both felt to be a little more than its actual worth. Pace reached for his brush and pulled it through the gleaming dark hair as he looked at his friend's reflection in the mirror. "I owe you for this Sonny." Then an unbidden thought of the woman he had come to know in those early-morning hours came sneaking into his mind, and a soft smile lightened his somber features. "And I owe you for a little something else, too," he added whimsically before turning to lead the way downstairs for supper.

Sonny followed closely in his wake. For once he was thoughtfully silent. Pace had changed, but Sonny was hard-pressed to identify exactly how. Then memories of the early morning rose to plague him, too. Surely not, he argued with himself. Why not, he rebutted. It was time Pace found someone gentle to temper the distrust, heal the scars, mend the overwhelming and awful hurt that watching Linda destroy his brother David had caused. It was a pensive Sonny who joined the others at the large dining table. More than one questioning glance met another at the evening meal. What had transpired upstairs to create such moody withdrawal in both Sonny and Pace?

IT WAS SEVEN TWENTY-THREE when Alisa awoke to a hard pounding on the frame of the French doors. It had been late when she had finally gone to bed, and for once there had been no dreams set in Central American jungles, no thump-swish of phantom machete blades cutting paths through dense undergrowth, no swarm of insects darting at her eyes and clogging her nasal passages, no gnawing hunger, no stifling terror. She resented the intrusion into a rare segment of dreamless, peaceful sleep. Turning away from the annoying sound, she faced the window as she forced her eyes open. A tiny crack between the newly hung shade and the window frame gave her a glimpse of the outside world, a glimpse that included the red and silver of Pace Lofton's pickup truck. All of a sudden Alisa didn't resent being awakened. She welcomed it.

Flinging on a robe, Alisa crossed through the living room and threw back the night-bolt, forgetting that her hair was unbrushed and unaware that she wore the mark of her pillow on her face. She had spent too much mental energy the previous afternoon and evening thinking about this man to be concerned about her rumpled appearance now. Besides, if her early-morning appearance yesterday hadn't driven him away, it wouldn't matter how she looked today.

"Good morning." Through the partially opened door, in a voice still husky with sleep, she warmly greeted her caller.

"Good morning," Pace answered with a wide smile. He slowly reached up to poke a lean index finger at the brim of his hat, an action which tilted it back from his forehead and lifted the morning shadows from his dark eyes. Leaning against the door frame, he tucked the fingers of both hands into the back pockets of the tight jeans riding low on his hard flanks. The smile widened as he took in her sleep-flushed features. "Now isn't this much nicer than beginning the day with a roll in the mud?" he teased with a knowing sparkle in his dark eyes.

"Mud baths are good for the complexion," Alisa rejoined as she held on to the door, a knob in each hand.

The ebony eyes scanned her smooth skin. "I don't think you need any treatment." She blushed and to hide her uneasiness at how quickly the spark of awareness had been rekindled between them, Alisa stepped back to usher Pace inside.

Pace declined. "I'm a day late in checking a wheat field, but if you think you can remember the right way to make coffee, I should be back in about twenty-five or thirty minutes."

"Maybe you should write down the recipe. Is that a third of a cup of coffee to a cup of water, or was it just the opposite?" she questioned coyly.

"Experiment," Pace directed as he crossed the weed-choked lawn in long purposeful strides.

"Breakfast?" Alisa called from the screened porch.

"At this hour?" Pace answered from the truck. "It's almost time for lunch."

A half hour later Alisa had showered, dressed in khaki shorts and a red shirt, brushed her sun-streaked hair until it shone, made up her bed, thrown open the doors to the Delta morning and had brewed the blackest, most bitter pot of coffee that she had ever tasted. This cannot be right, she thought as she took another assessing sip. Even with a splash of hot tap water it was still too strong.

When Pace returned, she had just convinced herself to pour the contents of the pot down the drain and start over. "Maybe he really should have written the recipe for me," she muttered as she held the pot poised over the sink.

"Whoa," Pace called from the doorway. "Don't spill a drop. It smells perfect." He crossed the kitchen floor on bootless feet and took the pot from her hand, sniffing appreciatively.

"I didn't hear you drive up."

"That's because I walked across the field." He looked down at his feet. "There were still a few wet spots from Monday's rain, and it seems that I stomped right through every one of them. I left my muddy boots on the porch." He plugged the coffeepot back into the outlet, set the dial to reheat and leaned his hips against the kitchen counter. "It should be hot as well as black and bitter," he explained, and then his eyes began to take in the changes in the kitchen.

"Nice, very, very nice," he complimented. "You've obviously been a busy lady." Then he cast a knowing glance in the direction of the living room. "But not busy enough," he laughed as he turned back to the shiny coffeepot and poured two cups of the thick, steaming brew.

"Pace, I can't drink this stuff," Alisa protested as she studied the inky beverage in her cup.

"Sissy," Pace goaded as he opened the refrigerator door for cream to add to Alisa's coffee. He stood for a long time with one hand on the door while he studied the contents of her refrigerator. "I thought you were going to lay in some food."

"I did," Alisa retorted as she set her coffee on the counter and slipped beneath Pace's arm to see what had happened to the groceries she had bought and placed in the refrigerator. They were all there.

Pace read the labels on cartons of yogurt and cottage cheese before opening the crisper drawer to peer at a bunch of celery, two cucumbers and a head of lettuce. He brought out a quart of skimmed milk, slammed the door shut and popped open the freezer compartment. He sighed at the four packs of frozen broccoli and cauliflower and the assortment of prepackaged dinners. Closing the freezer, he eyed the artistically arranged bowl of fruit on the Formica-topped counter. "No wonder you're so skinny," he muttered.

Since her ordeal in Central America, Alisa had become very sensitive about her weight. "I am not skinny," she snapped back as her hands flew to her hips in a defiant stance.

Pace stood peeling open the lip of the paper milk carton as he carefully examined Alisa. It was a thorough examination that started at the frosted polish on her toes, traveled up the slim length of her long tanned legs, lingered at the delicate curve of her hips, before stopping at the surprising fullness of her breasts. "No, it's my mistake, Alisa Fairlight. You aren't skinny at all. You're perfect...too damn perfect."

The last three words had been muttered beneath his breath as he poured a generous splash of milk into Alisa's cup. "In here or on the porch?" he asked in a blunt change of topic and handed her the pale-blue ironstone cup that repeated the color in the blue-and-brown plaid of the two place mats on the drop-leaf table.

Alisa automatically reached for the diluted coffee. "The porch," she answered softly and led the way outside. At the first sip, Alisa didn't even think of the flavor of the coffee. Her tongue never registered the underlying bitterness, which was only slightly masked by the milk. She was too busy thinking about what was happening between her and the man she had met a little over twenty-four hours earlier, a man unlike any other she had ever encountered.

Pace Lofton had come into her life under the wildest of circumstances and had fit in like a comfortable old friend. He had not pressed her about the circumstance of her experience in Central America. He had automatically helped her when she needed help. The man had not stood on any formality at all. He had been instantly and completely at home in her house, a house that she had yet to stamp with the imprint of her own personality. Considering the amicable side of Pace created a thinly drawn line between her slightly feathered brows.

"Leave it, Alisa," Pace instructed in a tight voice as he raised his feet onto the porch rail and slid lower into the chair.

Alisa's eyes flew to Pace, but he was studying the overgrown lawn. Had he read her mind? Was he as disconcerted as she about the direction their relationship seemed predetermined to take? Or was she imagining the tension that seemingly colored everything whenever they were together, the tension that she was positive was between them right now, when they were barely beyond the point where they should be calling one another by first names? Such thoughts had filled her head since she and Pace had climbed out of the ditch. Such questions persisted in tormenting her now, when all she really wanted to do was enjoy Pace's company, to get to know him.

Pace interrupted her reverie. "What are you planning to do with this yard? It's a wonder the snakes haven't taken over."

If there was only one thing capable of shifting Alisa's mind from one worrisome topic to another, he had definitely found it. There had been snakes in Central America. "Snakes!"

"Snakes. Good Lord, Alisa, you're camped not two hundred yards from the Bayou Macon. Snakes," he repeated for the third time.

"Poisonous snakes?"

"Among others."

Alisa set the cup down on the table. "I don't suppose you know of someone who would come in and cut the grass for me," she hinted broadly.

"I know where you can borrow a couple of goats," Pace replied dryly.

"Goats!" Alisa reacted with almost as much revulsion as she had when Pace had mentioned the snakes. "Goats smell horrible, and they don't discriminate about what they eat. They would just as soon eat the tires off my car as this overgrown grass," she protested expansively. "Besides, they leave...they leave droppings," she added fastidiously.

Pace looked over at the little blue sports car parked at the corner of the house. "I don't think there would be too much gone if they ate that whole thing," he teased. Her car would almost fit into the bed of his truck. "And the 'droppings' would work wonders in organically enriching the soil."

The green eyes glared at him.

"Okay," Pace yielded, "if you don't want goats, I'll bring over a bush hog and at least get the yard down so it can be handled with something more conventional."

This time there was no doubt that he was serious and Alisa was aghast. "You really mean it, don't you? I think I would rather have goats than pigs. Thank you, Pace Lofton, but no thank you!"

Pace's sock-clad feet hit the floor in a muted thud. "Pigs?" Then he burst out laughing. "Pigs!" he repeated and laughed louder. "Just where have you been all your life? Dear Alisa, a bush hog is a piece of equipment we use to clip pastures. It most definitely is not a barnyard animal."

Alisa fought a blush. "I didn't even know that pastures had to be clipped. I thought the cows *ate* the grass. There just aren't that many pastures in downtown Boston."

Pace felt as if he had received an unexpected blow to his midsection. The injustice of it all, he charged. Why couldn't she have been from rural Vermont, or the craggy coast of Maine? Why the city? But he should have known, he countercharged. It was all there. He wanted to smash something, anything. Instead, he asked in a tight voice, "Is that where you're from, Boston? Are you an out-and-out city girl?"

"Through and through. Is it important?" She didn't understand his mood change. It was a new Pace sitting across the table from her. The new Pace didn't answer. Instead he rose to his feet, placed his empty cup on the table and reached for his hat. Alisa rose with him.

"When do you start work at Poverty Point?" he asked as he tightened the curl in the brim of his hat.

"Whenever I'm ready." Something in her voice made him look up from his hat. "One of the things I had to promise my physician was that I wouldn't push myself."

"Physician? Your ordeal was months ago. Was it so awful?"

"While I was in the jungle I was numb, alert only to what I had to do in order to survive. But later, when I had time to remember exactly what I'd seen and experienced, it was terrifying. I had nightmares, headaches, nausea. I couldn't eat or sleep or work." She shook her head sadly at the memory of the complete wreck she had been. "Perhaps I could have handled it a little better if I hadn't had the added pressure of revamping my thesis. Even in my distress, it didn't take long before I realized that without the data from the site we had abandoned, as well as the sites we never reached, my research proved inconclusive, my thesis invalid. So now, instead of tracing the ceramic development of the ancient mound builders from the Mexican coast southward, with a concentration on the sites of Central America, I am beginning here at Poverty Point and ending with the last site from which I managed to salvage data.''

"How long will all of this take?"

"I'm allowing myself a full six months, which includes ample time for writing. Actually, I lack little, primarily collating the Poverty Point information with my previous research. By the end of November I should be ready to present the paper and take my oral examination.''

"After you finish at Poverty Point, couldn't you write someplace else, like back in Boston?"

"I could, but there won't be nearly so many distractions here." Alisa moved to the edge of the porch and looked out across the gravel lane to the lush pasture land. "You, of all people, can attest to the fact that I still have a little more healing to do after my first-hand experience with guerrilla warfare.''

Fleetingly, she remembered the diagnosis. The physician had told her that every case of post-trauma syndrome was different. He couldn't tell her how long she would suffer, but he had insisted that she take it as easy as possible for at least a year. He was the one who had encouraged her to extend her stay in the country. And with the encouragement of her father as well as her academic advisors, she had taken his advice. She plucked a fading blossom from a pot plant. "It has been suggested that this is a location conducive to the complete restoration of my former good health."

Alisa had trouble concentrating on her health, on Poverty Point, on her paper or the anticipated degree. What she really wanted to think about was right here on her porch. Whatever had happened to Pace? One reference to Boston and he had become as taut as a finely tuned lute. What had she done? What had she said? She could find nothing, so she forced herself to concentrate on their conversation—talk that she doubted either one of them would be able to recount fifteen minutes later.

"The location will be conducive as long as the crop dusters fly long loops around this section of land," Pace qualified.

"Or give me fair warnings," Alisa amended as she turned back to face him, puzzlement still in her eyes.

Although he had his feelings under surface control, Pace wondered exactly how attuned to his mood shift Alisa was. He wondered if she could possibly know how much he wanted to forget the fact that she would be in the area for only a limited time, to forget that sometime in the near future she would pack up the household goods, her clothes, typewriter and books and disappear from his life. When he thought of Alisa Fairlight, as he had done so often in the past twenty-four hours, it was never the end that he envisioned, only a beginning. He wondered if she had the slightest notion of how much he wanted to say to hell with his better judgment, to grab at what he intuitively knew could be between them, to let their attraction grow and grow until it reached the inevitable explosion. Could he not heed the fallout that was sure to follow? That he could even entertain such thoughts bothered Pace Lofton a lot.

But what he did next bothered him even more. After settling the well-worn hat on his head, adjusting it low onto his brow and slipping the tips of his fingers into his back pockets, the words he uttered came unbidden, and he couldn't seem to stop them. "Tomorrow night one of the chemical companies that manufactures most of the fertilizers, herbicides and pesticides we farmers use is hosting a supper for the members of the Delta Rivergrain Terminal. There will be some very informal business conducted, but primarily it is a social event. I'd like you to go with me."

Alisa turned back and answered without hesitation. "Thank you. I'd like to go."

"Good. I'll pick you up about six and don't dress up too much. The supper will be held at the fishing and hunting camp of the Triparish Timber Company." He crossed to the door and stepped into his boots. As he straightened up, he cast one last look over Alisa's overgrown lawn. "And someone will be over to clip this jungle of a yard for you."

There was no farewell as Pace shoved open the door and, two at a time, descended the steps, broke yet another trail through the overgrown grass of

Alisa's lawn and crossed into the wheat field, breaking off an occasional head of grain and rubbing it between his knowledgeable fingers. He did not turn back.

CHAPTER THREE

By Friday afternoon, Alisa was looking forward to a night out. Earlier in the day, a truck pulling a trailer loaded with a small tractor and bush hog had stopped in front of the house. Without conferring with Alisa or even acknowledging her presence as she watched from the screened porch, the grizzled driver had unloaded the equipment and immediately set about clipping several years' growth of grass and weeds from her yard. By the time the taciturn man, sent by Pace, had finished, reloaded the equipment and left, Alisa had completed the last of her unpacking. She had also finally arranged her furniture and household goods to her satisfaction, hosed down the front porch and screens to rid them of the dust the mower had created and was more than ready to climb into a relaxing tub of hot water.

But she had not been ready for the sight of Pace Lofton when he came to pick her up in the last glow of the spring afternoon. Although she had dressed with care, for some reason she had expected Pace to be in jeans, perhaps less faded than those he wore for work, in boots, more dressy than those she had twice seen encrusted in rich Delta mud, and to be

wearing a Western-styled hat. And she had definitely anticipated his arrival in the red-and-silver pickup truck. Instead, when a bare-headed Pace tapped
lightly on the glass door, he wore well-tailored
slacks and an intricately knitted short-sleeved
sweater that emphasized the muscular expanse of
his chest. The flash of gold at his neck and wrist
contrasted with the darkness of his skin tone. And
out on the gravel lane awaited an elegant smoke-
gray Lincoln. Alisa blessed the stars that had urged
her to reject slacks and select the bronze-colored
blouse and the slightly gathered skirt of cream-
colored linen.

"My, my, but you certainly don't look like a
farmer tonight, Mr. Lofton," Alisa offered lightly
as she opened the door to the now-orderly lamp-
lighted living room. Instantly, the soft smile around
Pace's mouth faded.

For a minute he stood silent. When he spoke, his
words were harsh, but she heard something else in
his voice, too. She couldn't identify the underlying
emotion. It sounded like disappointment. She
wasn't sure.

"Don't let the props fool you, Alisa," he finally
bit out. "I'm just a red-neck farmer, and I will
always be a red-neck farmer. I'm not even an agribusinessman. Don't ever make the mistake of
thinking I'm anything more." Before Alisa could
apologize for whatever unintended offense she had
given, Pace was stepping back from her arrested
welcoming gesture. "If you're ready, we should

go." He did not come inside, but stood on the porch, staring out over the darkening land while Alisa turned out lights, gathered her bag and locked the door.

In the quiet car, Alisa tried to think of something to say into the overwhelming silence, while Pace drove so aggressively the car seemed to eat the miles of back road. It was Pace who finally broke the uneasy quietness, his words unrelated to their previous conversation.

"Once upon a time, I wouldn't have dared to take anyone interested in Poverty Point to a gathering of local farmers. Even more dangerous would have been to take someone directly involved in the work at the Indian mound."

"Why?" Alisa asked with complete interest, the awkwardness of the past few minutes temporarily forgotten.

"The narrow strip of land that lies adjacent to the Mississippi River from Memphis south to the mouth of the river is perhaps the richest farm land in the world, a near perfect sandy loam. When the archaeologists first began to tout the importance of Poverty Point with any kind of authority, with any kind of plan for its development, the area farmers' first reaction was fear. They were convinced that the Department of the Interior would expropriate their beloved Delta land. For a while the landowners kept busy leveling anything that vaguely looked like it might contain artifacts and camouflaging what they could not plow down. The mere hint of possible archaeological interest in the vicinity sent the plowshares deeper into the soil and the graders rolling.''

''How very, very tragic,'' Alisa sighed. ''There is no telling how much was lost forever.''

''Yes, it was tragic, wasn't it, almost as tragic as taking away a man's land that he has worked and prayed for, sweated and sacrificed for, land he has agonized over and built into a heritage for his children by the calluses on his hands and the aches in his back.'' Again there was the same bitterness in Pace's voice that Alisa had heard when she mentioned his mode of clothing.

''Have you lost land to the preservation of archaeological sites?'' Alisa ventured cautiously. Something told her that Pace was not speaking of a threat against his land by state or federal expropriation. It was something far more personal, perhaps that same thing that had bothered him when she commented on his clothing.

''No.''

''Are there any possible sites on your land?''

Pace's response was a shrug of his shoulders, and Alisa didn't know if that was a positive or a negative gesture. She interpreted it to mean that he didn't know or he didn't care.

''Does any of your land adjoin the Poverty Point site?''

''No,'' Pace answered again. ''All of our land, Little Fork Farms, is on the east side of the Bayou Macon.''

For a while they talked about Little Fork, conversation that evaporated the previous tension as the big car covered more miles of near-desolate country roads. "How far is it to the camp?" Alisa asked.

"Not far," Pace responded.

"It seems to me we've already gone a far distance," Alisa idly protested his vague answer.

For the third time Pace's demeanor instantly hardened. "You're in the rural South, Alisa. There isn't a supermarket every half mile with a pharmacy, a boutique, three cocktail lounges and a gas station in between."

"And I can't walk to church or to the library nor is there public transport to compensate," Alisa snapped back in kind.

The dark head swiveled toward her, and gradually the big car slowed. "Is that how I sounded?" Pace asked quietly as he returned his attention to the road.

"Worse," Alisa qualified. "*You* had no provocation."

The car slowed even more, and in an electronic whirl, Pace lowered his window. The vibrant air of the early evening washed out the heady aroma created by the leather appointments of the luxury sedan. The smell of outdoors was vital—the full, rich yeasty smell of freshly tilled land, cut by the acrid scent of leafing pecan trees from a nearby orchard. The soft leather seats protested quietly as Pace shifted in his seat.

His next words came around a constriction in his

throat. "There's provocation, Alisa, more provocation than any one man should ever have to bear. Some cold, rainy night in December I'll tell you the whole woeful tale."

"I probably won't be here in December," Alisa supplied.

"How right you are," he agreed. "And that, pretty Alisa, just happens to be part of the provocation," he added cryptically, "but I will share this much with you now, even though it may only serve to cloud the issue of why I harbor such ambivalence toward you." He paused to glance at her before he continued. "I've learned the hard way that it's imperative for me to avoid—at whatever cost—any woman with a completely different background, with different values and different goals from those of the women who were born and bred to the life here. But," he stressed, "you are also everything that I admire in a woman. You are self-sufficient, aggressive yet sensitive, intelligent and—" he paused significantly before the last word "—desirable. When I think of you without the shadow of your past and the obvious direction of your future, I want to be with you, to get to know you. But when your past or your future intrudes, as a simple off-chance remark may cause it to do, I automatically react negatively. Most of the time, I am not aware of my rudeness. And that is as much of an apology as you will get tonight," he finished flatly.

"I don't understand," Alisa whispered in protest. "You know nothing about my past and neither one of us can predict my future. You aren't really making sense.''

''And you won't be around long enough for it to become much clearer, so let's leave it alone and enjoy the time we have together,'' Pace supplied as he braked the car and executed the turn onto a narrow road leading toward the densely wooded horizon. ''You are now on Triparish property, some of the best hunting grounds left in the state.''

Until Pace finally rounded the last twist in the rutted road, he kept the conversation on the role of the timber industry in Northeast Louisiana. They also spoke about the nationally publicized fight of the conservationists to keep the great wooded Tensas wildlife preserve. Pace was well-informed and enthusiastic, and Alisa wondered what part he had played in the conflict. But before she could ask, they sighted the camp, and there was no opportunity for more personal conversation.

The hunting lodge was set deep inside commercial timber property. It was a single-storied building of rough-hewn logs, surrounded on three sides by long expanses of screened porches. The fourth side was a covered cement slab that presently held tight knots of men gathered around portable butane cookers. When Pace opened the car door for Alisa, the smoky aroma of sausage and ham completely overwhelmed the scents of the deep woods. Alisa sniffed appreciatively.

''Jambalaya,'' Pace offered. ''And you can forget about that skinny food in your refrigerator. You won't find anything like that here tonight." Then his white grin flashed in the dark. "Well, maybe a light beer or a diet cola," he amended.

They walked up the shadowy gravel path toward the sheltered patio. As they neared, the all-male crew called warm greetings to Pace, which he returned in kind. In the yellow glow of the bug-repelling lights, Alisa easily read overt signs of curiosity about her identity on strangers' faces, curiosity that intensified as Pace made introductions. Somehow Alisa knew the interest of his friends, which sometimes more nearly resembled total incredulity, had nothing to do with Pace's references to her research at Poverty Point. It was something else. It was as if she seemed like a threat, not only to Pace, but to all of them. She didn't understand.

As Pace joined briefly in the conversations of first one group and then another, he kept his hand at Alisa's waist until he directed her into a large room filled with an assortment of tables, benches and folding chairs. Again he was warmly greeted. This time the salutations included soft feminine smiles and voices. As it had been outside, this, too, was a heterogeneous collection of people, ranging in age from the early twenties to a few whose appearances defied time.

Still touching her, Pace carefully surveyed the room, then with a little nudge he directed her toward a man who was leaning against a wall and studying a pamphlet with deep concentration. Alisa guessed the man to be in his late fifties or early sixties. He was a bit weather-beaten, but still handsome. His graying hair contrasted with his dark skin, and Alisa knew that his skin tone was due neither to sun nor time. The man's heritage was there, in his complexion, in the high cheekbones, in the slight upward tilt of his black eyes, a feline tilt only barely suggested in the mysterious set of Pace's eyes. Even before the introduction, Alisa knew the man was from Pace's family. Which American Indian tribe, she wondered, had left its mark on the Loftons?

"Dad," Pace began in strangely hesitant tones. He sounded as if he had an unpleasant task to perform and he wanted to get it over with as quickly as possible. The man looked up at the sound of his son's voice. "This is Alisa Fairlight. She's staying in the granny-house on the old O'Neill place while she does some work at Poverty Point. Alisa, my father, J.D. Lofton."

Alisa held out her hand. "Mr. Lofton, it's so nice to meet you."

At the sound of her voice, replete with clipped New England syllables, the black eyes narrowed. It was a long time before the callused, work-marred hand folded itself about Alisa's softer, far smoother one. And when he did touch his hand to hers, he quickly released it. "Miss Fairlight," J.D. Lofton answered too carefully. Then the hard, black eyes, eyes only slightly modified in his son, moved from Alisa's face to Pace's. "Do you know what you're doing?'' the man asked in dark, angry undertones.

A flush further deepened Pace's own swarthy skin. "It's all right, dad," Pace replied tightly. When Alisa's puzzled glance moved to follow the path of J.D.'s, hoping to determine the reasons for the older Lofton's attitude, Pace avoided meeting her glance by quickly looking around the room. "Have you seen Sonny?" he asked his father. At first Alisa didn't know if he was really interested in Sonny or if he was merely interested in changing the topic.

If Pace had wanted to change the conversation, he was successful. The older man did not continue his rude questioning, but neither did he relax. "No, I haven't seen him, but if he's here, he's probably still outside carrying on his usual line of foolishness." Then J.D. turned to Alisa. Intuitively she knew his anger still burned, even though it was no longer apparent. He was as good as Pace at hiding his feelings. "Have you met my son-in-law Sonny Carter, Miss Fairlight?" he asked with forced politeness.

"No, sir, I haven't," Alisa answered, wondering why this question instantly erased some of the tension from Pace's expression and brought a sudden flicker of amusement to his dark eyes. Then just as quickly as it had come, the playful light was gone.

Pace was once more questioning his father. "Did Sonny call after I left the house?"

"Not that I know of." J.D. patted his shirtfront absently. "What did I do with my pen?" He looked around the room. "I must have given it to your mother. Where is she, anyway?"

"We haven't seen her, dad, but if we run into her while we're looking for Sonny, we'll send her your way."

Just then a burst of loud laughter came from the area of the cookers. "I think you just spoke of the devil and he appeared. Want to make a bet that Sonny just arrived?" J.D. challenged as he once more futilely searched his pockets for the missing pen. Behind them the room began to quicken with noisy new activity. Looking up, J.D. offered, "Sonny just walked in."

Pace glanced over his shoulder for verification, suddenly tightening his hold on Alisa's back. "You need a beer or anything, dad?" he asked. "I'll bring you one, and then I have to talk to Sonny."

"No, I don't need anything, but if you can keep your mind on business long enough, I do want you to talk to the chemical representative about his new herbicide." J.D. sounded angry again. He fanned through the collection of brochures he had amassed, selected one and held it out to a very grim-faced Pace.

"I don't think that was called for," Pace accused as his dark gaze locked with his father's. "I've never let you down."

"Not yet, you haven't. But the future remains to be seen, doesn't it?" The two men stood silent for a long minute, and then J.D. once more extended the pamphlet to his son. When he spoke again, there was no apology, no explanation. And Pace seemed to need none. "Look this over, and then get back to me and tell me what you think. It sounds good to me, like something we could use on the Willow Bayou wheat. If we don't find something to stop that spread of wild onions, we won't be able to raise wheat there much longer."

Pace slipped the pamphlet into his back pocket. "I'll look into it, but right now, I think we'll see Sonny." The hand on Alisa's back pressed her toward a large circle of people near the door, barely giving her time to offer a polite comment on the pleasure of meeting the elder Lofton. If Pace knew the reason for his father's unpleasant behavior, he did not offer to enlighten Alisa. And once out of his immediate presence, Pace relaxed a little. He even managed a broad grin when Sonny hailed him.

"Hey, Pace," the red-haired man called as Pace and Alisa approached, "I see the cat scratch is healing. Once more, you lucky dog, it seems you have escaped without permanent damage. But one day, my friend, the fates are going to catch up with you, and you will have hell to pay."

"And I see Lou Ann left your cage unlocked, and you're out after dark," Pace rejoined, releasing his possessive hold on Alisa and turning his full attention to the woman beside Sonny. "Poor, poor baby sister," he commiserated in heavy tones of mock pity as he leaned down and brushed a theatrical kiss onto the cheek of the lovely, black-haired, black-eyed woman, a feminine replica of himself. The feline tilt in her eyes was more pronounced, and what in Pace was a wholly masculine feature became, in his sister, hauntingly female. "Wouldn't anyone help you get him back in?" Pace asked solicitously. "You should have called me, little sister. I would have waved a bottle of Jack Daniels through the bars, he would have walked right in and all you'd have had to do was slam the door behind him." The group laughed.

"Funny, Lofton, fun-ny," Sonny responded as Pace turned and clasped Sonny's hand in a firm two-fisted handshake. But Sonny's bright blue eyes were moving speculatively over Alisa. "Who is this pretty lady, Pace? She is uncommonly attractive and appears to have the normal amount of intelligence. Surely if she knows you at all she didn't voluntarily come with you tonight. Who got you this blind date, Pace, your mother?"

Again there was a loud guffaw from the people loosely gathered at the doorway. A boyish grin spread over Pace's face. With a move so subtle that Alisa wasn't sure it was intentional, Pace separated Sonny and Lou Ann from the others. His voice lowered intimately. "Don't you remember, Sonny? You got me this date." He draped an arm about Alisa's shoulders and pulled her closer to him, creating a new circle that contained only the four of them. "Sonny Carter, this is the she-cat herself, Alisa Fairlight. Alisa, Sonny, whom my poor little sister in a moment of unaccountable weakness had the misfortune to marry, is the pilot who buzzed your house Wednesday morning.''

Alisa was grateful that Sonny's next words were a hoarse croaking whisper, audible only to the four of them. ''The she-cat: long brown legs, pale-blue nightgown, flying tackle....'' As his voice trailed off, Sonny's mouth dropped open.

Lou Ann's eyes narrowed to target on Sonny, and Alisa's color rose to clash with the bronze of her blouse. ''Nightgown?'' Lou Ann repeated as she looked from Sonny to Pace to Alisa and back to Sonny again.

''I'll explain later, sweetheart,'' Sonny assured his curious wife.

''I think you'll explain sooner, *sweetheart*,'' Lou Ann mocked. She cocked a fine brow over her striking black eyes and again flicked a searing glance over the trio.

''Touché, Pace, touché,'' Sonny growled as he kept a wary eye on his wife.

Pace smiled broadly, enjoying every moment of his best friend's discomfort. Finally, he relented. ''Alisa, will you explain to my sister Lou Ann why Sonny knows the color of your nightgown while he and I get us something to drink? What do you want, a diet soda?'' he teased as he stepped away.

Alisa pulled a face at Pace's retreating back, turning just in time to see the speculation in Lou Ann's eyes. What was going on in his family? Why did her accompanying Pace create such strong reactions in everyone they encountered? She glanced back at Pace, but there was no help from his quarter, only more mystery.

Pace and Sonny had taken less than two steps toward the row of ice chests, filled with bottled and canned drinks, before they were stopped by a man whom Alisa remembered meeting outside. She saw the brief flicker of annoyance in Pace's eyes when the man followed them as they slowly made their way across the room. Fleetingly, she wondered what private thing Pace had to discuss with Sonny that was so important. Then she mentally acknowledged that there was a lot she wondered about when her thoughts dwelled on Pace Lofton, and now there would be even more. He was, above all else, a contradiction unto himself, the greatest human enigma she had ever encountered. Also a very sexy man, she added, then, dismissing her train of thought, Alisa turned to Lou Ann.

"I hope you aren't truly upset with your husband," she began as they edged toward a vacant table and sat down. Carefully, she explained the circumstances of her first encounter with Pace, and Sonny's role in that meeting. Lou Ann, who possessed a sense of humor almost as keen as her husband's, found the idea of her handsome brother covered in ditch water and mud extremely funny. Alisa breathed a relieved sigh as she concluded, "But I don't know anything about those references to a she-cat."

It was then Lou Ann's turn to explain. When Pace slipped into the chair beside Alisa and placed the bottled drink in front of her, Lou Ann had recounted the conversations and misunderstandings that had arisen in the Lofton home on the evening following Alisa's "rescue" of Pace.

The four of them had the table to themselves only for a short while. All too soon, for Alisa's comfort, the chairs around them filled with Loftons and with each introduction there was a slight hesitation when the newcomer learned of Alisa's origins. It was especially pronounced in Pace's mother who took the chair across the table from Pace and Alisa. But Mary Alice tried her best to mask her reaction as she acknowledged Alisa's introduction.

Even with the awkward moments, Alisa was fascinated by Pace's family. Ever since her tenth year, she had seldom been in the same room with all three members of her own immediate family at a given time. She had usually seen her mother one week, her father three weeks later and her sister whenever things were not going well. In fact, communication with any member of her family was not a simple matter. They were important people who were often traveling, and above all else they were independent.

Elizabeth Fairlight, Alisa's mother, was the antithesis of the ample-bosomed, thick-waisted Mary Alice Lofton. Mary Alice seemed to exemplify familial devotion and commitment to the home. Alisa's mother was a federal judge who aspired to a seat in the presidential cabinet as soon as her political party was restored to power. That seat didn't have to be the Attorney General's; Elizabeth would be satisfied with directing the department of Health and Education if need be. Every move that Elizabeth made was calculated to bring her closer to her goal, and she was constantly spending long hours working for her party, chairing this committee, attending that conference or symposium. She turned down nothing that would take her nearer the core of the exalted executive circle.

The same was true of her sister, Marlene, except Marlene's interests lay in the theater. Alisa couldn't remember the last time she had had a truly meaningful conversation with her older sister or when they had last touched and laughed together as Pace did tonight with Lou Ann. Their dealings with one another were so rare that Alisa wasn't sure that Marlene knew she had left Boston and come to rural Louisiana. Alisa surely didn't know the whereabouts of Marlene. In fact, not knowing how to reach Marlene was something that still bothered Alisa.

The last time Alisa had tried to find Marlene, right after she had made her decision to come to Poverty Point, Alisa had been told that her sister's phone was no longer in service. For days she had spent energy she could ill afford to expend, trying to remember the snatches of conversation she had overheard the day she had returned home after her ordeal in Central America. That day was doubly rare in that all four members of her family had been in the Fairlight home at the same time. But Alisa's weakened condition had not allowed her to concentrate on their interchanges. Consequently, she could not remember what Marlene had contributed. Later, Alisa had run through the usual sequence of Marlene's life, trying to find a clue as to her whereabouts. Had her sister announced plans to go into rehearsal out of town? Was that where she was? Was there a new gala opening on Broadway and Marlene had changed her phone number to allow for greater privacy during the surge of notoriety that usually accompanied such events? Finally Alisa had remembered a few quiet words. Marlene was in the process of shucking her latest live-in lover. That was Marlene's way of saying she was being dumped— again. With that realization, Alisa had ceased attempting to reach Marlene. She had known that by then Marlene had either moved in with a new man or she had gone off somewhere to "take the cure," as Marlene put it.

After the sour conclusion of every affair, and there had been enough conclusions to establish a pattern, Marlene checked into a hotel room where for a couple of weeks she would attempt to reach nirvana via the medium of alcohol or, if she acted more wisely, she checked into a mental health hospital. Alisa had hoped that if she were correct in her assumptions, Marlene had chosen the hospital.

Her thoughts drifted to her father, Thomas. Thomas Fairlight was an archaeologist of international repute, a man who traveled the world in search of the secrets of ancient times, who retraveled the world as he recounted his discoveries in lectures and symposiums. It was Thomas who had inspired her, who had whetted her intellectual appetite so that she, too, could not resist the call of antiquity. But Thomas was home only long enough to write articles for professional journals and magazine and to organize yet another expedition into yet another remote region.

Because of Thomas's frequent absences as well as Elizabeth's involvements with her own career, Marlene, at age thirteen, and Alisa, at age ten, had been sent to boarding schools. And because of an unexplained family rift there had been no grandparents, aunts, uncles and cousins to compensate for the lack of direct parental involvement in their lives. That was one reason Alisa had never been in such close confines with an extended family unit. She found the experience with Pace's family not only overwhelming, but also captivating. After a while she riveted her attention on Pace's parents. It was like a glimpse into another world.

Alisa had seen little of the inner dynamics of her own parents' marriage. She had no idea of the quality of their relationship, and it was only because of what she saw in Pace's family that she gave it thought now. She supposed that her parents' union suited their needs. She really didn't know.

As Alisa continued to observe the large family who had lived together with obvious success for a long time, she particularly noted the way Pace's parents interrelated. The Loftons didn't touch one another. In fact, Mary Alice sat beside Sonny while

J.D. remained across the table beside Pace. They rarely spoke directly to one another, yet it seemed they were in constant communication. When Pace and his father discussed the new herbicide in which J.D. had expressed interest, Mary Alice anticipated her husband's every move. Before he asked for the pamphlets and notes that he had dropped into the side pocket of his wife's purse, Mary Alice was sliding them across the table. The same had been true of his need for the pen he had sought earlier. On both occasions J.D.'s thank-you had been the most tender, loving smile Alisa had ever witnessed. She tried to remember if she had ever seen her father look at her mother that way, look at anyone that way. A memory that she couldn't quite grasp teased her. It was something from a long way back, and she couldn't make it gel. The vague image strangely affected her, and she was suddenly awash in alien emotions—a kind of sadness and hunger, a strange emptiness and maybe a touch of fear.

Alisa was sad that she had missed something so beautiful as growing up in a home filled with the kind of love she saw in the older couple. It was a love that was repeating itself in Lou Ann and Sonny, as manifested in Lou Ann's acceptance of Sonny's seemingly total lack of seriousness. And for the first time, she knew the source of a quietly nagging inner restlessness that had nothing to do with her life-threatening ordeal. She was hungry for emotional security, for some sense of permanence in her life, some sense of continuity, some sense of being

wanted. She longed for what all of the people seated
around her had. For the first time she understood
the term "roots," and she knew that she had none.
It wasn't that she couldn't trace her family. It had
been done on both her paternal and maternal sides,
and the results were stored in neatly bound volumes
in her father's study. But there was no depth to her
roots. They were like grass roots, whereas the Loftons' were like a giant oak's, buried deep in the
Delta soil. Beside these people, Alisa felt shallow.
She shuddered at the feeling.

A work-roughened hand clasped hers beneath the
table. Pace had been perfectly attuned to her, and
he leaned close and whispered low. "Are you all
right?"

She turned to face his questioning eyes. The grip
on her hand tightened. "Yes, it's nothing," Alisa
assured him, and with the same words she tried
assuring herself, too. The Fairlights were important
people. They were the movers and shakers of the
modern world. They were individualists. They were
independent. They couldn't function within the restrictions that family dedication required. As one of
them, she couldn't function that way either, she
told herself.

Pace prolonged his searching, assessing glance.
"Are you sure?"

Alisa smiled tenderly in return, because she felt
enveloped in a warm cocoon of care that seemed to
encompass them both. It was another new feeling
and far, far more pleasant. "I'm sure."

Alisa became aware of the attention she and Pace had attracted with their intimate posture, the overlapping of their arms as he held her hand firmly in her lap, his dark head so close to her fairer one as he sought an explanation for her sudden tenseness. As Pace spoke quietly with Alisa, he had his back to his father; he could not see the sudden hard line of J.D.'s mouth, the tightening of his hand into a hard fist. And he seemed oblivious to the questioning looks that flew between Mary Alice and Lou Ann. Those glances asked the same question J.D. had vocalized earlier: Does Pace know what he is doing?

Only Sonny Carter smiled knowingly, and when he did, all the dark eyes focused on him. He grinned wider beneath his red mustache and shrugged his shoulders. "Hey Pace," Sonny called across the table, effectively refocusing the attention, "let's get in line for our supper."

Pace still held Alisa's hand beneath the table, and he rubbed a callused thumb over her knuckles, gave her fingers a last reassuring squeeze and lifted both his hands to the edge of the table in preparation for shoving back his chair. The gleaming twinkle reentered his eyes. "What's the matter, Sonny? Did Lou Ann stop feeding you when she found out how much you lost pitching horseshoes out behind your hangar?"

"Indeed not," Lou Ann joined the teasing in defense of her husband. "Why should I, when he lost that money to me?"

"You're kidding," Pace scoffed in disbelief.

Sonny's ploy had been successful. J.D. once more seemed in control as he rose to his feet and corroborated his daughter's tale. "No, she's not, Pace. Lou Ann came in to do some bookkeeping for Sonny, joined in the game and took not only Sonny's money, but also mine and a few others' as well."

Lou Ann stood up and pirouetted prettily. The hem of her skirt belled about her trim legs. "I bought this outfit with my winnings."

"It's the truth," Sonny boasted. "I'm sponsoring her in the Fourth of July match. Your little sister is going to clean your plow, Pace Lofton."

"I doubt that," Pace contradicted. "She may have gotten in enough hours of practice to take care of you fellows, but I'm the one who taught her to play in the first place when she was about ten years old, down at the old house." The men moved away from the table, immersed in talk of past games they had played under the oak trees at the old family house.

When they returned, each carried two paper plates filled with steaming jambalaya, green salad, hunks of french bread and a thick square of frosted cake. Alisa looked with dismay at the quantity of food on the plate that Pace set in front of her. "I can't eat all of this," she protested in an undertone meant for his ears alone.

"The other morning you said you couldn't drink my coffee, but you managed." Pace had not been as discrete with the level of his voice, and again questioning dark eyes snapped in a quick circle around the table. Alisa could just imagine the interpretation they put on Pace's making morning coffee for her. Oblivious to the looks flashing from Lofton to Lofton and especially the burning questions within J.D.'s eyes, Pace continued. "Don't worry, Alisa," he teased, "you don't have to sit at the table until you clean your plate."

"It's a good thing, or I'd be here for a couple of days," Alisa muttered just before she took her first bite of the spicy food. It was delicious, but far more than she would ever be able to consume. She wondered how anyone present managed to keep from being grossly overweight if this meal and the size of the servings were typical. She glanced up and down the table and saw that many other half-filled plates were being pushed back from obviously sated diners. It was the plates that were nearly cleaned that amazed her. They included Pace's, and she knew for a fact that he carried no extra poundage.

At the lift of her brow, Pace answered knowingly. "Before you leave the area, I'll let you follow in my footsteps for one twenty-four-hour period. After that you will never wonder again what I do with all the calories." Grinning, he deftly transferred the square of untouched carrot cake from her plate onto his.

After everyone had finished eating, the groups realigned themselves, and Alisa once more found herself at Pace's side, moving as if in some intricately choreographed dance. She felt sure that she had met and shaken hands with every person in the room, and some of them twice. After a while she gave up trying to keep names and properties straight. She was satisfied to relax against Pace's proprietary arm and enjoy her new acquaintances' brand of teasing humor, sometimes as earthy as the land they worked.

As the hour grew later, Alisa felt Pace growing tense. She knew this tension had something to do with Sonny. It had been building in him since he arrived at the supper. She had become aware of a change as soon as Pace asked his father whether Sonny had called. She had observed that Pace had managed to maneuver Sonny away from the others several times, but each time he had been unable to maintain privacy long enough to broach whatever was bothering him. She knew the exact moment when Pace gave up the attempt.

He didn't try again until they were leaving the building. The few people who remained were busy wiping the tables, sweeping up and loading the filled garbage bags, butane cookers and big pots onto waiting trucks. Just outside the door Pace urged Alisa to walk in front of him beside Lou Ann, as he fell in step with Sonny.

CHAPTER FOUR

"DID HE CALL?" Pace began baldly the minute the four of them were out of earshot of the men on the patio.

"Right on time," Sonny replied, not asking who the "he" was.

"And..." Pace prompted.

"And he knew from word one that I was speaking for you." Pace's response was a deep groan. "But," Sonny quickly supplied, "it's still a deal."

"For how much more?"

"Nothing more. He took the first price I offered. The paperwork begins Monday morning."

"That's good," Pace sighed in relief. "Did you discover anything about his plans? Will he settle there? Will he send for the boys? Is he going to come back?" His voice lowered in a painful desperation as he asked the last question. "Is he with *her*?"

Again there was no need between the two men to name the new characters. "He didn't mention Linda and I didn't ask. As for the boys...." Alisa could hear the hesitancy in Sonny's voice. "I asked, but he hedged the issue. I begged him to get in touch with you, not only about the house and property, but about the boys. I tried to explain how important it was. Lou Ann got on the line and put in her two cents, too, but he's no longer the David we grew up with." Now it was Sonny's voice holding the pain. "Pace, she has him in such a tailspin that he can't think straight. She is making his life a living hell; my guess is that it's worse than it was when they were here. If you could just hear him, the hurt in his voice and the fear, you would feel sorry for him, give him a little more understanding." Sonny appealed to his wife for support. "Tell him, Lou Ann."

"I don't have to tell Pace anything," Lou Ann mumbled as she tucked in her chin and let her hair fall in a sable drape covering the sides of her face. It was obvious to Alisa that Lou Ann's emotions about the mysterious David were too near the surface for her to deal with. "Pace knows already. He was the first to see what was happening." Her voice broke. "I can't handle this." Immediately Lou Ann lengthened her stride, and Alisa thought she saw her wipe at a tear. Alisa was sure that Lou Ann's posture and quickened pace stated that she intended saying nothing more.

"Lou Ann's right, Sonny. I *do* know, and I do feel sorry for him. I honestly do." There was truth in Pace's tone, and then his voice hardened. "But he's a grown man with responsibilities, the prime one being his role as father, the care of his sons. He doesn't seem to want that responsibility, yet he won't cede it to me. He must realize, and soon, that he cannot have it both ways. It will not work. Dammit, it won't.'' The curse was a futile cry of frustration that lay on the quiet night air.

The four of them reached Pace's car in that oppressive silence, and Alisa felt like an intruder. She didn't know what the other three were talking about, but she knew it was important. That knowledge colored the hesitant good-night to her newly met friends and resulted in her saying nothing more when Pace reached around to open the door for her, absently assisting her inside and closing the door with a muted thud. Although Lou Ann continued walking silently across the graveled parking area, Pace and Sonny remained beside the Lincoln. Alisa didn't doubt that Lou Ann was as emotionally involved in the mysterious situation with the unidentified David as were Sonny and Pace, but, to Alisa, Lou Ann seemed either resigned to accept what was patently unacceptable to her brother, or she was incapable of fighting it.

As Lou Ann walked away Pace stuck his balled fists into the pockets of his trousers and hunched his shoulders. Inside the car, Alisa tried not to listen to his private conversation with Sonny. She felt she had already heard more than she should have, but a few of the words came clearly, words like medical emergencies, temporary guardianship, permanent custody. Finally, Pace's dejected posture straightened, and through the tinted glass she watched the two men's shadowy outlines merge in a firm handshake. She saw Sonny throw his arm about Pace's shoulders in a comforting gesture as he followed the taller man around to the driver's side of the car. When Pace opened the door, Sonny put forth one final point in their discussion.

"Either he'll come to his senses or you'll have to petition the courts, Pace. I know that an open battle will hurt not only you, but the rest of the family as well, especially J.D. Like you, I'm not sure that he can handle it, but it may come down to a question of which is more important—the boys or J.D. You might as well admit that sooner or later that may be your choice. I think you should begin preparing yourself emotionally and laying out a few hints to J.D. But whatever way you have to go, it'll work out, my friend. It *will* work out," he concluded on a reassuring note and then stepped back from the opened door.

"God, I hope so," Pace mumbled hollowly as he slid into the seat, but there was no evidence in his voice that he shared Sonny's optimism. He pulled the door closed, and Sonny walked away.

The trip homeward began in much the same attitude as their earlier journey. Pace was totally withdrawn and silent. Alisa was at a loss as to the details of the underlying cause and, more importantly, the cure. What a pair they made, she thought as the silence lengthened. Neither of them seemed able to cope very well with the curves that life was throwing them. They both seemed to share a penchant for dropping into a brooding black funk at the slightest provocation, shrouding themselves in emotional mystery. Yet, she had a feeling that Pace was not normally morose. Surely the man who teased and laughed and found humor in the daily hard struggle of earning his livelihood in an environment where nothing was assured except the uncertainty of the weather was the real Pace. The real Pace Lofton was the one who, without being asked, assembled her bed, hung her drapery rods, and sent a man over to "bush hog" her lawn. He was the one who shared a social evening with his family and thought them the best of company.

As the beam from the car's headlights vainly tried to outstrip the stretches of black-topped road, Alisa watched the working of a tight muscle in Pace's jaw. The green glow of the dash lights coupled with the milky-blue tint of moonlight cast a peculiar hue over his features. That strange light heightened the darkness of his beard, which had already begun to roughen his firm chin and the outer edges of his cheeks. It emphasized his infinite sadness.

She wondered at the cast of characters whom she knew must play important roles in Pace's problem. Who was David, and who was the evil Linda? Where were these boys of whom he spoke? What deal had Sonny sealed for him? And again and again the final question replayed in her mind. Why, oh why was such a basically good man so very, very sad?

"Pace," Alisa began in a small voice, "is there anything I can do?"

The dark head swiveled toward her then back to the dark surface of the road. The headlights caught the red reflection of a rabbit's eyes as the creature paused briefly before scurrying into the underbrush along a fence row. It took Pace a long time to respond. He took that time to shake off the betraying expression that told of the foreboding his conversation with Sonny had produced.

Reaching across the seat, he took her hand. "Yes. You can talk to me. You can tell me what you thought of the people you met tonight, of the evening in general," Pace directed with forced lightness. But the firmness in his clasp told her that his mysterious pain was still with him.

His request wasn't what she had expected, but it was better than continuing in the previous grave atmosphere. Alisa took a deep breath and began her critique of the evening. "First of all, I had an absolutely wonderful time." She thought of the infrequent dinners she had attended with her father or her mother, usually stately affairs at which she had always felt that her appearance had been requested, not because anyone desired her company or particularly enjoyed it, but because it made a nice showing. The memories of those stiff, formal occasions made her amend her statement. "It was a uniquely wonderful evening for me."

"You didn't find it too casual, too folksy... paper plates, beer out of bottles, some of the men straight out of the field still in their muddy boots?"

"I enjoyed every minute, including some of the

jokes that I didn't understand and you wouldn't explain to me," she teased. She had understood a lot more than she had let on, but she found it far less embarrassing if she sometimes kept a blank-eyed look on her face. From the quick squeeze Pace gave her hand, she knew that he had been aware of her ploy. "I really liked your family and I liked your friends. And I thank you for taking me." A heavy pause followed her statement of gratitude.

"But..." Pace prompted.

"It's nothing derogatory. It's just that the people seemed so bent on having a good time, almost compelled to make the most of the social side of everything. Oh, I know that almost every farmer there conducted business, spent time with the chemical representatives, but the business seemed insignificant, almost unimportant, something to get through as quickly as possible so they could get back to the primary purpose of being there—socializing."

Pace nodded his agreement. "A very fair assessment. Now on to the question of why. Not only do we have to 'make hay while the sun shines,' but everything else as well. Between now and the middle of July, almost every man you met tonight will be working as many hours as the weather permits, hard physical labor. We have to get our winter wheat out of the fields, get our soybeans into the ground and tend our young cotton, and our time is limited.

"From now until our crops are 'laid by,' any

social life we have will be when it's too wet or too dark to continue in the fields. But even then we usually have other pressing demands from equipment repair to creative financing. We also have to keep in close touch with our brokers so we won't miss booking the best price for our crops." He glanced at her once more. "I think you can see why many people tonight felt *compelled* to make the most of the social side of this evening—and any other evening in the next two months or so. Then in the fall, when it's time to harvest, it's the same thing once more. We have to gather the crops in before they ruin in the fields."

"Will it be like that for you, too, Pace?"

"Maybe worse," he answered grimly. "The Loftons aren't gentlemen farmers, Alisa. We have always worked our land ourselves, and this season we won't have my brother David to help us." She saw him swallow his bitterness before he added in a husky undertone. "It's a rough life, but it's a wonderful life. In fact, there is no other life for me."

David, she thought, Pace's brother. Younger? Older? She had one piece of the puzzle in her hand, but no place to put it. But in her heart, she knew that it fit against the subtle warnings Pace had given her when he commented on her being a "city girl." It fit with his comments about her future and his defense of his way of life. It also had something to do with the wary glances she had received from the other people at the dinner. It most definitely had something to do with J.D.'s thinly veiled hostility directed toward her. But what was Pace, as well as his family and friends, warning her against?

Once more the silence built between them, but she was determined that this time it would not last. Frantically, she searched for a conversational gambit.

"What does 'laid by' mean?" she asked.

"Laid by means left to mature unattended until harvest. There reaches a time in the growing season when there's nothing more you can do except pray and wait. In this area the farmers aim to have their crops laid by before the Fourth of July. Traditionally there are big family celebrations on the Fourth, celebrations that rejoice at more than the winning of national independence if their crops are laid by." The moonlight, filtering through the trees under which they passed, dappled the interior of the car. Alisa could see the warm smile play across Pace's features.

It was the Pace to whom she was inexplicably drawn, the Pace who spoke of his life lovingly instead of defensively. "On the Fourth of July, the Loftons celebrate. Everybody who can be spared heads into Mississippi to the Homochitta River. For three or four days we forget Little Fork, we forget subsurface moisture content, we forget the migration of boll weevils, army worms, soil depletion. We forget the land. We just lie out on the sandy river beach and relax."

"And play horseshoes," Alisa added.

"You remembered." He seemed pleased.

"What if you aren't laid by?"

"Then those who are still working, still work. The rest go on to their well-deserved holiday."

"That must be hard for those left behind."

"It is, but they know their day is coming. But enough about us Loftons and the horrors of working the land. What about you, Alisa? What will you do once you're finished here and have the last degree?"

"Before I took a leave of absence to follow the southern migratory lines and trade routes of the ancient Olmec Indian culture, I taught in a small private college in Boston. In mid-January my leave will expire and I must return to the classroom, Ph.D. or not."

"Is teaching what you want?"

"No. I like it because it keeps me alert, but it's definitely not all I want."

"More trips into the field?"

"Definitely."

Pace's voice tightened. "Central America?"

"Eventually. I really would like to prove my original thesis, for myself if for no one else. There's something about us archaeologists that just won't let go."

This time the grip on her hand tightened. "Even after all you've been through, you would go out there again?"

"Oh, Pace, the chances of something like that happening again are practically nil. Besides, the area won't always be in a state of civil war."

"What if by the time you feel you can go back

there, your situation has changed? What if you have a family, people who care about you?''

Alisa laughed. ''I have a family—a beautiful mother, a handsome father and a truly glamorous sister. And in their own way they care about me. They care about me enough to want me to have what I want, even if that means being up to my muddy elbows in crumbling relics.''

''That wasn't exactly what I meant,'' Pace replied. But he let it go at that, releasing her hand to turn the car from the paved highway onto the gravel lane that led to Alisa's rented house. As he pulled the car onto the grassy driveway and stopped behind her little car, the headlights raked the layers of wilting weeds and grass and the ragged stubble left by the bush hog.

When Pace came around the car to open the door for her, he surveyed the scraggly lawn. ''Looks like I'd better get you inside, claim my good-night kiss in a hurry and get on out of here. You definitely have tomorrow's work cut out for you, and you'll be needing a full night's sleep.'' He indicated the lawn with a sweep of his arm. ''In fact, I think you have a couple of days' work waiting. Do you have a rake?'' he asked as he held open the screened door and they entered the porch.

''Yes, I have a rake. There were some tools left here—the rake, a hoe, a shovel and one of those jagged-edged things used to cut weeds from ditches. And what makes you think you'll get a good-night kiss?''

"A sling-blade," he identified the last imple-
ment, "but you leave it alone. You might cut yourself and bleed to death before anyone could get to
you. And I'll get a kiss because singing for your
supper isn't allowed. It might start a cattle stampede," he teased as he leaned against the wall,
hands deep in his pockets, and watched Alisa wrestle her key into the stiff new lock she'd had installed
at his suggestion.

"I haven't seen cattle out there to stampede, and
besides I sing sweetly." The lock turned and the
door swung open. When she looked back, Pace had
removed his hands from his pockets and was push-
ing himself from the wall with a shake of his head.

"A kiss nevertheless," he insisted in a low voice.

She knew it wasn't the time to be coy. And the
time for teasing had ended as well. "Yes, a kiss,"
she whispered in warm agreement, for it was what
she wanted, too. Slowly, she moved into the arms
he held out to her.

But Pace did not kiss her. Instead, he wrapped
his strong arms about her and held her close. "Do
you have any idea how many times in the past few
days I've wanted to put my arms about you?" His
hold tightened. "And you probably know that is
not all I've wanted to do." One hand moved to
cradle her chin, to position her mouth for the first
coupling with his.

For an extended minute he watched her, delving
deeply into her shadowed eyes before moving his
burning glance to her mouth. In that still moment, a

moment ripe with anticipation, Alisa admitted to herself that his holding her had never been all she wanted from him, either. She only hoped that the intensity of her feelings was not stamped too clearly on her features, as inch by slowly measured inch Pace lowered his lips to hers.

And then they kissed. At first it was a soft caress, like a whisper, as sweet and as tender as a first kiss should be—but only for a fleeting second. They both responded with sudden passion, with equal and undiluted demand. When her lips parted at the nudge of the hard edge of his tongue his entire body reacted. His arm around her waist tightened, bringing her hard against his full length, closer and closer until she was pressed into him and could feel the desire in him grow as hers grew. The hand that held her chin began to move in a slow devastating caress, a soft gentle touch at odd variance with the hard hand that now splayed across her hips to keep them welded together. His moving hand wove into her hair and he wrapped handfuls around his fist, releasing the silky mass in a tumble so that he could slide his hand down her back and up again, threading through her hair once more. Somewhere in a corner of her mind she knew he wanted to touch her in other ways. But he didn't.

Her own hands wandered over him, over his chest and arms, finally repeating the pattern he laid for her as she mirrored his actions, entangling her hands in his thick hair. She was lost to him. She could not get enough of him, and she could not give enough to him. She told him so by her unconscious arching against him and by making greedy little sounds.

When Pace finally broke the embrace with an abrupt movement of his head, Alisa opened her eyes to find him staring down at her with an expression of a strange bewilderment and what she thought was a touch of fear. If it was fear, it was a fear she shared. No kiss had ever affected her like this one, and she knew that Pace was equally moved. Their desire had been born full grown, a living thing, and it was awesome. How were they to manage a passion like theirs, a passion that instantly dissolved all reservations, all inhibitions, all sanity?

"I didn't know a kiss could be so wonderful," Alisa whispered in weak admission. She could feel his body vibrating with suppressed desire, and she lay still against him, her head nestled into the hollow of his shoulder.

"I don't think one often is," Pace responded on the edge of a still-ragged breath. "But we should have expected it. There were enough hints all along."

"You wanted me that very first morning, right there in the ditch, didn't you?" she asked shyly.

"I thought that was my secret." She felt him smile against her hair. Then she felt that smile fade, and when he spoke, his voice was tight. "Alisa, we have a problem."

Alisa nodded her agreement. She didn't have to ask what he meant. She knew. Controlling the passion between them until they determined what direction it was to take and making the decision either to accept or reject that direction would be a nearly impossible task.

They sweetly held each other in the Delta dark, thinking, pondering the portent of the smoldering passion between them, a passion just waiting for the right southern breeze to fan it into a roaring conflagration. Alisa could feel the slow beating of Pace's heart, could feel his breath become more regular, deeper, suggesting that he, too, was pretending an emotional tranquility that wasn't really his. Then gently Pace eased her away from him until they were a scant inch apart.

"You know I like holding you, sweetheart, but we aren't addressing that problem." His hands moved to her shoulders and slid down to grip her upper arms as if to physically force some comment from her.

Alisa didn't know if the only possible comment she could make was what Pace expected to hear. But there were no other words forthcoming; it was almost like a conditioned reflex. After twelve years of watching her sister Marlene recover from being jilted by her last lover and knowing that each time she put herself back together she was never as good as she had been before, Alisa could not give a different answer. Whatever the reason, her words were more blunt than necessary. "I will not enter into a casual affair."

Instantly, Pace's hands were cupping her face.

His words were as free as hers. "I knew that the first moment I saw you. I might not know much else about you, but some things are obvious. But what do you know about me? Do you think that I could enter into a sexual affair lightly?"

Alisa didn't hesitate with that answer either. She had seen him with his family. That alone spoke volumes. "No."

The hands holding her gentled as he traced the line of her cheeks with his thumbs. "Help me, Alisa. What are we going to do?" He searched her face, but all he saw there was a mirror of his own anxiety.

"I don't know," she whispered. "I honestly don't know." She pulled away from him and stepped farther into the shadows. "You're rushing me. I need time." She turned back to look at him.

Pace's first response was a harsh expulsion of breath. "Time," he mocked. "You chose the one thing that is working against us."

"I don't understand."

"You've only given us a few months. Your stay here is temporary, remember?" There was a strange sound in his voice.

"I'm sorry," she whispered as she retraced her steps to stand near him, "but that is all the more reason to proceed with caution. I...no. We have the rest of our lives to live with whatever happens between us."

"How well I know," he agreed softly. For a long time he looked off toward the fenced grassland. Finally he turned his full attention to her. "Sometimes a lot can happen in a short time. Sometimes a lifetime is lived; sometimes a lifetime is lost." His tone was sad. Again, Alisa was besieged with burning curiosity, but there were no answers for her. "So wise Alisa and wise Pace will use their limited time to the best advantage. They will be very careful," Pace continued, "starting now." He turned his wrist so that the face of his watch was caught in reflected moon glow. "I don't want to, but I've got to go. I promised the boys I'd take them fishing tomorrow afternoon, which means in the morning I have to double up my work."

"Boys?" The second set of characters from his dialogue with Sonny made their appearance.

"My nephews, John David and Daniel, David's sons." Once more he was touching her, his thumb stroking the corner of her mouth as a thoughtful expression appeared on his face. "Will you come with us? I know it isn't the kind of date you're used to, but I need to spend some time with them and I'd also like to be with you." He sucked in his breath as if his next admission was hard bought. "I think I *need* the time with you, but I did promise them. Besides, if we share our afternoon with the boys, it will give us a good block of time together...easy time." She knew what he meant, and his concern strengthened her feelings for him. "Come with us."

She didn't need to think about her answer. "I'll come."

"Good. By the time you spend the morning

working on this yard, you'll be in need of some relaxation, although I can't guarantee just how much rest you'll get with two boys under age six." He smiled at some private thought of relaxing in the presence of his nephews. "I'll see you about three." The hand on her cheek pressed harder, and with lightning swiftness his demeanor once more changed.

"I don't want to start wishing my life away, Alisa, but I can't seem to prevent myself from wishing that we were somewhere in the future and that we knew it was safe to take the next step, in whatever direction it leads us. God, how I wish it." With that he adroitly turned so that Alisa was trapped between his body and the door frame. Again his lips moved hungrily on hers and his hands slid over her back to meld her hips with his. It was a quick, hard, possessive embrace, begun without preamble and just as abruptly ended. She didn't even have time to reach for his shoulders before he peeled away from her, turned her toward the living room and gently pushed her inside. By the time she turned around, he was down the steps.

Alisa did not turn on the lights. Instead, she secured the locks on the doors and followed the moon path streaming through the back windows. In her bedroom she prepared for bed in the semidarkness. She thought of the things she and Pace had said to each other. In retrospect, it seemed a moment out of time. How did they become so deeply involved so quickly? How much validity should she place on the emotion-charged discourse? Was she really ready for the kind of involvement that seemed destined?

Soon, less pleasant and even more disturbing thoughts entered her head. They were thoughts of Marlene. Was this how her sister had begun her seemingly never-ending cycle of romantic euphorias? Was this the same bliss that was followed by such heartaches when the affair ended so that Marlene sometimes required professional help to put herself back on an even keel? In the past, Alisa had always fled any personal relationship that vaguely hinted it might develop along the lines of Marlene's affairs. Should she flee now? Or was this different? Would she have more to offer than Marlene offered? And did Pace in return have more to offer than the men for whom Marlene cared? It was the first time she had faced those questions without instantly reaching a negative conclusion.

Before, she had never had to think about what a man-woman relationship could produce other than the obvious. Now, in just a few days, she had learned that there was more than just the appeasement of sexual appetites, and she had learned that she wanted that extra element. She knew in her heart that any relationship with Pace would also ultimately result in sexual appeasement, but it would be unlike anything she had ever dreamed. A shallow association would not suffice for them. In fact, it was already too late for that. In just a few brief encounters, Pace had created within her a depth of emotion and a sexual awareness hitherto unknown. But what she feared was something still unexperienced, something still completely hidden from her and only hinted at whenever either of them alluded to the future, the very near future—when she returned to Boston. In a few months she would finish her work at Poverty Point. Her research and her paper would be completed. Then, back in Boston, seated before a panel of learned men and women, Alisa would be questioned on her knowledge of antiquities generally and the mound builders specifically. She would be far away from the earthy Pace Lofton unless...unless.... That one conditional word tinted her thoughts, and after she had crawled between the crisp sheets and drifted to sleep future possibilities directed her dreams.

CHAPTER FIVE

JOHN DAVID AND DANIEL SAT on the seat of the truck between Alisa and Pace. Except for their shoes, they were dressed just like their uncle—western shirts neatly tucked into well-worn jeans held in place by wide leather belts. Instead of boots, the boys wore blue sneakers. Alisa, too, wore jeans, but her shirt was tailored and her shoes were topsiders.

From the very beginning of the outing, John David had chosen to ignore Alisa. He kept his eyes straight ahead and his lips in a firm silent line. Alisa wondered at his thoughts. For a while Daniel, too, was very quiet. He was so little that his legs stuck straight out from the seat and he could not see over the high dashboard. Sitting next to Alisa, he tried to content himself with a study of the toes of his shoes. But more and more frequently he cast a curious glance at the pretty woman beside him. Finally, he could bear it no more. "What happened to your hands?" he lisped bravely.

Alisa turned her hands palm up to expose several adhesive bandages as well as patches of angry red skin. "I raked my yard this morning and the rake

wore blisters on my hands." She indicated the
tapes. "Some of the places were worse than others,
and the blisters broke open. So I put medicine on
those and covered them with the bandages to keep
the dirt out."

"Did the medicine sting?" he asked in wide-eyed
sympathy.

"No, Daniel, I used an antibiotic cream. It felt
cool."

He thought about her treatment for a while before speaking again. "Sometimes when I hurt myself, grandpa puts monkey blood on me. It doesn't
sting either, but if he uses that other orange stuff,
he has to blow on it."

Alisa looked over the two blond heads to Pace.
"Monkey blood?" she mouthed.

"Mercurochrome," he explained. He touched his
face lightly and dragged his finger along the faint
line that remained where she had scratched him.
"Now I know what we did wrong with the Merthiolate. You didn't blow on it." He flashed her a
grin, and then in a shared instant, they both remembered what her failure to "blow" on the stinging
antiseptic had brought about, and the grin dissolved. "Didn't you wear gloves?" Pace asked
tightly as he, too, forced down the memory of the
feel of her breast under his hand.

"Yes, but they were thin, plus I simply did too
much for one day."

"You won't be able to hold a fishing pole."
Those were the first words that John David had

spoken since they left Alisa's house. On the shady front porch Pace had forced him to respond to being introduced to her. With this voluntary sentence Pace eased back into the seat. It was only then that Alisa realized he had been ill at ease with his older nephew's reaction to her.

"If Alisa can't hold a pole, then we may have to set out trot lines and give her the job of watching the bobbers," Pace announced as he stopped the truck before a huge aluminum gate bearing a No Trespassing sign and the Little Fork logo. He climbed down from the truck, flipped through a large ring of keys, selected one and unlocked the padlock on the gate. As he swung the gate open, he ran an expert eye over the flat stretch of grassland. Alisa followed his visual path over the lush pasture of grazing cows whose roan-colored hides gleamed healthily in the bright afternoon sun. Toward the far left of the expansive field three stately oaks, a pair of sweet gum trees and a thick stand of willows guarded the banks of a large pond.

When Pace drove the truck through the gate, Alisa didn't bother to tell them that this was her first fishing trip and that she didn't even know what a bobber was, much less a trot line. After securing the gate behind them, he directed the truck in a straight course toward the distant pond, right through the knee-high grass and any ruts it camouflaged. Alisa was too busy holding firmly with her sore hands to the edge of the seat to give thought to the plans Pace had for her.

The minute Pace pulled the pickup to a stop near the placid water's edge, the excitement began to build in the boys, and Alisa thought that at any minute they would begin clamoring to get out. "Okay fellows," Pace began, "rule number one?"

"Don't fall in," John David and Daniel chorused.

"And number two?"

"Keep your eye on your hook."

"Right. No hooks in your brother, no hooks in me, and no hooks in Alisa. My first-aid kit has the orange stuff you have to blow on. There's no monkey blood, so if you stick a hook in yourself be prepared to take it like a man." He issued this as a final warning. Pace opened his door, and before he had cleared it the boys tumbled after him, ran to the back of the truck and climbed onto the back bumper. Alisa exited her side far more cautiously, the talk of hook injuries making her wonder what she had let herself in for.

"Whoa," Pace ordered, just as the first small leg crossed over the tailgate. "I'll hand the poles and tackle to you. Once you get your arms full, you won't be able to get down." He reached into the bed of the truck and separated two cane poles from the several lying there. He handed one to each boy. To John David, he gave a tackle box and to Daniel, a paper container that reminded Alisa of the take-out cartons from Chinese food restaurants.

"Here, Alisa, you take these," Pace directed in the same tone he used with his nephews. Alisa ac-

cepted two small life jackets and a blanket, while
Pace gathered the rest of the poles and an ice chest.
In the shade of the largest oak, Alisa spread the
blanket at Pace's direction and sat on the edge to
watch as he helped John David and Daniel rig their
poles with lines, bobbers, sinkers and hooks.

John David sat cross-legged, his elbows on his
knees, his chin in his hands, his eyes on Pace. Pace,
kneeling in front of the open tackle box, seemed not
to register the added burden of Daniel, who leaned
on Pace's shoulder, his tiny arm flung lovingly
around his uncle's neck. The dappled sunlight
played on the three shiny heads, two so fair, the
third so dark. "Okay, Johnny, do you think you
can bait your own hook?"

In an instant John David was on his feet, a wide
grin splitting his previously solemn face. "Yes, sir,
and I'll be careful," he added for good measure.

"Then let Alisa help you with your life jacket."
The smile weakened only a little before he hurried
over to Alisa to let her fasten the buoyant jacket
across his narrow chest. Then he was headed for the
water's edge.

Pace now sat on the ground with Daniel positioned between his outstretched legs. Patiently, he
explained the reason for every knot he tied, the purpose of the lead sinker, the bobber, why he tied on
one hook and not a different-sized one. Every now
and then Daniel would indicate some colorful lure
in the hinged compartments of the tackle box, and
Pace would gingerly lift it out and detail its use. But

Alisa noted that he always kept part of his attention on John David, making sure of his safety.

Finally he had Daniel's pole rigged and Alisa was fastening an even smaller life vest around an even smaller chest. "Thank you, Miss Alisa," Daniel lisped charmingly. Alisa resisted the urge to throw her arms about him and squeeze him to her heart.

"I'll take it," Pace offered softly as he settled beside her.

"Take what?"

"That show of affection you just suppressed."

Alisa looked into the all-seeing eyes. Was she that obvious, or was it only Pace who could read her so well? And was his uncanny ability to know what she felt the greater part of his appeal? No, she reasoned. There was more. She didn't know exactly what just yet; it was too soon, but something more was there.

Pace watched the boys trail their lines through the water. After a while he held out his hand to Alisa. "Let's get a closer look at these fishermen's style." She placed her hand in his, but at the pressure of his firm grip when he pulled her to her feet, she winced.

"I'm sorry. I forgot," he whispered contritely as he examined her sensitive palms. Then his eyes lifted to her eyes, and his contriteness faded to be replaced by a more elemental emotion, an emotion that had nothing to do with the condition of her hands. His eyes never left hers as he lifted her palms to his lips and placed a tender kiss in the cupped center of each.

"Can't I even look at you without wanting you?" He mouthed the hungry words into her palm. "I don't understand."

"I don't either," she confessed in a small voice. "I thought about you last night after you left, and I'm afraid, Pace, very, very much afraid."

He placed one of her hands against his heart, the other he laid against his cheek. "We both are, Alisa. I'm fearful that...."

"Unc Pace!" Daniel screeched, cutting into Pace's confession. The moment was lost. "Look what I caught, look what I caught," he shouted jubilantly as he lifted a flapping fish above the water's surface. "And he's big, too," he pointed out as he struggled to keep the fish airborne. "We can keep him and cook him and eat him," he boasted as he fought to bring the fish in.

By then Pace had reached the boys and knelt behind Daniel to help him land the rainbow-hued fish.

Alisa stood behind Pace, taking in the quiet lesson on angling. "Alisa, hand me that carton," Pace instructed without glancing back.

Alisa looked down at the carton near her foot. It contained a writhing, wiggling mass of dirt-encrusted garden worms. Trying to control her natural squeamishness, she lifted the box by the lid and held it away from her body. To her dismay, Pace had turned to focus his attention on her, and she did not miss his knowing grin when he took the box of worms from her and handed it to Daniel. In open-mouthed amazement she watched little Daniel plunge his hand into the box and lift out a very healthy specimen.

"Look, Miss Alisa," he directed as he waved the wiggling worm about, "this fat, juicy worm is going to catch me another bluegill." He brought the worm close to Pace's face. "Won't he, Unc Pace?"

Calmly, Pace took Daniel's wrist and removed the worm from directly in front of his nose. "It's a great worm, a truly super worm, Daniel, but I'm not a fish. I don't like to eat worms, and you have this one dangerously close to my mouth."

Right then John David had a strike on his line. Rising to his feet, Pace carefully monitored the older boy as he landed, unhooked, and strung his fish just above the one that Daniel had caught. "Very good, John," Pace encouraged as he rebaited Daniel's hook. "You two are doing so well, I think we'll skip setting out the drop lines. You are now responsible for our supper, so keep up the good work. Alisa and I will be over by the ice chest."

At the blanket, Pace flopped down and stretched out full length, placing his hands behind his head. His voice lowered when Alisa sat beside him and leaned back on her elbows. "I prefer fishing with drop lines and set poles. Then you are free to go on about your business—hunting or watching the clouds float by or even more pleasurable activities." He watched the color rise in her cheeks then looked beyond her to his nephews. "But not with two little fellows checking out every move we make." Alisa relaxed and Pace filled the time by telling her anecdotes about his life with his nephews. After a while he moved to a sitting position and watched the boys. "How's it going?" he hailed.

John David pulled at the stringer and lifted a foot of shining, shimmering, flouncing fish into view. "Terrific," Pace called before turning back to Alisa. His expression darkened. "This hasn't been much fun for you, has it?"

"It's a new experience. I like being with you. I like being with the boys."

He plucked at a blade of grass and stared out over the water. "But will you want to do it again?"

She glanced down at her bandaged hands. "I will probably like it even more when I can fish, too." Then she grinned broadly. "Yes, I will want to do it again."

"As long as you don't have to select your own worm," Pace amended with a full-bodied laugh. He glanced back at the boys. "They have enough fish. The more they catch, the more I have to clean. The more I clean, the more *you* have to cook."

"Me?"

"Yes, ma'am. You. We didn't bring you along just for the ride, you know." He raised his voice. "Hey, fellows, take a break." He opened the ice chest and held up a soft drink. It was all the lure the boys needed.

By the time they finished their refreshments, the sun had begun to settle in the west. The air was becoming cooler, and Pace suggested they pack it in and clean the catch.

In no time, Pace had cleaned the fish and laid them in the ice chest, and Alisa and Pace were once more in the cab of the truck with the boys tucked cozily between them.

The conversation on the way back to Alisa's house was about the day's catch. When they reached the house, Pace lifted a small leather satchel from the back of the truck and handed it to John David. He accepted it reluctantly. Pace gave Alisa a grocery bag containing cooking oil, cornmeal and three large potatoes, and he brought the chest containing the fish and more drinks inside.

He set the chest on the kitchen counter. "Alisa, could the boys use your bath?" Pace asked as he placed the fish in the sink. At her nodded agreement, he eyed the neat kitchen skeptically. "Can you get the supper started while I draw their water? I'll do the cooking if you'll peel the potatoes, and maybe could you make a green salad?"

"I think I can handle that."

When Pace returned, he smelled less of the outdoors and more of bath soap. There was a dark watermark on the front of his shirt. "Daniel," he explained.

With an easiness that amazed Alisa, he moved about her kitchen, heating oil, breading the fish in cornmeal, slicing the potatoes for fries, and mixing a batter for hush puppies. Having completed the tasks that he had assigned to her, she leaned against the counter and watched.

"You're very good at this," she commented when he had the fish and several fat hush puppies frying in the oil. He leaned against the counter next to her.

"And you're very good at laying a pretty table." He nodded toward the table, set in gleaming glassware and shining silver, the plaid napkins of blue and gray and lavender picking up the blue in the ironstone and the flaming candles.

"So together we're both very good—"

He gave her no time to finish as he supplied the last two words. "At this." His arms slid around her, drawing her around to fit between his outstretched legs as his hips took part of his weight against the cabinet's edge. And then his mouth settled on hers, not forcing it open, but seeking permission with gentleness and a tangible need. Alisa had been waiting for this moment since early afternoon, when each lingering glance, each touch, both planned and accidental, promised that it was to come. Still there was something unexpected about the feel of his mouth on hers, the assessing probe of his tongue, the reality of his body stretched full length against hers, matching thigh to thigh, hip to hip, masculine breath to feminine. The embrace left Alisa helpless for a moment. Urgency and weakness ran together through her blood, and her heart beat wildly. Her legs seemed to lose their strength, and

Alisa, almost breathless, felt that she would have melted at Pace's feet had it not been for his arms molding her against him.

Pace moved his body against hers. He caught her gasp inside his own mouth when she became fully aware of the hardness of his limbs, telling her all too clearly of the intensity of his desire for her. His arms around her tightened, holding her still closer, and his hands moved possessively over her back and hips.

And then those possessive hands moved to tangle in her hair, to lift her a fraction away from him. "We *are* very good at this, aren't we, Alisa?"

"Yes," she whispered into his mouth.

"We are better with each other than we are with anyone else, aren't we?"

She knew he was asking for something else, and she didn't know exactly what. But for some inexplicable reason, she knew the answer without understanding the question, and she was compelled to give that affirmative answer to him. "Yes," she responded again and knew in her heart she spoke the truth.

She thought that Pace had kissed her with unbridled passion the night before. She thought no kiss could more clearly express his desire for her than the one of a brief moment ago. She was wrong. When he pulled her back against him, the other kisses faded into inconsequence. It was as if all the passion that had lain dormant between them since their first meeting centered in that one moment of mouth meeting mouth, of tongue touching tongue and in the way his hand drifted from her hair to her ribs, to hover just over her breasts. It was as if he sought permission to touch her, a permission she was incapable of denying. "Pace?" she whispered huskily.

"Are you kissing Miss Alisa?" a small lisping voice asked from the doorway. Alisa felt a different tension pervade Pace's hard body. Without shifting positions he settled one hand onto her waist and, with the other, tucked her head against his shoulder so that she, too, could view their intruder.

Daniel stood in the doorway between the kitchen and the living room wearing only a towel carelessly draped around his shoulders. Water dripped from his hair and ran down his cheeks. It drained from his white little tummy, down his thin little legs and puddled at his feet.

"Yes, I was," Pace answered straightforwardly. There was a thickness to his voice that Alisa identified as a touch of residual passion and a large portion of frustration. The hand at her waist tightened. "Is your rump showing?" Pace asked.

Daniel looked over his shoulder at the inadequate covering that left his pale bottom bared. "Yes, it is," he answered in perfect imitation of his uncle, and Alisa smothered a giggle against Pace's shirt. "You didn't put any clean underpants in the bag," Daniel accused.

"So put on the ones you took off," Pace suggested as he disentangled himself from Alisa and checked the progress of the food. Adeptly, he removed the fish and hush puppies from the oil and laid them on a waiting paper towel.

"They're wet."

"Why?" Pace spooned more hush puppies into the skillet.

"I stepped on them," Daniel lisped.

"Then you'll have to go without."

"Okay." As quickly as he had appeared, he disappeared back toward the bathroom.

Pace put the second cooking of fish into the oil with the hush puppies, took a handful of paper towels and mopped up the puddle of water. Only then did he turn back to Alisa, drawing her into his arms. But the white heat of their passion had faded. "Do we thank him?" She didn't answer, and more of their sexual need ebbed. He held her close for a while, and she could feel the familiar sadness in him, an emotion that she had come to associate with his feelings for his brother and for his nephews. She knew that they held his attention now, not she. Strangely, it didn't bother her.

Pace leaned his cheek against the top of Alisa's head. "Wouldn't it be wonderful if all their problems were as easily solved as what to do when you throw your underpants on the floor and then drip bath water on them?"

Alisa thought about her own family. Other than Marlene's never-ending cycle of heartache, the crises were few and far between. Elizabeth did not allow them. But if any problems did arise, they were handled with a minimum of fanfare, usually by her father.

It had been Thomas who had flown to Latin America to bring Alisa home and who had kept her name out of the press. It had been Thomas who had brought in the experts in post-trauma stress, and it had been Thomas who had negotiated the new parameters of her thesis. But as always, everything had been dealt with so quietly, so effortlessly, sometimes Alisa had wondered if it had even occurred. Just once she would like to see some show of real emotion, even if it were only yelling or crying, just some real proof of vibrant, vital love. She was not satisfied with the hybrid variety expressed by her mother and the aloof, expedient variety demonstrated by her father. And she definitely did not want the temporary insanity she associated with Marlene. She wanted something like what Pace showed for his brother's sons. Her arms around Pace tightened. From her own experience she gave the only answer she could think of. "We do the best we can and pray that it's good enough."

"And when it isn't?"

"Then we bear the pain," she spoke from her heart.

"Are you kissing her again?" a slightly drier Daniel asked from his former position.

"No," Pace answered as once more he broke his embrace with Alisa. "You didn't give me enough time. It's called cramping my style, my man," he teased lightly. It was obvious that Daniel didn't know what Pace meant. Pace smiled and finger-combed the boy's wild wet hair. "Where's your brother?"

"Cleaning the bathroom."

"Go help him."

"Why?"

"Maybe I want to kiss Alisa again?"

Daniel giggled and fled the room. And Pace did kiss Alisa again, but it was a quick buss on the cheek and then he turned to the stove. "Something strange is going on. Neither of them ever volunteers to clean. If you'll finish this, I'll check it out."

Alisa was just completing the meal when Pace returned with his nephews in tow. Ushering both boys to the table, he seated them next to one another. Pace held her chair for her, and as soon as he had seated himself, he and his nephews joined hands, leaving the circle broken for her. Alisa fitted her hands to complete the ring, one into the callused palm of Pace, the other into John David's. John said grace. It was a childish request for blessing, and Alisa smiled at the purity of his appeal, until his last plea. "And look out for my daddy, wherever he is. Bring him home safe." With the first word, Pace gripped Alisa's injured hand so tightly that tears stung her eyes and she had to bite back the cry of pain that rose to her tongue. The grip on her sore hand did not relax even as the chorused amen faded into emotional reverberations.

"Pace?" Alisa questioned as she tugged at her hand.

It was as if he returned from a place far off. "It's okay," he assured her as he brought her hand to his mouth, and for the second time that day he planted a kiss in her palm.

Both boys watched Pace carefully. "You must like kissing Miss Alisa," Daniel offered.

Pace grinned broadly. "I surely do, little man." He placed one of the bluegilled bream onto his plate and carefully peeled a strip of flesh from the bones.

"Alisa doesn't like to kiss you," John David injected quietly, his eyes fixed firmly on the center of his empty plate.

Pace's head jerked up to look at John David. Then he gingerly transferred the deboned fish onto Daniel's plate. Alisa wondered if she really saw his hand shake before he glanced over at her and then back at his older nephew. "Why doesn't she like for me to kiss her, John David?"

"It messes up her makeup and gets her dirty."

Pace opened his mouth to speak, but Alisa forestalled him with a touch on his arm. It was she who offered a rebuttal. She didn't know where she found the answer, but it came from deep within her. "You must be mistaken, John. I like it very much when Pace kisses me." She paused for a moment to give him time to think about her answer. "I would like it if you kissed me and Daniel kissed me, too. I don't think you will mess my makeup or get me dirty."

John David looked at her skeptically. Alisa was not to be deterred. She removed her napkin from her lap and slipped out of her chair to kneel beside the boy. "Will you give me a big hug and a kiss right now?"

"*I* will!" Daniel volunteered and made the initial motion to climb down from his chair to get to Alisa. His uncle's firm hand stayed him.

"If you don't want to hug me, then can I hug you?" She received only a slight nod from John David. It was enough. Alisa drew him close against her, resting her head against the shiny blond hair still damp from his bath. She held him until she felt a slight tug of resistance. When she drew back, John David looked at her a long time, then he chastely pressed his lips against her cheek. "Thank you," she whispered before rising to her feet. Instead of slipping back into her chair, she went to Daniel and accepted his noisy, smacking kiss and tight squeeze.

"And me?" Pace asked just before she seated herself.

"And you." Alisa leaned down, and Pace placed a tender kiss just at the corner of her mouth. "Okay now, let's eat." She took a fish onto her plate and began to strip the flesh from the spine, carefully examining it to make sure that none of the tiny bones remained in the meat. "I wonder who caught this fish. Was it you, John David?" He peered closely at the fish on her plate. "I bet it was, so why don't you eat this one?" She served the plate with potatoes, salad and hush puppies, then exchanged it for the empty one in front of John David. The boy beamed.

"I caught this fish, didn't I, Uncle Pace?" John David asked for reassurance.

Under the table, Alisa felt a hand on her thigh. Pace gave her a grateful squeeze. "You surely did, but I'm not sure who caught the one on my plate. What do you think, Alisa? Is this one of John's or is this Daniel's?"

"It looks like another of John's." She served herself another bream. "I have Daniel's, I'm sure. This is the one that flopped around on the bank for so long before John David could get him onto the stringer."

Both boys giggled in remembrance of the fish that gave them such difficulties. The happy mood took root and flourished throughout the meal. When the boys had finished eating, without being prompted they collected their plates and silverware and took them to the sink. Pace pushed back from the table. "I'll wash, you dry," he instructed Alisa as he gathered an armload of soiled dishes.

"I have rubber gloves. I can wash the dishes," she protested.

"But I can't put them away."

The boys sprawled on the living-room rug and entertained themselves with the toys and games from the bottom of the satchel that had held their clean clothes. Before Pace and Alisa had completed the dishes, the huge refrigerator door was covered with crayon drawings depicting their afternoon outing. Alisa was familiar with stick people, but it was her first time to see stick fish, especially ones that grinned from gill to gill.

When they had finished cleaning the kitchen, the adults joined the boys on the floor for a series of nonsense card games that all seemed to be a variation of Old Maid. It wasn't long until only Pace and Alisa held cards. Sometime during the friendly competition, the boys had fallen asleep. John David rested his head on one of the elaborately embroidered pillows from the sofa. Daniel lay in an ungainly sprawl on Pace's lap.

"I think I win this game, Alisa. I have two more donkeys and three more chickens than you do." Pace laid the last of his cards on the rug between them.

"You cheated," she teased him as she gathered the juvenile cards. She stacked them neatly and replaced them in their box.

"I don't think so," he denied as he carefully lifted Daniel off his legs and laid him beside his brother. Alisa would have risen to place the pack of cards into the satchel that now contained a plastic bag of the boys' wet clothes, but Pace stopped her with a hand on her arm and a husky whisper on his lips. "You're the one who took unfair advantage by looking so damn desirable. I know I'll hate myself later, but I have to do this." There was urgent insistence as he pulled her onto his lap and held her against his chest. "Just let me hold you for a little while," he begged, "and then I have to go. Just for a little while."

And that was exactly what he did. He didn't kiss her, he didn't touch her other than to wrap his arms about her. He held her close against his heart, his face buried in her hair. And then his arms tightened almost painfully. "What are we going to do, Alisa? This hasn't a snowball's chance in hell of working out, and you would think that I, of all the people on God's green earth, would know that." Suddenly he got to his feet and pulled her up with him. Thrusting a sleeping Daniel into her arms, he carried the heavier John David himself. Without an explanation for his abrupt behavior he placed the boys in the truck and stood by the open door ready to leave.

He looked off at the darkened wheat field. "Maybe it's a good thing that I have all this wheat to harvest, the fields to clear, the soybeans to plant. Maybe if I keep busy enough, I can handle this. Maybe."

"Does this mean that I won't see you until your crops are laid by?" Alisa asked. She knew he could hear the emptiness in her voice. She didn't care.

Pace leaned against the fender and once more drew her into his arms. "It would probably be better if the answer were yes, but I know that any time I can break away, I'll want to be with you. What it does mean is that our time together will be limited, and I won't be able to plan very far ahead as to when I can see you. Will you let me just drop in whenever I have a chance?"

"You know I will," she spoke against his shoulder. "Do I pray for rain?"

She felt his smile. "Only on cue, sweetheart. I don't want you making it rain at the wrong time so all my seeds wash away or my crops rot in the fields." He pulled her closer against him. "Tomorrow, I'm obligated all day." He didn't tell her he would be spending most of the day at the old house that he would buy from David, assessing its condition, making it secure against further deterioration. He wasn't ready to share his feeling for that house with anyone just yet. Sonny didn't count. He, like David and his mother, had always known his feelings for the house and for the Lofton land. He tried to deny to himself that he was afraid of what Alisa would say when she saw the vintage house. He also denied that it really mattered. She would be gone before the new year. But he didn't want to think about that. . . not yet. "So I won't be over. Monday I start on this wheat. Once we cut into it, we don't stop."

"And soon I'll start my research."

His voice grew strangely hollow. "And then you'll write your paper and be gone, in search of all of civilization's missing pieces."

"Let's not think about that right now," she said. "It's a long way off."

"Is it?" Pace's arms tightened, and he held her there on the darkened lawn for a long time. Alisa wished she knew what he was thinking.

"I have to go. The boys need to be in their beds."

"And so do you."

"And you." He kissed her sweetly, a kiss full of

promise, a kiss tinged with sadness, and then he was gone.

Alisa stood on the porch until the taillights faded into blackness. She felt empty, incomplete. And she knew that she didn't want to spend the rest of her life feeling that way. "Oh, Pace Lofton," she sighed aloud. "What have you done to me?"

CHAPTER SIX

WHEN THE SUN HAD BURNED AWAY the morning dew from the grain, Alisa awoke to the continuous rumble of engines and threshing bars and the hiss of grain pelting the metal sides of hoppers. Three big combines rasped through the wheat fields surrounding her house. Pace had begun the harvest of his winter wheat. Quickly, Alisa bounded from bed and pulled down all the windows. Dust and chafe rose in a thick cloud around each noisy combine, and light airborne particles had already begun to drift and settle in thin layers on her window sills. She watched in fascination from her bedroom window as the huge machines lumbered up and down the field, harvesting, threshing and cleaning the grain in one efficient operation, leaving in their wake a wide swath of stubble.

Parked at the end of the gravel lane was Pace's truck. Behind it was a portable fuel tank from which the men would refuel their combines. On the turn row, the strip of unplanted land between the ditch and the first row of wheat, sat a huge truck and trailer waiting to receive the grain when the hoppers on the combines filled. Every piece of equipment, including the fuel tank, bore the Little Fork logo. Pace might deny that he was an agribusinessman, but Alisa's observations, coupled with what she had overheard about the various phases of Little Fork operations, revealed that it took a very sound business head indeed to manage the massive Lofton holdings. Pace might take some kind of obstinate pride in the term red-neck farmer, but that term did not do his professionalism justice.

Alisa watched for a while longer, but she could not determine which of the machines Pace was operating, and as they moved toward the far end of the field she moved away from the window. She wondered how long it would take them to finish the section surrounding her house, how long it would take the dust to settle and how long it would be before she could open her windows and doors again. It would be a perfect day to spend at Poverty Point, she thought.

Sunday after church she had walked the grounds just like a curious tourist. She had climbed to the top of the bird-shaped mound, marveling that the immense earthwork, originally 110 feet high, had been created by dumping basket after basket of dirt until it stretched over an area 700 feet by 1000 feet. She gingerly touched the imprint of a basket, a press mark nearly three thousand years old, and felt an awesome thrill course through her body. She felt as if she were on hallowed ground.

It was difficult to discern the six concentric ridges that lay at the tail of the giant earth-bird, creating a partial octagon like a nest the bird guarded. Years of farming and erosion had worn the ridges down so they could only be seen clearly from the air. They, too, had been built one basket-load of dirt at a time, each ridge large enough to hold many houses. When she thought of the man-hours the seven miles of ridges would have required, she again felt the tingle of awe. And like all scientists before her, she wondered at their purpose. Were the ridges an astronomical observatory? Were the aisles, cut through the ridges, deliberately aligned with the summer and winter solstice sunsets? Or were their positions a statistical coincidence, as some claimed? She didn't like to think of their alignment being an accident any more than she liked to think of the purpose of the ridges as being so mundane as to be merely a convenient arrangement allowing the greatest number of people easy access to drinking water—the Bayou Macon.

As always, when she was on an actual site, the thought that she walked on the same land as an ancient people, that she touched the marks created by hands three thousand years dead, hands that had belonged to people who had lived and laughed and loved so long ago, filled her with a strange emotion. Sometimes it took her a long time to shake the mood, to reaffirm her purpose.

Yesterday, she had totally forgotten her scientific research. This morning she was anxious to get back to the Poverty Point archives, to fill her notebooks and pads with pages of her own strange shorthand

and detailed sketches. She wished that she could go right that minute. But the telephone company had promised to send a representative to install her phone early in the day. She would have to suffer the heat in the airless house until the serviceman arrived. She just hoped that early to him was soon. The heat was already oppressive, and it seemed to Alisa that each succeeding day was two degrees hotter than the one before. This day promised an even greater increase.

Alisa moved through the house slowly, performing minor chores—making her bed, hand washing her lingerie, preparing lemonade. At ten she took her second shower. She had just finished dressing when the serviceman arrived. An hour later she was backing her car out of the drive. Her briefcase held notebooks and sketch pad and two pieces of fruit. She was ready to begin her work on the second floor of the Poverty Point laboratory.

By five-thirty she was home, had taken her third shower, and dressed in white shorts and a white shirt. She stood in front of the big refrigerator contemplating what she would have for dinner when a familiar voice called from the porch. As easily as she had recognized the voice, she barely recognized the man. Pace was exhausted, dirty and angry.

"I saw a phone company truck in your yard this morning. Did their service man connect your telephone?"

"In the bedroom," she directed.

Pace looked down at his filthy jeans and shirt.

"I'm too dirty to come inside. Will the phone reach to the porch?"

"No, it's by my bed."

Pace turned back to the steps, stamped his boots and made several ineffective swipes at his dirty clothes, then gave up. "I hate to come in like this, but I've got to make a call before six and you're my only chance." He apologized as he removed his hat and wiped his dusty forehead on the sleeve of his shirt.

He did take time to wash his hands before he sat cross-legged in the middle of the hardwood floor of her bedroom, the phone nestled on his ankles. "Would you like some lemonade? Coffee? Or a beer left from Saturday night?" Alisa asked while Pace stabbed at a series of numbers.

"Lemonade sounds best, but you had better take a long time in pouring it. I don't want you to hear what I have to say to this man," he gritted between his teeth as he brought the receiver to his mouth and angrily barked a name into it.

As Alisa crushed ice for two tall glasses of lemonade, she looked out at the big machines still marching through the field. They were small specks on the horizon, but she could tell that only two worked. The third sat idle. It didn't take her long to figure out the purpose for Pace's call. His angry voice carried through the small house, and his words were not nice.

"Where is that part you told me you'd have out here by noon?" There followed a heated discussion which ended in Pace setting a time limit for the arrival of the necessary part, and then she heard the phone slam down followed by a long stretch of silence.

Alisa picked up the tall frosty glasses and crossed through the living room. She could see Pace slumped over the phone, his elbows on his knees, his head in his hands. "Pace?" she questioned lightly.

Pace looked up at her, utter exhaustion written in every line of his body. "I'm just so tired, Alisa, so damn tired. When the air-conditioning broke, I had windows to open, but the jackass who designed that combine didn't allow for the power steering to fail. When it, too, went out at about ten this morning, there was nothing to fall back on, nothing but manpower, namely mine. I don't even know if I can get up."

"Couldn't you have made do with the other two?" she questioned as she set the glass of lemonade down by him and lifted the phone from his lap to return to the table by her bed.

"There's a low front moving in. It should hit us Thursday or Friday, Saturday at the latest. Rain, Alisa. We wanted to finish here today and move on to the Willow Bayou property nearer the Mississippi River since it takes forever to drain after a heavy rain." He shook his head and reached for the lemonade. His hand quivered, and she wondered at the strain his muscles had been under.

"What will you do?"

"For the next forty-five minutes, I'm going to

rest. After that I'll hopefully oversee the repair of
the power steering in the combine, then move on to
Willow Bayou.'' He took a long draught from the
glass.

Alisa still stood over him. She turned to look at
her narrow bed. "Will you rest on my bed?"

"Don't tempt me, honey. I'm just too dirty."

"I don't mind."

"But I do." He finished his lemonade, handed
her the empty glass, and eyed her untouched drink.
She gave it to him, then took one of the pillows
from her bed and tossed it onto the floor.

He looked at her a long time before silently accepting the new invitation. "Are those clothes
washable?" He referred to the pristine white outfit
she wore. Alisa nodded her answer. "Make it two
pillows, set the alarm clock for forty minutes and
come lie with me."

"Lie with you?" she croaked.

He was not too tired to laugh. "Oh, Alisa, not in
the biblical sense. Even if I weren't too damn tired,
I have more pride than to make love to you when
I'm so dirty." He reached for the plum-colored
pillow and placed it behind him. "It was a stupid
suggestion anyway. I probably smell like those non-
discriminating goats you didn't want around last
week." He took another swallow of the iced drink,
handed it back to her, then leaned back against the
pillow and closed his eyes. "But do make sure that
I'm up when that mechanic and the new part ar-
rives."

Alisa stood looking down at him. He couldn't be asleep, not already, but he certainly gave that impression. Quietly she moved to close the blinds then left the room. Back in the kitchen she poured herself a fresh glass of lemonade and settled at the kitchen table with the notes she had amassed from Poverty Point. She knew she had her work cut out for her. The site had been carefully worked with every precaution taken in all excavations. Even so, the acidic soil, coupled with heavy rainfall, had caused much of the evidence she needed for her thesis to dissolve. Fortunately the clay figurines and unique cooking balls had survived—the cooking balls in such abundance that she had been given several. They lay on the table in front of her.

The clay cooking balls held her attention now. In all other mound-building cultures she had studied, none had cooking balls. These objects were so unique that they had come to be known as Poverty Point balls, and in each of the other hundred sites in Louisiana, Arkansas and Mississippi where they had been found, the cultures had been called Poverty Point cultures.

Alisa rubbed her fingertip over one of the dusty balls. It had the texture of unrefined Mexican pottery and left a rust-colored residue on her finger. She lifted one to her nose and sniffed it. In the nearly three thousand years since its creation it had absorbed the acidic smell of the earth in which it had lain. She wondered at the meals it had been used to cook—the deer, bear, rabbits and squirrels, the alligator, beaver and fish from the Bayou Macon and other nearby waterways. The most common food would have been fish, she knew, as the major rivers would have constantly replenished the supply.

Her thoughts drifted to Saturday afternoon's fishing trip. In her mind she placed Pace in the ancient Poverty Point culture and imagined him taking the afternoon's catch, not with pole and line or his favored drop lines, but with a basket trap, perhaps a basket woven by her own hands. She envisioned him hurling a weighted net into the water as the sun reflected off his bronzed body, covered only in a breechclout or perhaps completely nude. Her fingers tightened around the chalky ball.

She decided that both her fantasy about Pace Lofton and her projection into the Poverty Point culture were ridiculous. Little was actually known about the Poverty Point people. Archaeologists knew from small figurines that the women had worn short skirts and animal skins, but no one had the faintest idea how the men dressed, whether they had worn breechclout or deerhide pants or something else. And for all she knew, although it seemed highly improbable, the women did the fishing while the men hunted. Besides, she couldn't spend valuable time daydreaming about the man who rested on the bare floor of her bedroom.

Alisa refocused her attention and carefully reexamined the balls, searching for any familiar markings. She had noted the distinctive decorations imprinted on the balls in the archives, and soon she would begin cataloging those marks for inclusion in her paper. But her own samples were plain, without signs to indicate family groups or creative expression. Only one of the balls in front of her carried a mark, a faint impression that might be the mark of a finger or thumb. It was difficult to tell, and since the balls had been formed of moist clay, their original shapes often were distorted. They had been utilitarian objects—nothing to be treated gently. They had been heated in a fire, then placed in a pit. The food went on top of a thick layer then covered with more heated balls so that a crude oven was formed. A three-thousand-year-old crock pot, Alisa mused as she realigned the balls in a row across the table.

Through the window, she caught sight of a truck cutting across the field toward the idle combine. The mechanic, she surmised, rising and crossing to the bedroom. Pace lay in a careless sprawl on the floor exactly where she had left him, and this time there was no doubt that he slept. Alisa hated to wake him, but he had wanted to be there when the man began work on the machine. She knelt on the floor, sat back on her heels and stretched out a hand to his shoulder. Even before she touched him, the dark eyes opened and focused on her. The hand resting on his chest lifted to take her extended hand and bring it to his lips where he placed a kiss in her palm.

"This pillow smells like you." His voice was husky with sleep and his smile gentle, then it faded a little as reality intruded. "Is the serviceman here?" he asked.

Alisa nodded and Pace sat up, an action that brought him very close, so close that it took only a slight movement for him to brush a quick kiss across her soft lips. Although the light was rapidly fading and the closed blinds made the room even darker, Alisa could see that he wanted to kiss her again, but not in the same manner. He hesitated for a moment before looking down at his watch, turning it to catch the light from the living room. The shadow of desire faded and Alisa breathed more freely.

"I'll make sure that the mechanic knows what he's doing, and then while he works, you and I are going to my house for supper. If I have to move that machine to Willow Bayou tonight, I'll need a hot meal in me to keep going, power steering or not." He rose to his feet pulling Alisa with him.

"But your mother isn't expecting me."

"I told you about the way she cooks, and if it really bothers you, call her and tell her I'm bringing you." Pace was halfway down the front steps, ignoring her protest. "And we'll go in your car," he announced. "I don't want to unhook the gas tank from the truck, and I sure don't want to travel with it any more than I have to. I'll be back in a few minutes," he called from the edge of the field.

Before Alisa had time to decide whether to call Mary Alice or not Pace was back, telling her that she didn't need to freshen her lip gloss or run a brush through her hair. Her white shorts and tailored shirt were fine. He didn't even care if she had shoes. He just wanted to get home as soon as possible. He was hungry and he wanted to take a shower and get into some clean clothes.

Pace folded his hard frame into her car and made himself as comfortable as possible. "Damn, Alisa," he complained, "how do you stand this thing?"

"I don't drive it after I've tried to harvest five hundred acres of wheat in one afternoon." He smiled wanly and closed his eyes. "Pace, what about the other men? Don't they need a break, too?"

"Not hardly, they're the second shift."

She cast him a despairing look. "Then why are you still working and why couldn't the other men have taken turns with the broken combine?" She saw the coolness settle over him like a dark curtain and his posture stiffen.

"Of the four men who have run the other combines, two are well past their prime, the third is a partially disabled war veteran and the fourth is a neighbor helping out. That's why they were on the better machines, sitting in air-conditioned cabs. And the reason I'm still working and will be working again as soon as the equipment is repaired is that it's Lofton equipment in a Lofton wheat field on Lofton land. That makes it Lofton responsibility. There's no skin off the others' noses if we harvest before the rain or not. In the long run, it's nothing to them if Little Fork doesn't harvest at all. Some other Delta farmer will be happy to work them until the crops are laid by.''

Somehow she had once more hit a raw nerve. She let the silence, broken only by Pace's terse directions to his house, build between them. Alisa's eyes rose speculatively when she made the last turn beneath a wrought-iron arch that supported the Little Fork logo. The long drive, which wound around pecans and ancient oaks, branched after half a mile. Pace instructed her to take the right fork which led to a two-storied stone and cedar house. The other branch, not nearly in such good repair, continued beyond the well-tended yard, along the edge of a cotton field, then cut into a wooded area. Alisa forgot about it when she pulled her car onto the parking deck.

The Lofton house was a showplace. Light spilled from the great expanses of polished glass that overlooked magnificent plantings, a kidney-shaped swimming pool and an immense summer house, its lattice walls covered in the dark greenery of confederate jasmine. Alisa's eyes were drawn skyward to the chimney emblazoned with the Little Fork logo. To the right were neat barns and garages for the huge machines and farm implements. Alisa had grown up in the shadow of old Boston money, her father's estranged family's money. She was not impressed with properties, but she did know their value, and this property was valuable. Just a redneck farmer indeed, she mentally chided.

Suddenly Pace grasped her shoulder and spun her around to face him. His expression was forbidding, thunderously black with anger as he forced his words from between clamped teeth. "This house belongs to my parents, Alisa. It is not mine. Just like John David and Daniel, I live here at their invitation. It is *their* house," he reiterated and then released her and climbed out of the car.

Wondering again at his uncanny ability to read her mind, Alisa followed him past the triple garage, which held his Lincoln, a Chrysler and an empty slot. Parked on the grass was a large motor home. Pace didn't spare a glance at the impressive array of vehicles. When he placed his hand on the door to open it for Alisa, it was pulled from the inside. Mary Alice stood there with her purse on her arm. Pace tersely explained the situation. Again there was that silent flash of question at Pace's being with her, that mysterious expression she had seen so often a few nights earlier.

"J.D. hasn't returned from the brokers, some deal with a new foreign buyer. He just called to say they're having dinner or something, which means I have to go to Lou Ann's to pick up the boys. He dropped them off on his way out. I'll be gone a little over an hour, so you and Pace will have to serve yourselves." Alisa assured Mary Alice that she and Pace could manage their meal very well. Reluctantly, Mary Alice got into her car and drove away.

When Pace led Alisa down the hall past the kitchen, and she had a brief glimpse at the simmering pots on the stove, she knew she would never again doubt Pace when he said there was always enough for a few extra guests.

"I'm going upstairs to shower before I eat," Pace announced flatly when he ushered her into the living room. He was still angry, and, as always, Alisa didn't understand. More and more of the pieces were there, but still she didn't know what the finished puzzle would look like. In Pace's absence, Alisa returned to the kitchen and set two places at the bar which stood between the kitchen and the breakfast room. Mary Alice kept a neat, orderly kitchen, and Alisa had no trouble finding what she needed. Finishing her task, she moved back to the large living room and turned on the television. The weather segment of the news flickered on. For the first time in her life, Alisa gave more than cursory attention to a weather forecast. Just as Pace had mentioned, northeastern Louisiana expected heavy rains within the next three or four days. After the weather, there was a market report, but there was no mention of the traditional blue-chip stocks. It recounted the closing prices for corn, pork, beef, beans, cotton.

Alisa felt Pace behind her before she heard him. "Any change in the weather prediction?" he asked.

"No, but beans are up three cents."

She felt him move closer, sensed the hesitancy in him. "Alisa, I'm sorry." It was a quiet apology. "I wanted us to have time together. I wanted to be with you, but I didn't want it to be this way. I shouldn't judge you by another's standards. But I do. I can't help myself. I am sorry." His arms loosely circled her at the waist and drew her back against him.

Alisa slowly turned within that circle to face him. He was dressed in fresh jeans and a crisp work shirt. The sleeves were rolled up to his elbows to expose muscular forearms covered in surprisingly soft dark hair. He had shaved and shampooed, and she could smell the fragrance of his soap and shaving cream, a clean aroma, sandalwood, she decided. And to her, Pace looked much refreshed—except for his eyes. They were shadowed in pain, not physical, but decidedly emotional. "I wish I could explain."

"Why can't you?" He only shrugged, and as much as Alisa wanted to know what triggered his unsettling moods, she didn't press. "I've set places. Do you want to eat now?"

"Yes, I'm starved." He released her and followed her to the kitchen. There he dished up chicken and dumplings, fresh green peas and sugared carrots and laid on his bread plate a huge wedge of cornbread. He reached for her plate.

"No thank you. I'll serve my own." And she did, taking portions less than half the size of Pace's. "I sat on my backside most of the day. I don't need forty thousand calories to keep me going."

"You're just saving up for dessert," he teased as he settled on a bar stool beside her. His next comment was on her day's work at Poverty Point. That subject carried them through the meal.

When Alisa insisted that Pace take his coffee into the living room while she restored order to Mary Alice's kitchen, he didn't protest. Washing up took her only a few minutes. When she joined him, he was stretched out in a reclining chair, his eyes closed and the television tuned to a baseball game. "Watching with your eyes shut?" she teased as she moved to take a nearby chair. She didn't make it. His hand snaked out and grabbed her, throwing her off balance and tumbling her into his lap.

"Bottom of the third, Mets two, Phillies zip. Phillies at bat, one out, first man popped a fly to center, the second walked, third man up, the count is two strikes and one ball." He paused for the sound of leather striking leather and the announcer's comment. "Correction," he amended without taking his eyes from her mouth, "two strikes and two balls. And we have thirty minutes before that combine is supposed to be ready to move," he whispered softly as he smoothed her hair back with a rough palm. "Do you have any suggestions as to how we should fill the time?"

"Watching baseball?" she offered coyly.

He shook his head. "The Mets will win. Why watch when I already know the outcome?"

She placed a finger at her cheek as if giving deep thought to the problem of how to spend the next half hour. Then she snapped her fingers. "I know. I could make some more coffee and fill your thermos with it."

"One cup of your colored water per twenty-four

hours is enough." He rolled his black eyes toward the ceiling in veto.

"You could take another catnap."

The teasing tone left his voice. "Will you go upstairs and lie with me?"

"Biblically?" She wasn't teasing either.

He hesitated a long time. Longing marked his face, but it was mixed with something else. "Would you?" he finally asked.

Alisa dropped her cheek to his shoulder and an image of Marlene crossed behind her closed eyes. She didn't know enough about her own feeling, and she definitely didn't know enough about Pace's. She was not ready. Not yet. "No," she whispered.

"I didn't think so."

"Are you angry with me?"

"Angry? Why should I be angry with you?" He lifted his foot up onto the rest then raised her from his chest and propped her against his thigh so that he could watch her closely. "Alisa, the things that you feel are no different from those that I feel. Regardless of what some people say, my attitude toward casual sex is no different from that of any female who has been brought up in an environment with the same values. It doesn't mean I'm some moral fanatic nor does it mean I'm not tempted, and it probably doesn't mean that I wouldn't have had you up those stairs in thirty seconds flat if you had answered differently. I want you very, very much, as you have well known from the very beginning when you landed in that ditch on top of me.

I've been tempted over and over to say to hell with the future, to hell with the potential pain we can cause each other and ourselves. Sweetheart, I understand what you're feeling, and I know that we have to work together. We're too good with each other to mess it up by acting prematurely. Right?" he questioned softly as his hand stroked her cheek.

Alisa wondered why they couldn't always be this way with each other, why there had to be those horrible black moments that left him brooding and her tense and afraid. "Right," she agreed, "but we won't jeopardize anything if you hold me, will we?"

"Dear God, I hope not," he ground out, and he drew her onto his chest again and wrapped his strong arms about her. "How I hope not," he repeated as he pulled her around so that her body nestled more intimately against his. The combined weight of their bodies forced the reclining chair into a flatter position and she was above him, partially atop his strong body, and all she could see was the black fire of his eyes. She could feel his breath on her mouth and the hard thud of his heart against her breast. As she lay there absorbing the feel of him, the aroma of him, his heartbeat gradually increased in tempo, perhaps, she thought, in an attempt to match hers.

Alisa had frequently known the desire to taste his lips, but now it was stronger than ever before. She reacted to that desire by taking a timid initiative and faintly touching her mouth to his. At first Pace re-

sponded in kind with light, tentative kisses be-
stowed over and over on her lips. She didn't know
when the tenor changed, but suddenly those kisses
expressed full-blown passion. He had taken all of
her mouth into his, even her bottom lip and her
tongue. Passionate sounds came sliding up the back
of her throat, sounds that echoed around his own
hungry growl of need. Somehow her hands were in
the black silk of his hair, and he held her locked
against him, one jean-clad leg imprisoning both of
her bare ones. His hands were warm and strong as
he stroked her trembling back.

The kiss was shattering. She had not been prepared for it, especially not after their teasing and
their talk of sexual restraint. It was as if the center
of her universe had shifted and now lay somewhere
within Pace. She had lost her grasp of time and
space. Everything was Pace. He was the man she
wanted. And at that instant she knew it was forever.
That silent admission jolted through her like jagged
lightning. She broke the kiss, but Pace held her
close, speaking against her throbbing lips.

"I didn't mean for it to get like this, I swear I
didn't." He was as shaken as she, but she feared it
was not for the same reason. He stared up into her
eyes, and then with a yielding sound he took her lips
again, and reality was lost to her as his trembling
hands molded her breasts through the thin fabric of
her shirt. The response he got was involuntary.
Nothing mattered anymore but pleasing him.
Pleading, she reached for the buttons of his shirt,

baring his chest for the string of kisses she laid from his throat to his breastbone. She raised her head in time to see his eyes open and fix on her pale panting mouth. He kneaded her stomach and her hips and slicked his hands down her bare legs. They were trembling hands, but they were powerful and she was astounded at her own reaction.

In unison their eyes closed. The hands on her upper legs lifted her forward and once more their mouths melded. Pace's hands inched forward, slipping beneath the edge of her shorts to take the rounded fullness of her buttocks in his hands. He took her gasp in his mouth and gave it back as he repeated her name again and again in a passion-filled hoarse whisper.

"Alisa, oh God, my Alisa, you'll take my honor." She found it difficult to concentrate on his strange litany. "You will take my honor," he repeated again as gently, reluctantly, he slid his hands from beneath her shorts and lifted them to the tumble of her hair, pulling her head back so that he could stare into her eyes. His voice was thick. "Do you know how very, very much I want to take you upstairs and lock the door and love you?"

His face displayed his torture. She wondered if hers mirrored his. Tenderly, she lifted a trembling hand and touched his mouth. "I know because I feel it, too." And she did.

Pace closed his eyes and leaned back into the chair, urging her into the hollow of his shoulder. His large hand covered hers where it lay on his cheek. Beneath her, she could hear his heart pounding, feel the dampness of his hair-roughened chest and she felt him shudder as he forced himself into control. Gradually his heartbeat slowed and his breathing eased. For a long time they lay like that. Then he shifted beneath her.

"I think we have a bigger problem than we thought." He had tried to sound light; instead he sounded afraid. "Oh Alisa, let's get out of here before mom gets back. I don't want to make conversation, not now." Alisa raised up so that he could right the lounger and watched him button the shirt over his chest. At his gentle prodding, she rose.

"Besides," he added, "that mechanic should have finished, and if he hasn't he may need a little encouraging."

"You work too hard," Alisa protested in a small voice.

"I'll rest in July."

Was that it? Were they to leave it like that, so incomplete, so unresolved? Alisa needed a resolution. She needed to know where they were headed, what was happening to them, to her. He couldn't just get up and walk away like that. They needed to talk. Why was she suddenly so fearful?

The easiness between them during their drive back to Alisa's house was only on the surface. Pace lay back as best he could within the restrictive confines of the little car, trying to get a few more moments of rest before he settled into the task of moving the cumbersome equipment from one tract to another. When they had nearly reached her house, Alisa asked quietly, "How late will you work?"

Pace shrugged noncommittally before he straightened in his seat. "Let me out here," he instructed when she turned into the gravel lane. From the sweep of her headlights she could tell that the section fronting the mile-long lane to her house was completed. A bright pool of light marked the crippled equipment a few yards into the field past the turn row.

Alisa stopped the car where Pace indicated. He turned to look at her in the dim glow of the panel lights. "Someone will be in here tomorrow burning the wheat straw. Will you be all right? You don't have any problem with fire like you do low-flying aircraft, do you?"

"No. Will the burning take long?"

"No, not as dry as it is, but still it will smoke up the place for a while."

"That will provide a good excuse for me to get to Poverty Point early."

Satisfied that she would not be endangered by the wheat-field fire, he opened the door, but he did not get out. "Right now, I don't know when we can be together again. Without David, we're all having to double up, but most of his responsibilities have fallen on me. Today, I think you saw what the next four or five weeks can be like. If the equipment hadn't failed, you and I would have had no time at all together."

"I didn't request that in my prayers. I promise,"

she teased, trying to break his heavy mood as well as her own. She received only a wan smile in return before he turned his face skyward.

"If those rains come as predicted, and I see no reason why they shouldn't, I'll probably have a break while it's wet, but...."

"You have to spend the time with John David and Daniel," she finished for him sympathetically.

"Lou Ann has her own brood, and if it rains she'll want time with Sonny. He's in about the same situation as we are—he flies from sunup to sundown when the weather permits. He plays only in the rain. Besides, he, too, has a few acres of ripe wheat in the fields and beans to plant. And mom has already raised her family. She shouldn't have the full responsibility of David's children."

More of the elusive David's responsibilities had fallen to him, she thought. "I understand, Pace, honestly."

"I hope so, but that doesn't make it any easier." Suddenly, he was filled with frustrated anger. "Damn," he cursed, "how are we ever going to know what to do if we can't even find time to be together?" His fingers bit into his thighs as if he resisted touching her. "I can only promise that we'll get together when we can. There'll be time, and I'll find it, Alisa. I swear." He offered her the only resolution available.

"Yes, I know you will," she agreed softly as she reached up a hand to his hair, stroking it back from the temples. She didn't consider the familiarity of her gesture. This was Pace whom she touched, the man for whom she had acknowledged profound need only a short while ago.

"Since you make me feel the way you do, it might be just as well that any time we have in the near future will probably be with the boys." Pace was being open with her, as straightforward as her reaching out to touch him. And then he leaned over and kissed her, threading his hands through her hair. They shared a deep kiss full of residual longing, marred by fatigue, tinged with sadness. It was a kiss that said much and promised more. And then he lifted away from her, jammed his hat on his head and stepped into the darkness.

Alisa watched his shadowy figure cross the field toward the pool of light. When she saw him crawl under the giant machine, she turned on the ignition and continued down the lane.

For the first time, she found her little house infinitely lonely, and she wondered again if she had overdone the isolation therapy. She circled the three rooms several times, repositioning a lamp here, a potted plant there. She was restless, and nothing kept her interest.

Her work was still spread across the kitchen table, and she eyed it with mixed feelings. She turned to make a pot of coffee, spending a long time just watching the brown bubble burst against the glass dome of the percolator. When it stopped bubbling, she armed herself with a steaming cup of mild coffee, brewed exactly the way she liked it, and reluctantly settled at the table. She stared at the accumulation of two years' worth of index cards, photocopied articles, notebooks and folders. She flipped through the stack of papers until she found her outline of procedure: review all related literature, obtain information from all sources of data, define terms, arrange data to provide an orderly and systematic comparison of the cultural characteristics. Under the last item another list stretched: dates of occurrences, relationship to cultural area—the location, geography, natural resources—technology and resources, technology of livelihood and material culture, social organization. The list blended together, a string of nonsense words. For the first time since she was sixteen, Alisa Fairlight didn't care about the socio-political alignment of Indian cultures of the early Neo-Indian period, the formative period of history in North and South America. She wasn't interested in their economic structures, their kinship groupings, religious and ceremonial life.

For a while she sat at the table delivering herself a pep talk. She had come to northeast Louisiana for a purpose, to write a dissertation on the common traits found in the ceramics of Middle and North American Neo-Indian mound builders. The Poverty Point culture was to take the place of the missing Central American data. And she knew what had to be done. "Review all related literature," she muttered and forced herself to pick up an abstract on Poverty Point sites in southeast Louisiana. She put it down, took a sip of coffee, then picked it up again. It was no use. There would be no work tonight.

Through the window, she saw the mechanic's floodlights disappear and be replaced by the headlights of the combine. She watched the service truck make its bumpy way back to the roadway as Pace steered the lumbering machine out of the harvested field. She knew he would be following the trail of the others through the country back roads to the Willow Bayou fields where the equipment would be left in readiness for tomorrow's work. She looked at her watch. It was nine-thirty. In Boston it was ten-thirty. She thought of her many friends there, but there was no one she wanted to call. She thought about her sister. No, now was not the time to talk to Marlene, it would only cloud the issue of what to do about Pace Lofton. She wished her father was stateside, but unless there had been a change in his plans, he was somewhere in Peru. She prayed he was safer on his current dig than she had been on hers.

Feeling even lonelier and knowing exactly why, Alisa showered and dressed for bed. But she did not retire. Instead, she stood on the porch for a long time listening. She wasn't sure, maybe there was the shadow of a sound, the ghostly echo of a combine slowly wending its way eastward. She stood for a long time straining her ears.

For the first time since Sonny's low-flying plane had triggered her wild nightmare, Alisa suffered a series of bad dreams. She awoke several times during the night, and each time it was to a throbbing headache. Sometimes she was drenched in sweat, sometimes she was wrapped in the cold hands of fear. Each time she awoke she curled around the pillow on which Pace had napped. She willed the headache away and thought of Pace—Pace the mystery man, Pace the man of two faces.

CHAPTER SEVEN

THE NEXT TIME ALISA AWOKE, it was to the smell of smoke. One of the Little Fork workers had fired the wheat stubble. Alisa was grateful that the blaze had begun on the back side of the field, but after she watched the thick cloud of smoke for a while, she knew it would not be long in spreading across to the edge of her property.

Nursing a tender head, she quickly showered and dressed for work. Foregoing her usual cup of coffee, Alisa made breakfast of a granola bar and a can of apple juice. She had learned the hard way that caffeine only aggravated her condition following a headache. In her haste to flee the smoke, she arrived at Poverty Point far too early. She would have to wait for the curator, the park manager or one of the caretakers to open the doors, and it would be a long wait.

Climbing to the top of the observation tower in front of the museum, she looked down at the scale model of the site. It provided a perspective unattainable from the ground, and she marveled again at the magnitude of Poverty Point. While she stood there, all of her enthusiasm for her project returned.

The ridges and mounds had been built by hand from basket-load after basket-load of dirt loosened with shells or stones used like hoes. She had read that it took approximately 30 million 50-pound loads to build the earthen ridges, the giant bird effigy mound and another smaller mound.

How many man-hours and how many men had it required? Just how many generations had it taken to complete? What kind of society had possessed the foresight, the patience to sustain such a monumental task? What kind of chieftain had wielded the power to direct the earthwork construction, especially when those who began it would never see it finished, not even the chieftain himself? And what had happened to that society, a society capable of creating such a wonder before the Mayan or Roman civilizations had ever begun?

Voices intruded into her speculation, and she was surprised when she noted the time. While she had been lost in a world almost twenty centuries older than Christ, the park, museum and laboratory had opened. She could begin her own work on the second-floor loft that overlooked the main work area of the lab. It was here that a large portion of the archives were neatly stored.

She began work according to the second item on her outline of procedure: obtain information from all sources of data. And what wonderful data she had, a complete representation of the actual artifacts amassed from the site for the past hundred years—ornamental stones, bola and atlatl weights, clay figurines, cooking balls, stone projectiles, gorgets, beads and pendants, microtools. When she left at five she had even more notes and more sketches to add to the pile of papers on her kitchen table.

When Alisa returned home, there was no more of the golden wheat field. In its place lay a blackened expanse of burned-over land. By contrast the green pasture across the gravel lane seemed all the more rich.

Alisa dropped her briefcase by the front door and headed for the kitchen. Even before she changed her clothes, she slid an Oriental T.V. dinner into the oven. It reminded her of the meal she had shared with Pace, the comments he had made about her larder. She could imagine his reaction to her main meal of the day. Just out of curiosity, Alisa retrieved the box from the trash and read the nutritional information printed in impossibly small letters. Then she made a trip to the medicine cabinet where she swallowed a multivitamin tablet prescribed by her Boston physician.

After she ate her solitary meal on the porch, Alisa found the evening stretching out long before her. She found herself watching the clock and wondering what had happened to her self-discipline. She had to get some work done. With determination Alisa moved back to the kitchen. The previous afternoon she had placed her work there so she could keep an eye out for the arrival of Pace's mechanic. She had abandoned the papers where they lay, when she could not scrape together enough motivation to continue her work. Tonight she would move them into the corner of the living room, to the antique table that had served as her desk since she earned her first degree. On some strange whim, her father had bought and presented it to her as if it were an award for some grand accomplishment. It had been an unusual attitude for him, and she often reexamined that day, looking for something that still eluded her years later. Mysterious as were the circumstances of its coming into her possession, the desk was the one thing she was truly pleased had been shipped against her wishes.

Alisa was immersed in "reviewing related literature"—underlining and making notes in the margins, transferring some information to cards, other facts to a fat notebook—when the phone rang. She held her breath, knowing it had to be Pace.

"I take it we didn't burn down your house this morning," he began.

"No, but you filled it with smoke and soot."

"Are you sending me a cleaning bill?"

"Maybe. Would you pay it?"

"Maybe," he answered in kind.

"Did you finish the wheat at Willow Bayou?"

Instantly his tone became brittle with disgust. "Not even close, but I did send back one defective combine. We were all ready to get moving this morning and the damn thing wouldn't start, wouldn't even turn over. I tried everything I knew and so did the mechanic...when he got there. Nothing worked.''

"What will you do?''

"Without.''

Over the phone she could hear the sound of water running, the clink of dishes. She looked at her watch to find it nearly midnight. "Are you just getting in?''

"I've been in long enough to have supper. I'm putting my dishes in the sink and then I'm going upstairs for a shower and bed. How was your day?''

"Busy.'' She highlighted her day for him, not aware of her own enthusiasm.

"I don't know if you'll be able to pull yourself away from the dead Indians long enough to share my plans. I arranged the work schedule so that I'm the one breaking up the land by your house for soybeans. I know it isn't polite, but I thought maybe I could invite myself to supper. It'll save me a trip home, give me a longer break—'' his voice lowered sensuously "—and give us a couple of hours together.''

Her breath caught in the back of her throat. There had been no mention of the boys. "I'd like that, Pace. What time?''

"Seven. And Alisa, I will have been in that field about twelve hours with only a couple of sandwiches, a thermos of soup and a jug of water to keep me going,'' he warned.

"I can take a hint, Pace Lofton, and it doesn't have to be as big as a Little Fork barn. Believe it or not I can cook, and hearty will be the fare."

"Not out of yogurt, cottage cheese, three white grapes and a bean sprout it won't."

"Wait and see," she taunted.

"For the meal, I don't mind waiting, but for you, I'm not so sure that I can." His words were low and rasped sensuously across the line, and then he was gone.

NEVER HAD ALISA SPENT a more hectic day, nor a more ambivalent one. All day she had been alternately attracted and repelled by the priceless objects she handled. Intellectually, she still knew their importance. Emotionally, she kept blaming them with keeping her away from her house where Pace was working nearby and where she might catch a glimpse of him. Her work was keeping her from riffling through her closet to find the perfect outfit or from beginning her dinner preparations.

From the minute she had hung up the phone she knew exactly what food she would serve him—Italian: rich, wickedly fattening, old-styled Italian. It would take a little adjusting of recipes, but she would do it. She had already placed an order at the little country store on the road leading to Poverty Point. Just as she had expected, she had to substitute ground beef for the Italian sausage she would have bought under different circumstances. Again she spared a moment to forgive the storage company for its transgression of shipping south the entire contents of her apartment, for among the kitchen supplies were bottles and jars of herbs and spices, things the little rural store had never seen on its shelves, things that the proprietor had never even heard of. In fact, if the dairy-produce supplier hadn't been there at the same time as Alisa, she had a feeling that she would be substituting longhorn and American cheese for the necessary romano, mozzarella, and Parmesan as well. As it was, there was no fresh meat. The grocer had taken a frozen block of ground beef from his freezer and promised to have it thawed when she came by for it on her way home. How much longer was that now?

She looked at her watch for the twentieth time in the past hour. "Oh what the heck," she muttered and gave up, carefully replacing the items she had removed from the shelves, returning everything to its exact spot. So what if she left early today? She had months. What did an hour mean here and there? With a cheerful goodbye to the park manager and the attendants, she left the laboratory on buoyant steps. She missed the knowing looks they shared. She was too busy thinking about the upcoming evening.

All the way home she mentally inventoried the contents of her wardrobe. Everything she owned was there, including her winter coat and thermal underwear. She would find something to suit her exact mood. Then her spirits sagged. Pace would be coming directly from the field. In the last few days, she had watched the activities of the area farmers more and more intently. If he were breaking ground with one of those tractors without a cab, he would be covered in dust. In fact, most farmers wore filters over their noses and mouths to keep the dust from their lungs, and safety glasses to protect their eyes.

She knew her worry had been for nothing when she reached her house. There on the porch was a note and a familiar leather satchel. "I know you think it's getting to be a habit, but could a Lofton fellow use your shower once more? I promise not to be covered in mud like the first time and to do a better job of keeping the floor dry than the boys did the second time." It seemed that in her absence, Pace had used her porch as a place to eat his lunch. She frowned. If Pace had just let her know, she could have left the door open and he could have had a glass of cold lemonade, taken a hot shower, rested on her bed.

Alisa carried his bag in with her briefcase and then returned for the groceries. Within an hour she had a deep dish of lasagna ready for the oven, a zesty salad in the refrigerator and seasoned green beans in a boiler, needing only to be heated. She had purchased a long, narrow loaf of unsliced bread at the little store. It was labeled French bread, but it had a soft crust. Alisa brushed it with butter and hoped that a short stint in the oven would improve it. Since there wasn't time to make a dessert, she settled for ice cream and one of several toppings she had bought. Given different circumstances she might have done better, but in a pinch and since

Pace had issued his own invitation, she thought she had done very well.

She almost brought out the china and silver that she had stored beneath her bed, and then thought better of it. She would put on the ritz when there was no soybean field claiming Pace's attention. Then they would be able to have a meal together that didn't serve the dual purpose of being his rest break as well. She set the table with the plaid mats and blue ironstone she had used before and candles of the same pale blue. When she had raked the lawn on Saturday, she had discovered a rose bush, protected by an old boundary post. In the fading light she ran out and cut all the blossoms to form a bouquet large enough to complement the heavy dishes. The flowers were of a dusty rose, nearly lavender, and they repeated the mauve hue in the napkins and place mats. She stood back and studied the table critically. Pace had admired the setting before; he would remember. Should she do something different? Was there time? She studied it a while longer, moving a knife a fraction of an inch upward, brushing an imaginary dust mote from the table. Except for the flowers the setting was exactly like the one Saturday night, she admitted, yet she found it was so very, very different—softer, more romantic, decidedly more intimate. It was all in the eye of the beholder. She laughed and headed for her bath.

She finally decided on a sun dress, full-skirted and low-necked. It wasn't an inspired choice, but she liked the soft knitted cotton of muted rose that clung gracefully to her lithe frame, molding the full-ness of her breasts, hugging her trim waist. She slipped her bare feet into low sandals and made a last check through the house. Sliding the lasagna into the oven, she set the timer and waited for Pace.

He was right on time, and for all the lines of ex-haustion on his handsome face he took the steps two at a time. Alisa didn't stop to think. Before the screened door had slammed shut behind him, she had hurled herself into his arms. As he held her tightly against him she realized that she had been waiting all day for Pace to hold her possessively against him as if nothing in the world mattered but the two of them. He did not disappoint her. His mouth found hers, covering it in a trail of slow fire. It burned its way through her and set aflame her al-ready preheated senses. Running his hands over her body and down to her softly rounded bottom, he pulled her tightly into the cradle of his loins, and she knew his masculine need matched her feminine one. Alisa whimpered as she buried her hands in the midnight thickness of his hair.

When she would let him, he pulled his mouth a millimeter away. "I know, honey, I know," he said hoarsely. The words were breathed into her mouth. "You can't imagine how hard it was for me to keep going from the moment I knew you were home. It's been hell, a living, torturous hell." He recaptured her lips, moving his mouth hungrily across hers in devouring possession, seeking the honeyed moisture within.

Alisa knew she was out of control. It was as if they couldn't get close enough to each other, as if they had been lovers in another lifetime, and now the previous feelings of love and need and passion were wholly revealed to them through a corridor of timeless sensation. It was all right to surrender. It was more than all right—it was necessary, it was urgent. But the urgency was a fantasy, an emotional excuse to forget the world around them. It was a dream, shared by both of them, but only a dream. They had responsibilities in the real world—fields to husband, antiquities to investigate, nephews to nurture, papers to write, goals to pursue. Somewhere through the emotional haven their touches and tastes and needs had created, rationality rudely intruded.

"No, baby, don't," he begged, dragging his mouth away to bury it in her fragrant hair. Slowly reality returned for her, too, and she caught a ragged breath. Pace rocked her in his arms, a slow, gentle motion.

"I'm sorry." She apologized for her wanton behavior, embarrassment in her voice. She hadn't realized that she was capable of losing control like that, not the cool, intellectual Alisa Fairlight. She didn't know how to handle it.

Pace forced a distance between them so he could see her face. "Don't ever apologize for feeling that way. It is a gift from God, through you to me, and I am humbled by it, Alisa. Nor do I want you to think that I am rejecting you." His eyes dropped lower to the shadowed cleavage revealed by the low-cut dress. One gentle hand reached up to brush knuckles across a distended nipple jutting against the confines of her clothing. Alisa caught a jagged breath. "Don't you know how proud it makes me to know that your body responds to me this way, and how hard I pray it's not this way for everyone?"

"It's not, Pace. I swear that it's never been this way with another."

His smile was like melting chocolate. "And I, too, swear, that it's never been this way with another." He took her hand in his and traced his finger over the healing blisters and then lifted her hand to his mouth and placed a kiss in her palm before he whispered, "That is why, even if you would let me, I would not take you like some cheap lay a man picks up for his lunch break. We both deserve better than that."

He drew her tightly against him, speaking huskily into her ear. "That doesn't mean that we will deny ourselves the pleasure of holding and touching one another. But you have to help me tonight, because I want you so very much. Promise?"

Alisa resisted her desire to lean into him, to fight his decision that he would not take her quickly, to fight her own decisions that she must be sure before committing herself. Pace had vocalized her feelings, too, as hard as they were to hold on to, given the heat of the moment. "I promise," she whispered into his collar. They stood like that for a while, as more of the heat of the moment seeped away. Finally, she took a deep shuddering breath. "Do you want your bath now?" she asked as she stepped back a half inch.

Pace's smile was marked with residual passion, his eyes half-shut. "I think you know what I want right now, Alisa, but I will settle for a bath."

Determined to do her part in keeping them both sane, Alisa pulled her arms away and stepped back. "I already have everything laid out for you in the bathroom. By the time you finish, I'll have the meal on the table."

"Does this mean you aren't serving me a neat bourbon in the tub while you scrub my back?" he teased as he reached for his satchel lying by the bedroom door. He didn't have time to duck the pillow she snatched from the sofa and hurled at him.

Alisa fled to the safety of the kitchen, calling back, "If you want a beer, there's one in the refrigerator. Get it for yourself, and I didn't get your back dirty, so I shouldn't have to clean it."

"I guess this means I also have to shave myself. Beer," he teasingly complained in an exaggerated voice. "I thought surely you would serve me something exotic. Beer," he grumbled beneath his breath as he crossed through to the bathroom. He laughed out loud at her rebuttal, which came just before he closed the door.

"At least it's filling."

When Pace returned from his bath, smelling of soap and shaving cream and manly cologne, Alisa was setting the lasagna on the table. He made no comment on her menu until after he had sampled the first bite. And then he gave an exclamation filled with surprise. "Fantastic!" Alisa smiled to herself.

"And how was your day?" Alisa asked as she watched Pace eat his meal with gusto.

"Not bad, really. With the air-conditioned cab, stereophonic system, and power steering, the biggest chore was staying awake." He saw her mouth drop. "I'm teasing. But I do have to fight boredom...up and down, back and forth. It's all physical. It's not even like building rows, where you at least have to concentrate on keeping a straight line, so that when you come back to cultivate you don't run over your crops on account of the crooked rows beneath the foliage. I had forgotten just how much I hate this part of the job."

"Has it been that long since you've broken ground?"

"Actually, yes. I usually get one of the workers to do this—a mindless task anybody can do—or at least I would share it with David. I was out there today strictly so that we might have this time together."

"What would you be doing if you weren't breaking ground?"

"If I could be spared from harvesting wheat, I would be running tests on a backlog of soil and water samples, checking for insect infestations on the cotton, taking a culture from a sick cow we have in isolation, that sort of thing."

"In short, working as a scientist."

"A farmer," he corrected.

"Do you have a college degree?"

"Two. Bachelor of Science and an M.Sc. in entomology from L.S.U."

"Do you perform these experiments and analyses only for Little Fork?"

He looked up from his plate with a cold, hard stare. "No, I don't."

"Do you have your own company?" She knew he was becoming angry with her, but she was curious. He insisted on billing himself as a farmer, disdaining any other title. However, the more she came to know Pace, the more she knew there was nothing simple about the man, not his profession, his education nor the depths of his emotions—and definitely not in the way he made her feel.

"Alisa, I run these tests for my friends and neighbors because it is a skill and knowledge that I have and they don't. I have not charged them in the past. And I damn well will not charge them in the future. When that neighbor came over yesterday and ran that combine for eight hours straight, stopping only to answer the call of nature, he was making payment for work I did in my lab for him." He held his fork poised over his plate in a white-knuckled grip. There was a blazing black fire in his eyes.

This time Alisa did not back down. "Whatever makes you think I give a care whether you charge for your services or not? It's no skin off my nose, as you so frequently put it, how you run your business. I stepped into this mess out of an effort to make conversation and because it puzzles me as to why you continuously have to downgrade yourself in my eyes. You haven't asked for my motivations and I don't remember asking for yours. So why are you coming down on me with black thunder in your face?'' She hurled her napkin on the table and rose, grabbing her plate and glass, stalking to the kitchen to lean heavily on the counter while she ran a sink full of hot water.

He was right behind her, slipping his arms around her waist, trying to pull her resisting body back against his. Finally, she gave in, but she was determined not to let it go, determined not to accept a sweet hug and pretend he hadn't deliberately offended her integrity. "Why do you react this way, Pace? Does it bother you that I've come here with no visible means of support? Do you think I plan to ask you to take care of me, that I'm assessing your worth? Is that why you call yourself a simple farmer, why you warned me about the clothes, the car, your parents' house, so that you can discourage any ambitions that you think I might harbor? Do you think I believe you're rich? Do you think I'm out to get my hands on as much of your money as I possibly can?''

The arms around her almost cut her breath. "It's happened before," he bit out. She tried to twist around to face him. He wouldn't let her.

"To you?"

"No."

She made a logical second guess. "David?"

Instantly she was released. "Yes." His answer was delivered to the ceiling as he threw back his head in pain before spinning around and leaving the room. From the kitchen she saw him flop down on the sofa, his chin on his chest, his legs sprawled in front of him. It cut into her heart to see him so dejected. She knew why Pace did not trust her. Poor Pace, she thought, how wrong can you be? She personally might not have the great material wealth that she had come to suspect backed the efforts of Little Fork Farms and thus backed Pace Lofton, but it was there, in her family. She had never thought about tapping into the Fairlight reserves. She had never needed to, for in her own right she was not poor. There were trust funds from her paternal grandfather, money she seldom touched. She did not need Pace Lofton to finance her way into a better life-style. She was Dr. Thomas Fairlight's daughter, and in her career circle, although she had never consciously capitalized on it, that counted for a great deal. Being Elizabeth Ardoin Fairlight's daughter opened a different kind of door, in other circles. And if she chose, she probably could claim some merit in being Marlene's sister. But most importantly she was an educated woman about to become better educated. She was in a secure position that money could never buy.

Alisa stepped forward to tell Pace so, to prove to him that she was not like the villainess in his brother's life. Something held her back. Pace didn't trust her. That much was obvious. He wanted her and she believed that he might even be on his way to loving her, but he did not trust her. And trust was something that had to be earned. She would have to find a way to show him she was trustworthy.

Alisa knelt before him, looking up into his sad face. It was Pace who spoke. "David's gone, Alisa, and I don't think he'll ever be back. God help me, but I don't know how I feel. Sometimes I'm actually glad he's gone so that I don't have to see him suffer, see him torn apart by what he wants to do and what he needs to do. But I miss him so much it's hard not to cry. I've never told anyone, but sometimes I wake up at night and think I'm six years old and he's nine and he's in the bed across the room, big and tough and able to keep me safe. I'm so scared, and I call out to him just like I must have done a hundred times back then, but he isn't there anymore. He's gone." Pace took her face in his hands, smoothing her cheeks with his thumbs.

"You keep insisting that I'm an agribusinessman. I'm not, but David is. He can create a market for snowballs in Greenland, for sand in the Sahara. He did create a market for our soybeans in Japan." There was a flash of pride that instantly faded. "He was on a flight back from the Orient, where he was sent on behalf of the co-op we had established, when he met Linda. She came like you, almost out of nowhere, a pretty blue-eyed, blond-haired stewardess. Suddenly, every time we turned around, David was in Memphis or New Orleans or Houston, meeting her flights as they came in. And then he brought her home. Pretty little Linda took one look at Mom's house, the number of acres in Little Fork, did a quick inventory of the equipment, the livestock and thought she had struck gold. She didn't need a calculator to multiply the number of acres in Little Fork to come up with a sum to keep her in clover for the rest of her life, but at the same time she ignored the fact that everything belongs to the cooperation, family owned, but nonetheless a cooperation. David failed to make her understand that the success of that cooperation, known as Little Fork Farms, depends on the efforts of every one of us as well as the people we hire and the people around us. If I can show a neighbor how to clear his field of army worms, there won't be a migration from his land onto Little Fork. If David found a market that demanded more bushels of beans than we could produce, we only got that market if our neighbors supplied also. It's a game of you scratch my back, and I'll scratch yours. It's also a game Linda doesn't play.

"No," he repeated. "The only games she plays are the ones that make her happy. Traveling makes Linda happy. She insisted that David could get away during planting time—if he really wanted to. She insisted that he could get away during harvest time—if he really wanted to. She never acknowledged that he could not leave and be fair to the rest of us. And money makes Linda happy, not assets, but ready, spendable cash. She insisted that David bill our neighbors for broker's fees every time he—" He stopped abruptly and drew her head down to his knees. "She didn't understand our life, and she didn't understand our way of doing things. We couldn't make her happy here," he finished flatly, and Alisa sensed that he regretted telling her about David and Linda. She also knew there was more, but it was not hers to know this night.

"Maybe I don't know anything about running a farm, but I'm not like Linda," she spoke against his thigh.

Pace lifted her face and brought it close to his. "And I am not like David. No one will ever do to me what Linda did to him. No woman that I ever love will hurt my family through me like my family has been hurt through David. Neither my father nor my sons will ever end every prayer and every grace at every meal with a plea for my safety because some woman has woven a magic spell over me while she had me in her bed. And the mother of my children will not abandon them, even if she and I cannot make a go of it. I will make sure of that." The words were directed to her and each one was like a stake in her heart.

"So now you have a little of your curiosity appeased. And with that in mind, what do you suggest I do now, Alisa? Do I allow myself to give this thing between us its head and hope it burns itself out in the time you have here? Do I take as much of you as you will let me in that time and hope it will be enough? Do I turn my back right now, deny there's anything between us, so that when you go it doesn't matter anymore? What, Alisa? What do I do?''

''What is there between us, Pace?'' It was a question she had to ask. ''Forget about David and Linda. Think only of us. Are we talking about something other than the mating instinct?'' Alisa knew where she stood, she had to know about him.

He dropped his hands from her face and leaned back into the sofa. He took a couple of deep breaths. ''Right now I believe that the 'mating instinct' is the primary link between us, but I don't think that's all there is. I can't deny the possibility I might be coming to love you. More than once I've thought that perhaps I'm already in love with you. I've confessed, nearly from the beginning, that you have most of the traits I admire in a woman. Add to that the undeniable physical attraction between us, and you know what can develop.''

''Would that be so terrible?'' she asked in a small voice.

''No, Alisa, I think loving you and being loved by you might be the greatest gift that a man could ever have. But it would never work between us.''

''Do you see so much of Linda in me?''

''Yes,'' he stated baldly. Then he quickly qualified his answer. ''I don't think you are as mercenary as Linda; I don't think another human on this earth could possibly be that grasping. It's other things, not nearly so unflattering, but just as important.''

He rose from the sofa and crossed to the darkened porch. There he leaned against a slender column, his hands stuffed into his back pockets. After a while Alisa followed. Finally she touched his arm, turning him to face her. "Will you tell me what these things are?"

He looked at her a long, long time. "It would serve no purpose since this discussion of things that may or may not be between us really serves no purpose until you understand one important thing." Again there was a heady silence between them, and then he laid it all at her unsuspecting feet. "For the record, Alisa, before we become any more involved with one another than we already are, you have to know that whatever else happens between us, I will *never* marry you. And once you leave here, Alisa, whether it's tomorrow, six months from now or ten thousand years, I'll never come after you... never," he declared in absolute finality.

When Alisa found her voice, it was thin and reedy. "And when did you decide this?"

"There was never a decision to make. I have always known it."

Alisa didn't know where to turn. Suddenly her brain wouldn't function; she couldn't seem to string two consecutive thoughts together. "Well, I guess that's that," she managed to say. She made a slight move to turn away from him.

Pace stopped her and it was his time to question. "What do you mean?"

"That we won't be seeing each other again."

"It doesn't have to be that way." He waited.

"All it means is that any relationship that develops between us is not as open-ended as it might otherwise have been. What it means is that there are directions that our relationship will not take." His voice lowered. "I still want you and, if it's possible, more than before." There was open pain in his voice.

And there was pain in hers, but she was also angry, angry that he could presume so much without yielding even the possibility of hope. "I'm not some starry-eyed teenager who assumes that every relationship she has is *the* one. But I'll never settle for a casual affair. Never," she repeated words she had spoken to him once before. And they were not just words learned from observing her sister Marlene's disastrous life. They came from her own rich moral fiber. Nonetheless, her next words referred to her sister.

"You once questioned my having a family that cared about me. And I listed among them a glamorous sister. Well, Pace, she isn't always glamorous. There are times when she is hideously ugly, and those times invariably come when some man tells her exactly what you have just told me. But in Marlene's case, it's usually after she has committed herself... in all ways possible. As I see it, the only difference here is that you're telling me first and assuming that I'll not care. You misjudged me, Mr. Lofton. My answer is the same. I will not enter a casual affair."

Her words seemed to sting him, and he dropped his hand from her arm. "You know there is nothing casual about the way we feel for one another."

"I thought there wasn't. I'm not so sure anymore." She slumped into a deck chair, her legs weary of holding her.

Pace moved restlessly about the porch. He plucked the blossom from a begonia and crushed it between his fingers before turning to stand in front of her, staring down with his black eyes. "What has changed between us, Alisa? What?" he repeated.

She looked up but could see nothing there. She told him the truth. "Hope."

He knelt in front of her, again taking her face in his hands. "What did you hope for, my Alisa, what?"

She opened herself to him, for what did she have to lose? Wasn't her pride gone already? "That you would care for me."

"I do."

"That you would let me care for you."

"I will."

She held nothing back. "That we could love."

"Physically?"

"Yes."

"There's nothing to stop us, not really, not anymore. Had I not felt that I owed you this...this moment of truth, we would have loved before now."

She knew he spoke the truth. Neither of them alone could have prevented their ultimate union. It had taken the combined will of both. "And I had hoped that we could love emotionally," she confessed.

He looked at her a long, long time before answering. "I've fought that since we crawled out of the ditch, my Alisa. But as God is my witness, I won't fight it anymore. Will you?"

She didn't tell him that she had probably never fought it, merely questioned it. She answered simply, "No."

"What has changed between us, Alisa?" he requestioned.

She wished that she could see into his eyes. "The possibility of permanence," she whispered.

"Whatever comes between us will last as long as it needs to last. It will last as long as you are here with me. But it will be between the two of us, no one else, not my family, not yours, and not the courts. What has changed, Alisa?" he asked urgently. She felt herself being drawn from the chair, down to her knees to face him.

"I'm afraid of you," she admitted.

"You weren't before. I'm the same man. I won't hurt you."

"You will destroy me," she separated each word, forcing their counter rhythm against the dance of some horrible dark images playing in her mind, images she didn't want to identify. Yet, she could not resist looking past him into the awesome shadows. She could hear old words echoing, words so familiar, words cried against her shoulder again and again and again by a shattered Marlene. Alisa wrapped her arms around her middle as if she herself had already become the image, and as that miserable phantom, she held herself together against that time in the future. "You will destroy me," she whispered again.

His hands on her shoulders bit into her flesh. "Oh no, I won't destroy you," he bit out, "because you won't allow me to, just as I won't allow you to destroy me. I've taken the precautions to ensure my survival, and you will take yours—whatever they are—and I will either accept them or I will reject them. If I reject them, I will close the door between us and walk away." He gave her a hard little shake. "You have that same right. Either stay and accept my limitations or reject them and walk away—now. Do you understand?"

And suddenly she did. She was not Marlene, and Pace did not in any way resemble the men from her sister's life. He was a man of character. He was a man capable of great depths of emotion. He was a man with an overwhelming sense of permanence. Essentially, weren't he and she both after the same goal, total commitment to one another? Wasn't it simply that each had a different perception of that goal and of the best way to achieve it? Alisa didn't have everything all worked out, but suddenly she again felt the ray of hope flicker to life. In that faint glow she acknowledged that Pace was right. He could do nothing to her that she would not allow him to do. Nothing had changed between them, and if she were careful, she could keep her hope alive. "Yes," she confessed. "I understand." *But do you, Pace Lofton, do you?* she silently asked.

"Okay, Alisa, I think we do understand each other." His next words were tight. "Only one more question. Are you walking away from what we have?"

Again she did not need to think before answering. "No, Pace. I will stay. For now."

He drew her into his arms again and held her tenderly. "I wish it could be different. God, how I wish!" He held her like that for a long time before he pulled them both to their feet.

"We have a lot to think about. I'm leaving now to let you begin." He swept back her hair. "It will all come right, Alisa. It really will. Whatever we finally decide will be right."

"I know, Pace." She secretly felt that she knew better than he.

"The same situation prevails. I don't know when I can break away. I was truthful earlier. I do need to get that lab work done, but I do promise I will not bury myself in the lab when it rains." He smiled. "Then again, there seems to be a pretty, unemployed lab assistant in the neighborhood. Maybe—"

"Oh no you don't. I don't know the first thing about insects."

"Or snakes," he teased.

"Those either."

"Okay, no lab work. We'll have to think of other rainy-day activities."

"I thought you already had one in mind."

"Don't, honey, not now," he pleaded. Alisa's teasing innuendo had once again pushed them back into the realm of sexual tension. "Another thing that I cannot promise. I can't promise it's going to be easy. One kiss, my Alisa, and then I'll go."

"One kiss," she repeated as his mouth met hers. They both held back, as if by mutual agreement.

"Good night, my sweet," he whispered against her temple and then he left.

Alisa stood on the porch, waiting. It did not surprise her when she heard his truck engine start up, nor was she surprised to see the lights flood the turn row. Pace was not returning to his field. Alisa smiled to herself. She understood. For the second time in as many weeks, Pace Lofton was ignoring his responsibility to the land. He was going home...to lie in his solitary bed and give much thought to their future.

But Pace was not to be the only one to spend the night lying awake. Alisa, too, spent little time sleeping. She might not have all the facts, she reflected, but she had enough to draw conclusions. Pace's brother David had broken the rule her fellow scholars called endogamy—a rule of marriage that requires a person to take a spouse from within the local kin, status or other group to which he belongs. Evidently the results had been disastrous. His actions had threatened the security of the Lofton family group and caused them great mental anguish. David had abandoned his tribe, committing the worst offense of all, leaving his sons behind.

To Pace, Alisa was an outsider, and, although he acknowledged that she did not bear the offensive character traits of David's spouse, he would not risk breaking the rule of endogamy again. He would not be responsible for jeopardizing the security of the Lofton family.

Or so Pace must have rationalized. But hadn't he, underneath all the denials, offered her the possibility of something of equal value to that which he withheld, perhaps something of greater value if their feelings for one another continued to grow in the same direction? They both had confessed the presence of the embryo of their love. They both had expressed a desire to nourish it. And should this love survive the ordeal of birth—never in all of nature an event without trauma—they both would care for it and value it. As to life expectancy, in Alisa's heart their love would live forever. She knew that, and one day Pace Lofton would know it, too. And when he did, he could lay to rest the dark memories, his absent brother's legacy to him. With these thoughts the flame of hope glowed just a bit brighter for Alisa.

CHAPTER EIGHT

CONFIDENTLY DETERMINED that everything would come out right between her and Pace, Alisa went about her business the rest of the week with normal enthusiasm. It didn't bother her to see a strange blue truck parked on the turn row, indicating that someone else worked the land adjoining hers. It didn't bother her to take her evening meals alone, to work late into the night organizing her research, outlining her paper, reflecting on the marvels of Poverty Point. She knew the rains were coming.

But they did not come soon enough. The phone beside the bed rang. It was Marlene, hysterical, sobbing, inebriated. Alisa didn't even ask how Marlene knew where to find her. She assumed the information had come from one of their parents. For an hour Alisa listened to her sister berate herself, weeping that she was getting old with nothing to show for the passing years, wailing she was fat and ugly, that no one could love her. She denigrated her talent, swearing that she wouldn't get the part for which she was to audition on Friday. She was scared. She wanted Alisa with her for the audition.

She would make the reservations, meet her at Kennedy, pay for the flight herself.

It was a strange plea. Marlene had never wanted Alisa with her. In fact, like Alisa, Marlene asked nothing of the members of her family. After Marlene finally ended the depressing call, Alisa sat for a long time thinking about her sister. Had that call been one of those distress signals sent out by people who are about to do some irrevocable harm to themselves? Should she call their mother? Should she call some friend of Marlene's? But Alisa didn't know any of Marlene's friends. As she understood, their mother was on the West Coast and their father was still in South America. What was she to do?

Alisa searched through the stacks and stacks of boxes stored in the corner of the small bedroom until she found the neatly bound stack of letters and cards Marlene had written her over the years. After a while, she found Marlene's agent's name, Leo Steiner. It was the best she could do. Not caring about the hour, she called New York.

At the first word Alisa knew the disembodied voice was too mechanical, it lacked life. God, no! Not an answering machine. Nervously, Alisa left a message and after hanging up doubted that her words made sense, and if they did, knew that they had in no way conveyed the urgency of Marlene's distress. She paced the floor, wringing her hands. Then she sat by the phone again, this time dialing a familiar series of numbers. She didn't know what she expected, but when a tired voice answered, she cried in relief. Her father was home after all. He would take care of everything.

Thomas Fairlight listened carefully to his distraught second child. "Alisa, take it easy. It'll take me a while to get to Marlene, but in the meantime, I'll send someone over to stay with her. She'll be all right. I promise you. I'll take care of her."

"Should I go to her?"

"I'll let you know. It may be that she needs you, and then again with the morning light it may all be over. If this audition is as important to her career as she has indicated, maybe she will need you there. But for the moment, you are not to worry. I'll take care of everything."

The urgency of the situation did not allow for any other exchange, not even the usual inquiries about health. But when Alisa hung up so that her father could arrange immediate support for Marlene, she kept the echo of her father's words in her heart. "I'll take care of everything." There was familiarity in those words. Yes, she had heard them before. The last time had been when he tucked the covers around her and urged her to rest, that first night in her own bed after so many nights in the jungles. "I'll take care of everything." Yes, Thomas Fairlight had taken care of her. And although he had not said anything, she knew that it was because of Thomas that her unusual request to work independently within an established research unit had been accepted. Thomas had pulled rank, called in favors, to facilitate her dissertation, to see that she did not jeopardize her fragile health. She tried to hold on to the warmth of her father's love, but more pressing problems displaced it.

At the moment her concern was for Marlene. Carrying the burden of worry for a family member was new to Alisa. She thought about Pace and his concern for his brother. Now she was more appreciative of his anxieties, and she wanted to talk to him about her feelings, not only about Marlene, but also about her father as well. If only the rains would hurry. But they took their own time.

IT WASN'T UNTIL SHORTLY AFTER NOON on Tuesday that a light drizzle began, but by midafternoon thunder rumbled, flashes of lightning threatened the firmament and Alisa smiled. *It won't be long,* she said to herself, feeling almost content.

Pace didn't even call. Just as she was stepping out of the shower, he splashed onto her porch, announcing his arrival with the thud of booted feet as he nearly missed his footing on the rain-slicked porch.

Alisa girded her bathrobe tightly about her waist and opened the door in time to hear Pace use a few choice words directed at his own clumsiness. He grinned sheepishly at being overheard. "If I'd hit the deck, instead of supper and drinks in the city we'd be here all night with my slacks under your hair dryer," he complained while he wiped a dripping forehead with the back of his hand.

"I think it's your tongue that needs a good soaping this time," she muttered as she ushered him in and headed for the bathroom to fetch a towel. When she raised herself up from a low cabinet, an emerald green towel in her hand, he was standing directly behind her.

"I missed you," he spoke huskily as he reached for the towel, unfolding it to drape, not around his own neck, but Alisa's. Shortening its length, he pulled her closer.

Alisa took an end of the towel and blotted Pace's cheeks and neck, standing on tiptoe to reach his hair. Her voice was husky with emotion. He was finally close enough to touch. "How did you get so wet?"

"It was raining," he teased through a lopsided smile. Then the charming grin faded, and he pulled the towel closer. "But not anymore. Now you're with me, and the sun is shining, and all is finally right with the world."

Alisa swayed toward him, her eyes held captive by his hot dark gaze. Pace released his hold on the towel, letting it drop to the floor at their feet. Then his arms were around her, pulling her still closer, pressing her the full hard length of him, and his mouth was only a millimeter from hers. She heard his hard little intake of breath, felt the sudden quickening of his heartbeat as his hands slid over her hips and he discovered what lay beneath the soft fabric of her robe—only her warm flesh, newly bathed and fragrant with soap.

"I'll not keep away this long, not again, not ever again," he whispered. She melted against him, giving herself totally to the scorching kiss. They swayed together, mouths fused, straining to get closer, as if quietly trying to absorb one another, to become one, not only physically but in another dimension as well. They kissed until she was dizzy. Then they drew shakily apart to gasp for breath, to stare in open admission of the wonder of it all and then to kiss again.

Their lips met softly the second time, his as if in apology for all the pain he had caused at their last meeting, hers in understanding. When he slowly released her, she asked, "Where are John David and Daniel?"

"At a birthday party complete with cake and ice cream and balloons and—" he hesitated dramatically before the last item "—water pistols!"

Alisa stooped to pick up the fallen towel. "Do I hear regret in your voice that you weren't invited?"

"I *was* invited, and it was pretty hard to choose between kissing you and water pistols. I really do like water pistols. On second thought...." He dug into his pocket for car keys. With a big grin, he caught the towel she tossed at his head and placed it neatly on the bar.

Alisa turned to the bedroom. Pace stood against the door frame and watched her lay out her clothes. She matched her outfit to Pace's casual slacks and knit shirt, choosing a wrap-around skirt of turquoise-colored poplin and topping it with a striped lavender and turquoise polo shirt. She rummaged through the drawers and added a little pile of lacy underwear. As she turned to find the shoes she wanted, Pace lifted from his easy position and crossed to the stack of frilly things. "Put these back in the drawer," he instructed, pointing a dismissing finger at a pair of sheer panty hose, then he turned to the living room, closing the door behind him to give her privacy.

When Alisa opened the bedroom door, Pace lay sprawled on the sofa engrossed in an article about the prehistory of Alaska. "I'm ready," Alisa injected when Pace turned a page. Reluctantly, he closed the magazine and replaced it on the cocktail table. "You may borrow that magazine, if you haven't finished the story," she offered.

"Thanks, I'll take it."

"You're welcome. Now how do we get to the car without drowning?" It had been a valid question, for there was no sidewalk, only an obstacle course of puddles of varying depth between the front steps and Pace's car.

Pace looked at the pretty silk umbrella in Alisa's hand, then down at the clear plastic rain boots she wore over her shoes. "Can you carry me?"

She stuck out her tongue at him. "Where is your rain gear, your umbrella?"

"My slicker is in my truck, and umbrellas are for sissies."

"At least they're dry sissies," she countered as she popped open her own umbrella and urged him to share it.

THEY SPENT AN EASY EVENING TOGETHER—until they returned to Alisa's little cottage on the edge of the Bayou Macon. Maneuvering around the mud puddles, he walked her onto the porch, and followed her inside for the coffee she had offered. He stood in the kitchen doorway as she filled the percolator. "Mom asked that I invite you for supper Friday night. Will you join us?"

Without turning to look at him, she reached for the cups. "I wish I could give you a definite yes, but I may have to go to New York Thursday night." Both her father and Marlene's agent had called. Everything seemed under control for the time being, but in Leo Steiner's opinion Marlene still seemed too anxious about the audition, too tense. She still might need Alisa. Thomas had expressed a similar opinion.

"I want you here." Pace's cold, harsh demand was alien to Alisa, and the last attitude she had expected.

Slowly, carefully, Alisa closed the cabinet door and turned to face Pace. "And I would like to be here, but it is something I cannot guarantee. You have to be reasonable. There will be other suppers. Surely Mary Alice will understand and invite me another...."

His words that played under hers were low, perhaps not even meant for her ears. "Yes, Mary Alice will understand all right, just like the rest of us. God knows we've heard these words before," Pace muttered bitterly before addressing her directly.

"Yes, Alisa, there will be other family dinners, but I've asked you to this one. Why can't you come?"

"There are problems in New York. Leo Steiner thinks it might help if I'm there and my father...."

Suddenly, his hands were on her upper arms, and she knew Pace fought the temptation of trying to shake loose the answer to his next impossible question. "If you find the idea of a simple family gathering not sophisticated enough for your cosmopolitan tastes, come straight out and say so." He didn't give her time for rebuttal before leveling another charge. "Or is this Leo your real reason for holding back on me? Is that it? Is he someone worldly? Someone who lives an exciting life?" He bit the last three words from between tightly clenched teeth as if he had latched onto an absolute truth. "I want to know. Who is he?"

Alisa was dumbfounded. She didn't know this man in front of her and she fought to wiggle out of his menacing grip. "I'm not meeting any man."

"I don't believe you." She didn't like this newly discovered side of Pace Lofton, not at all. He was making her angry with his unfounded accusations, and that anger fueled her next words.

"Well, that's just too bad," she snapped as she finally shrugged out from under his hold. "If you can't take my word that I'm not meeting a man, if you can't even wait long enough for me to explain that I'm going to see my sister and the reason why, before you jump to these totally unfounded accusations, there's not a thing I can do to create belief, is there?" And like Pace, she barely paused for breath and did nothing to temper her words. "You aren't the only person who has a family. We Fairlights may not live in one another's pockets, but that doesn't mean we are insensitive to one another's needs, and right now my sister needs me. I've told you how she lives, and I've told you the pain she brings on herself. And self-inflicted as it may be, it is, nonetheless, something which she frequently needs help in coping with."

She paused to catch her breath, and new ammunition filled her argument. "And just where do you get off questioning me, anyway? I don't remember giving you the right to question anything I do. In fact, it's none of your affair if I've two men waiting in New York and five in Boston. None whatsoever!"

It seemed that Pace was to ignore the seed of explanation in her heated words. "You think not?" he charged.

"I know not."

"And you're probably right," he responded flatly. With that he turned and before Alisa knew what had happened, Pace was gone. She was alone in the little house, alone and empty, more alone and more empty than she had ever been, and she couldn't even cry. All she could do was ask herself over and over what had happened. One moment they were so comfortable and the next they were raging at each other. Now her only comfort was that she had not made that physical commitment she had wanted to make to Pace Lofton. She had resisted her own urges.

Then she questioned another scene between her and Pace, a scene where they had made another kind of commitment, hazy as it had been. She wondered what had happened to that man, a man who had claimed he might be falling in love with her. Mentally she derided his words. If this raging distrust was his idea of falling in love, his notion of a platform upon which to build a solid relationship, it was just as well that he had shown his true mettle tonight. Just as well, she repeated and then she said it again. But there was no real comfort there, either.

She sought solace in her work. Wednesday, Thursday and Friday as well. Now her phone rang more than ever, but it was not Pace with an apology. Her father and Leo Steiner, as well as Marlene, had called again to deny the need for her to come to New York. So each morning Alisa was at Poverty Point, waiting for the lab to open, and when her work at the site was finished, she would bend over her antique writing table, hour after long tedious hour, reading, taking notes, organizing, rechecking data. She forgot about the possibility of stress; she ignored remembered warnings; she did not worry that she might revive the nightmares. She was determined to get her work finished and get out of the area as soon as possible. She worked until her eyes would no longer focus, until her shoulders and back ached from lack of proper exercise. This was not the place for her, she kept repeating as she massaged a throbbing elbow. Again she suppressed the idea that if she didn't watch her step, she would become ill again. At present she only wanted to get away and soon. It was time to be around her own kind of people, people who could make her forget this new emptiness.

That was the homily she was repeating to herself late Friday night when twin headlights strafed her living room. Alisa looked up from the table and her breath caught. Even before the car engine stopped, even before he climbed the steps and crossed the porch, she knew it would be Pace. Rising slowly, she waited until he reached the French doors, open to the fragrant Delta night.

Pace stood in the doorway with his hands stuck in the back pockets of his jeans, looking fit and handsome, but as tired and as lonely as she. "You really should get a guard dog or something, Alisa." He chided her for the open doors tentatively, softly, as if he expected her to rage at him, to pitch him out on his ear. Alisa did none of those things; she merely waited.

"You didn't go," he added after a while. Still she said nothing, and the tension mounted between them. "I missed you tonight," he began, shifting from one foot to the other.

Alisa moved from behind the desk; her words were wary. "What do you want, Pace?"

"You aren't making this easy are you?" He re-shifted his stance, and again Alisa did nothing. "Alisa—" His voice broke and he began again.

"Alisa, I'm sorry. I'm so very, very sorry." His voice dropped even lower. "I warned you how it could be. And yet I can't promise that it won't happen again."

"Linda, I suppose." Alisa hadn't meant for her words to sound so harsh, but like Pace, neither could she promise to control her emotions whenever Linda influenced their relationship.

His answer was another apology. "I'm sorry."

"What do you want?" she asked the second time.

"Maybe I want you to acknowledge that I do have the right to question." There was no arrogance in the statement, only a tinge of desperation.

"But you don't."

He looked at her for a long time, and when he spoke this time, his words were a pain-filled whisper. "I know I don't. But maybe you can tell me that I haven't killed what was between us. Alisa, I need you, especially tonight. Please, please, be here for me."

Her answer was small, too. "I can't, Pace. Not now, especially not after...."

Pace was quick to read her interpretation and quick to qualify. "I don't mean for you to go to bed with me. I simply need to be with you. I need you to hold me and tell me that everything will be all right. Alisa...." He turned back to the darkened porch, and his manly shoulders slumped. "You're right. I'm sorry." This time he did not apologize for their last encounter. He apologized for the now, and it was more than Alisa could withstand. When Pace made the first step toward the door, she was there, directly behind him.

"Don't go."

Those two whispered words were all he needed. Turning, he enfolded her in his arms, holding her against him, tightly, possessively. There was nothing sexual in his touch; there was only desperation. Finally, he loosened his hold. Then he lifted her and carried her back to the softly lit room where he lowered her onto the sofa, cradling her tenderly. "Do you know how I felt when I thought it was over? Do you?"

"Yes, I know, Pace," she confessed.

"What would I have done had you been gone?" It was a question he asked of himself as he stroked her shining hair. He grew even more still, so very, very quiet, as if he contemplated a future without her. "What *will* I do?" The last words were spoken so quietly Alisa wasn't sure she had heard them.

"I would have come back," she softly addressed his first question, trying to assure him, but he seemed not to hear. After a while he sighed and pulled her closer into the shelter of his arms.

"What happened, Pace?" Alisa broke into the silence. "Is there something bothering you besides us?"

Again he sighed heavily. "It's David. Always, it's David." He buried his face in her hair. "For the first time in months and months, he called me. Oh Alisa, I don't know what to do anymore. I just don't know what to do."

Alisa waited wordlessly and after a while Pace continued. "David always believed in family, just like the rest of us, but earlier this evening when I suggested that his sons need him, he didn't sound interested. He didn't even want to talk about them. What happened to him, Alisa? What could make my own brother ignore the basic needs of his sons? What could make him treat our parents this way, especially dad? Especially dad," he repeated on a pain-filled cry. Then he cleared his throat and continued.

"All I asked was some form of legal permission, a temporary guardianship for the boys. If he isn't returning soon, I need it." His words grew harsher. "Do you know what he said to me? He said he would talk to Linda. That woman hasn't seen Daniel since he was a few months old, yet David has to talk to her to give me permission to seek medical treatment should the need arise." There was anger in his voice, anger and disappointment, but more than that, he was hurt.

Alisa brushed back the fall of his hair. "How have you managed so far?"

"David was in and out until December, and, thank God, so far there hasn't been anything major that required his presence. Dad's cousin who is in family medicine has looked the other way and performed any minor medical service we needed." He was quiet for a while. When he spoke again he seemed to be musing aloud. "I think if I offered enough money, I could get Linda to give me permanent custody."

"And David?"

"Without Linda's influence he would do what is best; I *know* he would. But she has him wrapped around her finger. He is incapable of seeing what sort of woman she is."

"Do you have the kind of money you think she requires?"

"Not liquid. And the only way I could get it would be to sell some things that I don't feel I have the moral right to sell or...or I could go to my father. I'll not do that."

"Why not?"

"I can't, Alisa. I'd have to tell dad the truth, and I am convinced that he cannot take it. He's changed since David left. Sometimes I think I hardly know him anymore. I worry for his health. I think, Alisa, that one more blow would destroy him. I can't be responsible for that. I just can't."

"What will you do?"

"I honestly don't know. I'm damned if I do and damned if I don't. Whom do I sacrifice, Alisa? Do I sacrifice my father or David's sons?" They sat like that for a long time, quietly holding each other, each mulling over the situation. And then he added one more candidate. "Or myself?"

As the quietness settled around them Alisa thought it was time to bring up the issue that had caused their anger with each other. She sensed that for some inexplicable reason, Pace didn't want to acknowledge that the hostile scene had ever happened. But she knew that wasn't wise, so she imperiled the moment of warmth between them.

"Pace," she injected softly, "the trip really would have been for my sister." And then Alisa talked about what had happened. She did not remind him again of Marlene's penchant for disastrous love affairs. Something held her back, but she talked about Marlene's inability to deal with frustration and her feelings of inadequacy. She dwelt on Marlene's fear concerning the auditions. She also told him about the recent thoughts that she had entertained about her father, how perhaps she had misjudged his concern for her and for her sister. And she talked about Marlene reaching out to her, about the newness of being needed and the newly found sense of unity she had discovered in her own family.

She wondered if Pace listened, if he heard her at all, for he made no comment. Finally he spoke. "You don't really know how lucky you've been, Alisa. You may someday wish that this New York sister had forgotten you completely or that you will have come to forget her. You may long to forget obligations to your father. Take my word for it, family unity and being needed isn't everything it's chalked up to be. When someone really cares for you, there comes responsibility to that person, responsibility that you cannot shirk, no matter what you want for yourself." Alisa found Pace's words strange, not at all what she had expected. He offered her no advice, no sympathy and no apology for misjudging her. Instead he turned to her and presented his own needs for understanding.

That night and during the next few weeks, it seemed that the restrained tenor of their physical encounters seemed the only consistent element in their relationship. Alisa felt as if she were on an emotional roller coaster. There were euphoric highs when Pace would drop by late at night, and they would sit on the shadowy porch and talk about their work or about the boys. Somehow they never talked about her sister or about his brother. Each time he stayed only a little while, but she lived for those few minutes.

There were horrible lows when she wouldn't see him at all for days at a stretch as he fought the elements to get the fields of Little Fork planted. But Pace and the area farmers were not the only ones under the pressure of too much work and too little time. Collating her new findings into her old research was proving far more difficult than Alisa had first thought. That difficulty, coupled with the drain on her mental energies caused by her relationship with Pace Lofton, took its toll on her, too. Sometimes, on the rare occasion when Pace had a free evening, and he called to ask her to a movie or to dinner, Alisa would have to turn him down. As much as she wanted to grab at the chance to be with him, she did not always feel free to chance losing her train of thought. She knew he didn't understand, even when he said he did. She could hear the doubt, the mistrust, in his voice.

What kept her going was that those lows were counterbalanced with the seed of hope, a hope that continued to grow the more Alisa understood Pace's deep sense of obligation to the emotional welfare of the family unit, a welfare that David had threatened when he married a woman who was an outsider. Alisa knew she was not like Linda; the things they had in common were surface things, and therefore totally unimportant.

Sometimes when she took a break from her books and notes, she would make lists, trying to see what it was about herself that alarmed Pace. The list was brief. She and Linda both came from urban backgrounds, neither of them had ever experienced the isolation of the Delta farm lands. Alisa didn't know about Linda, but she herself had never witnessed the closeness, the near clannishness of the Delta family units. And the longer she stayed in the area, the more she came to realize it was a unity not unique to the Loftons. It was indicative of the area. It seemed strange to her that in an era when mobility ate at the sanctity of the family unit throughout the country, in this little isolated corner of Louisiana it still reigned supreme.

Alisa did not feel herself a threat to Pace's family. She had no intention of breaking it up, and someway, somehow, she was confident she would convince Pace of that.

Her confidence was short-lived. The one thing she had counted on had not helped. When Pace learned that she, unlike Linda, didn't need his money, that she had social position of her own, it had shored his belief that whatever developed between them could be only temporary. That conviction had been in his face, in his posture and in his voice when he came to return the magazine he had borrowed. Wordlessly, he laid the magazine on her writing table opened to an article about her father's contributions to the field of archaeology. The article focused on her father, but there was space devoted to her mother and her sister. It was the culminating paragraphs that had upset Pace. The article had ended with the hope that one day Alisa would follow in her father's footsteps.

Alisa hadn't yet seen the article, and Pace gave her time to skim through it. "Why didn't you tell me?" he accused.

"Tell you what?"

" 'My sister the actress has problems. She can't handle her love life and she drinks,' " he mimicked. "You didn't tell me that actress was Marlene Ardoin. I had never heard of Marlene Fairlight, but Marlene Ardoin is a different story."

"What does my sister's fame have to do with anything?"

"It isn't just your sister, but the whole lot of them."

"What are you talking about?"

Pace's anger gave way to dejection. "You really don't know, do you? Just how long do you think you can be satisfied living outside the limelight?"

"It's their limelight, not mine," she protested.

"But you're one of them. Weren't you just the other night ranting about suspicions of your father having a more active role in your life than you had believed? Do you think he will allow you to waste away here in the boonies? And if there's any truth to the article, you should have inherited your illustrious family's compulsion to achieve. Even if you haven't, which is most unlikely given the way you burn the midnight oil around here—and I might add against your physician's advice—it is expected of you. Something is causing you to tear through the research, to put me off because of some rusty lump of clay. You obviously have this need to hurry back to the exalted circle." Then his voice lowered painfully. "You know, Alisa, on occasion I really thought we had something going here, I really thought you were different. And in some ways you are, but not enough. Not enough at all. There is no way I can ever keep you content here with me, me— the good ol' red-neck farmer. I can no more keep you than David could keep Linda. When you get ready to leave here, there won't be a damn thing I can do to stop you any more than he could stop her." With those words he had slapped his hat against his dusty leg and returned to his fields.

It was several days before she heard from him again, a tight little phone call near midnight. Before the call she had thought that Pace had deliberately killed his feelings for her because of the article and his newfound knowledge of her family. But when he spoke, there was no mention of their last meeting. And Alisa refused to confront him on the phone with the fallacy of his reasoning. She didn't know when there might be enough time to talk, because Little Fork had reached the crucial stage that allowed them only the late-night phone calls.

Clearing up this new misconception would have to wait until the crops were planted, if not laid by. Alisa became as anxious as any native for the fields to be planted and the pressure on the farmers to ease. She knew it would still be a hectic season, but Pace would not work late into the night as often, and they would have the time they needed together.

Finally Little Fork was planted. Pace and Alisa resumed seeing each other, but it was not the same. Alisa believed that the change between them had been caused by Pace's recent assumptions about the Fairlights. In her heart, she felt he was more determined than ever to disavow the possibility of permanence between them. A new kind of anxiety quickened in her heart. He must come to know the real Alisa before it was too late.

One Sunday afternoon she and Pace lay on loungers by the pool. In the absence of his parents, Pace was keeping one sleepy eye on the children in the water, and Alisa thought it a good time to broach the subject of her own family. Evidently, so had Pace. It was he who began, but not as Alisa would have wanted.

"Alisa, do you really want to follow in your father's footsteps?"

She looked over at him, but his eyes were narrowed to a tiny dark slit through which he watched Daniel paddle across the shallow end of the pool. "My father has made several very important 'finds,' and I imagine he will continue to formulate theories and then set about proving them. He's a very brilliant man. I would be satisfied with a quarter of his present accomplishments within my entire lifetime. To answer your question directly, yes. I want to be where the action is. I want to see the secrets brought to light. I want to make a contribution. I want to practice my profession."

There was no trace of emotion on Pace's face. "How often does your father go out on these explorations or digs or whatever they're called?"

Alisa didn't know where Pace was leading. "It depends on the financing. When everything is going well, I would suppose he makes a major new evaluation every five years or so."

"And in between?"

"There are frequent revisits to sites already being worked, trips to gather more data or to examine new finds made by his friends and associates."

"And how long is he absent from home, how long is he out in the field?"

A frown crossed Alisa's brow. "It depends. Anywhere from several weeks to several months. One time he was in Peru for an entire year."

"What did your family do?"

"Do? My mother did what she has always done, wooed the king makers. I was at school and my sister—"

"Took a new lover," he supplied for her.

Alisa caught a tight breath. "That's not fair. My father's career is not responsible for Marlene's unhappiness."

"What is?" Pace asked flatly.

"You are being simplistic," she charged angrily.

"Perhaps." He chose not to pursue her accusation. Instead, he asked her to detail the locations of the places her father went and the places she herself had gone. The more information she revealed about her father's career and her anticipated future, the darker his expression became, until finally he muttered an obscene word and abruptly arose and sliced into the sparkling water, leaving her in the middle of a sentence.

It was after that brittle exchange that her hope for their future together grew dimmest. Alisa felt Pace would never trust her to be satisfied wherever he was, specifically the sparsely populated northeastern corner of Louisiana. It was then that she wondered if she shouldn't take his hints and end their relationship.

But during the last week in June after they had been holding themselves in sexual check for nearly two months, not daring to take the slightest liberties with one another for fear they would be caught up in the whirling maelstrom of their physical need of each other, Pace told her he loved her.

The evening had started out as a precelebration dinner in anticipation of Little Fork's being laid by in time for everyone to make the annual camping trip to the Homochitta River. So Pace and Alisa had picked up Sonny and Lou Ann and crossed the Mississippi River into Vicksburg. There were just the four of them. "Absolutely no children," Lou Ann had insisted, neither hers nor John David and Daniel.

Pace drove, as usual setting the automatic cruise the instant they were on the interstate and reaching for Alisa's hand to haul her away from the door and near to him. "Damn panty hose," he muttered when he slicked up the hem of her dress to lay his hand upon her knee. Alisa knew that Sonny and Lou Ann pretended not to hear.

They went to Top o' the River, a restaurant that boasted "catfish exceptionale." Because of the restaurant's popularity they had a long wait before being seated at a table. Alisa and her party spent the wait in the Riverboat Lounge, enjoying live entertainment. Good music along with the potent drinks that were served in canning jars elevated their already high spirits, and they were reluctant to leave the lounge when their table was finally ready.

Lou Ann had wanted to eat on the deck overlooking the river, but Pace and Sonny flatly refused. "I didn't come this far to be toted off by mosquitoes," Sonny complained.

"But maybe we'll see the raccoons," Lou Ann pleaded. Raccoons frequently came up the river bank to the edge of the deck and begged for scraps from the tables.

"Next time Pace and I try to save a corn crop

from the 'coons, you can come along and see all you want. We're eating inside." There was a distinct finality to Sonny's announcement.

"My romantic husband," Lou Ann pouted as she yielded the argument. It was Alisa and Pace's turn to pretend not to hear Sonny's comeback which featured a not-very-oblique reference to a privately romantic incident that had occurred while they were dressing earlier in the evening. Lou Ann blushed and hid behind her menu.

The menu was limited. Catfish. It came on a large platter with french fries. With it came jalapeno cornbread in a cast-iron skillet, coleslaw in a tall pottery crock and mustard greens in a little pail. Pace served Alisa's plate. "And try some of these fried dill pickles," Sonny suggested. Alisa thought they were awful. No one disagreed. "Every place has its gimmick," Pace commented as he moved the thinly sliced rounds of pickle to the edge of his plate. "Maybe we should have eaten outside after all. Maybe the raccoons like fried dill pickles," he suggested.

"I keep trying these things, but they don't get any better," Sonny admitted.

"Then why are you foisting them off on me?" Alisa asked.

"Well, I figured that if your tastes ran to the likes of Pace Lofton, you'd probably think fried dill pickles were absolutely delicious."

The teasing banter between the two men continued throughout the meal. Pace might have a blood relationship with Lou Ann, but he and Sonny definitely had a joking relationship, the classic pattern of behavior—mild to taunting to ribald joking—that expressed a privileged familiarity. It made for an emotionally warm evening, especially when they moved back to the Riverboat Lounge for after-dinner drinks. Pace leaned back in his captain's chair, angled so that he could throw a casual arm about Alisa's shoulders. It seemed an unconscious gesture whenever his hand drifted up to caress her nape or knead her shoulder. Whenever he leaned forward to make an indelicate remark to Sonny, his hand would drop to her knee and each time that he encountered the thin layer of nylon, he would look back at her with a line between his dark brows. It was one of the few tactile pleasures he had maintained over the past months and he was making it clear that he resented her keeping it from him by wearing panty hose.

As it does when companionable people are together the time flew. Lou Ann was the first to notice the late hour. "Sonny, you'll be in the middle of the morning getting that baby-sitter home." It was all the reminder they needed of full days ahead if they were to meet the July fourth crop deadline.

The men laid out bills for the bar tab, and they reluctantly moved outside to the parking lot. While holding the door open for Alisa, Pace studied the heavens. "Hang in there, clear skies, until I run that plow through those beans one more time," he intoned.

"Amen," echoed Sonny. Although Sonny's acreage was only a small fraction of Little Fork's holdings, he, too, couldn't leave until his crops had been laid by.

Pace started the car and pulled onto the city street. As soon as he had the car on the interstate, he reached for Alisa's hand, as always pulling her closer to him. While the conversation flowed back and forth across the seat, his hand moved to Alisa's knee and he pushed her skirt back to stroke his thumb against the inner flesh. At first Alisa didn't notice that he had dropped out of the small talk; she was too comfortable, too content. Out of habit she rummaged in the bottom of her purse and found her lipstick. Opening the top, she rolled out the stick and lifted it to her mouth, but she never made contact with her lips. Pace's hand stayed hers. "Uh-uh. It'll just get all over us." He spoke the words under Lou Ann's account of an argument she had overheard in the grocery, and it was the only thing Pace said until he braked the car in the Carter driveway.

"Hey, Pace," Sonny began, "since it's on your way, would you mind running the baby-sitter home?"

Pace's answer was low and final. "I certainly would."

Sonny was obviously taken aback at Pace's refusal to carry out the simple favor. "It's not like I'm asking you to pick up the tab, my friend, all I...ouch!" Lou Ann had kicked him. "Yea, well, I probably needed to ride by my hangar and check on the planes anyway,'' he grumbled as he headed for his own front door with Lou Ann close behind.

Even before Sonny had the front door closed, an extremely silent Pace had pulled the car back onto the road. But instead of taking the turn that would direct them to Alisa's house, he followed a little-traveled lane until it narrowed to a mere trail. He barely had the car stopped beneath a shielding tree when he slid from beneath the wheel and had Alisa in his arms, curling her into his lap. "I know this is puerile, but I couldn't wait, not even long enough to run that damn baby-sitter home. I just couldn't wait a minute more,'' he whispered in her ear before dragging his mouth across her cheek and onto her parted lips. Maybe it was because they simply were not thinking that caused them to let down their guards. Maybe it was simply that they had kept the lid on their boiling passion too long. For whatever the reason, the minute their mouths joined restraint seemed impossible.

His lips were hard and sure, and Alisa opened to him without hesitancy. He speared his tongue into her mouth, sliding it along the roof only to withdraw it and repeat the act. Her arms slid around his neck, and her hands threaded through the black silk of his hair, bringing him closer until nothing else existed. The kiss went on and on with burning intensity, an explosion of passion. He held her so closely, so tightly that she could feel the buttons on his shirt biting into her flesh. Her breasts ached from being flattened against the iron wall of his chest and from the passion charging into them.

Pace slid lower onto the seat, twisting to place himself nearer the unyielding steering wheel pressing her against the soft upholstery. That movement pinched her breast, causing her to cry out. "Oh God, I've hurt you. Where?" he asked in alarm against her lips. His voice was wild with remorse, yet so soft. Alisa couldn't find her own voice to explain, so she took the tips of his fingers and stroked his hand against the sensitive tissue. Pace's hand froze. It had been weeks since he had touched her breasts. It had been too provocative an act for him to trust to his thinly worn control. Now she had done it for him, and the control dissolved. In slow motion, in deliberate movements, he laid his hand fully over one breast. And in the same manner he slowly lowered his mouth to hers again. This time the rhythmic flow and ebb of his tongue was repeated in the kneading of his hand, and Alisa thought she would lose her mind. She wasn't sure she had a mind to lose when his free hand slipped beneath her dress to cup a nylon-clad buttock in the same rhythmic clasp, urging her beneath him. She could not endure the torture, for that was what it was. She wanted to move against the masculine fullness that throbbed against her thigh. She wanted to touch him. She wanted him—inside her!

Those things could not be, not then, not there. And to deny them was nothing less than torture. It was Alisa who tore from his mouth, trying desperately to control her rasping breath. That alone took so much effort, so much concentration, that she wasn't sure she had heard him.

"I love you, Alisa."

She didn't have to control her breath anymore. It was as if she had stopped breathing. "I love you," he repeated. *Passion's voice, Lust's tongue,* her heart cried. And then the dappled moonlight played on his face. Lust did not create the tears that filled his eyes.

He silently mouthed the three words one more time and then pulled them both upright and leaned his head back against the seat, closing his eyes from her wondering gaze. Without looking at her, he urged her head against his chest, cradling her in his arms like a child. After a while, when the raging heartbeat beneath her ear had slowed, he spoke. "I'll take you home now."

He did not utter another word until after he had walked her to her door. On the shadowed porch Pace watched Alisa fit her key into the lock, waiting until she had the door open. Only then did he speak. "I've got a lot to think about. I'm taking the time between now and the Fourth of July camping trip to do it in. Mom or Lou Ann—someone will be in touch about the plans. You will come with us," he ordered in a tone not to be denied. He didn't declare his love again; he didn't kiss her again. All he did was brush his knuckles across her cheek and murmur an emotionless good night.

CHAPTER NINE

A WOMAN IN LOVE, a woman loved—that was what she was. Knowing that Pace Lofton loved her should have made Alisa Fairlight the happiest woman alive. She should have been ecstatic. She should have felt warmed and comforted. Knowing how Pace felt should have softened her view on life. It hadn't. She was cold and lonely. She was afraid, and she had nowhere to turn. Not even her work helped. Everything she did was mechanical, flat. After a few days she yielded to her questions about Pace. Where was he? What was he thinking? What was he feeling? How would he resolve this admission of love? When she saw him next, would he pretend it had never happened as he so often pretended things between them had never happened? Would his confession of love negate his pledge never to marry her and never to come after her if she should leave? Would he now see her as she was, without the preconceptions he had developed because of David's wife and her own family? Would it allow him to place her past, her future—their future—into perspective? Would it allow them to look beyond the narrow confines of the immediate present?

She didn't know. And she hated not knowing.

Alisa soon discovered that she was not the only one with doubts and questions. Although veiled and filtered through Lou Ann, there were inquiries from Pace's mother. From those questions she deduced that Pace was seldom home, and his extended absences were not caused by the concerted push to get the crops laid by. Wherever he went, he did not take Sonny into his confidence, that much was apparent from the more direct questions that Lou Ann asked.

GRADUALLY TWO WEEKS PASSED, and the holiday weekend approached. The second of July was a blisteringly hot, clear Friday. True to Pace's word, Alisa had been included in the holiday plans and kept informed every step of the way—but not by him. From Lou Ann she knew they were leaving that morning. From Mary Alice she knew that the motor home had been pulled onto the Lofton driveway, given a thorough cleaning and packed with supplies. Campers and trucks of relatives and close friends were readied, a few having left the day before. Still no word from Pace. At ten Alisa received a final call from Mary Alice. Little Fork was not laid by. Pace would be staying behind—alone.

There was no time for Alisa to react. Even before she hung up the phone, Lou Ann and four hyperactive children were in her driveway, sounding the horn, urging her outside. Before Alisa could thoroughly assimilate the fact that Pace would not be going with them, Lou Ann was charging through the house, pulling down windows, turning off the lights, closing the zipper on Alisa's bag. "Let's go, let's go," she urged, rattling Alisa's house keys in an attempt to get her moving. Outside, the car horn blared again. "For goodness' sake, Alisa, get a move on! Listen to those hellions. We've got to get these kids to the campground before they drive me stark raving mad."

"Pace isn't finished," she offered flatly. "I'm not going."

"So what? Neither is Sonny. They'll be there when they can, and Pace will expect to find you." She paused in her frenzy to really look at Alisa. "He expects to find you," she repeated more decisively. "Now come on." Lou Ann was not to be denied and before Alisa knew it, she was squeezed into Lou Ann's overloaded station wagon with a wiggling Daniel on her lap. By the time they reached the campground, she was enjoying herself so much she was sorry for delaying the trip even by a few minutes.

As soon as the car doors opened, the children spilled out and scattered in four different directions. "Wait," Alisa called in alarm. Not one errant child heeded her.

Lou Ann placed a comforting hand on her arm. "The only danger those children face is sunburn. For the next few days, there is only one rule for the kids—don't fight. There are no others, but that one is a hanging offense. We've all come here to enjoy ourselves, so let's get unpacked and begin to enjoy."

As soon as they had stashed the things from the station wagon, some beneath the edge of the big motor home where Lou Ann and Alisa would be sleeping, some into a camping trailer belonging to a cousin, all semblance of structured life disappeared. It was a lazy time. Alisa spent most of hers in the river, which was so shallow she placed a lounge chair right in the stream and the cool water only lapped at her bottom. With profound relief, she found that the blazing sun baked out some of her accumulated tensions.

It wasn't until late that first night she felt the muscles in her neck tauten. The all-too-familiar headache that felt like a vise across her forehead and sent excruciating pains down her neck and into her shoulders came after the campground had settled down. She again felt frightened and lonely when the only light was the moonlight and the muted glow from simulated Japanese lanterns strung along the front of elaborate campers and motor homes.

But Alisa did not seek restorative slumber in the neat, narrow bed that Mary Alice had prepared for her in the big motor home. She had volunteered to sleep in a small tent pitched on a wide sandy ledge just below the regulation sites with their water and electrical hookups. Her tentmates were three little boys, all below the age of six and not even collectively brave enough to sleep outside without an adult. "If Unc were here, he would stay with us. He always stays with us," Daniel had whined piteously when told by his grandfather that if he wanted to sleep outside on the hard ground, to be his guest, but he wasn't going to sleep with him. One by one the boys had made their rounds, meeting the same response everywhere. Finally, Alisa relented and helped them to pitch their tent in the soft sand. In three minutes flat the tent was filled with sleeping bags spread from wall to wall. Any left over room was taken by flashlights and little stores of cookies and fruit.

"Okay, fellows," Alisa addressed the giggling crew, "and just where am I supposed to lay my weary bones?" Finally, she shifted the boys around so that there was room for her air mattress as well as a narrow path to get in and out without stepping on little arms and legs. The first night Alisa had to get up three times to take her sheets outside to shake the sand from them. She learned it was futile to lie down until the boys were sound asleep and the only sand they sloughed off fell into their own beds.

The second night she helped them to settle, and then she sat near a dying campfire waiting for the giggles to subside. In the darkness she deliberately kept her mind away from Pace Lofton. She didn't know if he was really cultivating beans or cotton or if he was avoiding her. She sat for a long time, watching the play of light on the water. Finally, the persistent buzz and bites of hungry mosquitoes drove her into the tent and she slipped out of her shorts and bra, leaving on the long T-shirt and tiny briefs she had selected as proper night garments for the co-ed sleeping arrangement. She lay quietly, waiting for an onslaught of emotional pain. Mercifully, it didn't come. The second day in the sun had exhausted her, and gradually she dozed off.

When Alisa jerked awake, she knew it was late by the position of the moon. She was surprised to find neither pain nor an echoing memory of a bad dream, yet she knew something specific had awakened her. She lay in her gritty bed listening. And then she knew.

In one quick movement she was out of her bed, nearly tripping in the tangle of sheets. She fought with the zipper of the tent door, silently pledging to rip it apart if it didn't open instantly. There was no need. Hands as shaky as hers had taken over, rasping the pull up from the other side, and then she was in Pace's arms, hauled hard against him.

"I couldn't find you," he managed to say through a rain of kisses over her eyes, lips, cheeks, nose and throat. It was a hungry random sequence that not once repeated itself. "I stumbled through every bed in the camp looking for you. I thought you weren't here."

"I thought you weren't coming."

"We were both wrong." He was hard against her, fitting her tightly into the cradle of his loins, burning against her, needing, anxious. "Make love with me...now Alisa...tonight."

She had no thought of denial. "Where?"

"Here!"

"Pace, this tent is full of kids!"

He used a curse word she had never heard him use before. And with it some of the heat sapped from his body. "You're right. I'm not thinking." He loosened his grip on her. "Okay, then I'll just sleep with you. Sleep. That's all. Just hold you in my arms and sleep. I must have that much. Okay?"

"Do you really think we can manage that?" She couldn't camouflage the doubt in her voice, nor the tinge of disappointment. This was the man who loved her; this was the man she loved. She didn't want to "just sleep."

"We'll have to, won't we?" He lifted his hands to cradle her face and kissed her deeply. When the kiss ended, he pulled back to look at the results. "Don't look at me like that, Alisa. We're about to put enough to the test as it is." His voice was hoarse with desire and she felt him repress a shudder. "I guess the sooner we get to sleep the better. There'll be no rest as soon as those boys know I'm here." He had tried to sound practical. "Waiting and thinking about it is only going to make this worse, so let's not put it off. Let's try it now. If it doesn't work, I'll have to sleep outside." He had managed to sound desperate.

"Pace, this isn't going to work," Alisa insisted. He looked down at her and then reached for the tent flap, pulled it back and pushed her in, following close behind.

"Just help me a little and we'll make it," he promised tightly.

Alisa eyed her narrow bed, dappled in moonlight

filtered through the screen window. "We'll both fit," Pace whispered. The confines of the canvas room was filled with the sounds of Pace undressing, boots dropping in a muted thump, the clank of belt buckle, the zip of his jeans. He stepped around her and knelt by the bed, quickly restoring order to the tumble of linens, pulling the corner of a sheet taut before retucking it beneath the edge of the air mattress. The moonlight streaming through the mesh window illumined the startling whiteness of his briefs against the dark tone of his skin. It played across his naked shoulders and Alisa wanted to reach out and touch him, to lay a string of kisses down his spine. "Inside or outside," Pace asked without looking up.

"Inside," she answered in a small voice, and he moved so that she could get in before him. Alisa was conscious of every inch of her flesh as she bent to the bed. She was acutely aware of the ribbing along the vee-neck of her shirt; she felt the weight of the soft fabric on her shoulders; she was conscious of the seams, the way it clung to the points of her breasts; she mentally marked the elastic in her briefs, the light airy silk hugging her hips and buttocks. Every nerve in her body was so sensitized that the grains of sand on the bed seemed like small boulders as she stretched on her side and waited for Pace to lie with her.

When he had settled beside her he pulled her against his side, nestling her thinly clad pelvis against the jutting hardness of his hip. Alisa had never had such a sense of belonging. Suddenly she knew everything would be all right. Pace shifted, pulling her partially over him so that he lay more fully on his back and she lay tucked into the shelter of his arm, one leg between the muscular length of his, her head on his chest. He stroked her hair, her back, her silk-covered hips, each foray sliding the shirt higher and higher until it bunched just beneath her breasts. Although that one stroking hand was the only movement between them, she could feel the heat of him straining against her. She knew he could not go on; she could not go on.

"We are deliberately driving each other crazy," he verbalized her thoughts and then she was beneath him, the shirt over her breasts so that her silken feminine flesh lay against his hair-roughened masculine chest when their hungry mouths met. He pressed hard against her, and she was flooded with a moist heat, a heat she knew seared through to burn him with her need. "Alisa, my Alisa," he choked out and then in an instant he rolled off and turned her, fitting her back against his chest, his knees tucked up behind hers. Every hard line of his body dared her to move; his arms around her were so tight that she could barely breathe. But she knew not to protest. One blink of an eyelid and they would be out of the tent. She would be slung across his shoulder like a pagan mate as he searched for a place in the underbrush to throw her down and take her in the rites of old.

They lay like that for a long time, too wary to

move, too tense to speak. And that was the way they drifted to sleep. When Alisa awoke, it was to find Pace's face buried against her breasts, his hand beneath the cover thrust intimately between her thighs and Daniel just blinking his eyes, trying to focus on the sleeping man across the narrow aisle from him. She could see the presence of his uncle slowly beginning to register.

"Pace," Alisa hissed as she reached beneath the sheet to move his hand. The dark lashes slowly lifted over dark eyes. The hand moved suggestively and his head lifted.

"You disturbed a great dream. Was it to make it a reality?" His mouth was poised tantalizingly near her breasts, but if she let go of his hand.... She twisted her legs. "Pace, we have an audience," she pleaded desperately. The dark eyes snapped shut and his head dropped heavily onto her bosom. The concealed hand stilled.

"Don't tell me. Let me guess. Daniel Holt Lofton."

"That's me," lisped a chipper voice and Pace groaned.

"I know I should have dropped him in a pond the day after he was born."

"Pace!" Alisa scolded as she wrestled her shirt down over her hips, finally dislodging his hand. Pace rolled onto his back just in time to catch Daniel as he came sailing over the other children to hurl himself at Pace.

Daniel's squeal of delight brought the others up,

and in the resulting commotion, Alisa tugged her shorts up over her hips. That was all she managed to accomplish before she, too, received a wallop with a pillow that sent her sprawling into the jumble of sleeping bags. In self defense, she was forced to retaliate, and her rich feminine trill was added to the high squeals and Pace's deep full-bodied laughter as he managed to best them all.

"Enough," he finally called and sent the children trooping off to the bathhouse. Alisa lay among the downy rubble of the pillow war, trying to catch her breath. Pace looked at her a long time, marveling at the beauty of her tumbled hair, the flush of her skin following the early-morning exercise. He knew she would look like that after other morning exertions, exercise of a far more intimate nature. His desire resurged. He leaned over and kissed her slightly parted mouth. "Good morning," he spoke against her lips.

"Good morning," she repeated.

There followed another brief, deep kiss. He smoothed her hair back. "Who made breakfast yesterday?"

"Your dad."

"That's my job when we camp. Will you help me?"

"Yes." They lay for a while longer, content just to hold each other. "The troops will be back soon," Alisa reminded him.

"I know, and if I hear Dan ask one more time about what you and I are doing, I am going to auction him off. Some little old lady has got to give me at least a dollar and a half for him." He rose to his feet, pulling Alisa with him. While he dug in the tangle for his clothes, Alisa began folding sleeping bags and stacking pillows, gathering her own kit for the bathhouse.

When she returned from her morning ablutions, Pace had already showered, shaved and started breakfast. In his usual manner, he had enlisted the help of the boys. While he tended to the bacon and sausage in the electric skillet he had placed on the end of one picnic table, the boys, under his direction, had set another table with a cloth, plastic forks and spoons, paper plates, cups and napkins. "Pancakes or scrambled eggs?" he asked and received a chorus of "Pancakes!"

"And you, Miss Alisa, can pour me a cup of coffee." He nodded toward a pot on the bench.

"Yes, sir." Alisa poured his coffee and her own, found a jar of orange juice and a container of syrup.

"Where's Susan?" Pace asked with a scowl as he sipped his coffee and kept an eye on the pancakes. It was the first time he had stopped long enough to realize that his niece was not with all the boys. Alisa explained that the only girl had spent the night across the river with a cousin on her father's side.

"Too many fellows, huh?" Before Alisa could comment, the other adults began to stumble into the picnic area from campers and motor homes. A cousin whom Alisa had met the day before grumbled a good morning and reached for the coffeepot.

"I sure hope you found whatever you were looking for last night," he growled at Pace as he pilfered a slice of bacon. "You woke up everybody in the camper."

Pace glanced at Alisa. "I found it." He lifted out the first pancakes and poured in a half dozen more. His father was next with his complaint about Pace's search for Alisa.

"What the hell was wrong with you last night, Pace?"

"I couldn't find my bed," Pace answered bluntly and ignored his sister's startled expression. "Okay, fellows, line up." He filled their plates. By the time the children were nearly finished, he had enough pancakes cooked to feed the rest of the family. "I quit. If anyone gets left out, there are the ingredients." With that he filled his own plate and settled down between Alisa and Daniel. The rest of the children were already on the beach.

The curiosity about Pace's demeanor upon arriving was momentarily forgotten over the breakfast table. "Man, oh man, am I glad you made it, son," J.D. mouthed around a napkin he used to catch a drip of syrup. "One day of cooking breakfast for this mob is enough to last me a lifetime." He speared another forkful of the pancakes. "By the way, exactly what time did you get in? From all the rummaging around you were doing, you must not have realized how late it was."

"Oh, I think I knew," Pace hedged.

"Everything okay? Did you get everything done?"

"Everything is all right."

"Good." He reached for the coffeepot to fill the cup that Mary Alice held out. "Where'd you finally bunk down? Alisa had your usual bed. She's been keeping the boogers off the boys in your place."

Daniel, trying desperately to wipe a big smear of syrup from his hands with a dry paper napkin, piped up, "He slept with Miss Alisa."

Pace caught his mother's coffee cup before it hit the table. Very casually, he spooned sugar into the cup, stirred it briskly and handed it back to her. "Alisa, will you take Daniel inside the motor home and help him get the syrup off? Otherwise, the ants might pack him off and then I wouldn't even get my dollar and a half."

On wobbly legs, Alisa directed Daniel to the bathroom. She knew that her helping him to wash was just an excuse for Pace to talk to his family. Two minutes in the river water and Daniel would have been squeaky clean. She washed him anyway, lingering over her task. When she could stretch it out no more, she returned to the outdoor breakfast table. Pace was gathering up paper plates and throwing them in the trash, his father was gazing with hard unseeing eyes through the trees to the blindingly white sand. Mary Alice was pleating and unpleating the hem of her shirt. At Alisa's appearance, a strangely quiet Lou Ann and Sonny excused themselves under the pretext of checking on the kids. Other than J.D. and Mary Alice, the remainder of the family, which had included a few odd cousins and an uncle or two who had wandered over to share morning coffee, was nowhere to be seen. Alisa supposed Pace had found errands for them, too. Or perhaps they had fled the pervading tension in the air, a tension that rivaled the heat.

Casting a nervous glance around, Alisa moved to help Pace clear the breakfast things. She felt Mary Alice's eyes on her and turned to see her wipe a tear before forcing a smile as she rose to walk around them. Slipping an arm around both of them, she gave them a squeeze. "You two go on down to the water. I'll finish this up."

"Thanks, mom." Alisa knew that Pace's gentle words were not a gratuity for Mary Alice's taking on the job of cleaning up. Getting out of kitchen patrol would not have relaxed the forbidding line of his jaw, would not have replaced the pain in his eyes with a grateful gleam, would not have caused him to turn to his mother, to take her in his arms and hold her for a while. What had he said to his family? And what had Mary Alice accepted that was so important to Pace?

Whatever it was, he didn't give Alisa a chance to question him. He kept her busy. He had brought a dozen inner tubes in the back of his truck. With a tank of bottled air he inflated them, had Sonny drive them three miles upstream where he and Alisa accompanied the youngsters on a slow float back to camp. The water, the sun and time worked their magic on their appetites. By the time they returned, even Alisa was so hungry she didn't protest the overly generous servings Pace piled on her plate. She ate everything including the wedge of watermelon Sonny handed her, not caring that the juice ran down her elbows and dripped onto the ground between her bare, sandy feet. Finally she could hold not another bite. "I think I had better wash before the ants pack *me* off," she teased Pace. "You maybe could get a dollar seventy-five for me when I'm all cleaned up."

"I'm offering two and a quarter, dirty and untried," one of Pace's cousins bid suggestively.

"Bid rejected," Pace snapped and there was no jest in his voice. All eyes flew to Pace but he was turning to Alisa. "Go ahead and shower, honey, and get your gear together. We'll be leaving in an hour or so."

Alisa saw the way glances moved from one to another. There was a nudge here, a raised eyebrow there. Somehow Alisa knew people's reactions had something to do with the conference Pace had held with his family earlier in the day.

"But I thought everyone was staying another night. I thought there were fireworks and things later on."

"We've got *things* to take care of back at Little Fork."

Alisa knew those things were important. She knew it from the way J.D. hung his head. She knew it from the misty shine in Mary Alice's eyes. She knew it from the way Lou Ann picked at her nails, the way Sonny pulled at his mustache. She knew it from the way Lou Ann sneaked a look at Sonny, the way Sonny watched Pace. And most of all she knew it from the way Pace looked at her. She excused herself to take her shower and gather her gear.

As soon as Alisa had her things together, she and Pace made the trip home alone. There was little conversation between them. For the first time, he didn't haul her over to sit next to him. In fact, it was as if he didn't want her touching him, not yet. When he pulled the truck onto the paved lane that led from the highway to his parents' house, Alisa thought that to be their destination. When he didn't slow to take the right fork she knew differently. Pace continued past Mary Alice's neat yard, followed the lane until the paving gave way to rough gravel and then to a seldom-used trail that curved back into the wooded strip bordering the Tensas River. He stopped in front of a rambling house of pre-Civil War vintage.

In the late-afternoon light, she could see that someone had been working there. The grass was roughly cut and there were signs of recent repairs. Yet Alisa knew no one had lived in the house for fifteen or twenty years. She wondered whose house it was.

For all its state of neglect, it was a graceful house, a house built to last, made of the virgin cypress and hardwoods from the surrounding area. Resting on handmade brick pillows, it stood off the ground nearly four feet. Alisa knew that had been the custom before the surrounding rivers had been tamed behind levees, weirs, locks and dams.

Built in the old planters style, the bottom floor was cut in two by a wide hall to let in cooling breezes. A steep stairway led to the second floor, which she knew would probably contain four huge bedrooms, lighted by windows in the gable ends. She supposed that at one time the hall had been open. Now it was closed on both ends by heavy doors surrounded by fanlights and side panels. The windows in front extended from the porch floor to the ceiling and the sunlight picked up the flaws in the old glass to create rippling rainbows. There were four chimneys rising through the cedar shake roof. Alisa speculated at the firewood it would have taken to keep them going through the three months or so of Louisiana winter.

"Would you like to see inside?" Pace's voice was tight with an emotion Alisa could not read. She knew only that he waited.

"Yes, please." He held her door open, but still he did not touch her. Taking a key from behind the third long shutter, he opened the raw cypress door.

Inside, all the rooms on the ground floor opened onto the hall and most held furniture, shrouded in yellowing dust sheets. The left side contained a parlor, dining room and a third room which they did not enter. Instead, Pace directed her to the other side, which showed signs of alterations although it, too, had once contained three rooms of equal size. Now the middle one had been divided into a bath, walk-in closet and either a small sitting room or nursery. She couldn't tell which. They returned to the last room, now a kitchen.

She looked at Pace. "The original kitchen was not attached to the house, but it was torn down sixty or seventy years ago. This has been the kitchen ever since."

What she saw was no seventy-year-old kitchen. It was in the process of being remodeled, but it was obvious that no work had been done in several years. Pace opened a door to reveal a utility-room, complete with washer and dryer. He frowned. It was as if he had not known they would be there.

"Pace, whose house is this?"

He closed the utility room door and turned to her. "Mine."

"Since when?"

"About four weeks ago."

"And the things in it, the appliances, the furniture?"

"Everything comes with the house."

"Who lived here last?"

"My grandfather." She waited. "After my grandmother died poppa moved into the house with mom and dad. In a year or so he gave this house to David, his namesake. When David decided to marry Linda, he began improvements on the house—insulation, new plumbing and wiring, central air-conditioning and heat, modern kitchen,

baths and—" he nodded toward the door behind
him "—obviously a utility room. But Linda hated
it. Oh, not the house, but its location. What good
was a house of historical importance if it was so far
in the country that there was no one to see it? I'm
not even certain that she ever set foot inside it. According to mom, the minute she understood what
David intended for them, she started screaming
bloody murder. She didn't stop until David had her
installed in a house in Tallulah, the best he could do
and still hold up his end at Little Fork. It was the
scene she created over this house that first exposed
her to the rest of us. Too bad David never did see it.
And he still doesn't," he added bitterly. "Just after
you came here, he asked Sonny to find someone to
loan him money against his interest in Little Fork. I
got Sonny to offer for this house because I was
afraid he would sell it outside the family. Fortunately, when David realized that I was the buyer,
he didn't change his mind."

Alisa walked around the kitchen. The changes
were well thought out, just as the divisions in the
middle room that had probably once been a seventh
bedroom. She wandered back into the hall and
opened the back door which led onto another
porch. In the back lawn there were more of the
magnificent oaks that graced the front. From one
the ragged remnants of rope hung. "Did you swing
in that tree?" she asked.

"I think I fell out of it more than I swung in it."
Alisa could envision a black-haired, black-eyed boy

trying bravely not to cry as he picked himself up from the ground.

"Why have you brought me here?" There, she had finally asked him.

Pace came and stood beside her, not looking at her but gazing out over the backyard. "I want you to come live with me, Alisa, here, in this house."

Alisa spun to face him. And then she knew. He was not asking her to marry him, only to live with him. "I see," she whispered. "Live with you."

He pushed his hands into his back pockets. "I told you that I cannot marry you. And I still won't come after you when you leave me. But I love you Alisa, and I want the time that we can have, and I want to give you the love that I can—while you will let me."

"Is that what you told your parents this morning?" He nodded his answer. "And what do they think? What do they feel?"

"It doesn't matter." He peeled a splinter from the porch railing and twisted it between his fingers.

"I think it does, Pace."

"For the most part my mother feels guilty. She somehow thinks she is responsible for the limitations I have placed on my relationship with you."

"And is she?"

"No." He swung around to stare at her. "She is not responsible for anything that I do, and she shouldn't feel guilty because she has allowed me to see her pain."

"Won't this give her more pain, more guilt?"

He looked at her then, and she knew her question had been unfair. She was asking him to measure his needs against the needs of a member of his family, something he had obviously already done. "I don't know. I hope not. That was one of the reasons I told them what I planned to ask of you. Although no one approves of this, everyone has accepted my feelings for you—except for dad. I don't know what he feels anymore. I don't know what he thinks anymore. I just know there hasn't been much of anything left over for me since David left. David sucked that up, too." He tossed the splinter over the porch railing.

Alisa didn't know what to say about J.D., about David, about living with Pace. She didn't even know what she felt. They had both admitted they could not condone a casual affair, but she had never expected this. She'd thought that when he confessed his love, so much would be different. She'd hoped he would be willing to work with her in resolving whatever their differences were. She had been wrong. He was going to ignore them.

Crossing to the steps, she sat on the top of one. After a while Pace came to sit beside her, still not touching her. He had not really touched her since they had left the tent that morning.

"If I come to live with you, how long will we have, Pace?"

He sighed heavily. "We've been through this before, Alisa."

"We'll just go through it again." The words were

snapped. Alisa was hurting, too, and he wasn't making it easier. "How long?"

"Until you go."

The silence hung between them again. The daylight began to fade. "I don't see anything in this plan that takes into account my needs, the things I want from life."

"Exactly what needs are you talking about? Emotional security? I'll give you that. I will be faithful. You will never have to doubt that."

She hadn't. It was other things. "What will I do with myself? What about my career? My goals? Do you honestly think I can be happy here without those things?"

"No, and that's why it must be this way, but while you're here, you'll be happy if you'll let yourself. Women have lived here for centuries and been content."

There was to be no compromise. But she had known that all along. And there were some things about which she had no intention of compromising, either. "I will complete my degree."

"That is your choice. I won't stop you. I can't stop you. I'm not even sure I'd want to stop you."

"And if I continue with the rest of my plans, the explorations, the field trips, the digs in faraway places?"

He laced his fingers together, an action that seemingly required an inordinate amount of his attention. "Then you'll go, won't you? And I will stay here and that will be that."

"It doesn't have to be."

"But it will be." There was brutal finality in his tone.

Pace did not understand that she wanted unrestricted commitment from him, and she knew it was pointless to force the issue. She did not have the skills nor the tools to cut through the layers of scar tissue to expose his heart to the reality of who she was. She could only hope that time would give them to her. For the moment, she would have to follow his rules.

"What if I never leave?"

"Then it will be forever, won't it?"

"And what about the money?" Alisa knew he scowled. She didn't see it on his face because she refused to look at him. But it was there in his voice.

"What money?"

"The money it takes to support me. I'm an illustrious member of the illustrious Fairlight family. You don't think I'll come cheaply, do you?"

"Is that what worries you? Is that what all this talk about degrees and careers and travel is all about? Money? God, you're more like her than I thought." There it was. The final proof that he still judged her by his sister-in-law. Subconsciously, she had held onto the false hope, prayed, that he now looked at her for her own worth. They had been wasted prayers. "Just how the hell much money do you need? A new Cadillac every year? I can manage it. Your own charge account at the fancy dress shops in Monroe or Vicksburg? I can manage that, too. This place fixed up? Find your decorator. I can pay his bill. But everything stays here when you leave, the dresses, the jewelry, the cars, the furniture. And you won't sell them, either, and pile the funds up in a bank account, not even if it means I have to run a weekly inventory. It will all stay here; I don't care if the clothes rot in the closets, but every penny I spend on you stays here when you go. When you leave here, you take nothing of mine. Nothing!'' He was looking at her now, a black flame in his eyes, but she wondered if he even saw her. She wondered if he were role-playing, saying the things that he had wanted David to say to Linda. It was a terrifying thought. It shook her to her soul.

"Don't worry, Pace, if I ever leave here, I won't take anything of yours—not even your love.''

The flame still burned. "Especially not that.'' He had said the one thing she had desperately wanted him not to.

Alisa looked away. Her own voice was tired. "You will love me here, but not anywhere else.''

"I will love you here. I *do* love you here.'' And she knew it was the truth. It was one of two things that kept her from leaving him right that moment. The other was that she loved Pace Lofton.

Pace's anger cooled, and he reached a hand over to thread in her hair, turning her to face him.

Alisa pulled back from his touch. Drawing her feet up to the step directly below the one on which she sat, she leaned her head onto her knees. "You know, Pace, I've never met Linda, never heard her name mentioned by anyone but you. And you've told me so little. Yet this unknown person is doing all of this to me, to us. She is controlling our lives, mine and yours, dictating to me what kind of relationship I can and cannot have with you. It hurts, Pace. It hurts like hell.'' She fought to keep her voice from breaking.

"I wish it could be different, I really do, but I think I'm asking you to live with me for the right reason, because I love you. I am asking you to live with me in this house because it is my house.'' He rubbed his hands together. She knew that her withdrawing from his touch had upset him. She couldn't help it. Not now.

"Would you live with me anywhere else? Would you live with me in one of the nearby farming towns? In Delhi? Or Tallulah? Lake Providence?''

"I don't know,'' he answered sincerely. After a while he asked, "Is the house that bad, Alisa?''

"I love the house,'' she answered sincerely. "There are pieces of furniture here that belong in a museum, and I long to get at them with cleaners and polish. A little paint, wallpaper, drapes—it could be a magnificent home.''

The rasp of his work-marred hands rubbing together stilled. "Could be?''

"How long have you thought about our living here together, Pace?''

He shrugged. "I guess I've thought about it off

and on for two weeks, plus every moment of every day last week.''

"Don't you think it only fair that I have time to think about this, too?"

"How long?"

"I don't know."

He again reached for her, turning her so that he could see her face. "Will you stay with me tonight...here, down the lane, your place...I don't care where, just stay with me and let me love you?"

As much as it pained her, she gave him her answer. "No."

CHAPTER TEN

STAYING AWAY FROM PACE was the hardest thing Alisa had ever done. By the time she arrived at a decision, she had become an expert at controlling the headaches and tension that left her as drained as all the arguments she had had with herself. She had tried to approach the problem with scientific detachment. That definitely didn't work. She had viewed his proposal from a purely selfish standpoint. What was in it for her? The entries on the debit side far outnumbered those on the credit. And those debits were major.

The first was emotional insecurity. It didn't matter what Pace said to the contrary. All her life she had led a strangely solitary existence, a kind of limbo. For the most part she had been without family. Her youth had been spent in boarding schools and summer camps, out of the way of her parents while they pursued their diverse careers and made their marks in the world. It had been the same for her sister, Marlene. Just as they reached their teens, both Fairlight children were receiving only limited attention. Oh, their parents showed up for the usual special occasions—birthdays, awards days, parents' days. And she and her sister were paraded about when it made good press, especially when it seemed Elizabeth was ready to make another move upward or Thomas had added another feather to his cap. Conversely, when any of their actions could create bad press, the walls went up.

In the past few weeks, she had become aware that perhaps there was more to her family relationships than she had realized, but there was still something missing. Somewhere in the back of her mind she had thought that if she and Pace got together— within a union of marriage, of course—the Loftons would fill that void. But if she went to him as he proposed—lived with him without marriage—she would be no better off than she had been with her own family, living on the periphery.

She mourned what could have been. Married couples had close community and family ties. If a problem arose, they had built-in support. Couples living together did not have that support in most cases. She was sure that J.D. would reject their arrangement and so would almost all of the rest of Pace's family. Perhaps Sonny and Lou Ann might accept them, maybe even in a limited way Mary Alice would also, but Alisa had her doubts about the others, especially here in the Delta where the old ways still flourished.

She thought about that for a long time. And one thought led to another. Wasn't Pace threatening her in some way? Wasn't he saying that as long as she stayed beside him, he would love her, but if she took one step in the wrong direction or a step that he felt he could not take with her, that would be the end of his love? And he had sworn that he wouldn't even try to salvage their relationship. If she displeased him, wouldn't she become a kind of persona non grata with him, much as she had sometimes felt she was with her own family?

But what if she took the chance and went to Pace? Would he give her enough time, enough room to prove him wrong before it was too late? Did she have enough energy to show him that she could have everything she wanted without taking anything from him? Could she teach him that their two worlds could work together, and prove to him it was the thrill of knowledge that drove her on, not the possibility of fame? There was no answer.

And the wild, painful thoughts spiraled on. What if he didn't give her enough time? What kind of legacy would the death of their relationship mean? Would she, like Marlene, look for quick replacements? Would she find herself in a cycle that began and ended always in loneliness, each lonely period unlike any she had known before? That was too horrible to contemplate, so she forced the thoughts to take another twisting turn.

She knew also that she would be charged with social stigma. She wondered if she could handle that. She knew it would be more difficult here than in many other places. The Delta was unique.

But the biggest price Alisa felt she would have to pay would be moral guilt. She was no moral prude, but there were circles within circles to her sense of right and wrong. Unlike Marlene, Alisa was morally uncomfortable in defying the conventions of society and her religion, in establishing a family unit, be it only the two of them, without the sanction of church and fellow man. Maybe she had spent too many years in those church-affiliated boarding schools, but then Marlene had spent just as long. She didn't know why she felt the way she did. All she knew was that her heart told her it was wrong. It *was* wrong!

And then she looked at the lone credit. She looked at it long and hard, day after day, night after night. Finally she accepted its truth, too. It outweighed all the debits. It balanced the emotional insecurity, the social stigma, the sense of wrong. How wrong could something be that burned with such a bright, purifying light as did her love for the man Pace Lofton? And if she went to him, she would go out of love. For as long as it lasted, she would love and be loved; she would belong—to him. Wasn't that as much guarantee as any relationship offered, even those blessed with legal sanction and the highest of church benedictions? She could want for more, the right to bear his name, but even if he should grant her that right, it would not improve what was between them now. With her heart wrapped in the credit, on the sixth morning Alisa packed as many of her belongings as would fit in the little car and locked the door behind her. She would not be coming back, ever. Pace would have to attend getting the rest of her things. Right now she had to see about making one of those rooms in the old house fit for her and Pace to sleep in. If that was where he wanted them to start, so be it.

It was midmorning when she drove up the rutted drive of the old house. She sat in the steaming car for a long time, just looking, trying to see the house as Pace saw it, trying to see it as Linda must have seen it, trying to see it as it had been when Pace's grandparents had lived there as newlyweds, and as it would be sometime in the future. She had never had a real home, or by Pace's standards, a real family. Thomas and Elizabeth had flitted in and out of her life like glittering stars on a summer evening. They were names on checks, smiling faces in magazines, voices on the phone, signatures below letters mailed from faraway places. That wasn't a family as she now understood it, and boarding schools and apartments with impressive names were not real homes. She didn't understand Pace's lust for the land. But she knew there had been something missing from her life, and this was it. She would learn about his land. It was important to him; it would become important to her.

Stepping gingerly through the poorly cut grass, she searched for the overgrown brick walkway. She chided herself for her caution as there was the likelihood of snakes in the grass that spread over the sidewalk as anywhere else. With two suitcases in hand and a coffeepot under her arm she climbed the wide, tall steps to the front door. The key was exactly where Pace had returned it, behind the long shutter on the third window. She cringed at the thought of the crawling things behind that shutter and quickly withdrew her fingers, clasping the old-fashioned key tightly.

The lock groaned when she twisted the key, and the door groaned even louder when she eased it open. She knew intuitively that Pace had not been back since they had closed the door behind them. She wondered if he would know to come now. Should she look for him, tell him of her decision? Somehow she knew he would learn of it and that he would be with her that night.

Her first act was to raise the windows in the huge front bedroom and let the occasional puff of sun-heated air do what it could for the fusty smell left after years of disuse. Beyond that she didn't know where to start. She had never been given to domestic engineering nor had she really ever had the need. The most she had ever done was arrange her household goods in the little granny-house. But it had been clean and freshly painted when she walked in—unlike this place, where she was to begin a new phase of her life, a life with Pace Lofton.

Moving to the wall switch that controlled the long-bladed ceiling fan, she flicked the switch back and forth. Nothing happened. The same was true of the overhead light. No electricity meant no lights and no water and no air-conditioning, she thought, as she traced the power line from the corner of the house to the first utility pole while wiping a rivulet of sweat from between her breasts. That was when she saw the approaching car. It was Mary Alice, Lou Ann and the two women whom Mary Alice frequently employed as domestics.

Alisa moved to the porch and watched them pile out of the car with boxes and brooms and mops and pails as well as a basket of food and a large ice chest. She didn't know where they had put it all and still found room to sit.

"I saw you pass by the house," Mary Alice offered as she tied a bandana around her hair. "I thought you could use a little help." She didn't look Alisa in the eye and she offered no comment on the portent of Alisa's being there. Instead, she sent Lou Ann to throw the breaker to restore power to the house. Ignoring all of the upstairs as well as the huge salon and dining room, she directed her crew with the skill of an army drill sergeant. The accumulated dust and cobwebs of years flew before them. The debris of the carpenters, who had left their jobs unfinished, disappeared. Soon the high-ceilinged rooms yielded their musty odor to the bouquet of scouring powders, glass cleaners, disinfectants, lemon oil, and wax. Woodwork glowed softly with the patina of age and windows sparkled in the sun.

"It's a good house," Mary Alice commented softly as she wiped the last streak from a wavy window pane in the side panel of the front door, "a good place to start a life." Then she turned to Alisa. "I don't know about other places, but there's a tradition around here that we've always kept. When an offspring moves into a home of his own, he takes the furniture from his bedroom with him.'' She looked off down the lane, wiping her brow with the back of her hand. "That's probably the truck bringing Pace's bed and clothes and what-have-you now.'' It was.

"Does Pace know?'' Alisa asked as two burly men set up the king-sized bed.

"About the tradition, yes. David took his and Lou Ann took hers. Pace had to help load them both, raising sand the whole time.'' She pulled open a box and lifted out freshly laundered linen, snapping it smartly onto the bed as she directed Lou Ann to grab the other side.

Lou Ann saw the doubt in Alisa's face. "I think he also had to help Sonny when he brought his to our first house. Sonny and I still sleep in my bed, but our boys have the furniture from Sonny's house.'' Then she added quietly, "It's always done.''

By late afternoon, the five women had done what they could. Any further improvements would have to be accomplished with something other than spit and polish. With groans and protesting muscles, they began to load up the cleaning supplies. As Mary Alice tossed the last pail into the trunk of the car, she gently instructed, "You take a long hot bath and grab a little nap. You've put in a hard day.'' Her voice gentled, and her expression softened. "If it's safe to judge you by my son, then you've probably put in a hard week as well." She placed a tender hand on Alisa's arm and addressed the real problem. "He really loves you, Alisa, he really and truly does. If I harbored one doubt about that, I would not have been here today. I wish for both your sakes, as well as my own, that it could start differently. I'll never accept this arrangement as being right, but I've lost one son. I'll not lose another. Nor will I stop praying that with time, this union between you two will be made right." With that she got into her car.

Even after a shower Alisa was too restless to lie down. She wished there was more for her to do, anything to keep busy. Picking up a dust cloth, she opened the door to the parlor. Unlike the other side of the house and the kitchen, David's workmen had not touched these rooms. It would be wasted effort to do anything in them. Turning back, she left the house to walk the rough-cut lawn, and she waited for Pace. Afternoon faded into early evening and still he did not come. She bathed again and dressed in fresh shorts and the mimosa-colored shirt that Pace liked so well. She got out a long white night-gown and laid it across a chair, ready for when he came, when they would make love.

Finally she gave up, pulled out a sheaf of notes and climbed into the middle of the big bed, wishing that she had asked those men who had brought the bed to go and get her desk for her. As she worked at organizing her notes for inclusion in her paper, she gradually eased into more and more comfortable positions, deeper and deeper into the pillows. It was her undoing. Mary Alice had been right; she had put in a hard day. She had lived a hard week.

And that was the way Pace found her, asleep amid her papers and books. Trying not to disturb her, he gathered the scattered pages, notebooks, and rings of index cards and neatly laid them on the chair with the gossamer white nightgown. He fingered the silken fabric before he turned back to the soundly sleeping Alisa. When he tugged the pencil from her loose grasp her lashes fluttered open.

"It's a fine thing when a fellow doesn't even know where his bunk is and has to come hunting for it," he chided her tenderly as he sat on the edge of the bed and lovingly stroked the tumbled hair away from her sleep-flushed face.

"I didn't know about the bed thing...the tradition of taking it with you." He could see the uncertainty in her face. "Your mother was so insistent, and those men brought it and put it together. I didn't know what to do. Since we're not married, maybe you would rather...."

He placed three fingers on her lips. "Sh-h-h. This bed belongs in this house, in this room and you belong in it." He smelled fresh, of soap and shaving cream, as if he came straight from the shower.

"You stopped to shave," she accused lightly.

He rubbed an assessing hand over his chin and jaw. "I didn't exactly stop for that purpose. Not really. I guess I've been kind of semiconscious since last Sunday. Tonight when I came home, I went directly upstairs without speaking to anyone. I don't even remember if I turned on the light. I just walked through my room to the bath, showered and shaved. It was when I went to dress that I noticed everything was gone." He smiled tenderly. "If these clothes hadn't been in the wash, I would have had to put on my dirty things again. You must have been pretty determined to get me here. You didn't even leave me fresh underwear," he teased.

"Did you know where everything was?"

"When I turned and saw that the bed was gone, yes." He studied her as she lay in the pool of soft lamplight. "Have you been sleeping long?"

She smiled guiltily. "Long enough. I was supposed to be studying. Did you have supper? Are you hungry? There's food in the kitchen. Lou Ann and your mom brought it." Alisa knew she was rattling on. This moment was what they had both been waiting for, and now she felt so clumsy, so inept. Where was the passion, the fire, the breathless anticipation? What had happened to their almost uncontrollable need to consummate their relationship?

Again Pace's quietening fingers rested against her lips. "I'm fine." He stroked her cheek, then the bridge of her nose, defining her brows, her chin and her lips. Her lashes fluttered shut.

"Alisa," Pace called her name quietly. The green eyes opened. "I've touched you through your clothing; I've held you against me in the dark, but I've never seen you." His voice was barely a whisper.

"Show me now. Please," he added even more hoarsely.

"I. . . ." Her voice faltered and she had to begin again. "I have a pretty nightgown to. . . ." The fingers were there a third time to stop her words, and the dark head shook to deny her proposal, causing the lamplight to play on his black shiny hair. It looked like liquid silk.

"Please," he repeated huskily, "show me." His words rasped over her, stoking the dormant embers, touching the hidden kernel of sexual heat.

With shaking fingers, Alisa pushed the buttons on her blouse through the holes. Pace did not help her. Nor did his eyes waver from hers, not even when she had shrugged out of the shirt and lacy bra and lay before him wearing only her shorts. Still without breaking the visual lock of green eyes with black, he reached for her hand and brought it to his mouth, to place a tender kiss in her palm, then to lay it on his cheek while he leaned forward to repeat the kiss, as soft and as gentle as misty Delta rain, on her mouth. As if in slow motion he raised himself from her, still pressing her hand against his closely shaven cheek, still watching only her eyes. Slowly, ever so slowly, the burning black glance began its downward journey, pausing at her mouth for a long time, almost as if he lingered to watch the little puffs of frightening breath, little pants that stopped when his vision traveled lower and lower until it reached its mark.

The muscles in his jaw jerked beneath her hand

and his sharp intake of breath was audible. Just before he removed her hand from his cheek to place it at her side, she felt him swallow hard. Then in synchronized movements he lifted both his hands over her. She could feel the heat of his moist palms as he hesitated above the aching mounds. Then he slowly fitted his fingers around her and it was she who sucked in an audible breath.

"I thought you would be dark, like your arms and legs and the parts of you that show in your bikini. But you're not. You're pale and clear...and so very, very beautiful." There was awe in his voice, reverence in his touch, as he traced the line that marked the edge of her tanned flesh before cupping around her again. His thumbs rubbed back and forth on the lower slopes, nearer and nearer the peak of supreme sensitivity. "Look, my Alisa, how dark I am against you."

Like a magnet her eyes were drawn to his dark hands. The peaks thimbled and strained upward, as if searching for the tactile relief, reaching up for the thumbs that barely grazed the distended buds. How could she have doubted the passion, the fire, the breathless anticipation, the uncontrollable need? It was there in a spiraling focus in the points of her breasts. It was there in a molten flow at the center of her being. Her hand reached up into Pace's silken hair, to draw him down to her.

"Oh, Pace!" she cried as he settled his wet, hot mouth on the dusky-rose nipples, suckling as if he drew substance. She tossed her head from side to side, calling his name over and over while every pulse point in her body throbbed her need. And Pace attended.

"Alisa, my Alisa—my love." He was on top of her and she buried her fingers in his hair, pressing him to her as wave after wave of rushing need, need as she had never known it, raged through her trembling body. She was a smoldering mass that burst into wild flame everywhere his lips and tongue touched. And he touched and tasted everywhere, memorizing the textures and flavors of her body as he worshiped her. He laved the hollows of her throat, trailed a moist foray across her chin, pausing to dip into the sweet cavity of her mouth before moving to outline the shell of her ear, and then retrace his path back to the pulsating, throbbing breasts. He sated his need to drink from them again, turning her into a writhing wild thing as his second foray took a different direction, sliding downward to drift lower to her abdomen. He drew a wet line above the waistband of her shorts then crossed it, nudging down the fabric. She moaned and arched her body against him. His trembling fingers tugged at the button and zipper of her shorts, and she raised her hips to help him and felt the last two garments slide as one, down over her hips and the length of her legs.

The exquisite pain-pleasure stopped. He sat back on his heels and stared down at her for a long time. And then the lean fingers reached out to gently trace a newly exposed sun line. He ran his fingertips lightly across her flat belly, down her thighs to her ankles and up again hovering over the valley of her femininity. He bent his dark head to kiss her in ultimate intimacy.

And then he rose from her to stand beside the bed and his hands went slowly to his shirt front. They were no longer unsteady, but deliberate, full of purpose. He shrugged the shirt off and lowered the zipper of his pants. Alisa lay still gazing up at him, her eyes wide and nearly as black as his as her wild pupils reduced the green to a tiny, thin line. She marveled at the unstudied grace of his movements as he sensuously revealed his magnificent body to her.

He moved his trousers down his muscular thighs, and she caught her breath at the straining need of him. When she lifted her hand to touch him through the soft fabric of his briefs, he threw his head back, filling his lungs with a burning, hissing intake of air. He looked down at her as he covered her hand with his own and pressed it more firmly against him. It was her turn to be awed at the feel of the hot throbbing life in him. When she would have peeled off the fabric that kept him from her, he sighed and caught both of her hands.

"Wait," he managed to say raggedly. With dark eyes devouring her, he reached to the night stand.

"Pace, I have already taken precautions. I . . . ."

His voice was shaky, yet emphatic. "No, my love, it is my responsibility. I will take care of it . . . including tonight." He knew he hurt her, but he had no choice. At her next words, he did something he thought impossible. He loved her more.

He loved her more when she rose onto her knees and encircled him with her arms, placing her cheek against his, whispering her words into his ear, perhaps too timid to say them aloud, perhaps too full. "My love, my life, do what you have to do or let me do it for you, but don't ever stop loving me. It would mean the end of me." She pulled back and looked into his eyes. "I love you." It was the first time she had ever said it, and his heart swelled at the strength in her voice. She repeated it a second time, as if in prayer. "I love you."

And then she lay back and waited for him. "I don't deserve you," he groaned when he lay with her and buried his face in her hair. She moved against him once and all else was forgotten as flesh seared flesh and they grew closer and closer, finding one another. "I love you," he whispered in a husky voice that trembled. "Oh God, please don't leave me. Please don't ever leave me," he cried as he slipped into her and her moist heat surrounded him. And with that cry echoing in their hearts, he took them into a world where they were inseparable— one in soaring spirit as well as one in earthbound flesh.

A long time later, Alisa stirred. Pace did not. His hair lay damply limp across his forehead—as limp as she felt, inside and out. A tiny smile hovered about her mouth. Replete, surfeited, sated, slaked, sexually satisfied, gorged on love like a Christmas goose! It couldn't have been like that, not their first time! But it had been. She raised a tired hand to caress his cheek, which lay between her breasts. In his sleep, he nuzzled her, drawing her closer to him and then he settled again. Alisa stealthily stretched over to turn out the light. The hand on her hip tightened and a deep line settled between his dark brows. "Don't ever go," he mumbled in his half-sleep.

"It's all right," she assured him as she clicked out the light. "I'll be here as long as you let me stay."

In the darkness he sighed a long shuddering breath and grew heavier on her. She knew he would not remember rousing, would not remember the small moments of his own insecurity. Holding him against her, she waited until the deep darkness yielded to the gray of dawn and then the bright yellow of a hot July morning full blown. She slipped from beneath him and bathed and dressed for church. When she returned to the bedroom he lay in a sprawl on his back, the sheet twisted low on his loins, one hair-roughened leg exposed.

She sat on the edge of the love-tumbled bed. "Pace?" she called only once, and the dark eyes opened, slowly focused and a soft smile crept across his face as he remembered.

"Thank you," he offered in a voice thick from sleep as his hand stroked her cheek. Alisa raised a neat brow in question. "For loving me," he explained. Suddenly the gentle, sensitive look faded as he finally noted the sophisticated dress she wore, the shimmer of silk on her legs, the trim high-heeled sandals. "Church," she explained. The scowl deepened.

"Will you pray for me?"

"Not the way you think." She offered no other explanation, he asked for none. "I can wait if you want to dress and come with me," she offered. But she knew he would not accept. He had too often voiced his opinion of the people who attended her church. He felt them narrow-minded and more socially oriented than could possibly be good for their souls.

He plumped up a pillow and propped himself up against the headboard. He did not restate his opinion of her fellow parishioners. "No, I'll see about getting your things over here and check on the boys." For a minute there was a cloud in his dark eyes. "I'll need to talk to them...about us." His expression cleared. "Besides, I can get a lot done in the time it takes you to make the round trip to your fancy church in town."

"Maybe I will pray for you after all," she threatened with a flip of her silk skirt as she rose to gather her purse and prayer book.

"No goodbye kiss, my Alisa?" he asked huskily.

"No goodbye kiss, Pace, but maybe a good-morning kiss," she qualified as she returned to the bed. It was very difficult to remember that she was on her way to church.

It was a long trip there and a long trip back. She considered trying one of the local rural churches.

But after the first impulse, she knew that wouldn't do. Sixty miles or not, she needed her own denomination; she needed the ritual she had experienced since childhood. She would make lots of compromises for the man she loved, but this was not one of them.

On her return, when she neared the fork in the private drive leading to her new home, Pace's car barred the way. A note stuck to the window told her Mary Alice had lunch ready and they were waiting for her. Alisa eyed the driveway and breathed a little easier. There were no extra cars, she would be facing only Pace's parents after her first night in his bed.

Alisa didn't know why she entered the Lofton house so quietly, almost timidly. Maybe she didn't want to draw attention to herself. She wasn't yet familiar with the person she had become the night before. She didn't know exactly how to handle the new her. Her own body, as Pace had introduced it to her, was suddenly an alien thing. That was part of it. She wasn't sure that *everything* didn't show. What if his mother should look at her and tell where Pace had touched her? What if his father should know how Pace had loved her and she had loved him in return?

All that was forgotten the minute she crossed the threshold to the living room. Something was going on. It was written in Pace's posture, in J.D.'s face, and in the way Mary Alice stood between the two men, a hand on the chest of each, not as if she held

them apart, but as if she were the link that bonded
them together.

From Pace's clothes, Alisa assumed he, too, had
been to church after all. He wore dark-blue slacks,
a pale-blue shirt, its long sleeves still secured with
hammered gold links. On a nearby chair lay his
blazer and tie. Pace turned to reach for his jacket,
breaking contact with his mother. It was his father's
words that held him back. "Don't you know what it
did to us while we watched David throw his life
away, lose everything he had, including his family?
Do you really think we can survive that again, son?
Do you? Don't you remember what it was like for
all of us, especially you?"

The dark head snapped up and back. Pace's eyes
shut as if in denial of his father's words. His hands
balled into fists as if he could physically fight the
harsh memories. "Remember?" The one word was
like a welcome weapon in his depleted arsenal. "Remember?" he hissed again before turning to face his
father. "When would I have had the chance to forget? As hard as I pray to forget, you pray that I
won't. 'Look after David, Lord,'" he mimicked in
pious overtones. "'Bring David home safely, Lord.'
I'm sorry that you're ashamed of the way I've chosen
to live. But there is no shame in the way I feel about
Alisa and the way she feels about me. Shame doesn't
enter into it at all because even if we had spent last
night in our legal marriage bed, I could not love her
more. No, dad, I do not feel dishonor, except that
which I am forced to commit against her."

Abruptly his voice lost its power. "Do you know what I do feel, dad? I feel fear, the fear that my love will not be strong enough to keep her here. But rest assured, when she goes, I won't be leaving with her. She knows that. And it would be better for all of us if you, too, would accept the fact. And it wouldn't hurt if *you* tried remembering a little something, also." He paused only briefly before he spoke the words, each one separate from the other, each one flat and lifeless. "I am not David."

With the last word he turned again, picking up the discarded jacket and shrugging into it, carelessly flinging the tie around his neck. Not until he turned to the doorway did he see a pale Alisa standing there, tears spilling down her cheeks.

In three long strides he had crossed to her to wrap his arms around her. Heedless of Mary Alice and J.D. standing there, Pace blotted those tears with his lips, sponged them away with a sweet lick here, a tender taste there.

"I've rounded up a crew to help move the rest of your things, but they won't show up until late this afternoon. So if you feel up to another long ride, we have time to drive into Lake Providence for lunch or Delhi or Tallulah, or wherever you prefer."

"You will do no such thing," Mary Alice injected in a voice that brooked no argument. "I have a perfectly good meal cooked, ready to be placed on the table which is set with a place for each of you, and you have been invited. You will eat here."

Alisa could feel the tenseness in Pace's body as he spoke to reject the demand. "I don't think...."

"J.D.?" Mary Alice snapped. Intuitively, Alisa knew that it was a rare occasion, if indeed not the first time, that Mary Alice had addressed her husband in such a tone. She did not have to repeat it.

J.D. directed his words to the floor, but they were distinct enough. "I'll round up the boys while Alisa freshens up after her long ride." He turned to the patio.

Instantly some of the tension eased from Pace's body, and with a gentle nudge he moved Alisa toward the downstairs powder room, following directly behind her. When they were both inside the narrow room, he closed the door. "You know that I wouldn't have had you witness that for anything, don't you? I would never consciously hurt you."

She thought about his words while she lathered her hands at the basin. In reality, there was only one thing that Pace had ever done to hurt her, and she knew that it would be the only thing he would ever do: he had no faith in her love for him to overcome the obstacle that their backgrounds had placed in their paths. That was the only problem between them, and she would eventually solve that. No, what she had overheard had not directly hurt her. It had been an indirect wound—through Pace to her. They might have problems with the others accepting their relationship, but she had come to Pace Lofton with her eyes open. As he had told his father, she knew the limitations, and even with that knowledge, she and Pace, in the dark Delta night, had created something out of themselves that was different from any joining that had gone before—because it was theirs. And that something was glorious enough to overcome her hurt at his mistrust. It was enough to nurture her hope.

Watching his dark image in the vanity mirror, she reached for the plush hand towel and slowly dried her hands. "I love you, Pace Lofton," she addressed that worried image and instantly found herself jerked against him with his mouth closing over hers. The flame roared as she felt the deep thrust of his tongue.

They barely registered the creak of the door opening. "Unc, I'm starving to death," Daniel lisped in mournful exaggeration.

Pace dropped his forehead onto Alisa's. "Me, too, my man."

"Well, everybody is waiting for you and Miss Alisa. When are we going to eat?"

Pace brushed a last hot kiss on Alisa's mouth. "About an hour or so from now?" he whispered to her alone before lifting a hungry Daniel onto his shoulder and leading Alisa to the dinner table.

CHAPTER ELEVEN

FOR THE MOST PART, their days had not changed. Alisa still reported to the site. She conscientiously spent the odd hours in the archives, writing her paper if she came in earlier than Pace, or forcing herself to study. Although she had never thought it possible, spending time on her work took every ounce of her self-discipline. It was an ongoing battle, a battle fought in a passionate pool of obsession with Pace Lofton.

Pace still went about the vast acreage, checking the fields for maturity. When the weather became dry and the crops were threatened, he supervised the laying of the portable irrigation system, pumping water from the Bayou Macon, from the Tensas River, from ponds dug on Little Fork for that express purpose.

It was the hot Delta nights that had changed for them both. They were nights of love, nights where only the two of them existed, without a past or a future. They both were just...in love.

Alisa and Pace made love every chance they got and in every way they could think of—sometimes in a mode as desperately passionate as their first joining, sometimes slowly while they savored every nuance. They made love merrily with Alisa's light bubbling trill threading through and around Pace's rich laugh. They made love languidly, like a spoiled old sultan and his favorite concubine. And each time was more fulfilling than the last. Everything gave them pleasure but the greatest pleasure was pleasing each other.

Even the old house gave them pleasure. With the same care that she gave her own studies, Alisa researched the history of their home. What she could not document, she copied from nearby houses of the same period. Before she let Pace put one brush into paint, if she didn't know exactly what shade had colored what wall in 1858, then she knew what shade of what color had tinted a similar wall in Tallulah or Vicksburg or Vidalia.

Since the front bedroom was the center stage of their life together, Pace insisted that any improvements begin there. Hesitantly, she showed him what she wanted to do. "Fine," he agreed. "Everything but the mural painting. No mural on the wall. I will not make love to you with some wild-eyed swamp creature looking over my shoulder."

Alisa looked at the sketch. There wasn't anything in it that vaguely resembled a wild-eyed swamp creature but she yielded. Instead of her original plan, she and Pace and two tobacco-chewing men he covertly called "jake-legged carpenters" covered all four walls in pale-green paper...because Alisa had decided the mural painting would look even better on the dining-room wall. After Pace hung the long antique-satin drapes, she took a long hard look at the contemporary chest, dresser and night stands. In Mary Alice's house, Pace's furniture fitted well. But not in their home.

Pace eyed her warily. "No. We will make love and sleep in this bed, not another. It is important to me!" She didn't have to ask what he meant, it was important to her, too. "Besides, you will not smother me in a damn feather mattress and that is exactly what the beds in this house first had."

Two weeks later, he took a headboard Alisa had found in a storage area under the eaves to a cabinet maker in Natchez. He ordered a copy to be made to fit their king-sized bed. By the middle of October, Alisa planned to have their bedroom furnished in the style of their house, and she and Pace would continue their nights of love on the bed he had brought to their relationship.

The summer days were long and enervating, but they found the energy to turn the house into an attractive and inviting home, a task made simpler by David's earlier structural work. Even before the house was truly presentable, a strange thing happened. Gradually, members of Pace's family began to drift in and out of the old house. Beyond Mary Alice and the boys' daily visits and Sonny and Lou Ann and their children's frequent calls, Alisa came to expect the aunts, uncles and cousins, who still eyed her askance, but nevertheless spent an occasional quiet evening on the long porches, sipping

tall glasses of iced tea and talking crops and weather
and federal programs. But all too often the purpose
in those visits became clear when the conversations
became light gossip that pointedly made allusions
to yet another marriage faltering because an urban wife could no longer tolerate the rural life-style.
Or they talked about the disappearance of another
family who had wanted to get "back to the earth,"
but couldn't handle it. Sometimes an overly sensitive Alisa could sense the things still unsaid,
the words that condemned the unblessed union
under the roof of the old family house, words that
would have told her she, too, would soon be gone.
At those times she wanted to scream at them
that she and Pace would resolve their difference,
that he would soon realize that her leaving for expeditions or conferences would not threaten what
they had together. She wanted to banish those
doubting people from her home. On those occasions she longed for even more isolation, wishing
that she and Pace were the only two humans on the
face of the earth.

Even worse were the rare occasions when J.D.
came and sat in the shadows and covertly watched
Alisa and Pace together and waited, waited as if he
expected Alisa to sprout another head as absolute
proof that she was not like them, that she did not
belong, could never belong and the sooner she was
on her inevitable way, the better they would all be.
Those evenings left her drained and anxious to curl
against Pace, to assure herself that he was still there

for her, still loving, still wanting, still needing. And that reassurance was never lacking.

As time passed, Alisa realized that Pace did not interpret his family's visits and words as she did. She learned better control of her fears. But she found no self-assurance the first week in August when John David was to register for kindergarten. Alisa had gone to the school with Mary Alice to enroll her grandson, thinking it would be a quick stop and then they would drive into Monroe. Mary Alice wanted to shop for clothes for a cruise she and J.D. intended taking as soon as the crops were harvested, and Alisa needed to collect books for her comprehensive examination from the Northeast Louisiana University library. The stop had been quicker than either had imagined. They had no copies of John David's birth certificate, his vaccination record, and no one had legal guardianship over him. The forms were left incomplete.

"I feel like an idiot," Mary Alice confessed as she got back into the car. "You would think I'd know John David needed a birth certificate."

"Mary Alice, can we find it? Do you think there's a copy at your house, in David's old office, in some of the things stored in your attic?"

Mary Alice could hear the panic in Alisa's voice. "This will upset Pace, won't it?"

"He's been trying so hard to get David to act, to set things up to prevent this sort of thing."

"I know. And J.D. hasn't helped. He refuses to believe that David isn't coming back tomorrow.

Every night he says *tomorrow*, and he has done that every night for nearly a year. He won't listen to Pace. Pace told him after David had been gone six weeks that he would never be back. That's as close as I ever saw the two of them come to losing their tempers with each other." She shook her head. "There are things at Little Fork that need to be done, but J.D. keeps saying that David will take care of it when he gets back. It's not fair to Pace. Nothing David has done in the past six years has been fair to Pace." She looked at Alisa sadly. "Especially what he has done to make Pace treat you the way he does."

"Pace loves me," Alisa countered vehemently. "Pace loves me."

"I know he does. But he hasn't married you. It's not right, the way you two live." Alisa managed to swallow the gasp that tore from her throat. Mary Alice had hurt Alisa to the core. Until that moment, she had thought Mary Alice had finally come to understand; she had thought Pace's mother could see beyond the present to what would be. Her attitude in some measure had made up for J.D.'s overt disapproval. Alisa felt as if she had lost something precious.

"Have we shamed you, Mary Alice?" Alisa asked quietly, staring down at her hands.

"Yes...no...I don't know, Alisa. When I look at you two and see how much you love each other, I tell myself it doesn't matter that you're living the way you do. And then I get to town and...."

"Somebody says something," Alisa finished for her.

"Never to my face, just in a loud enough whisper so that I hear them, or it's camouflaged in a question. 'And just how is that handsome son of yours, Mary Alice? Still giving the ladies in Tallulah a rough time? And when is Pace ever going to settle down and marry?' You know the kinds of questions I mean. Oh, the real friends don't say anything, not to me or anyone else. Nor does the family. But it still hurts, Alisa, it still hurts more than I can tell you. Sometimes it's all I can do to hold my head up in church when the Sunday School lesson seems directed at my very own son, and it's even worse when it's the sermon. It makes me want to stay home."

Alisa could offer the older woman no comfort, for she doubted that Mary Alice had borne half the burden Alisa had.

Instead, Alisa returned to Little Fork with Mary Alice, and they turned the filing cases and storage areas upside down, searching for records on the children, but they found nothing. When Pace discovered them still at the task he slumped dejectedly into a chair in front of the desk that had been David's. "He wasn't always an uncaring bastard, Alisa. He really wasn't." Those were his only words.

That night while Pace found comfort in too much bourbon, Alisa typed out letters requesting duplicate records, not only for John David but also for Daniel. She wondered if their immunizations were current, if they would have time to bring everything up to date before school started, if Uncle Douglas, the family-member doctor who treated the boys without legal permission, had taken it upon himself to give them the injections. She hoped so.

When she had completed the letters, she took them into the bedroom for Pace to sign. He was lying on the bed, staring at the slowly turning blades of the ceiling fan. "I'll need checks to go with these," she informed while he slashed his bold signature across the bottom of the pages.

"Well, write them," he snapped as he flopped back onto the pillow.

Merely to prevent a scene, Alisa had penned her name on the signature card Pace had shoved at her one day. She had never written a check on their account. Under different circumstances, she wouldn't have written one that night.

She returned to the study she shared with Pace. Pace had once done most of his work at his desk in his lab. But the lab was in the narrow wing of his parents' house that also contained his father's office and David's office, so he now worked at home to be with Alisa. At his new desk Pace prepared Little Fork's paperwork before turning it over to the accountants. It was yet another job once held by David. It was also his new desk that Pace kept records of his personal investments, the property he owned independent of Little Fork. As if invading something very private, Alisa moved to Pace's desk and pulled out his checkbook.

It was a thick commercial book, not like the little foldover she carried in her wallet. But what held her attention was the last check written, never detached from the stub. It was made out to J. David Lofton III for a sum that startled Alisa. She knew it wasn't for the house. That transaction had gone through the banks. This was something different and probably accounted for a large portion of Pace's inconsolable black mood.

She thumbed back through the stubs. Four weeks earlier there had been another payment to David, almost as large. The book did not go back beyond that. Returning to the latest entry, Alisa wrote the checks to pay for copies of the records and slipped them into the envelopes with the letters, leaving them unsealed on Pace's desk for him to look over before taking them to the mailbox on his way out the next morning.

The next morning when she checked to see if Pace had remembered to pick up the letters, she saw a telltale tatter of blue in the trash can—the check to David torn in quarters and then torn again. Not nearly so intimidated as she had been the previous night, she opened the drawer and found the checkbook. There in Pace's bold penmanship was a glaring void written on the stub and an adjustment made in the bank account balance.

That evening he directed, "If you have time, go get the paint for the outside of the house tomorrow. I've already called in the order."

"I thought we were to wait."

"We did a little better this month at the commodities market than I thought." It was the first lie he had ever told her. To finance the painting of the exterior of the house—an expensive job at best because of the size of the house, a more expensive job because the wood had been bare for years and would require three times the normal amount of paint and labor—they were to use the money he had planned to send David.

"Are you sure?"

"Positive. You want it to be as pretty outside as you're making it inside, don't you?" He bent down and kissed her. "I love you, Alisa."

Two days later the "jake-legged carpenters" were back, this time with scaffolding. Within two weeks the house gleamed a muted coral, toned and accented by raven-green shutters and white trim. Alisa had left the front door a natural woodgrain and spent hours hand rubbing pints of tung oil into it and thinking about the strange situation between Pace and his family, between David and his family, Pace and her, and between her and her own family.

Her own family, she mused at length. She had been in the South for nearly four months and had heard little from any of her own people. Marlene had not communicated with her again. From a magazine, Alisa had learned that her sister had earned the prized part she had panicked over. She supposed that her sister was reasonably happy again. She also knew that her father was still at home. He had called just before he had sequestered himself to write the papers on his latest field adventures. And Elizabeth had written twice. From the letters as well as an item buried deep in the front section of the newspaper, Alisa knew that at the moment her mother was up to her elegant eyebrows in some controversial rulings in the realm of education. Although there had been changes in her address as well as her telephone number, neither parent had commented. Alisa wondered at their thoughts.

In the case of her father, there had been ample opportunity for him to learn that she no longer lived alone. More of her father's associates than she had thought possible wandered in and out of the Poverty Point complex. Any one of them could have picked up on local gossip and taken news back to him. She wondered if her father had scowled and puffed deeply on his pipe, thinking she was more like Marlene than any of them had ever imagined. She longed for a closeness to him, a familiarity that would allow her to tell him of her happiness with Pace and her fear that it could not continue. But she did not know how to approach a man like Thomas Fairlight. She had not learned the skill as a child.

She wondered less at Elizabeth's reaction. Elizabeth would think only in terms of her own ever-upward movements, how this latest controversy would influence her. Whatever conclusion she reached, Elizabeth would draw several contingency plans around it and shrug off what she could not control. Elizabeth would not waste energy on useless causes.

Was her relationship with Pace a useless cause? Alisa didn't want to think so. All in all, at the moment she was content. Pace was content. What more mattered . . . at the moment?

As awkward as Alisa sometimes felt when Pace's family came calling, she was equally at ease when, at her frequent invitation, her fellow scholars from Poverty Point came to the big house on the Tensas River. She did nothing to hide her living arrangements from them, and unlike Pace's family, when they came and sprawled over the galleries and lawn, speaking the shared language of antiquities, they found nothing untoward in her life-style. There were never underhanded references about their hosts, nor whispered conversations that ceased when she walked into the room. But Alisa also had the wisdom to acknowledge that these summer people were outsiders like her, for the most part urban scholars, bred in a society less narrow, less restrictive. And it was then when she and Pace entertained her fellow workers, that she relaxed in her role as hostess.

Alisa was at ease with them until a few days before the Louisiana State University team was to leave the area, when she invited some of the members over for drinks—a kind of farewell gathering. That night Pace and Alisa had their first serious and threatening rift, a rift that left her with no assurance at all that she and Pace would ever resolve their difference about the direction of their united lives.

At Alisa's request, one of her fellow archae-ologists quickly scanned the first draft of her paper while others moved about the property in small groups or sat on the porch reviewing their summer's work and making plans for the fall. Just as her friend turned over the last page of her rough draft, a few people drifted into the small room that served as a study, a room carved of space left over when the carpenters had made the downstairs bath and huge closet. "You know, Alisa, you really should take in the Writtles symposium. He's covering mound builders within the continental United States." He tapped the paper. "I don't think you've missed anything in your thesis, but why take the chance? Catch his presentation."

Alisa sat on the edge of her chair, excitement in every line of her body. "Writtles? Where? When?"

"Atlanta, two weeks from now. How did you miss the publicity on it?"

Alisa didn't volunteer the reason. She didn't think those dedicated scientists would understand. "Is it sold out? Do you think I can get in?"

"It's probably not too late to reserve an admis-sion ticket. You might not get into the small study groups you want, but you'll hear Writtles' presenta-tions, see his wonderful slides. You're going, aren't you, Wesley? What do you think?"

Wesley, director of the summer dig, nodded his agreement as he absently stirred his coffee. "I know for a fact it's not too late, and you really should go, Alisa. It's a good place to be seen as well as a place to see. If you don't intend burying yourself in this backwater forever, you should begin making your move, the sooner the better."

"Do you have an application or a number I can call?"

"No, but I can get it for you," Wesley offered.

"Great," Alisa accepted. It was then that she noticed Pace leaning against the door frame, a hard look in his eyes, a brittle expression that did not fade even as the conversation shifted and reshifted again. It was still there when her friends were gone and she gathered the cups and saucers and overflowing ashtrays and took them to the kitchen. It was a small task usually shared by them. Tonight, Alisa did it alone.

When she had everything neat again and the house closed up, she entered the front bedroom to find Pace standing at the foot of the bed, staring down with unseeing eyes. She moved to stand behind him, wrapping her arms around his hard body. For the first time there was no response. It frightened her.

"Pace?" she questioned.

"The beginning of the end. I had thought we would have longer," he stated firmly.

"I don't understand."

"When I can't supply all your needs in this 'backwater,' as your friend so aptly called it, you'll look somewhere else. It's already started."

She stepped around him, wedging herself between him and the foot of their bed, forcing him to look at her. "If you're talking about this trip to Atlanta, it has nothing to do with us. It's for my paper, nothing else. You are misinterpreting this whole thing."

"Now who's being simplistic." The black eyes bored into her as he made his desperate plea. "Don't go. Don't do this to us, please."

"Pace, it is important."

"Is it more important than us?"

She did not hesitate in her answer. "Nothing is more important than us, but this is part of us, a part that contributes to who I am—my work. It is something I have to do, just as there are things that you must do for Little Fork. When you flew to Memphis about the soybeans, I didn't feel threatened. And how you feel about me, about us, didn't enter into your carrying out that task. My going to Atlanta doesn't affect us, either."

Pace chose to ignore her parallel. He didn't even point out that he had not been gone overnight. "Can you complete the paper without going away?"

"I can, but it may not be as good."

"And do you have a guarantee that it will be better if you go to that symposium?" His hands came up to close around her shoulders as if he could transfer his urgency into her. He stepped nearer, hauling her into his arms, hard against his strong body. "The day when you leave and don't come back will come too soon as it is. Don't chip away at us before that time. Don't go."

Then a new thought struck Alisa. Maybe she was acting prematurely, perhaps she was jeopardizing everything, but this might be her chance to show Pace that she wasn't like Linda. She would go and come back without altering their relationship, prove that she was not a threat to him or to his family. She waited a long time before answering, weighing the risks. "I am wrong and you are right; this does have to do with us. And that's why I'm going, Pace, not only for the sake of the paper, but also for the salvation of us, to prove that I can be trusted out of your sight, away from Little Fork. I'm going."

She didn't know what reaction she expected, perhaps a show of temper, perhaps that he would plead, that he would try to use their physical passion to persuade her. Instead, he turned away and stood at the long window that looked out over the country lane leading to his parents' house. "I have to," she reiterated. "Will you let me come back?"

He turned and looked at her for a long time. "I really have no choice, either, do I?" He left the room, and Alisa followed the sound of his footsteps as he took long strides down the hall and down the back steps into the Delta darkness.

Ten minutes later he was back, lifting her in his arms, wordlessly placing her on the big bed, expressing the depth of his love the way he knew best. Finally her own heart settled so that she could hear above the thudding of her blood. She heard the depth of his fears with his first words. "Promise me you'll come back to me, promise," he repeated over and over. And then she discovered there were more than beads of perspiration dampening his cheek.

"I'll always be back as long as you let me. As long as it is what you want and what you need, I'll be here," she pledged.

His hold on her relaxed, and with a shuddering sigh he separated from her, positioning her in the cradle of his shoulder. "You are my love," he mumbled as he drifted to sleep. And Alisa let him sleep. It would be all right, she told herself. It would be all right. The brief separation would show him.

But the storm clouds gathered. "Don't go," she heard from Mary Alice. "Are you sure he's ready?" asked Sonny. "He is *not* ready," claimed Lou Ann forcefully. "Are you leaving us, Alisa?" lisped Daniel with huge tears in his chocolate-sweet eyes. Worse than those had been the silent accusations...from Pace and John David. Alisa wondered if she would have been persuaded to forego further research, to give up the symposium had it not been for J.D.

For the first time since Pace had made clear his intent toward Alisa, J.D. sought her out. "You know he'll never marry you. I won't let him. So whatever he's paying you to come back, I'll pay double for you to keep on going." Slowly he peeled bill after bill from a thick wad and laid them on the little drop-leaf table. Alisa stared down at the ever-increasing stack of currency, trying to control the rage within her, trying to keep her hands from shaking so obviously when she picked up the money, folded the bills into an unwieldy wad and slowly stuffed it into J.D.'s shirt pocket. With one last hard poke of her index finger into the denim shirt, she stepped back. She was too hurt to guard her tongue, and the words were crisp and distinct.

"The only reason Pace doesn't marry me is because of his love for you, but he loves me, too, and it would hurt him beyond compare to know what you have suggested. My sympathy has always been with you, J.D. Lofton. Now I wonder if it was misplaced. Judging by your actions today, maybe your role in losing David isn't so innocent as everyone believes. Maybe some misbegotten plan, like the one you had today, went awry. Is that why you're so hard on Pace, keeping him guilt-ridden and feeling so responsible for your emotional well-being? Aren't you afraid, just a little bit, that if I leave as you suggested, just like David, he might come after me? Aren't you?"

The sun-blackened hands balled into fists, and Alisa would always wonder what would have happened had Pace not chosen that moment to charge up the back steps, a laughing Daniel high on his shoulders. At the kitchen door, he stopped abruptly and carefully set Daniel aside.

"Dad? What are you doing here? Is something wrong? David...."

Alisa was quick to assure him. Looping her arm through his in a possessive gesture more intimate than any she had ever allowed J.D. to see, she leaned against Pace. "J.D. just came by to wish me a good trip and to see if there was anything I needed." She knew that Pace didn't believe a word she said, but it was so much better than his hearing the truth. Turning to the silent J.D., she asked, "Can I get you something to drink?"

"No...thanks...I got to be going," he mumbled. With that he settled his straw hat on his head and headed down the hall toward the front door. Pace looked from her to his father's retreating back. Alisa turned to the refrigerator and poured a glass of lemonade for Daniel.

"You want something cool?" she asked Pace. He shook his head slowly and watched her move around the kitchen. "Leave it alone, Pace," she instructed in a voice that told him he had no choice.

Alisa found Pace watching her more and more as the day for her departure neared. Since she no longer reported to the dig, Pace dropped in at odd hours and they made love, desperate, frightening love. Alisa sometimes thought that Pace actually tried to come by for a morning coffee break and not take her into the front room. She would sit across from him at the little drop-leaf table, answering his questions about how she thought they should handle the long-neglected lawn and watch the muscles tighten in his jaw. One time he even made it out to his truck. Watching from the hallway, she saw him open the door then slam it violently. In overlong strides he recrossed the brick walk, took the steps two at a time and flung open the door. "Damn you," he muttered just before he sealed his mouth to hers and lifted her in his arms to take her into the front room.

Those were the same words he used when he kissed her goodbye just before she left for Atlanta. They were the words he used a week later when he met her incoming plane. But when they reached the old house, he used different words, words that told of his loneliness, of his love. She had left and come back. And nothing had changed. Pace wanted her. Pace loved her.

But she was wrong. Something had changed. Sometimes she would come into the study and find Pace staring down at a map or studying articles in her professional journals, always accounts of far-away digs. She never saw him do so, but she knew he had read her dissertation. More and more he questioned her about what she expected after she completed the requirements for her degree. Again she told him that she wanted the full spectrum of her career. She had thought her leaving and return-ing had shown him that she could meld both worlds, her life as an active archaeologist and her life with him. Instead, Pace seemed more positive that their time together was quickly diminishing. They were no closer to resolving his mistrust than before, especially when so many of her professional friends had been at the symposium, and now that they knew her whereabouts, post cards, little notes, phone calls followed, telling her of their own plans, filling her with the excitement of their dreams and

ambitions. More of her old life intruded into the
Delta flatlands. And each day brought more tension. There might be valleys and peaks in the flow
of that tension, but it seemed to Alisa that each
peak was higher than the last, each valley less
broad.

Ever since her return from Atlanta, Pace, his
father and their employees had been in the fields
again, this time to pick cotton. Acre after acre of
white stretches of land were reduced to black,
scrubby stalks as the mechanical pickers lumbered
through the land, stripping the fluffy bolls from the
burrs. There had been no more coffee breaks.

Such work sapped Pace's time and energy and he
found himself behind in the paperwork. Finally,
when there seemed no catching up, Pace reluctantly
asked Alisa to make out the checks for accounts
due. It was in that capacity that she stumbled across
the reason Pace had not sent the check to David.
And the tension peaked again.

While she was opening the business mail that
Pace had tossed unopened on her writing table, she
inadvertently opened a typewritten note from
David. It had been in a plain white envelope with no
return address. Alisa had automatically assumed it
contained a circular. Instead, inside was an appeal
to Pace to reconsider David's request for several
thousand dollars, promising that this time he and
Linda would sign the papers giving Pace temporary
guardianship, that this time he would keep his
word. He would not break his promise again. He

was also sorry that Linda had not sent the boys'
records to Mary Alice, but she had mislaid them. It
ended with another appeal for money. There was no
inquiry about his sons, just the request for cash.

Alisa replaced the letter in its envelope and
propped it against the desk lamp where Pace would
be sure to notice it. That night she asked point
blank why he kept bothering to ask David and
Linda to voluntarily grant him guardianship, why
he didn't simply appeal to the courts.

Instantly his expression hardened. "I told you a
long time ago about my father, Alisa. Those reasons are even more valid now. I have added to his
fear by caring for you. We both have added to his
pain by the way we live. I can't hit him again."

Alisa wanted to argue the point, show him the
fallacies in his logic, but at the first word of her
rebuttal, he stopped her with hurtful words. "It's
my family and I know what I'm doing. Leave it
alone."

And so she did. But her confrontation with J.D.
had watered down her hope, and Mary Alice's feelings about their affair had undermined Alisa's
belief in a future for them. On top of this, Pace's
way of burying his head in the sand instead of deal-
ing with the custody suit frightened her. But soon
there came pain that would make her other worries
pale, a peak to shadow all else.

Since the middle of September Pace and the other
men had been putting in horrendously long days.
Sometimes they stopped on Sunday, sometimes

they didn't. Frequently, when Alisa dressed for church, Pace sent along little prayer requests. They always had to do with the weather, and getting in the cotton and the beans. Things were looking good, he'd rather not be thrown any curves.

But one bright Sunday morning, Alisa was thrown a curve of her own. The Sunday before, there had been an appeal by the church's women society for church members to place their houses on tour. The proceeds would fund a scholarship to the church-affiliated university in another state. For a long time Alisa had studied the application in the bulletin, even going so far as to get out her pen and put her name in the blank. Although the Lofton family home was out of the way, it was of historical importance and by the time of the tour, it would be well worth the trip. And if necessary, she could talk Mary Alice into opening her home, too. Mary Alice's gardens alone would be incentive enough to travel the thirty miles. And then she thought again. It was not her house to volunteer, not really. She had folded the application in half and slipped it into her purse and that was the last she had thought of it.

Bright and early, just as she pulled on her robe after stepping out of her morning bath, she was re-minded. The phone rang. It was a woman whom she recognized from her church. The things she had to say were not very charitable, beginning with her opinion of Alisa's having the nerve to show up in a house of God Sunday after Sunday while living in sin with Pace Lofton, to the utter affront in Alisa's supposing any decent human being would want to parade through a house in which such "goings-on" occurred, even if it had been built before the Civil War. Without saying a word in defense of her relationship with Pace or to remind the caller that she had not submitted the application after all, Alisa quietly replaced the receiver.

Next Alisa replaced the little dress and jacket she had taken from the closet. She put lingerie, the panty hose, the little clutch purse and the strappy little shoes back where they belonged. Crawling into the bed, she curled into a tight ball and pulled the covers close around her.

She did nothing when Pace came in a short while later. In his usual demeanor, he gave her a playful slap on the rump. "You'll be late," he directed as he continued on his way to the shower. Still Alisa lay without response. Slowly, he retraced his steps. "Alisa?" She did not answer. "Aren't you going to church?"

"No," came her hollow answer.

Pace came to sit on the edge of the bed. "Don't you feel well? Maybe you picked up a virus or something. Do you have a fever? A stomachache?" He reached a solicitous hand to her forehead; the other insinuated itself low on her belly. "A little morning nausea?" There was something ugly, something unloving in the last question that tore into her, far more sharply than any of the words on the phone.

Alisa jerked away from Pace's touch and rolled to her feet, out of his reach. She wrapped her robe more tightly about her and turned to face his narrowed glance. And her words were as ugly as his had been, her green eyes as glaring. "And what if I have? What will you do, Pace? Where will our child fit into this misalliance? Will you love him as long as he plays in this house and yard, but disavow him the moment he leaves the homestead? Will you care for him only as long as he fits your preconceived mold of a proper Lofton offspring? What if your father doesn't approve of his gender or the color of his eyes? Will you even give him your name? What will you do, Pace Lofton? What *will* you do?"

Now he, too, was on his feet, rounding the bed to stand over her. "Are you pregnant?" He separated each word before forcing them between clenched teeth.

"If I am, it certainly isn't yours. When ever did you allow for the possibility? You've damn well made sure that, just like marriage, whether we have a baby isn't open-ended in this relationship, either." She moved to charge past him, but he caught her arm, pinning her against the wall.

"It's absolute that you haven't been with anyone else, but that I kept you safe isn't," he bit out. "Are you pregnant?"

"Safe?" she derided. "If you had wanted to 'keep me safe,' you would have left me that night you first told me that you wouldn't marry me."

"Alisa!" Her name was a black warning of all the emotions he kept in check.

The defiant thrust of her chin was adamant. Then she haughtily pulled herself free to step around him. "No, Pace, I am not pregnant, but it seems the only person you have kept safe around here has been yourself," she hissed over her shoulder as she snatched slacks and blouse from the closet. She didn't turn back before entering the bathroom and snapping the door closed behind her.

When she came out, Pace was gone, and she didn't really care. The rest of the day she spent at the antique table, not even looking up when Pace came in to stand in the doorway, watching, waiting. Afternoon became evening and still she worked. She heard Pace in the kitchen, in the bath, in the front bedroom. Still the pages rustled and the typewriter clacked.

Alisa didn't know how late it was when he came into the study the last time. "It's time to go to bed, Alisa." There was nothing in his voice to reveal his feelings.

"Then go," she answered without looking up.

"Not without you." This time there was something, and it caused her to look up. "Not without you, never again," he whispered. There was pain in his voice but more in his eyes and his posture. Only then did she realize exactly what her going to Atlanta had cost him. How was she to measure her own pain against that of the man she loved, a man in as much emotional anguish as she, a man who was her beloved Pace?

"Dear God, what are we going to do? What's to become of us?"

"I don't know, Alisa, but I can't give you up yet, not yet." In three strides he was around the table, lifting her from the chair, crossing into the next room, to place her on their bed. "I know you think that I don't give you enough, my Alisa, that I put everything and everyone else ahead of you, the boys, my father, my job, the land," he whispered as he began easing her clothes from her body. "But I give you all that I have. I give you my love and I give you my body." By now she lay completely naked in the flickering light of an open fire he had built in the fireplace. He rose to stand over her, staring down for a long time, devouring her nakedness as if he were seeing her for the first time.

Eyes wide and dark with infinite sadness and overwhelming desire, he stripped off his own clothes, then lay down, fitting his hair-roughened muscles into the soft curves of her body. "When will I ever have enough of you, my Alisa? When?" he softly cried in a hot breath between her breasts as he began the rituals over which she had no defense, rituals that would bring her to a state of readiness as great as his own.

Alisa didn't even pretend to resist. This was Pace. And when he became all throbbing power in his final sensuous assault, taking them both to the edge of sanity where the only escape was through the gateway to oblivion, she was right there with him. But when the gate began to swing open, he brought them a step back. Sweetly he tormented her, only to be sweetly tormented in return. Alisa begged with her body for him to take her through the door, to remove the honeyed agony, begged with his name over and over and over, but he held them back. "You are mine. You must give me everything, my love. Give me everything," he commanded thickly.

Alisa did not know that she had more to give. But she did, and she offered it to him and received double in return. Finally, he entered her with a force that shocked them both. "Oh, God," he breathed at the wonder of the moment and then he kissed her. Lying still, they paused to savor the awesome height of the pleasure plateau they had already achieved before the ancient rhythm resumed slowly, then boldly, in perfect synchronization, rising higher and higher until they lifted beyond the atmosphere and there was no more oxygen. They broke free and clear of earth's pull, earth's trials and restrictions, she on a cry of bitter-sweet torment, he on a hoarse whisper of his beloved's name.

CHAPTER TWELVE

As the days of October passed, there seemed no relief from the tension building between them. Alisa was hard pressed to find a reason. Nothing had changed in their relationship unless it was that Pace loved her more, and she returned that love. She should have felt settled instead of so very anxious. And then Mary Alice presented her with an explanation for her uneasiness.

"I know this is sudden, but Sonny's mother must have surgery, and she'll need someone to care for her when she leaves the hospital. Lou Ann feels that she should be there," Mary Alice explained. Would Pace and Alisa keep the boys while she and J.D. took their long-awaited cruise?

"I know it's an imposition, and we could change our plans, but J.D. needs to get away. He really needs to get away." There was a kind of desperation in her voice. Alisa was quick to see that Mary Alice also carried her share of worry, and she was as quick to assure her that keeping John David and Daniel was no imposition.

Pace's voice cut through the room like a knife. "Will this interfere with your plans to present your paper and take your comps? I didn't think you had much left to do.''

"I hadn't planned to leave until the middle of the third week of November. Your parents will be back before then. Even if they decide to stay for a few extra days, you can manage the boys alone for that short while.'' She watched the hard working of muscles in his jaw. "We'll keep them, Mary Alice,'' she assured Pace's mother, then walked with her to the door. She could see the concern in the older woman's posture. "You go on with your packing and don't worry about this. It will be all right.'' She watched Pace's mother drive away and then turned back to the study where Pace still stood staring out the window. For a long time they shared the room in silence. When he finally spoke, his voice was flat.

"When exactly are you scheduled to present your paper and take your orals?''

Alisa now realized that specifics—exact days, dates, flight numbers—were things they had never talked about. She supposed it was something they both tried not to think about, especially since her return from Atlanta. They were not ready for another test. In many ways, they had barely survived the others. "I present the paper on the Friday of the week before Thanksgiving, my orals are the following Monday and Tuesday.''

She could almost hear the words before he articulated them. "Don't go.''

Crossing the room she caught him by the arm and turned him to face her. "Didn't you learn anything? I'll be back, just like the other time. I'll be back for Thanksgiving. I promise."

With a shuddering sigh he pulled her against him. "But for how long this time, my Alisa?"

"What are you asking of me?" She pulled back and looked into the blackness of his eyes. "That I give up everything?" Suddenly it all seemed too much. "All right, Pace, I yield. I'll complete the requirements for the degree and come back here. Do unpaid independent research at Poverty Point if necessary. I'll assist the director there, I'll help in their summer field schools. I'll stay right here with you, sleeping in our bed every night for the rest of our lives. Is that what it will take to prove what I feel for you? Is that what you want of me?"

She didn't know what reaction she expected from Pace, but it certainly wasn't the grim look, the working of a hard muscle in his jaw. "I never thought you believed me naive. I know you better than you give me credit, my Alisa. You can promise all you want, but it won't last."

"I'm willing to try. Will you let me try?"

"You have always had the right to do what you need to do. I won't stop you in this either." He picked up his work gloves and the thermos of coffee he had come for and returned to his work.

It will give me more time. In more time, you'll learn. You will, Pace Lofton, she told herself as she watched the pickup bounce down the rutted lane. *You have to.* But her conviction was fading.

And she again told herself everything would be

all right when Pace brought the boys and their trea-
sured possessions a few days later. It wasn't the
added work or the responsibility that bothered her.
In fact, since Mary Alice had insisted that her cleaning woman report to Alisa daily, she probably had
less to do in keeping house than at any time since
she and Pace had moved in. Her worry was that she
had never been around children, not really. And
whenever she'd been with John David and Daniel,
Pace had always been there, too. After the second
day, she realized her fears were groundless. She enjoyed the boys. John David was at school all day,
but Daniel was home with her, and she genuinely
liked his company. She never grew tired of his questions, for she had introduced him to the world of
antiquities.

In one of the upstairs cupboards there had been a
box of what Daniel and John David called "arrow
heads," gathered from the Little Fork fields years
ago. She didn't have the heart to tell them that not
one of the points in their collection was an arrow
head. They all predated the use of the bow. During
the day, she and Daniel lay in front of the fireplace
in the front bedroom, an area now filled with all the
fancy pillows that had so annoyed her and gotten in
the way when she first came to the Delta. For hours
they lay and classified the projectiles as she filled his
head with stories of the way the Indians had lived.
Together they filled pages and pages with crude
drawings to go along with the stories she told. At
night Pace would sit in his lounge chair with both

boys on top of him and listen to Daniel embellish and retell the stories, visual aids included.

When Daniel told his uncle the "bird-woman" story, the tale of a creature with the body of a woman and the head of a bird and of the spreading of bird effigies to ensure good harvests and human fertility as well, Alisa had to leave the room. But Unc Pace, managed to keep a straight face. John David thought they were all stupid and he told them so.

In the afternoon, Alisa and Daniel would ride out to the highway and wait for the bus to bring John David. Then she and the boys would work on another project, the making of an atlatl to fit their small sizes.

Alisa, feeling intellectually guilty for allowing a misconception to be perpetuated, had finally told the boys that their "arrow heads" weren't for arrows at all, but probably for atlatl-enhanced spears. She carefully explained that atlatl was the Aztec word for spear thrower and the atlatl itself was a device made of wood or bone that cradled the socketed end of a spear, serving to lengthen the throwing arm and thus give it greater force. Alisa had learned the art of spear throwing with the enhancement of an atlatl from the Poverty Point manager. Once she finally made herself clear, the boys seemed anxious to try.

Under her direction they attached several of the projectiles from their precious store to cane they had cut from the riverbank. Under Alisa's ever watchful supervision, they learned the rudiments of hurling a spear, aided by the ancient launcher. The afternoon they gave a demonstration to Pace, he was duly impressed.

It was a moment out of time, a time out of context. Again they lived without a past, without a future. It was as if John David and Daniel had always been their children. And both knew it was a dangerous game to play, especially when they remembered that Sunday morning in late September.

One night, after the boys had been with them for over a week, Pace settled his young nephews in the room Alisa had prepared for them, and then he and Alisa lay on the bedroom floor in front of the fire, their favorite place since the evenings had become cool. "Do you know that in a week and a half you have done more with John David than Linda did in three and a half years?"

Alisa knew that Pace carefully watched her with the boys. Just as carefully she tried to keep her reactions to them natural and honest. They had been pulled in enough directions. They did not need to become pawns in any more games. "Pace, from everything you've said, Linda felt nothing for John David." He nodded his verification as he sipped from a neat bourbon. "Why did she have another child?"

Pace shifted so that she was tucked closer against him. "When John was born, dad gave Linda a very impressive piece of jewelry as well as cash, supposedly for the baby. We don't know how much, but he was generous. John David was his namesake. Naturally David expressed his joy over his first born, too, his namesake as well. And I am not without guilt. Linda made a very nice return on her nine months' investment, and I firmly believe that she thought when Daniel was born there would be another round of goodies for her."

"And was there?"

"There was, but nothing so impressive. A few months after Daniel was born she left, taking every negotiable asset that she could cram into a bag. David tried to find her. He hired detectives and personally went to everyone whose name he had ever heard her mention. It took him almost eighteen months, but he found her. And when he did, he came home long enough to liquidate everything he owned outright and a few things he didn't," he added bitterly. "That was a year and a half ago. He hasn't been back, and other than a few cards to mom and dad, a couple of calls to Sonny, three or four calls and letters to me asking for money, no one has heard from him."

It was one of the few occasions Pace had ever told her much about David and Linda, and Alisa wanted to find out as much as she could. "Your father is so irrational when it comes to David. I'm surprised that David doesn't appeal to him. Wouldn't he stand a better chance of getting the funds he seeks from J.D.?"

"I don't know and probably neither does David. As far as I can figure, he hasn't chanced it. I've intercepted every piece of mail he's sent, federal offense or not. You read that letter he sent to me. You know there was nothing there but an appeal for a handout, and that would be okay—if he were in need. He's my brother, he's my father's son, he's a Lofton. If he has needs, we should and would take care of him. But David has no need, other than to come to his senses. Oh, but does Linda have *wants*!" He stopped and took another sip of his bourbon. For a minute Alisa thought he would change the subject as he usually did. Surprisingly, he continued.

"With the money I paid him for this house, my sources tell me they bought an imported luxury car, a new wardrobe for her, four nights at a casino and some jewelry. It doesn't seem to me that there would be much left. And that's all right, because I got something for the outlay that time. I got this house for us. If dad had financed that splurge, what would he have gotten in return? Another plea for more money, that's what."

"What did you get for the last check you sent him, Pace," she asked quietly.

"I got his worthless promise that he would give either me, dad or Lou Ann temporary guardianship over the boys."

"Pace, don't you think this has gone on long enough? We must petition the courts."

"I know it will come to that. I know, but not yet, my love, not just yet." He buried his head in her hair and she knew from the change in the feel of his body against hers that he had finished discussing his brother.

An oak log broke in the fireplace, sending a shower of sparks up the chimney. "Do you think they are asleep yet?" he whispered as he shifted her onto her side, pulling open the loose knot of her robe's belt. "I didn't know you owned so many nightgowns," he protested, finding a garment instead of the bare flesh he would have revealed had the boys not been staying with them.

With infinite patience he opened the row of tiny buttons down the front of the pale-yellow gown that stopped a few inches above her knees. When he was finished he did not peel back the folds of the concealing garment. Instead he raised her arms and wrapped them around his neck, kissing her sweetly on the mouth, stretching out the moment before he would feast his eyes on her naked body. Slowly, even while his mouth still fed on hers, he separated the edges of the gown. The lingering kiss ended and he pulled back to look at her.

Even after nearly five months he was still awe-struck by the beauty of a naked Alisa, especially when her breasts swelled and hardened with her need of him, when her nipples thimbled into pleading pouts, begging to be touched, stroked, kissed. Leisurely, his eyes wandered over her, tracing the feminine line of her graceful body from the slow rise and fall of her breasts to the juncture of her thighs. Just as slowly his fingers followed the path of his eyes to hover tauntingly, teasingly over her then, wanting to prolong the prepleasure, he returned to the starting point of her generous bosom.

Gently he cupped her breasts in his hands and lifted them slightly. "You are so very, very beautiful." He spoke the often-repeated words, words of which she never tired. She didn't know if she were really beautiful, but when he held her like that and stroked his thumbs across the taut peaks, she felt bewitchingly beautiful.

Slowly he continued his reassessment of her sensuality. It was unnecessary. He knew her body almost as well as he knew his own. Alisa's lungs and throat ached with constricted muscles as she waited for him to quicken the pace. She outlined his lips with her forefinger before drifting down to the buttons on the soft flannel shirt, then laying his chest bare to her own caressing, assessing hands. "Please," she murmured and drew his head down to her. Still unhurried, he settled his mouth, hot and wet, over one dusky crest. At the flick of his tongue, she surged against him, rocking against his hard tension. His hand against her hips clasped her firmly to him, denying her movement. At her deep moan of frustration, the blood pounded through him. The sound was the essence of her. Combined with her scent, her taste, the texture of her skin, the feel of her body, it had the power to drive all rationality from him.

She felt the muscles in his back bunch, and in one unbelievable effort he lifted her from the floor, crossed the room and lowered her onto their bed, easing the loosened gown and robe from her shoulders before disrobing himself. Alisa wound her arms around him, glorying in the novelty of the moment though it was as old as Eve.

AFTER PACE FELL ASLEEP, Alisa held him against her for a long time, staring into the fading fire. Sighing heavily, she nestled deeper into his sleeping arms. From nowhere came the unbidden thought that it was only a week before she had to return to Boston. It would be the ultimate test of their relationship and she was frightened. Would it ever be the same between them when she came home again? Home, she breathed deeply. That's where she was now, in Pace's arms, home. She could only hope and pray that what they had would not change, ever. Gradually, her eyes grew heavier and finally, she, too, slept.

It was not an amorous Pace who awakened her in the wee hours as he so often did. She didn't know why her sleep was disturbed. She hadn't had bad dreams in months. She listened again. One of the boys was crying. Maybe *he* had dreamed badly. She eased Pace's arm from around her and rose on one elbow. The cry came again and instantly she was fully awake. That was not the sound of fear, real or imagined. It was the sound of pain.

"Pace," she called urgently as she shook him hard. Frantically, she searched for her robe. At the sound of the alarm in Alisa's voice, Pace was awake, pulling a pair of jeans over his naked body.

In strides that outstripped hers, he reached the boys' room first. John David was huddled in his bed sobbing quietly, his eyes big and frightened. It was Daniel who screamed in pain. Pace seemed at a loss, but only for a second, and then he was at the little boy's side, reaching for him, scooping him up into his arms, covers and all. Daniel was in too much pain to tell his uncle where he hurt, and as Pace dropped his lips to a flushed cheek, he felt the raging fever. "Get Uncle Douglas on the phone," he instructed Alisa as he headed with Daniel toward the bath for cold compresses.

Alisa made the call, knowing before the doctor answered what he would say. She went directly to Pace's car and started the engine, turning the heater on high. Not bothering with undergarments, she, too, donned jeans and shirt, slipped her bare feet into her shoes, the whole while urging John David to hurry and dress, also. In only a few minutes the four of them were in the car, a sobbing Daniel in Alisa's arms, a grim-faced Pace concentrating on his driving. Alisa had never felt their isolation so much as she did during those moments she held the burning little body in her arms while Pace took the country highways at breakneck speeds. She was sure they had set some kind of record in reaching the hospital in Tallulah.

"It's appendicitis. We'll have to operate," Douglas told a distraught Pace, a shaken Alisa, and a frightened John David.

"Then do it."

"Son, I'm in family practice. You know that. I haven't performed surgery in years."

"Then get someone in here who does." Pace was wild.

"Who will sign the release forms?" the calm physician asked.

Pace's answer was instant. "I will."

"Pace, they know you here. They won't let you get away with it. We'll have to call in someone from the courts. It'll only take a short while to get a representative from juvenile courts in here."

"No." Pace was adamant.

"Pace, be reasonable. It will absolve you of any responsibility." Alisa could see the worry in the man Pace called uncle although he was really J.D.'s cousin.

"This is Pace you're talking to Uncle Douglas, not David. I don't want my responsibilities absolved. Does Daniel have to have the surgery right now, tonight?"

The older man raked a hand over his balding head. "No, the antibiotics and painkillers are working, but the thing needs to come out, within the next six hours or so."

"Then I have time to move him to Vicksburg where they don't know me." He turned to the pale woman beside him. "Alisa, call Sonny and tell him to pick up John David at Uncle Douglas's." He turned back to the doctor. "You will keep him for that long, won't you?"

Pace had offended his relative. "I'd keep him

forever if the need arose, you know that. But I don't approve of what you're doing. It's going to have to hit the courts sooner or later, Pace. You're just putting off the inevitable." With that he stalked toward the desk and Alisa saw him bend over a clipboard. She caught the silver reflection of his pen moving across the paper to release Daniel.

Alisa took John David into a little niche outfitted with vending machines. She asked him if he wanted chocolate milk. He shook his head. "Alisa, is Daniel going to die?" Alisa looked at the sober-faced youngster. She had been too concerned about first Daniel and then Pace to heed his distress.

"Oh no, my little love, Daniel won't die!" she exclaimed, holding him tightly. As best she could, she explained what was happening to his brother. He seemed satisfied—about that. She did not find his next question so easy to deal with.

"Alisa, what did Uncle Pace mean about my daddy?" The wide trusting eyes watched her carefully.

"He meant that since your daddy isn't here, he wants to look out for you and Daniel."

"And you, too, Alisa."

"And me."

Pace had been tracing and retracing a short path across the floor, waiting until he could get Daniel. He paused in his last turn to look at John David. Then he stepped over to them and flopped down on the sofa beside Alisa. He looked ragged. Wiping a hand over his rasping beard, he monitored John David, watched him nervously peel at the address label on an old magazine. "Come sit on my lap, Johnny." Dutifully John David placed the magazine on a nearby table and crossed to his uncle. Pace held his arms wide and John David crawled into them.

It was John David who offered comfort. "Daniel has appendicitis and you are not to worry. He will be fine. Alisa told me."

Pace threw a loving look at Alisa. "Yes, he will and I will be fine, too, as soon as my number-one nephew gives me a great big hug." Pace got a bear of a squeeze. "I want you to go home with Uncle Douglas. In a little while Sonny will come for you. Is that okay? Will you stay with Sonny and Lou Ann while Alisa and I look after Daniel?"

"Yes, sir."

At that moment, a nurse's aide signaled that Daniel was ready. While Pace collected Daniel, Alisa delivered John David to his Uncle Douglas, leaving him with a kiss and another promise that all would be well with his little brother.

IT HAD BEEN A DIFFICULT PROMISE TO KEEP. It was not that Pace had trouble in admitting Daniel. In fact, no questions were asked. The surgeon accepted the signed release without batting an eye. But Daniel's little body had rejected the antibiotics in a vicious allergic reaction, and a secondary infection had set in. Although the problem had been discovered promptly and proper counter-measures taken, Daniel was a very sick little boy, and for several days neither Pace nor Alisa left his side. When there were definite signs that he was on the mend, they began to feel easier, but still they stayed.

Lou Ann chided, "Alisa, go home, get some rest. I have a sitter for Sonny's mom and my kids are in school. I'll stay in your place." She chose the exact wrong moment to take Alisa to task. Daniel had drifted awake.

"Alisa stay," he lisped piteously. All three adults in the room knew that there would be no getting her away after that appeal.

"I'll stay," Alisa promised softly. "But would it be all right if unc goes home? Someone needs to check on Little Fork. Remember that grandpa and grandma are still on vacation and what if that old bull has broken the fence again?"

"Okay," he whispered then drifted off again.

Pace slipped an arm around her waist. "Is this alienation of affection or what?" he teased.

"Have you taken a good look at yourself, unc?" Lou Ann asked. "I'm not even sure a mother could love you." Pace grinned and ran a hand through his bristly beard.

Neither Alisa nor Pace had left the hospital in four days. Members of the family had brought them clothes, and Uncle Douglas had offered to rent them a room in a nearby motel. They declined his offer, and the fresh clothes didn't stay fresh long with the abuse they gave them. Even though they both tried to keep clean, Alisa had not washed her hair, and Pace hadn't shaved. "He's on the mend now, Pace. Go on home and get a good night's sleep. Maybe in the morning I can take a turn.''

Pace waited until he had seen Alisa eat a good meal before he kissed her goodbye, and, promising to rest well, he reluctantly left. By eleven-thirty he was back. "I honestly tried, but I couldn't sleep in that bed without you. I'm not sure I'll ever be able to,'' he explained as he eased into the huge reclining chair that served as bed for both of them and pulled Alisa down on top of him. For a long time they lay, watching the sleeping Daniel. "He should be out of here in two more days, three at the most. We'll go home then...together,'' he promised. That proved an easy promise to keep.

When they finally did go home together, Alisa asked a relaxed Pace, "Do you think the Loftons would mind having Thanksgiving dinner in a dingy dining room? We could give it a good cleaning, and with lots of flowers and candles and maybe a colorful tablecloth instead of the traditional white it wouldn't be too, too bad.'' Daniel lay on the seat between them, his head in Alisa's lap, his feet in Pace's. Alisa stroked his hair lovingly. "And if you built a fire in the fireplace, I don't think anyone would notice the flaking paint and the threadbare rug.''

The car slowed as Pace exited the interstate, his easy manner vanished. "You're leaving for Boston tomorrow night and you won't get back until Wednesday afternoon. Don't you think that would be pressing things a little?'' As usual, when he mentioned her leaving, his voice was tight.

"I have postponed my presentation and my orals." She bent down and placed a kiss on Daniel's forehead. It was cool and dry.

"When are they rescheduled?"

"They aren't. I'll take care of that later." Pace was silent. "Well, what do you think about Thanksgiving? You're finished in the fields for a while and we'll both be home. Will anyone mind if we have it instead of your mom?"

"Will you stuff the turkey with bean sprouts?" Alisa knew he teased to cover his emotion.

"No, I had in mind watercress, cucumbers and three white grapes," she answered in kind.

"The family will love it."

"Without doubt."

"Alisa," Daniel interrupted, "couldn't grandma stuff the turkey?"

"Good idea, Dan," Pace agreed.

Suddenly their world was nearly whole again, temporary as the mending might be, and Alisa had that confirmed when she overheard Pace calling the "jake-legged carpenters" that night. The Lofton clan would not be having Thanksgiving dinner in a dingy dining room after all.

Mary Alice and J.D. returned Monday before the holiday and quickly made their views known about not being told of Daniel's illness. Somehow J.D. managed to make it all sound like Alisa's fault, not only that they had not been called home, but that

Daniel had become ill as well. He balked at having the holiday meal at the old house. Neither Pace nor Alisa needed to ask the reason.

"It's okay, J.D. We don't have to have the meal here." Alisa turned to the window, took a deep and calming breath and turned back, trying her best to show that it really didn't matter. "I haven't bought the turkey or anything."

"There will be a Thanksgiving meal on the dining-room table in this house and every member of the family is invited to share it with us. If there is no one here but Alisa and me, so be it." Pace stood firm against his father.

Alisa placed her hand on Pace's arm. "Don't," she urged quietly.

Pace shook her hand off. "Yes, I mean it. The rest can do what they want, but you and I will eat here." There was absolute finality in his pronouncement. "I'll get the boys' things." With that he turned and left the room. J.D. quickly followed suit, although he left not only the room but the house as well. He sat outside in his car, waiting until Pace had stowed the suitcases and toys in the trunk and placed the still-recuperating Daniel into his doting grandmother's arms.

When his parents' car pulled away, Pace returned to the little study. "We have a lot to do in that dining room. There won't be time to send the table out for refinishing, but it won't matter," he rationalized. "It'll be covered with a cloth anyway."

Wary of Pace's new mood, while Pace and his

two cronies concentrated on hanging the wheat-colored paper, Alisa kept her ears shut to their colorful expletives. She polished and repolished the window glass, mentally planning and replanning a menu that could be adapted to serve either two or forty-two people. She laid in her stores for the larger number and waited. Every day the telephone rang. Aunt Sadie would bring pecan pies. Lou Ann would take care of the fruit salad. Before it was over, Alisa had little to do but to learn from a plantation cookbook the way to make cornbread dressing and bake the biggest turkey she had ever seen.

Dinner in the South is the noon meal, and by mid-morning, most of Pace's family had arrived. There were moments of uneasiness when Alisa entered a room and knew that the conversation had been about her, about J.D., about the ultimate outcome of their affair. The uneasiness increased when Mary Alice opened the front door and behind her stepped a very reluctant J.D. But the awkwardness was shortlived. Sonny's quick wit saw to that.

Everyone seemed determined to make it a real thanks-giving—for Daniel's health and a bountiful crop with a good market. It seemed that all would go well until J.D. began to express at length his disappointment that David was not with them. "Maybe he'll call later," he finally concluded, then wandered into the unheated, unfurnished salon. After a moment Pace followed him. No one ever knew what he said to his depressed father, but in a short while they returned together and Pace brought out the bourbon, cigars and cards. Most of the relatives and near-relatives stayed to snack on turkey and ham sandwiches for supper, to nibble on the pies and cakes, to sip at the mulled wine Alisa had prepared, to open the second and then the third bottle of bourbon, much to one of Pace's more pious aunt's disapproval.

Late that night, after Alisa had realized that for the first time the huge refrigerator was filled to capacity, when the last of the dishes were in the dishwasher, the table linens in the laundry room waiting to be washed, the last candle extinguished except for the ones that now burned in their bedroom, Pace drew her down by him onto the pillows in front of the fire. "I suppose I should get the jake-legged fellows back in tomorrow to do the living room."

Was there an underlying motive in his readying the living room? She held her breath.

"We have to have some place to put a Christmas tree," Pace offered.

"The hall?" she suggested, perhaps too lightly.

"Maybe, but I'd like it in the living room." Alisa could almost feel him frown as he stroked back her hair. "You will be here for Christmas, won't you?"

Her breath caught. There it was. "I have to go sometime. If I wait too long, I'll have to start my reviews all over." She didn't know why she bothered to appeal to his logic. When it came to discussing anything in their future other than another season of crops at Little Fork, there was nothing logical about Pace Lofton.

"After Christmas. Wait until after Christmas." This time, when he laid back the folds of her robe, there was nothing to delay his pleasure in her...or hers in him. But nothing had been settled.

CHAPTER THIRTEEN

AND SO ALISA STAYED, and December was perfect, too perfect to last. Pace was home most of every day, foregoing his usual season in the hunting club to spend the time with Alisa. They listened to the boys' Christmas wishes and fulfilled as many as they could. Only Alisa heard the one they could do nothing about. "Alisa, I wish that my daddy would come home for Christmas." John David did not make the same wish to Pace. Intuitively, he knew that it would hurt the man who loved him so much. "So do I, Johnny," Alisa agreed, but for more than his sake alone.

Alisa and Pace did not have the family in for Christmas dinner. That privilege went to Lou Ann. Instead, they had them all over on Christmas Eve. Alisa searched the cookbooks for a good wassail recipe, Pace laid in a supply of bourbon. Alisa searched the woods for mistletoe, which Pace dutifully shot down with his rifle. He searched the highways for fireworks stands; she protested loud and long. He said she would change her mind. She said fireworks would make Christmas like a Chinese New Year.

He was right . . . and so was she.

Again life was new, love was wonderful . . . until
Pace asked Alisa to drive his car into Tallulah to be
serviced. For the most part, they had spent their
time on Little Fork. Their rare outings had taken
them to Vicksburg or Monroe where they had dinners, saw plays, danced, attended concerts and college football games and were lost in the crowds of
the city. On many of those jaunts, Sonny and Lou
Ann went with them or sometimes a cousin or on
occasion a lifelong friend of Pace's. But for the
most part, their small circle of friends was the family. Since the scathing call from the woman in her
church, Alisa had not thought about the opinion
that outsiders held of the life she and Pace led, she
did not think of the rest of society . . . not until then.

She was to drive the Lincoln to the garage late in
the afternoon just before closing time. Pace would
be right behind her to explain what he wanted done
and to pick her up. Then they would have dinner
before returning to Little Fork. She had no trouble
finding the mechanic, but Pace was not directly
behind her. Alisa got out of the car and walked to
the grubby workbench where an even grubbier man
tinkered with some internal part of a car's engine.

"Excuse me," Alisa began. From the corner of
her eye she saw another man, also wearing an iden-
tical blue shirt with the same logo, leave what must
have been a washroom. "I've brought Pace Lofton's car. Where shall I park it?"

The man at the workbench looked her up and

down in a way that made Alisa uncomfortable. "You just pull it right in here, sugar." He nodded toward an empty bay.

Alisa turned to go back to the car. She was out of their sight, but she still could hear every word the two men exchanged, horrible words, ugly words, words that froze her in her tracks even though, more than anything, she wanted to clamp her hands over her ears and run.

"Who was that?" the second man asked.

"Must be Pace Lofton's woman," the man who had called her sugar supplied.

"Didn't know he had married."

"That ain't his wife. The two of them been living together over in old man John's house since the middle of the summer. The fine piece of stuff that just walked out of here is Pace Lofton's night comfort, his hot piece of—"

Alisa had seen the word written on the walls of dirty rest rooms, in public telephone booths, subway stations. She had never heard it used. It was outside her realm of imagination that it should ever be directed at her. It was worse than the woman from the church. She could understand how she might have given offense to her, but these men had never laid eyes on her. They didn't even know her name.

"She can come play house with me any time." There followed vulgar descriptions of Alisa's attributes that the men found interesting and still she could not move, not until one small part of her numb brain registered Pace's truck stopped behind the Lincoln and Pace getting out. On wobbly legs she stepped toward him.

"Alisa?" He had never seen her like that, lips tight and white, a strange hue to her complexion. "Sweetheart, what's wrong? Are you sick?" She could only shake her head, if she opened her mouth, she *would* be sick. "Let me help you." He reached for her arm, but she sidestepped him. "Alisa?" he called after her as she continued toward the truck and crawled into the passenger's seat. He took two steps toward her, stopped, then went inside the garage. In a few minutes, he returned to pull the car inside the bay, talked a minute more with the mechanic before returning to the pickup truck.

He sat there for a long time watching her. She was huddled into her coat, the collar pulled up around her ears, her chin dropped onto her chest. There was really nothing for him to see beyond the shining curtain of her hair...except the absolute emotional trauma her posture screamed. "Please take me home," she squeezed out around the constriction in her throat.

It seemed to Alisa that it took forever to reach Little Fork, a long, silent forever. As they neared the juncture that led behind his parents' house to theirs, she asked him to stop. "Your mom made a big pot of beef stew this afternoon. I'm getting out here to walk the rest of the way home. You go have supper with your folks."

"Alisa, it's cold and it's damp out there. You can't walk three miles in this." He leaned over and held the door closed, his arm across her chest like a steel band. "Dammit, talk to me. What's wrong?"

"I need time to think. I need a few hours by myself. Please." It was a desperate plea. The arm across her chest eased, then lifted.

"Take my sweater." He peeled off his jacket, then tugged the vee-necked sweater over his head. As if he undressed and dressed a baby, he unbuttoned her coat and eased her out of it, pulling his soft wool sweater, replete with the warmth of his own body, over her chest and hips. Just as carefully he rebuttoned her coat. Alisa neither protested nor helped. "Wait here a minute," he insisted and opened the door. Standing beside the open door, he gave a shrill whistle. An answering bark came from the distance. Pace whistled again and waited. In a few minutes two dogs came running from the area where they stored the huge machines. Pace circled the truck and opened Alisa's door. "Keep the dogs with you," he instructed then placed a kiss on her unresponsive mouth.

It was the first time she had ever failed to kiss him back. "Alisa, I love you."

She stared down at the ground between his boots. "I know you do, Pace. But tonight it doesn't seem to be enough," she replied cryptically. Stuffing her hands into her coat pockets, she started walking down the lane to their house, the two dogs by her side. Pace stood watching her until the narrow road curved and took her out of the twin beams of his headlights. Alisa didn't hear his fist smash into the metal of the truck fender, or if she did, she probably thought he was slamming a door. And if she heard the truck start up, she probably thought he was going to his mother's supper table.

The truth was she was too lost in her own misery to hear anything. She didn't doubt Pace's love, nor hers for him, but she did doubt her strength to live the rest of her life as it was, discounting the problems with her career. She had thought she could. She had thought she could manage J.D.'s hostility, Mary Alice's restrained disapproval, not of herself, but of her unsanctioned union with Pace. She had thought she could handle Pace's not trusting her, a mistrust that led him to believe she might deliberately conceive his child without his knowledge. She had thought she could live happily with him without legal sanction. She had thought public opinion did not matter. What she and Pace had between them was so beautiful and so rare, so very, very right. But those men had made it dirty and ugly. Pace was a well-known man in the area, an area of old-fashioned morality. Their relationship had probably been discussed in barber shops, barrooms and back rooms, front rooms and kitchens throughout the whole territory. Subconsciously she had always known that, but she had never thought it would be discussed in the terms she had heard that afternoon. She had thought.... She had never thought.... Now she didn't know anymore.

She and Pace had been living together for six months. Together they had created a lovely home. For him and for the caring of his nephew she had postponed her degree. He didn't know it, but when she didn't return to her teaching position the second of January, she had given up her job, too. Her mind made a selfish circle. What had he given up for her? Self-respect? No. Even in the present enlightened age, most of his peers may have raised an eyebrow at their living arrangement, but it didn't lessen their feelings of respect for him. She was the wicked one. She was too wicked to worship in her church without giving offense. It was as if she wore a brand as glaring as Hester Prynne's, but those men in the garage, trash that they were, had not condemned Pace's role, only hers. Money? Just as he had said, he had spent nothing on her that wouldn't stay behind if she left. In fact, she had flatly refused anything for herself. Of course, Pace had frequently asked if she needed clothes, if there was some little piece of jewelry she wanted, but she had always found something for their house instead. Had he given up family? No, they were all there, in and out of their home, privileged guests, even his father who secretly taunted her with veiled looks and cutting remarks, who had tried to bribe her into leaving. Nor had their relationship influenced his job, threatened his beloved Little Fork. But that was not true of Alisa. She had passed up more than one interesting sidetrip, several workshops and symposiums, had even resolved to change her career goals—all to keep Pace happy, to keep him from feeling threatened.

For the first time, she felt the utter injustice in her love of Pace. And with it the tears began to fall, for there was nothing she could do to rectify the inequities but to leave. But not yet, she didn't have the strength. However, one day, just as he had predicted, she would have to leave him, not just for a week to get the degree, not to attend a conference or participate in an evaluation or a dig, but she would leave never to return. She would not leave because she did not love him; she would not leave because he could not or would not provide her with the material goods she wanted; she would not leave him because of the rural life-style they lived. She would leave him because it would be the only way she could survive, the only way she could keep her self-respect, the only way she could ensure her own emotional stability. He was slowly destroying her with his lack of faith that she could handle both worlds—the one at Little Fork and the one on the outside. He could tell himself whatever he liked, but the reason he had sworn he would never marry her and that if she left, he would never come after her was because he could not share her. She had promised that she would stay as long as he let her. She could not stay without room to grow, the one thing he seemingly could not give her. It was a circular resolution; it was no resolution. She would have to go.

She climbed the steps to their house, not feeling

the damp cold that blew in off the swamps and rivers and bayous. The coldness in her heart numbed her to everything else. Fitting the key in the front door, she looked down at the two dogs, thumping an arhythmic tattoo on the porch floor with their tails, asking with mellow eyes to be let in from the cold. Their appeal was not lost on the emotionally sensitized Alisa. Opening the door wide, she snapped her fingers and they trotted in ahead of her.

Inside the bedroom, she set a match to the fire Pace had laid earlier. Like familiar visitors, the two dogs, heads on their paws, lay on the hearth rug and watched Alisa move around the room. She wondered absently if she were subconsciously committing everything to memory for when she was no longer there. She hoped not, for that would mean she hadn't much time left, and as inevitable as her leaving was, she wanted to postpone it as long as possible.

Alisa took a bath, hot and long, sat with the dogs before the fire and drank hot chocolate laced with coffee liqueur. The bath, the fire, the drink, the lethargy that follows great emotion, the absolute silence broken only by the crackle of the fire and the sighs of the dogs all combined to work their medicine. Tossing her robe across the foot of the bed, for the first time in over a half year Alisa crawled into the big bed alone.

She didn't know when Pace came in, she did not hear him order the dogs out. She was oblivious to the familiar thump of his boots as they hit the closet floor, the shower running, the poker scraping along the firebricks as he banked the fire for the night. She was unaware that there was more than one reason he sat on the edge of the bed and watched her sleeping form instead of reaching for her with the desperate hunger he felt. She knew nothing of the way he hung his head and sighed her name before easing his frame down to lie beside her. She didn't feel him wince as she shifted in her sleep to nestle with familiarity into the curve of his body. She knew nothing. . . not until morning.

Pace was in the bathroom when she got up, a cup of coffee on the edge of the vanity, the first-aid kit open beside it. He had already showered and shaved and made coffee. He kept his head averted as she stood in the doorway watching him replace tape and scissors, a bottle of Merthiolate. She waited. He could not spend the rest of the day rearranging the contents of the kit. Finally, he turned.

"Good Lord!" she gasped. "What happened?" He had secured butterfly bandages to the corner of his left eye and to his lip. There were scrapes and bruises along his chin and his hands were a mass of cuts. "Oh, Pace! Were you in a car accident?"

"No," he bit out, shoving the first-aid kit into the vanity drawer, slamming it closed in near violence. "I, my Alisa, was in a barroom brawl, a fistfight." He pushed past her, stooping in front of the fireplace to kindle flames with slivers of lighter pine. The crisp fragrance of the resin-rich kindling filled the room as it caught up and flared against the spent ashes. He laid on several small oak limbs, then a log. The flames intensified. Pace stood up and watched his handiwork. After a moment, his manly shoulders slumped and he released a heavy sigh. "I didn't know what else to do. They had hurt you, and I didn't know what else to do." He placed his marred hands on the ancient mantle and leaned forward, a study in dejection. "I didn't know what to do," he whispered once more.

Nor did Alisa. Given their present circumstances, nothing either of them could do would make things better. She wanted to go to him and tell him it would be all right, but it wouldn't be. He couldn't beat up every man who vocalized a dirty thought about her, about them. She was too afraid to make him choose between her and his father. He couldn't understand her need to fulfill her potential within the world of antiquities. She couldn't understand his narrow perception of her role in his life. It would not be all right. With a sigh, she turned toward the bathroom.

"Alisa?" She stopped, but did not look back. "You aren't leaving me, are you?"

"No." Then for the first time she expressed his greatest fear. "Not yet," she added sadly.

With those two words, their love and their lovemaking changed. There were no more evenings leisurely spent before the fire, languidly loving, stroking, teasing, laughing. The end was in sight and they were desperate, desperate to reaffirm their love for each other, desperate to hold on. More and more they isolated themselves from the outside world, from his family.

The only members they did not avoid were the boys. It seemed to Alisa that their desperation had spread to encompass them. During the day, Pace kept Daniel and Alisa with him any time he left the house. They all three made the trips to buy supplies, to pick up equipment, to check fences and live-stock. It was Pace, Alisa and Daniel who waited at the end of the lane for the school bus to let John David off, Alisa in the middle of the seat, Pace gripping her hand painfully. Pace helped John David with his homework so that they could all four play games. Gathered around the little drop-leaf table, Alisa across from Pace, her feet in his lap resting under his shirt against the bare flesh of his hard stomach, they played Chinese checkers, Yatzee, Go Fishing, and nonsense games that Pace made up.

Pace, who had criticized her dietary habits, now requested the boys' favorite foods. They lived on pizzas, hamburgers, hot dogs, and colas. He lost weight; she lost weight. The boys did not. At eight they would take the boys down the lane to his par-ents' house where Pace and Alisa would supervise their baths, their prayers, and their tuckings-in, Pace choosing not to notice his father's ever-deepening dark scowl, Alisa feigning indifference.

When they were home again, he would fix a cup of hot chocolate for her and a glass of neat bourbon for himself. He would turn on the television or the stereo, settle in his chair in front of the fire, open the paper and rustle pages. She would thumb through a journal, pages of a professional newsletter, and the old house would become deathly quiet. There was no conversation between them now. They were afraid to speak, except when they were in bed. But in bed there was no need. There they communicated with their bodies, and the message was always the same . . . passionate, desperate, fearful love. Time was running out.

Cold, damp and bitter, January came. Alisa slept wrapped in Pace's arms, not only out of habit and to share his body's warmth, but because that was where she needed to be, to have all that she could of him before she left. That is exactly where she was when he jerked bolt upright in the bed in the middle of the night. "David!" he cried out in a distressed whisper.

When Alisa reached for him, her hands encountered perspiration-slicked skin. "Pace?" He didn't answer but lay back down, a hard shiver passing over his damp body. The dream that had disturbed his rest had not awakened him. Alisa felt hard, cold fear rise up the back of her throat. Stealthily, she rose from the bed, shrugged into her robe and slippers, stoked up the smoldering fire and readjusted the thermostat for the central heat. In the same quiet purposeful manner, she pulled her little rocking chair near to the fire, positioning it at an angle so that she could watch Pace in the dim firelight.

For an hour she watched his restless turnings, watched his irregular breathing, watched his fist opening then closing then opening again. She saw him when he reached for her and didn't find her. It was only then that his dark eyes opened and he lifted on his elbows to look for her.

"I'm here, Pace," she spoke quietly from her place by the fire.

"Something's happened to David." His voice was hoarse, but he sounded very, very sure of what he said. Alisa rose from her chair to kneel beside the bed. Tenderly, she brushed back the silken hair from his damp forehead. Pace caught her hand in his, pressing it against his cheek. His other hand he entangled in her hair, drawing her head against his chest. He lay on his back, staring at the fire-shadows cast on the high ceiling. "We'll never see him again," he stated in an empty voice.

Alisa didn't know how long they stayed like that, waiting and waiting. One hour, perhaps two. The only sound was the fire; the only movement, their slow, careful breathing. Around four o'clock the lights of an approaching vehicle raked the front windows and Pace's clasp tightened. When the car door slammed and the first booted foot hit the steps, his breathing caught harshly in his throat.

The brass knocker hit the plate twice, then three times more. "Pace, it's Sonny," his brother-in-law's voice rang out through the hollow night. Alisa broke Pace's hold and rose to her feet. Pace's dark eyes closed and grim lines settled between his brows and along the edges of his mouth.

When Alisa led Sonny into their bedroom, Pace had pulled on jeans and a flannel shirt that hung loosely down his sides. He made no attempt to button it, nor did he turn when Sonny came to stand behind him. Pace leaned against the mantelpiece as he had done the morning when he told Alisa he had fought the men who had said bad things about her. "It's David, isn't it?" He did not look up from the fire even at Sonny's affirmative answer.

"He died in a car accident three or four hours ago. I just got the call."

Alisa saw Pace's body tense. "Why you and not me? I'm his brother."

Sonny shrugged, but Pace did not notice. "A business card from the flying service in his wallet or something." Alisa watched the stiff posture of the two men. Finally, Sonny drooped. "Pace, I didn't stop by J.D.'s. I...I don't know how to tell them." His voice broke and the bushy red mustache quivered.

"Alisa and I will take care of it. Thank you, Sonny."

"Pace...." The glib, smooth-tongued Sonny Carter was at a loss for words. Then he knew there was nothing he could say, nothing anyone could say. "Call me." He patted Alisa on the shoulder as he turned to leave, and still Pace did not move.

Alisa was like Sonny. She didn't know what to say, where to start. Afraid she might make the situ-

ation worse, she waited while Pace stood, as if
frozen to the mantel. Finally she could stand the
silence no longer. He had to move, had to react, at
least to speak. "Your mother will be up starting
breakfast soon," Alisa offered lamely.

"I know. We'll go over in a little while. Will you
make me some coffee?"

"Yes," she agreed quickly. It would give her
something to do. When she returned with the bitter
brew, Pace had showered and shaved and their bed
was made, neatly, precisely. On the bedside table
stood a bottle of bourbon. "Pace?" she questioned
when he added a generous splash to his cup.

"I'm cold, Alisa."

It seemed that neither of them would ever be
warm again. Pace, with Alisa at his side, told his
mother and father of the death of their first born.
Then he told John David and Daniel about the loss
of their father. Uncle Douglas came with his numb-
ing drugs, but he had nothing to take away the
awful cold.

And then in the midmorning the mourners came.
From where, Alisa did not know. They came bearing gifts of food and drink and mouthing witless
platitudes. *I'm so, so sorry.... He was such a good
man.... Such a loving father.... Such a good boy
when he was growing up.... His poor little boys
will never know their daddy.... I'm just so
sorry....*

Alisa thought she would scream. How could
they? Good father, indeed! It was Pace who had

taken the boys to Sunday school, it was Pace who had taken them fishing, to the movies, for pizzas, who had helped with their homework, who rocked them and bathed them and kissed them good night. Where was the loving father when Pace lied to get Daniel proper medical help? A good man? Where had this good man been when J.D. prayed for him, when Mary Alice planted yet another thousand caladium bulbs to control her own fears and anxieties? Where was this good man when he spent the money that Pace had worked so damn hard to earn, spent it on a selfish, uncaring, frivolous, no-count woman. It wasn't fair!

Alisa bit back the words until it seemed they would spew forth in spite of her best efforts. She took a jacket from Pace's lab and slipped outside. She didn't hear the footsteps behind her. She didn't know she had been followed until a freckled hand grabbed at her. Sonny Carter tucked her arm into the crook of his.

"It isn't working out, is it, sweet lady?"

"No, Sonny. We aren't going to make it." She surprised herself at the ease with which she verbalized the truth.

"Yet you love him and any fool can see that he loves you."

"That's the worst part, Sonny."

"It's still David, isn't it? Pace is still blinded by his pain."

Alisa shrugged. "David, Linda, J.D., me, him, archaeology, the Delta, I don't know anymore.

Maybe he's one of those men who will never trust a woman, maybe he's one of those men who need a woman at his beck and call, a man who can't allow his woman any life of her own. I don't seem to know anything anymore.''

''Nor do you seem to have much stomach for the comforting words that our many friends brought.'' Alisa shook her golden head. ''Would you have them speak the truth?'' Alisa shrugged. ''No, I don't think you would. Let J.D. and Mary Alice pretend for a while. After the newness of the pain is over, they'll remember how it really was. Maybe J.D. will see that it wasn't only Linda, and then Pace can see. Maybe. But for now, let them keep the dream.''

They walked along in silence for a while. ''What are you going to do, girl?''

''I'll have to go.''

It was the answer he had expected, and when he responded his voice was infinitely sad. ''Pick your time carefully. Just pick your time carefully,'' he sighed, and they turned back toward the house filled with more newly arrived mourners, mouthing more mindless words. They both kept their own council.

It was Sonny who flew to Nevada to claim David's body, to supervise its being loaded into the cargo bay. It was Sonny who brought David home.

Late in the damp afternoon, Pace and Alisa waited at the small airport for the little plane to land. Not only were they early, but so was the long gray hearse. No matter how much she tried to direct Pace's attention away from the vehicle, as if to a magnet he was drawn back. Finally she gave up.

Fortunately, the plane was on time and Sonny brought it in smoothly, not far from the waiting car. With hard muscles flexing in his jaw, Pace stepped forward. Then Alisa saw the others—two cousins, two men who worked for Pace, a man from the adjoining farm, another man whom Alisa had never seen before. They stopped leaning on the fenders of parked trucks, stepped out from the sides of buildings to grind out cigarettes and moved in a unit behind Pace as he directed his steps toward the plane.

Sonny, looking tired and old, stepped down from the cockpit. He spoke awhile with Pace and then moved to the small cargo bay. Alisa held her breath. A man ought not to have to do what Pace did, she thought, never in a lifetime. When Sonny swung back the hatch, it was Pace who reached in for the bronzed handle and with near superhuman strength dragged the heavy casket forward. The other men surged around him and together they carried David's body to the waiting hearse.

The gray door slammed shut, and Pace began a slow, angry return to the plane. Alisa's breath came shallowly. Linda, the root of all their problems was on that plane, Linda, who might not be safe from the anger and the hurt that Pace had held inside for so very, very long. She watched Sonny and Pace cross to the far side, but no dainty feminine foot stepped down, no shining blond head posed between the black and the red. The plane was empty, except for a briefcase, a suitcase and a paper carton bound in twine. Pace and Sonny brought those to the car and placed them in the trunk. A grim-faced Pace shook hands with Sonny then urged Alisa into the passenger's seat. He didn't start the engine, he didn't look at her, he didn't express any emotion.

"As best as Sonny could determine, Linda left for South America with some big spender two days before David's death." That was all he said until they entered Little Fork property. "I have to tell my folks that Sonny brought him in and that Linda didn't come," he supplied tersely. They didn't stay long.

Back at their own home, Alisa made coffee and sandwiches while Pace built a fire in the study. When she brought in the tray, he had brought the things from the trunk. He had placed the briefcase on his desk, the carton and suitcase on the floor. Not even asking what kind, he refused the sandwiches with a silent shake of his head, but he accepted the coffee, added bourbon and took an assessing sip. He nudged the carton with his foot. "Not much to send home, is it?"

Alisa didn't reply. After placing his cup on an end table, he reached into his pocket and brought out a knife, deftly slashed the twine around the box and popped open the top. His one exclamation was obscene. Inside were neatly packed evening clothes, including a pink ruffled shirt, a plaid cummerbund, silk hose and garters, things that had no place in Pace Lofton's life. When they dressed to go out Pace was stunning, and feminine heads turned for second looks, but there were no silks, and there were no synthetics. He wanted fabrics against his skin that came directly from the good earth. He wanted linen and cotton and good honest wool and leather. He disdainfully lifted a silk smoking jacket, patent leather shoes, English jodhpurs. In the bottom was a book on vintage wines, another on ordering in French restaurants. The third was a popular book on status symbols. She could almost feel the dead David's desperation to understand the alien world he had entered in pursuit of his wife, the errant Linda.

The contents of the suitcase were much the same. Only two things did Pace set aside, a silver buckle for a western belt and a well-worn money clip. "This money clip was our grandfather's. I gave him the belt buckle when he graduated from high school. The boys should have them." He placed them on the mantelpiece, finished his coffee in two gulps and refilled his cup, omitting the coffee this time. The rest of the things he carelessly tumbled back into the cardboard box then deposited it on the back porch. "Dad and mom gave David the leather suitcase when he went off to L.S.U." He separated a key from the many on his ring and opened the gun cabinet. Taking a cloth dampened in the mink oil he used to treat his gun cases and holsters, he wiped down the piece of luggage then placed it on a shelf in their closet.

The phone rang. John David was giving J.D. and Mary Alice problems, throwing a temper tantrum, refusing to bathe, pinching and kicking at J.D. and biting Daniel. J.D. wanted Pace there. He might help to settle the distraught child. When Pace pulled on his jacket, he did not suggest that Alisa do the same. She knew without being told that J.D. was pulling the circle of his family closer. Alisa was being left on the outside. Pace did not return until dawn.

Pace was the tower of strength for his mother and his father. He supported them through the death rites of their faith. He maintained his poise at the cemetery even as the pallbearers and ministers unpinned their boutonnieres and laid them on the coffin, each intoning a final farewell. "Alas, my brother... Alas, my brother...." As the red-eyed, grim-faced men circled the bronze-hued casket, embracing the immediate family members, kissing them on each cheek, stoically Pace endured. He helped his mother and father to the waiting car. Alisa stood back on the fringes and waited; she knew Pace's grief had to be expressed. She just didn't know what form it would take. Her pulse quickened when Pace told Lou Ann to drive their parents home and then directed Sonny to pull his car aside so that the others could maneuver around it on the single-lane drive through the cemetery.

Alisa looked questioningly at Sonny. He ignored her. And Alisa waited. The long cortege of cars exited through the winding roads of the burial ground. Only the long dark-gray Lincoln stood alone, Sonny propped on the front fender, arms crossed over his chest.

Out of the corner of her eye, she saw two workmen exit from an inconspicuously parked van. Still Pace did not move. Efficiently, the men stacked and loaded the folding chairs, rolled back the green mats concealing the mounds of raw dirt. Alisa placed a hand on Pace's arm to draw him away. He shook it off. In desperation, she appealed to Sonny, who remained in his deceptively casual pose against the fender of Pace's car, also watching, also waiting.

Pace did nothing when the casket was lowered into the ground or when the ropes and racks and pulleys were stored with the other paraphernalia. It was when the overall-clad men scooped up the first shovelful of dirt that Pace lost control.

"No!" It was an order barked with absolute authority. "No!" he repeated to the men who stood poised with the first spade unemptied, staring at the raging mourner who stalked toward them purposefully.

Alisa looked at Sonny, back at Pace, to Sonny and to Pace again. Sonny had not moved, but his narrowed blue eyes were trained on his best friend. Oblivious to the mud into which her heels sank, Alisa chased after Pace. She reached him just as he snatched the shovel from the workman. "Back off," he ordered. The men looked at each other and over at Sonny, and at Sonny's barely perceptible nod they stepped back.

In a crisp movement Pace sank the shovel into the rich Delta soil. Alisa held her cheeks in her hands, watching as he began to fill in the grave. The rich mud caked onto his soft leather shoes, it clung to the legs of his trousers. He stopped only to fling his suit coat to the ground, to loosen his tie, to roll his sleeves over his powerful wrists and forearms.

The earth mound rounded. He emptied the last shovelful. By then the tears were streaming down Alisa's cheeks, filling her eyes so that she could barely see through them. Pace reached for the blanket of flowers that had rested atop the coffin, the red roses his family had offered to honor the lost one, blood-red and forest-green now punctuated with the white rosebuds from David's death attendants. He tried to lay it on the mound; it was unwieldy and his aching muscles could not manage its awkward bulk. He could not make it lie straight. He turned his desperate expression, a silent plea for help, to Alisa. Stumbling over the clods of dirt, falling to her knees once, twice, getting up without bothering to brush away the clinging soil, not heeding ripped stockings and ruined shoes, she helped him to arrange the floral tributes around his brother's grave.

There was no more to do. Pace stood for a long time looking at the raw mound of dirt. Finally, he stooped to pick up his coat, and with dirty hands he pulled it on, turning the collar up, buttoning every button. "I'm so cold, Alisa." For her it was impossible to speak. If she opened her mouth, she would wail endlessly, not for the dead David, but for the living, aching Pace. Placing her arm around his waist, she led him toward his car where Sonny had the door open. Pace looked back once at the flower-covered mound resting under the green awning. Beneath her arm, Alisa felt the muscles tense and bunch. "Take down that goddamn awning," he shouted angrily at the gawking workmen. His next words were directed to no one. "It's cold out here. He needs the sun." And then his first tear fell. "It's so cold," he muttered as he crawled into the back seat. "So cold." He reached for Alisa and then great, racking sobs shook his body.

They drowned out Sonny's words. "Thank God," he mumbled as he closed the door and got behind the wheel, "he finally let loose."

CHAPTER FOURTEEN

SONNY DROVE RIGHT PAST J.D.'s and Mary Alice's house where cars lined the drive almost to the highway. "Why are there so many people there?" an aghast Alisa asked Sonny.

"After the funeral all the family and close friends get together for a meal."

"But they need their rest; Mary Alice is at the breaking point. None of them, but especially her, need all those people around them." She was appalled.

Sonny shrugged away her concern. "Under the same circumstances, you might prefer to be alone, but Mary Alice and J.D. would be destroyed if their friends and family didn't come to comfort them. Their pain didn't end at the graveside. It has just begun and their friends are showing that they understand. It's the way it's done." It was obvious that he saw nothing wrong with the tradition.

"As soon as you change your dress and shoes and wash your hands, I want you to go on back there, too. A lot of folks will be worried about Pace. You need to tell them that he's okay...now. In the meantime, I'm going to take Pace in and run him through the shower, fix him a stiff bourbon, and then he and I will join you.''

Pace lay heavy in her lap, his arms around her waist. At Sonny's words, he lifted, wiped a hand over his eyes, finger-combed his hair, reached into his pocket for a handkerchief and blew his nose. ''I'll have the drink first.'' His voice was thick, but steady.

While Alisa changed her clothes and shoes in the bedroom, the men stayed in the study, sipping their drinks and talking. She could hear the deep reverberations of their voices, but she could not distinguish their words. Dressed in gray flannel slacks and an off-white fisherman's sweater, she entered to tell them she was leaving. She was pleased to note that Pace's eyes were clearer, his voice firmer. ''We'll follow in a little while, Alisa. You take the Lincoln, and Sonny and I will come on in the pickup.'' He brushed a dismissive kiss across her forehead, a casual caress unlike any that she had ever received from him. It was so matter-of-fact, so automatic, so unfeeling. Quickly her eyes scanned the room. David's briefcase was on the desk where Pace had left it the night before, but there was one difference. Now it lay open and a few papers lay outside of the stack of manila folders. Pace and Sonny had something other than showers and clean clothes on their minds, and Alisa had the distinct feeling that Pace was telling her she was in their way. Suddenly, she felt the chill settle around her backbone, and she knew firsthand the coldness of which Pace spoke.

It was a coldness that stayed with her down the country lane to Pace's parents' home. It was still there when she entered the front door. Gritting her teeth, Alisa made her way through the throng of sympathizers. She had thought that at one time or another she had met all of Pace's family. She quickly learned that she had encountered only the tip of the familial iceberg. And there were awkward moments for her when some of the newly met members could not, or simply refused, to understand her position in the family, in Pace's life. This lack of understanding might have triggered the conversation she overheard, a conversation that deepened her chill.

"Is *she* the reason Pace never petitioned for guardianship of John David and Daniel?" Alisa did not recognize the male voice nor the one that answered.

"That's the way we all figured it. What social worker would recommend granting custody to Pace when he was living openly with her? Did you know that neither one of them has ever tried to hide the fact, not from day one? It's common knowledge from Tallulah to the Arkansas border." Alisa's knees gave out and she slumped into a nearby chair. All this time she had honestly thought Pace had done nothing to change the custody status of his nephews out of deference to his father. Every time she had asked, pleaded, cajoled, that was the reason Pace had given her. And she had believed him. Even with the two men still discussing the pros and cons of her influence upon the children, she still believed him. But now she knew the issue had been more complex. Now she knew that perhaps Pace had always harbored the inner strength to defy J.D., the strength to chance whatever the consequences might have been in fighting for the boys. But wiser than she, Pace had known it was wasted effort as long as they were together. What would have been the point in subjecting his father to more pain if he knew beforehand that he would have lost any legal appeal on the moral issue of their relationship? And in the meantime, he would have drawn attention to the boys' condition, possibly causing them to be declared wards of the state. They might have been placed in foster homes, maybe even separated. One never knew anymore.

The two voices droned on. "Well, he'll have to do something now," the first prophesied. "The child welfare people will be out here within the week, you mark my word. Even if they overlooked the case, some busybody would call their attention to it. If Pace wants to keep those boys, he'll either have to marry that girl or get rid of her."

"Yeah, that's the way I see it, too. That's a shame. Most of the family says she's really nice, but I also heard more than one say that Pace swore he would never marry an outsider, that no one would ever have the chance to do to him what Linda did to David, God rest his soul. And J.D. has made no bones about how he feels. I guess he figures one outsider per family is enough. Poor J.D. In his case, one proved too many." Alisa could just imagine the man sadly shaking his head and scuffing his shoe on the carpet.

"Yea, he'll be getting rid of her, all right, because I haven't heard one person say that he's changed his mind even though they seem to get along all right."

Neither had Alisa heard differently, and it seemed to her that she should have been the first to know. Well, she had always said that she would stay until it was time to go. It seemed to her that it now was time. Rising from the chair, she crossed to the kitchen. There she set about making herself useful, rinsing dishes and silverware, making a fresh pot of coffee, setting out more trays of food. With a kind of numbness, she moved throughout the house, emptying ashtrays, picking up abandoned glasses, cups and plates containing half-eaten sandwiches.

Her actions were automatic, for Alisa kept most of her attention on the main door. To her it seemed that she had spent the last four days waiting, and now she was doing it again. Finally, Pace and Sonny came in. Pace was freshly showered and wore crisp jeans, a burgundy vee-necked cashmere sweater over a pale-blue shirt and his highly polished dress boots. Her breath caught at his masculinity, and she wondered if she would have the strength to do what she had to do. She prepared both men plates of food and set them on the bar between the kitchen and the breakfast-room. When Pace settled on the tall stool, he seemed preoccupied, and Alisa let her imagination have free rein at guessing his thoughts. It didn't matter. No matter how imaginative she was, she always returned to one issue. Pace was deciding how to resolve the problem of keeping her and having the boys. And she knew that under the present circumstances, it was not possible.

Gradually the visitors thinned until only close family was left. Mary Alice secluded herself in her room, J.D., Pace and Sonny, as well as Uncle Douglas and a few more male Lofton family members retreated to the corner of the living room, around a bottle of Kentucky bourbon. Lou Ann had gone home taking John David and Daniel with her. Two old aunts talked quietly around the breakfast room table. Alisa paced the floor. What was she waiting for, she asked herself. When would leaving be easier? Would it be easier after Pace asked her to go? No. She had to do what she must, just as Pace would do what he must, and she was wasting time. Finally, she approached Pace.

"I'm going home."

He looked up from the contents of his glass. "Do you want me to drive you?"

Alisa eyed the nearly empty glass knowingly. "I don't think so, and it might be better if you walk when you come." She tried not to sound disapproving, but Pace had been consuming inordinate amounts of his favorite bourbon for the last two and a half weeks, ever since the day she had overheard the men in the garage. He knew her feelings on the matter although she had never verbalized them. Today, he shrugged off the unspoken criticism.

"I'll drive him, Alisa," Sonny offered. "Don't worry about him getting home safely."

Alisa thanked Sonny before going into the guest room to get her coat. Pace followed. "If you really want me to, I'll come with you. Sonny and Uncle Douglas will stay with dad as long as he needs them."

"I think you should. You and I need to talk, just the two of us." At her words, the dark eyes narrowed speculatively, and Pace reached a gentle hand into her hair, turning her face to the light, studying her intently. She didn't know what he saw there, but she knew it was something he did not like, something that brought an even deeper sadness to his already-soulful eyes.

"All right," he finally agreed, "just let me tell the others."

Alisa pulled on her coat and followed him to lean tiredly against the door frame of the living room. She listened with only half an ear as Pace began to tell J.D. that he would be going home with Alisa. She was not too tired or too indifferent to miss the quick hard glances J.D. threw her way before he dropped his face into his hands. The older man's words were too muffled for her to hear, but she knew from the shift in Pace's posture that they had been effective. He would not be returning with her after all. Alisa did not expect, nor did she receive, an explanation when Pace turned back to her. He merely suggested that she go on without him, promising that he would be along as soon as he could.

Again there was the dismissive kiss before he turned to rejoin the men, to settle on the sofa beside his father. This time the kiss had been on her cheek. To Alisa it was even more significant than the one before, and it served to steel her resolution.

By the time Alisa reached the old house, she knew what she must do. She had probably been formulating a plan in her mind for a long time, she reasoned, or she could not have decided so quickly. She was going back to Boston. She could stay in her parents' apartment while she looked for a new place of her own. From their rare communiqués, Alisa knew that Elizabeth was in residence in Georgetown and her father was on a lecture tour of the West Coast. She could sneak in and have the place to herself. There she would stay while she healed her emotional wounds. And when she knew that she could function without him, she would complete the requirements for her doctorate. After that she might return to St. Thomas and lie in the tropical sun. It seemed appropriate that in a year she would have come full circle, back to where she had started— healing.

A determined Alisa spent the next hours planning her immediate future, what she would take, what she would have Pace ship to her and what she would leave behind. She began as she had once before— with a list.

As the evening began to darken, she listened closely for an approaching vehicle that would signal Pace was on his way. In her mind she rehearsed what she would say. But the words lay dormant in her brain, and she could not call them forth.

While Alisa wrestled with the problem of what to say to Pace, the hour grew later and later, until it was easy for her to convince herself that it was too late to initiate a conversation of such grave import, especially after a day like the one they had just had. Not knowing whether she was relieved or not, Alisa acknowledged that at least they would have one more night together. So she built a fire in their bedroom, bathed and waited for Pace. One more Delta night of pretense, as had been all the others, she whispered to the leaping flames.

Alisa fell asleep among the embroidered pillows, waiting for Pace. The previous weeks as well as the last few days had taken their toll on her. She did not awaken, not even when Pace finally came in and lifted her from the pile of cushions and laid her on the bed. In his own physical and emotional exhaustion, he didn't even bother to shower; he just stripped off his clothes and tossed them in a careless heap on a chair before falling heavily into the bed beside her, too drained to attempt rousing her, not even to assure her that he was safely home.

The next morning Alisa awakened in a cold bed in a cold room. Pace had come to bed with her and left again without waking her. It seemed like the final blow. On the bathroom mirror was his note. He was having breakfast with his father. Later he had appointments with his lawyers and didn't know when he would be back, probably not until late afternoon.

"Now you do what you have to do," Alisa ordered herself as she set about sorting through her things. Her belongings had seemed like such a lot jammed into the tiny three rooms of the rented house. Here her property had been assimilated just as she had been assimilated, and it took great effort to find the pieces to make the whole. She decided she didn't want the things she had shared with Pace. She wanted only the things that had remained solely hers—the books, her typewriter, her clothes and the antique writing table. With the exception of the table, it would all fit in the little car. Once she had made that resolution, it didn't take long to assemble her property. Again she found herself waiting.

This time she received a phone call. Pace was at his parents' house. He couldn't leave his father. He would be in when he could. Alisa moved her cases to the car and this time, for the first time ever, Alisa spent the entire night in the big bed alone. Under those conditions, she found it impossible to sleep. Consequently, when Pace came in the next morning for his shower and fresh clothes, she was awake and waiting for him when he came into the kitchen for coffee.

She saw no reason to stall, no reason for preliminaries, not even for the social amenities of asking about his father. And so she began. "I'm leaving today."

The dark hand wielding the coffeepot halted midair, the manly posture stiffened. Pace did not look up from the cup. ''When will you be back?'' Knowledge was in his voice, but he continued to play the game, to continue the pretense.

''I won't be coming back.''

Slowly Pace lowered the coffeepot to the counter top. ''I see.''

''No Pace, I don't think you do. In fact, I don't think I did either for a very, very long time. You pledged this day to me, and you've never gone back on your word. You predicted that one day I would become dissatisfied here and have to leave. I didn't believe you because I knew that I would never stop loving you, and I knew that you loved me. At the time, I recognized our problems, but I honestly thought our love was enough. I thought that, armored with that love, I could fight the reason you didn't trust me, the reason you had no faith in that love.'' Her voice thinned. ''And worst of all, I really thought that I had identified our problem. That was my biggest mistake. All this while, Pace, I've thought that I needed to overcome, to wage war against, the precedent that Linda had set in the Lofton family.'' She laughed without humor. ''No wonder I've lost that battle and I've lost you. I was fighting the wrong enemy.

''The enemy was you and J.D. and all the 'good ol' boys' who don't understand us females, outsiders or otherwise. Linda was just an excuse, perhaps a valid excuse, but an excuse nonetheless. Oh, I don't doubt that from the very beginning Linda was as horrible as you say. She would have to be if she could abandon those wonderful sons and, if David was half the man you are, leave him for someone else.'' For a moment her voice hardened. ''But then again, maybe everything that happened here in your precious Delta wasn't all her fault. What did the family offer her, Pace? Did you hold out to her the warmth you give one another? I doubt it. I think you offered her what you have offered me—conditional love. As long as she fit into the mold of the traditional farmer's wife, as long as she functioned as a one-dimensional woman, content to sit at the hearth and tend the family, mind her knitting so to speak, you would let her stay. But something tells me you didn't allow for her needs, her right to individualism, her right to function independently. I feel that you denied her the right to grow in her own direction, just as you have refused to allow me.'' And then came the hardest part.

''I love you, Pace Lofton, but just like you, I know that it is never love that would allow a human to destroy another. It is not love that cuts off your breath. It is not love that denies. Love gives. Love creates. There's a part of you that doesn't love a part of me. That is what I cannot reconcile myself to and that is why I must leave.''

She stopped then and let the silence settle around them. ''Have you nothing to say to me, Pace?'' Again the silence shifted.

Finally Pace spoke, but his words were not at all what she had expected. Later on she would think about that. She would decide that she had expected him to refute her defense of Linda. Or perhaps she still held on to the hope that he would give her what she needed. Instead, he offered what he had long withheld. But now it was too late. Now she knew that it was not enough and had probably never been enough. "I'll marry you." It was a thin proposal. She asked that he repeat it. "I said that I will marry you."

Alisa stood for a long time, watching the set of his shoulders, the hands that gripped the counter edge. "Why?" She had to know. Was it to give the boys a mother? Was it to keep her there so long that she would become incapable of leaving with dignity or perhaps incapable of ever leaving at all?

"Why?" he repeated. "I will marry you because it is what you want."

Alisa had thought she was incapable of being hurt more. As in other things, she was wrong there, too. "No, Pace. Once I thought that was all I wanted from you, but not anymore. I won't marry you, because you were right. If to appease me is the only reason you are marrying me, it would end just the way you have always believed it would. I know that you don't understand, and I don't know if you ever will. I wish that I knew how to make it clearer. I wish to God that I did, because if you don't understand, then you'll never forgive me."

He turned to face her then, and his expression almost dissolved her intellectual resolve. "I love you, my Alisa."

She thought surely she must yield, but she held on. "I know you do, but David loved Linda and the good ol' boys loved the girls from town. Where are they today, Pace? Where are they today?" With that she turned to the little drop-leaf table and laid down a piece of paper, on which she had written a Boston address. "You can do what you want with everything else that I brought into this house, you can continue to use them, you can put them in storage for the boys, or you can have a bonfire. All I ask is that you ship my writing table to me."

She looked at the paper and gave a bitter little laugh. "You once said that when I left, I would take nothing of yours. I'm going you one better, Pace. I'm leaving with a lot less than I came with."

"I lied, my Alisa. You will be taking something of mine when you go. You will be taking my love after all."

She choked back a sob. "That's unfair."

"Perhaps, but I'm not feeling very fair right now." He took a step toward her, but Alisa backed away.

She spoke her last words. "And I leave mine with you."

CHAPTER FIFTEEN

ALISA MOVED TO THE WINDOW of the elegant Fairlight apartment. To the left she could see a patch of late February sky, gray and heavy with snow. She shivered at the cold seeping through the window. Once that bitter, damp cold wouldn't have bothered her. But today she hated it. She hated the weather, she hated everything. In her mind she reviewed the past three weeks in Boston.

She had used the anonymity of the city to help her put herself back together. She had cruised the dress shops, the great department stores, the boutiques and specialty stores. She never bought anything and doubted that she could describe one garment she had touched, one chair she had sat in, one wall covering she had brushed fingers over. She stopped the browsing and window-shopping when she found herself gravitating to departments and stores that specialized in antiques and interior design. Subconsciously, she was looking for something to do to the second floor of their house, hers and Pace's. The next day she watched television for fourteen hours straight. Then she had placed a call to the director of her graduate program.

Other than the formality of being granted the degree in commencement exercises, Alisa had finished her post-graduate program. She had withstood the hours of grilling by the learned panel; she had defended her paper. She might have the right to use the title of doctor before the formal presentation. She didn't care enough to find out.

Moving from the window, she went into the kitchen where she brewed a pot of the blackest, most bitter coffee that had ever stained a Fairlight cup. It was as if Alisa took substance from the awful beverage that she had served so often to Pace. The thick inky liquid had become the staple in her diet.

"So what do I do now?" she asked herself aloud.

"A very valid question," agreed a masculine voice.

Alisa whirled to face the doorway. There stood her father, looking almost as weary as Alisa felt.

"Dad, what are you doing here? I'm sorry. I assumed. . . I thought you would be away for at least another two or three weeks." She placed the coffee cup on the edge of the counter and rubbed her hands together in a nervous gesture. "I can be out in a couple of hours." She made the initial move to leave the room. As she came abreast of him, Thomas Fairlight caught his daughter by the arm.

"Is there more coffee?"

Alisa looked down at the hand staying her and back up at the sad green eyes absorbing her emaciated state. "Yes, I'll get you some."

Thomas took off his overcoat and draped it over a chair before taking a seat at the breakfast table. He watched the agitated movements of his younger daughter. "I hear you are to be congratulated." A puzzled Alisa turned with the cup and saucer in her hand. "The Ph.D.," he supplied.

"Oh, that." She set the cup in front of her father. Thomas frowned at her tone. Her spirits were worse than he had thought.

"Won't you join me?" Alisa still stood, absently wringing her hands, but at her father's urging she retrieved her abandoned cup and sat across from him.

Thomas grimaced and bit back a comment at the bitterness of his coffee. He also hid a look of near awe as Alisa sipped from her own cup, which didn't contain either a masking dollop of cream or a sweetening spoonful of sugar, items that Thomas now added to his coffee for the second time.

As he stirred the milky beverage, he began his gentle probe. "I didn't just happen to return today, Alisa. Dr. Crowell called me. The gist of the conversation was that after nearly a year, you seem to be in no better health than when you made your way out of the jungle." Dr. Crowell had been Alisa's advisor throughout her doctoral program. He was also a friend of her father's, but Alisa had not thought them that close. Thomas waited a while. "Robert Crowell doesn't think that your problem is physical, and now that I've seen you, neither do I. You're too intelligent to allow a physical problem to go unattended. I want to know what's bothering you." He waited for an answer not forthcoming. "Has it something to do with a man named Pace Lofton?"

If Thomas monitored his daughter for response, he was not disappointed. Without volition, Alisa's blond head snapped up before she had time to mask the open pain there. And it wasn't pain caused only by the surprise of hearing a name she had refused to whisper aloud, even in the complete privacy of her lonely bed. "Pace?" Saying his name was an emotion-filled action. "What do you know about Pace Lofton?" Her throat was dry, her heart raced.

Thomas sighed. "Probably not the things I need to know. I do know that the two of you were very involved, that you stayed far longer than was necessary at Poverty Point. I know that the people who saw you together never thought your relationship would end so soon." He wiped his hands over his face, then rested his chin in his palm. "You tell me what I need to know, Alisa."

Alisa looked at her father for a long time. What was he asking? Why was he asking? Was this something else he could unobtrusively "take care of"? She didn't think so, not this time. "There's nothing to tell," she whispered.

"Alisa," Thomas said gently, "it may be too late to correct a mistake I made a long time ago, but I'm going to try. First I want you to know that you and Marlene are, and always have been, wanted and loved children. My mistake was in forcing you to grow up too independently. I was too late in realizing that my error has nearly destroyed Marlene. I hope it's not too late for you.

"The mistake began before you were born. It began when I was a child, when my father set about to force me into a mold I did not fit, that of orthopedic surgeon, like him. It didn't matter that I hated medicine; it didn't matter that I wanted something different. Consequently, there was a parting of the ways when I declared my intent to study archaeology. That is why you and Marlene have generous trust funds and I inherited nothing," he interjected lightly.

"Even though I made the break and made my way without my father's help, I never stopped feeling guilty that I had disappointed him. That guilt was one thing I was determined that my children would never feel. When each of you began to outgrow that 'I want to be a fireman-nurse-policeman-cowboy' stage, I thought I was setting you free. I thought by sending you to school, you would be away from my influence, and independence would be a natural thing, not something you had to wrench from me like I did my father. I wanted you to feel free to be and do whatever you wanted, but most of all I wanted you never to suffer the guilt of disappointing me.

"Naturally, I was so very, very proud when you decided to become an archaeologist, but I am just as proud of Marlene. I only wish she were a happier person."

Thomas got up and came to stand by his daughter. "Even if I didn't see that I was wrong to stay so aloof from your lives, even though I knew I had never abandoned you, I should have been a little more overt in showing my affection. But all too soon keeping my role in your life covert and acting only when I saw that you were in trouble had become a habit. But it is a habit I am breaking, right now. I love you, dear daughter, I love you and it is breaking my heart to see you this unhappy." For the first time in many years, Thomas held his child against his heart.

"And mother?" Alisa questioned against his shirtfront.

She felt her father shrug. "Your mother doesn't need us, Alisa. She doesn't need me; she doesn't need you. But I need her," he confessed sadly and held Alisa tighter.

THAT ADMISSION went a long way in causing Alisa to look at Thomas in a different light. A new open relationship between father and daughter was not quick to develop. But Thomas was patient even when it took him weeks to piece together exactly what had happened to his daughter the nine months she had spent at Poverty Point. Finally when he thought he had heard enough, he repeated the question he had overheard her asking herself upon his arrival. "What do you plan to do with the rest of your life? Another expedition? Do you want to go out in the field with me?"

Alisa shuddered. "No." Of the last two field trips, in the first she had nearly lost her life; in the second she had surely lost her heart. There were no more expeditions in her immediate or long-range plans. In fact, there were no plans at all.

"Another teaching position? There are probably lots of small colleges that could use a newly minted Ph.D." Thomas met with the same response. Alisa shook her head. "Curator in a museum? I have a few useful contacts." Alisa sighed, a fatalistic sound that Thomas had grown to hate. "Well, what?" he pressed.

"I don't know," Alisa wailed.

Thomas was running out of sympathy. His daughter was killing herself. "Did you stay in the South so long that you've developed the Scarlett O'Hara philosophy—you'll think about everything tomorrow?"

Alisa rose from her chair to pace the floor. "Dad, you aren't helping me!"

"If I helped you, I'd put your skinny little bones on the next plane to Louisiana, that's exactly what I would do. But you won't let me help you." With that he stormed out of the room and out of the apartment. Alisa followed his departure with amazement. She still hadn't adjusted to seeing this emotionalism in her father. He cared, he really and honestly cared that she was unhappy, and he was *showing* it.

When he returned he looked for a long time at his listless daughter, the daughter he had always thought so very, very beautiful. Now she was a limp shadow of the image he had always carried in his heart. He shook his head. "Damned red-neck," he muttered to himself. Stiff-necked red-neck. Pace Lofton didn't deserve his daughter; he didn't deserve to be shown the error of his ways. But neither did his beautiful daughter deserve to suffer so. He gave his agile brain full rein.

The next morning Alisa found his note stuck on the coffeepot. "Off to see a man about a dig," he offered and nothing more.

For two more weeks, Alisa spent a lot of time in her room, doing little, if anything, other than staring at the ceiling and sighing or sitting at the window in the salon wondering what Pace was doing. Would he be fertilizing the winter wheat or readying equipment to prepare the land for the cotton seeds? She was at the window when she saw the taxi pull up in front of the apartment and a familiar man step down. Her heart stood still.

J.D. Lofton! Oh God! Something had happened to Pace! He was hurt, he was dying and had asked for her. He was already dead! Why else would J.D. come to her? By the time J.D. had placed his finger on the bell, Alisa was at the door, flinging it open, ready to have her worst fears confirmed.

She began her questions without preamble. "What's wrong with him? Will he be all right? He can't be dead; he can't be."

For a moment, J.D. looked stunned. Perhaps his shock was caused by the questions, maybe it was by the physical appearance of Alisa. J.D. remembered her as a beautiful woman who had tried to take his son from him. She wasn't so beautiful now.

"It's nothing like that. There's been no accident or illness. Nothing like that," he repeated, and then he paused and looked down at his boots.

It was then that Alisa realized they were still standing at the entrance. "Won't you come in, J.D.?" She opened the door wider, and hesitantly J.D. followed her inside. She offered to take his coat, his hat. She offered him a seat, a cup of coffee, a glass of bourbon, something to eat. He shook his head in answer to her hospitality and chose to stand by the fireplace, hat in hand. Alisa wondered if he was cold. She was. She couldn't even remember the last time she had been warm. Had it been Christmas Eve? Or perhaps the week before Thanksgiving? It didn't matter. It was a long time ago.

Alisa, too, did not sit. She nervously waited near the window for J.D. to explain why he had come. When he did, it was in a voice almost too low for her to hear. She stepped nearer. "He's not hurt, but he's hurting, Alisa." He said nothing else for a while. Then his shoulders slumped. "I wanted you to go. I really wanted you to go. I prayed for it, and I thanked the Lord when He answered my prayers. But I think I've lost my second son, too." The voice filled with pain. "All Pace does is work and work and work, like a damn slave. I hire people to help him and he fires them. When he's not working, he's on his horse and he rides to Poverty Point and he stands on that hill and he just stands there...in the rain and in the cold, it doesn't matter. Or he goes over to the old house, and he sits there. He doesn't light a fire, and half the time he doesn't even turn on the lights. He just sits there in the dark. He just sits.''

Pace's father turned to the woman whom he had always thought to be his enemy, repeating a gesture she had seen his son make a dozen times. He worried the brim of his hat, tightening the curl. "I'd rather see him in his grave like David than see him this way. He's not dead, but neither is he any more alive than is David." Alisa knew what the words had cost that proud man.

"I want you to give him back to me, Alisa Fairlight. I want you to set him free. I want my son back.''

"J.D., there's nothing I can do," she wailed. "There are things that you don't understand." She did not qualify that they were things a man with his background and of his generation could never understand.

"I'll share him with you, Alisa. I'll do whatever you ask, just help him," the man who had never begged of anyone but his Creator begged.

"I can't. It isn't that simple.''

"It would be simple enough for you to see him. Come back with me, talk to him.''

"He doesn't want to see me, J.D. That was part of the deal. When I left this time I was not to come back, and he was not to come for me. It is over. Don't you see? It is finished.''

"It's finished all right. He's killing himself as surely as David killed himself." He received no satisfaction from Alisa's sharp intake of disbelieving breath. "It was in the coroner's report. I thought you knew, and I certainly thought that you knew exactly how alike David and Pace are. Didn't you have any idea of why I fought you so? It was because you held such power over Pace, just as Linda held it over David. And now I'm asking you to join with me, to use that power to save him, because as surely as I'm standing here Pace is doing the same thing as his brother, only it won't be as quick."

"My going back won't help, J.D." She continued to deny.

"Since it is the only thing left untried, I don't see where you really have a choice, not if you love him the way Mary Alice and Lou Ann say you do."

"What if it makes matters worse?" She was beginning to yield. "I won't know what to say to him."

"Do you still love him?"

"Yes."

"Then you'll do and say whatever it is that you have to."

Alisa didn't have the heart to tell him she had done exactly that when she left the Delta. Instead, like Thomas, she'd left a note on the coffeepot. Only Alisa's was a much longer message.

TWENTY-FOUR HOURS LATER Alisa stood in the little study in front of her writing table, still positioned as she had left it. Pace had never crated it and sent it to her. The room was cold, and she shivered in the Delta dampness. Drawing her coat closer around her, she lifted some of the papers that littered its top. They were maps and plats, many with strange notations in the margin. There was something in those notations that captured her intellect, but it refused to come into clear focus. In this house emotions, not intellect, ruled.

Suddenly, a hand rested on her hipbone. It was such a familiar gesture, so right, so absolutely right, that she automatically leaned into the tall hard frame behind her, a frame that fit so neatly, so perfectly against her own. She, as always, possessed no defense against it. The hand slid across her belly and pressed suggestively into her. If Pace were after a remembered response, he got it. And with that response, Alisa remembered, too. Turning quickly she faced the man who touched her so intimately, so possessively.

"Pace." It was all she could say, so she said it again.

"I understand that it's *Dr.* Fairlight now." The soft-spoken specter from all her lonely reveries wasn't smiling the sweet, loving smile she had dreamed so often. She reached an unsteady hand up to his lean face, relished in the rasping rough growth of his blue-black beard, felt the hard tension of his facial muscles playing beneath the polished bronze of his skin. It was her beloved Pace, so thin, so tired looking, so sad, but nevertheless her Pace. He clasped her caressing hand firmer against his cheek, holding her spellbound with his burning black eyes. And when he spoke, his voice was liquid pain.

"What are you doing here, my Alisa? What new torture do you have for me?"

"I heard that you were not well. I came to see for myself." The dark eyes narrowed before they drifted down her own care-worn body.

A scowl marked his weary features. "Where did you hear that?" he asked in puzzlement.

"It doesn't matter," Alisa hedged. "I thought maybe if we talked, we could help each other some way, put some ghosts to rest."

Pace released her then and turned to stand in the doorway of the adjoining bedroom, their bedroom. "There's only one ghost for me, Alisa, and he keeps asking the same question, over and over and over. 'Why, my Alisa, why?'"

"I told you why. There was no choice; you know that." As she spoke he pulled the door closed to the other room, as if he could not trust himself with it open. When the lock softly clicked, he turned back to her. She could barely handle the pain in his face. It took all of her energy, and that was why she didn't know the extent to which Pace fought to keep his hands off her, fought to keep from declaring that nothing in the world mattered but the two of them, fought to keep the door closed and the two of them in the study. He controlled the physical; he did not resist the words that came from his heart.

"I know only one thing when it comes to you,

Alisa Fairlight. I know only that I love you and that I cannot function without you.'' There was undeniable truth in his voice. He lifted himself from the doorjamb on which he leaned. A muscle worked in his hard jaw and his hand rubbed up and down his thigh. Even in the gathering twilight, it was not difficult to discern the infinite pain consuming him. It was everywhere, not only in his eyes, but also in his voice, in his posture, in his every movement. It was Alisa's turn to fight. She wanted to go to him and take some of that pain away, in the way that came easiest for them both. But, like him, she controlled the physical impulse.

Pace spoke again. ''I know what you told me, but at the time it sounded like something from one of those women's magazines. I didn't accept it. I searched for my own reasons. At first I thought you had left me because you couldn't accept the responsibility of rearing the boys, children that were not yours, children not of our own flesh and blood and love. I thought that if I gave them up, let Lou Ann have them or mom, you would come back to me.''

''You didn't really mean that,'' she rebutted gently. ''You could never walk away from them. You love them too much, and they belong with you. They always have.''

''Couldn't I?'' he challenged. ''*You* belong with me and *you* love me, but *you* walked away.'' His voice was filled with angry accusation.

''That was different. It was for my survival.''

''And leaving my nephews to come after you

would have been for my survival.'' There was something so adamant in his voice, that Alisa had no choice but to believe him. Pace Lofton would have come after her! Would have. . . would have. What had changed his mind?

He waited for a while as if waiting for some of his anger to abate. ''For a while I thought Linda had taken enough from me, and I became determined that I wouldn't allow her to take you, too. If I couldn't have you because of her sons, then she would have taken you from me as surely as she took David. I would not let that happen.''

His voice lowered to a near whisper, as if he imparted a secret, or something so awesome, he dared not approach it boldly. ''Do you know, Alisa, when I had convinced myself that you had left because of the boys, and when I decided that I would follow and either bring you back or stay with you wherever you wanted to be, I thought, so this is what it was like for David. For the first time I understood what drove him. Just like him, I was willing to give up everything for you, Alisa, everything. And just like David, I would have followed you to the ends of the earth, done everything within my power to give you anything you wanted.''

He crossed to her writing table and trailed a callused hand over its mellow surface. ''I had my bag packed, my plane ticket bought, and then I knew that what you wanted, that what you needed was here all the time. You needed more room to be yourself, and that included space to practice your trade and, Alisa, I didn't know how to give you that.''

Alisa's agile mind snapped at one word. *Didn't. didn't.* The ember of hope that she had thought long dead sent out a spark into the center of her heart.

Pace slid open the long drawer in the writing table and took out several tubes of tightly rolled papers. ''I was surprised to find you here. I had planned to bring you my idea when I was more sure of myself.'' He shrugged. ''It is probably best that you came. I might never have been brave enough to show you this.'' Slowly he unwound the first paper, another map, but this one was more neatly drawn, had a more finished look to it. Again, as with the others tossed carelessly across the table top, there was something oddly familiar about the style of the sketch. But Alisa didn't have time to think about it. She was too excited by a new thought. Pace had intended following her; he had a plan for them.

''One of the first things that I told you about this area was of an old battle between the farmers and the preservationists. I told you that battle was dead. It is, but while it raged in its full glory, a lot of farmers grew accustomed to keeping their mouths shut about what is on their land. In the last two weeks I've combed the area and located some unexplored mounds. I've touted the tax advantages available to site owners and explained easements as if I really knew what I was talking about. Through sheer generosity and by my calling in a few favors,

I've gotten you permission to evaluate several virgin sites throughout northeast Louisiana and northwest Mississippi and to proceed in whatever direction you see fit in their development. The only catch is that you will be working under a grant from a national foundation, which means some traveling. But they promised me that you would have input selecting your teammates."

He looked up then from the map, now hesitant and unsure of himself. "It is the best I can do for us, my Alisa, and I know it doesn't seem like a lot. It can't be nearly as exciting as the jungles of Central America, nothing to compare with the awesomeness of directing work at Poverty Point, with the vastness and importance of the sites in Peru." His dark eyes burned into her, his posture begged. "But if you will look upon it as a starting place for *me*, a place where I learn to let you go so that I can keep you, I promise by the love that I hold for you that I will understand when it's time for you to reach out for the other, no matter where it is . . . how very, very far away—" his voice became a whisper "—as long as you promise to come back to me."

The tension built between them. "Just tell me what more I can do. Just tell me." And then he used the ultimate argument. "I love you, my Alisa."

He reached out for her then, pulling her into his arms, against the hard demanding length of his body. "If this isn't enough, I'll go with you. I'll take some refresher courses, work with you. Just tell me what it takes."

He was willing to give up what she could not, and in doing so neither had to sacrifice. "It is enough, my love. You don't have to leave the Delta. And it will work. We'll make it work." There was time for no more words, for Pace captured her mouth with his. It was a kiss confirming that all their wishes had come true. He had found a way for them.

Pace and Alisa were too busy to know they were no longer alone. Neither heard the first "ahem," not even the second. Thomas Fairlight thought he would either have to tap them on the shoulder or, at the rate things were escalating, quietly close the door behind his departure. He rattled the keys and change in his pocket instead and cleared his throat once more. This time he succeeded in getting Pace's attention.

Carefully, tenderly, Pace pulled Alisa's arms from around his neck and turned her to face the doorway. "Dad!" And then she knew what was so familiar about the map. It was her father who had helped Pace to work out their problems. Once more, he had taken care of her. How could she ever have compared him to other fathers and found him wanting? And then she was hurling herself into his arms. "Thank you, thank you, thank you." She couldn't seem to say it enough.

Finally Thomas pulled away from his clinging daughter. "I have one request before taking care of you becomes someone else's responsibility. I want you to have a big wedding, here or in Boston, that much doesn't matter. I want you to have the elegant dress, the bridal cake, the champagne reception. For once I want to *publicly* play the doting father. Would it be asking too much?''

Alisa glanced over her shoulder at Pace and said, ''You can ask for the moon and I will gladly fetch it for you. A big wedding it shall be.''

''But soon, Thomas,'' Pace interjected. ''Soon.''

AND THOMAS DID HIS BEST. With Mary Alice, Lou Ann and a host of Pace's female relatives, it was almost soon enough to please even Pace. Almost. They had sipped champagne from a shared glass, they had fed one another heavily iced cake, they had danced together and with what seemed a thousand guests each.

''If we don't get out of here soon, we won't be alone until the crops are laid by. Let's sneak out, my Alisa, now,'' Pace urged impatiently.

''What about the garter and my bouquet?''

They were standing in the shadows. ''Give them here,'' he ordered as he shielded her body from the view of the happy wedding guests at the same time he eased her gown up and peeled off the lacy blue garter. Even though it was fleeting, Alisa felt the way his fingers lingered over her silk-encased thigh.

''God, Alisa, will it always be this way for us? Is it always this way for a man and the woman he loves?'' he said huskily when he had the garter in his hand. For a moment he dropped his forehead onto hers. ''You are the woman that I love, you know that, don't you? There has really never been

another, and we both know there will never be another.''

"I never doubted that, Pace, never for one moment. And I never stopped loving you, I never
will." She looked deeply into his eyes. "Let's go,
please."

"Yes." And with a deft flick of his wrist, he
hurled the garter and the bouquet into the dancing
throng, and in the same motion he urged Alisa
toward the exit. The scramble for the favors kept
the guests too busy to realize that the bride and
groom were escaping. Alisa looked back, trying to
get one more glimpse of her proud father and
mother mingling with the Delta farmers, but when
Pace tightened his hand on her waist, she willingly
turned and followed him.

For once Pace did not protest her hose as he
clasped her thigh in his hand while he maneuvered
the car over the backroads of the Delta countryside.
Alisa leaned her head against his shoulder, and as
usual paid no attention to the passing scenery. They
had planned to begin their marriage in their own bed.
There could not be a traditional honeymoon until the
crops were laid by. But when Pace flung open the car
door, they weren't at the old house. They were at
Poverty Point. "Okay, my Alisa, we've said the
vows for the state of Louisiana, we've said the vows
for your church and for mine, we've said them for
my family as well as yours. Now we will say the ones
that really count. We'll say the ones for ourselves."

Taking her by the hand, Pace directed Alisa to

the narrow paved walk that led to the giant bird
mound. In the moonlight, her wedding dress shim-
mered like a thing alive with the spirit of the Delta
night, and she was sure that the ancient bird-woman
watched over them and blessed their union. Hand in
hand they made the long walk across the six ridges.
It was a very silent procession of only two, but each
step was taken in joy. Slowly they climbed the
wooden steps to the breast of the bird, the ancient
holy high altar.

Pace knelt and drew Alisa down beside him.
From his pocket he removed two candles and gave
one to Alisa. The private ceremony began. By the
light of the flickering candles, he made her promises
too intimate for others to hear. She made pledges
that, like his, were for their ears alone. And then
Pace slipped onto her finger a third golden band, so
thin it was barely noticeable beside the wider one he
had given her earlier. "With this ring, I promise to
love you enough to let you go."

Alisa thought she would surely weep. They still
knelt on the ancient earth, facing one another.
"Don't cry, my Alisa," he whispered and then he
turned her slightly to look back down the ancient
holy mound. "Just there, the sun is rising and right
across the way our bed waits...as it has waited
since we were last in it. Shall we go home?"

"Yes, my husband, let's go home." They planted
their candles in the hard dirt, earth as old as their
love. Alisa touched her fingers to her lips and then
carried the kiss to the holy soil. Maybe, just maybe,

three thousand years ago, a handsome brave with hair like liquid silk, secret night, and a fair green-eyed maiden had brought their baskets of rich Delta soil to the top of the mound hoping...hoping....

EPILOGUE

THE FIRE CRACKLED as a log broke and sent a shower of sparks up the chimney. Pace, leaning back in his reclining chair, rattled the magazine as he turned the page. Alisa smiled her secret smile. He didn't fool her, not for one minute. He had really wanted to reread the article she had written. Somehow it always seemed different in print, on the slick page with even margins left and right. But he hadn't read a word since she had entered their bedroom and taken the little rocking chair across the hearth from him.

"Don't you feel like a sideshow?" he finally questioned.

"Jealous?" she asked across the top of the little mop of silky black hair and smiled wider. Tiny Mary Elizabeth smacked her lips hungrily against Alisa's breast and wide-eyed Daniel, leaning against Alisa's knees, gasped in awe.

"Damn right," Pace muttered. Taking a sip of bourbon, he replaced the short glass on the table and added, "But not for the reason you think." Alisa raised a shapely eyebrow in question. "Later, Mrs. Lofton, when the fan club of my daughter and your bosom has retired for the night."

A pajama-clad John David sat at Alisa's feet, his legs crossed tailor style, his elbows on his knees and his chin in his hands. He watched the baby closely as it kneaded Alisa's breast with its tiny hands. "Randy Hailey's little sister takes a bottle," John David finally offered.

"Your little sister is a breast-fed baby. It will make her healthier, keep her from getting sick because of immunities she will get from Alisa's milk. She will take a bottle later," Pace answered John David's non-question.

He turned and looked at Pace, not even caring that he didn't understand about immunities. "Then can I hold her while she eats?"

"Yes, and Daniel can, too." He finished the last of his drink in a gulp. "Okay, fellows, the show is over for the night. She'll be here tomorrow, I promise. Bedtime," he announced amid double groans. Placing a marker in the magazine and laying it in the rack beside his chair, he rose with the boys. First one and then the other kissed Alisa's cheek and then the new baby's head. "G'night, Alisa; g'night Maribeth."

In the hall John David questioned, "Uncle Pace, when Maribeth can talk, will she call you and Alisa daddy and momma?"

"Probably, unless Alisa teaches her some Yankee variations."

The young boy let that pass just as he did the information on immunities. "Is Maribeth really our little sister?" This question was delivered on the first stair.

"Johnny, I showed you the papers that made you and Daniel our sons, mine and Alisa's. I even had copies made and gave you one to keep in your desk. Maribeth also has papers that say she is our daughter. That means she is your sister." Pace could envision the inner workings of the child's thoughts. He monitored him carefully while urging both boys not to dawdle.

Just as Pace had surmised, John David was far from finished on the subject of his new sister. "Maribeth's not going to understand why me and Daniel don't call you daddy and Alisa momma and she does."

"Maybe not at first." Pace pulled back the cover on John David's bed, then on Daniel's. He tucked them in neatly.

"Wouldn't it be better for Maribeth if me and Daniel called you the same thing that she does?"

Pace held his breath before giving the same noncommittal answer he had given before. "Probably."

John David looked Pace straight in the eye in his manly fashion. "Well, I think it would, so I think me and Daniel will start calling you daddy and Alisa momma. Okay?"

"Okay."

"G'night, daddy." John David tried out the new appellation.

"Good night, son," Pace answered around the lump in his throat as he leaned down and kissed his older son on the forehead.

"Me, too, dad-dy," piped up Daniel, stretching out the syllables in Pace's new title. And Pace duly planted another tender kiss on another tender brow.

Downstairs Pace stood in the doorway watching Alisa shift his greedy daughter from one breast to the other. He came closer, and much like his sons, knelt down to watch in awe. Finally he found his voice. "She doesn't look very much like you, does she? I thought she would have blond hair and big green eyes."

Alisa thought he sounded just a bit disappointed. "You are absolutely right. She doesn't look at all like me," she agreed. "She's too busy looking exactly like you—the hair, the little tilt to her eyes, the high cheekbones." She looked down at their daughter. "Well, maybe she has my nose?"

Alisa could almost see Pace's chest swell with pride. "Do you really think she looks like me?"

"How many times do you have to hear it? Everybody says the same thing."

"But they were looking through all that safety glass in the hospital's nursery. Part of the time she was in an incubator and the rest in one of those awful plastic bassinets."

"Those who stopped by here this afternoon and passed Maribeth from hand to hand weren't getting a distorted view, and every one of them said how much she favors you."

Pace grinned sheepishly. "I was too busy being a nervous father his first afternoon home with the new mother and baby to notice what anyone said."

The infant instinctively nudged into Alisa's breast. "She has your appetite, too," Alisa teased. Her teasing stopped when Pace leaned forward and kissed her full breast right above his daughter's suckling mouth. Wordlessly he peeled back the folds of her robe, completely baring her torso. With a tender fingertip, he traced the veins threading throughout her breasts. He reached higher to follow the line of a delicate gold chain that ended in a huge pear-shaped diamond, winking and sparkling in the flickering firelight, his gift to her for presenting him with his daughter. He lifted it from between her breasts, turning it this way and that, watching the brilliant reflections play against her breasts and his daughter's cheek.

"Are you hurt that you received no birth present from dad?" There was pain in his eyes although he had never vocalized his own feelings.

"J.D. has come a long way toward accepting me, in laying the past to rest. So, no, I am not hurt. I understand that it would have brought back too many memories. I'm saddened only by the fact that it hurt your mother...and you." She reached up her free hand to brush back his silken hair, hair the color of night. "It will always be present enough for me that he reared such a wonderful son who has given me such a perfect daughter."

Pace laid the jewel back against her smooth flesh and sat back on his heels. "Oh, my Alisa, I have always thought that your breasts could never be more beautiful than when you were filled with desire for me. But now, seeing you with our baby like this, I know that I was wrong." His adoration was a wondrous thing that stole all words from Alisa's tongue.

"How long have we waited for this, Alisa? To be a real family, you, me, Maribeth, our sons upstairs?" he asked huskily.

"In how many lives have we loved?"

"If ever, I think never like this."

"No, never like this."

He lifted the sated, sleeping baby from her arms and cradled it in the crook of his elbow, helping Alisa to rise with his free hand. Together they took their daughter into the room that had once been their study. A tired Alisa instructed him in settling Maribeth into the little cradle with its lace-edged linen. Leaving the door open between their room and the new nursery, he next helped her to prepare for bed, taking the great blazing diamond and laying it beside the two intricately carved gold bracelets he had given her on the day their adoption of John David and Daniel had been finalized.

"I think you overdid it today. Alisa, are you sure you'll be strong enough to have the family in for Christmas Eve?"

"What's the matter, did you and Sonny and the rest of the crew drink up your supply of holiday bourbon the night Maribeth was born?"

He grinned sheepishly. "We shot up a hell of a lot of the fireworks, too."

"Good, with Maribeth's Yankee grandparents as

well as her fabulously famous Aunt Marlene coming for the christening and staying through Christmas, that was probably a blessing in disguise."

"One would think so," he teased, "if he didn't know Sonny Carter had bought some more."

Alisa groaned in mock despair. Then she eased onto the bed. "The way our family pitches in to help, what I'm not able to accomplish someone else will have done before I even think to ask. But I'll be ready and so will your daughter."

"Our family. I like to hear you say that." He crossed the room to bank the fire and secure the screen. Just before he lay beside his wife, the phone rang. Quietly he listened, and after saying the one word "pierced," he replaced the receiver then slipped into bed beside her. "This year it will be all right if I turn the holidays into a Chinese New Year. I think we've had Christmas three weeks early."

Alisa turned, a question in her expression. "That was your unobservant father-in-law. I think it reasonable for you to expect earrings within the next couple of days." There was a smile on his face and peace in his voice. Gently, he took her into the tender shelter of his embrace, holding her against his heart through the dark Delta night.

The Fourth
Harlequin American Romance
Premier Edition

GENTLY INTO NIGHT

KATHERINE COFFARO

Emily Ruska and Joel Kline
are two New York City police detectives
caught between conflicting values
and an undeniable attraction
for each other.

Harlequin Intrigue

Because romance can be quite an adventure.